THE PATH OF THE SYNTHESIZER

THE BLESSED OF THE DRAGON

Book One

Patrik Martinet

CONTENTS

ACKNOWLEDGMENTS

I would like to thank my friend, Daniel. Without you patiently reading early drafts, enduring numerous discussions when I needed advice or someone to bounce an idea off of, this book—and those soon to follow—never would have happened.

Thank you, Elayne Morgan, for your amazing editing skills. Thank you, Jake, of J Caleb Design, for capturing a pivotal moment with your incredible cover. And thank you, Zach Bodenner, for bringing Dradonia to life with your wonderful map.

A list of acknowledgements wouldn't be complete without also thanking all those who have helped me one way or another along the way. To each of you, I say thank you.

MAP OF DRADONIA

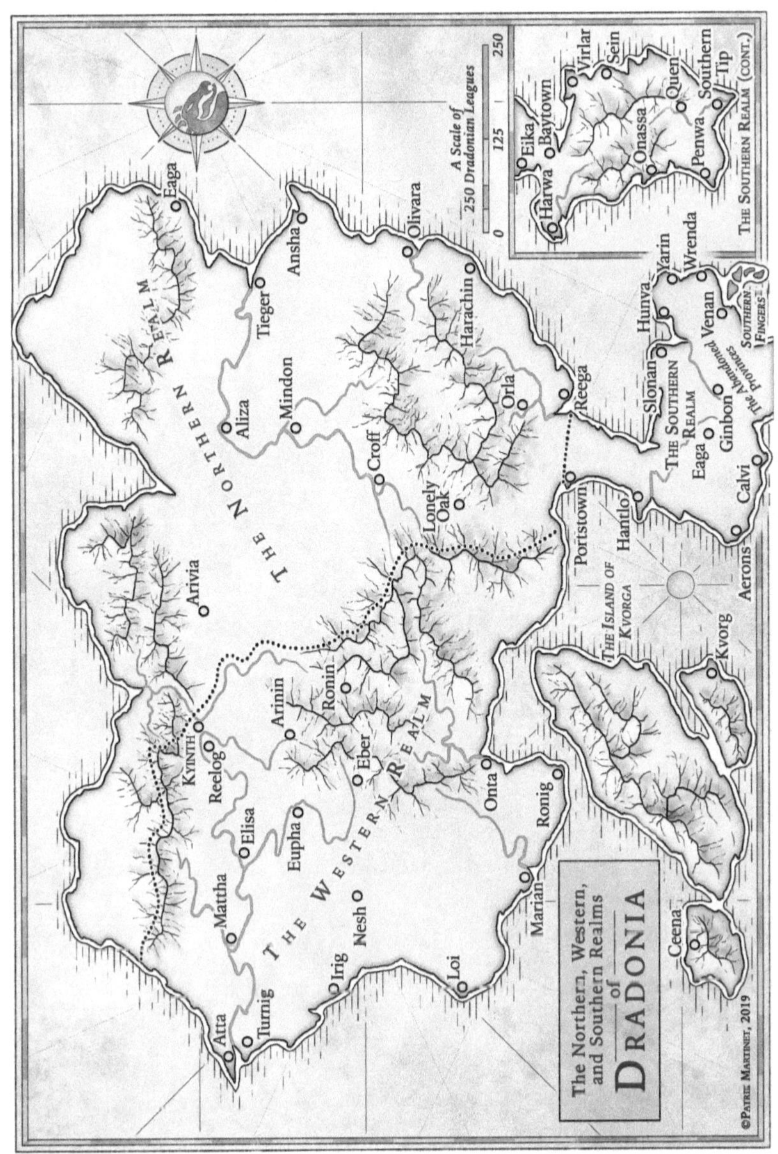

THE PATH OF THE SYNTHESIZER

BEFORE

389 United Era

Drenan did not see the Overseer approaching until he was nearly upon him. The black armor the Overseer wore, which matched his own, veiled his presence on the moonless night.

"Everyone's in place," the Overseer said.

"The tavern's secure?"

"Yes, Your Majesty."

"You're sure?" Drenan said, even though he already knew the answer. The tavern stood alone, away from the town, surrounded by four Overseers and four dozen soldiers. He had planned this mission carefully and was taking no chances. He would not squander this opportunity to rid the empire of its last real threat.

"Yes, Your Majesty."

Drenan nodded. "Get into position."

The Overseer turned toward the tavern and faded into a shadow after a dozen feet.

Drenan allowed the Overseer time to take up his position with the soldiers under his command, then signaled to the two assassins, wearing close-fitting black clothes, standing next to him.

They both nodded and silently moved toward the tavern.

Drenan placed his hand on the hilt of the black dagger tucked into his belt and reached out with two threads of Energy until he felt the heartbeat of the two assassins. Their pulses reflected the calm with which they moved.

The minutes passed while he waited alone in the sea of wild grass, away from the solitary building. He thought about his previous failures to kill Danavin. His fingers drummed lightly on the bone dagger. *Not tonight,* he thought, forcing his fingers to stop. Tonight, he would finally avenge Therese and Cara.

Unable to see anything but the tavern's dimly lit windows, he listened. The only sounds disrupting the peaceful night were the babbling of flowing water to his left and chirping insects in the distance.

The assassins' pulses quickened.

Drenan gripped the dagger tightly, and his other hand formed a tight fist. The scars on the backs of his hands stretched.

One of the heartbeats stopped.

He took a step toward the tavern.

The other heartbeat stopped.

The thought of failure forced its way back into Drenan's mind. His hatred for Danavin begged him to go and finish the man himself, but he clenched his jaw and ignored it. The plan was already set. The Overseers and soldiers were in place. He'd prepared for this possibility.

Drenan took one quick look toward the sleeping town down the road, then siphoned more Energy from the dagger. Using the heat pooling inside him, he sent Energy to the front wall of the two-story wooden structure and set it ablaze.

He continued feeding Energy to the fire and waited tensely as it grew. He forced himself to remain where he was, trusting his unit to stop Danavin from another escape. However, as the fire spread, memories of countless missed opportunities overwhelmed him and compelled him to move. He drew the dagger from his belt and strode through the grass toward the tavern.

An explosion boomed, freezing him in mid-step. "*Danavin*," he said through clenched teeth. He broke into a run, the small scales of his armor permitting fluid and unrestricted movement. When he arrived at the road, the Overseer and leather-clad soldiers guarding the front of the tavern were moving around the sides of the building. "Hold your position!" he yelled, and the soldiers returned to their formation in the middle of the road. There was a stone annex attached to the side of the wooden building, and he moved quickly down the cart path between the annex and the creek.

At the back, corpses littered the ground around a gaping hole in the annex. Rubble was scattered into the distance as far as Drenan could see by the light of the fire.

A bell rang in the distance.

Drenan picked his way through the rubble and fallen soldiers. He entered the remains of the kitchen and stepped over the body of a woman lying in a pool of her own blood.

"He's dead," an Overseer said.

"Where's his body?" Drenan said.

The black-armored man gestured at the door that divided the kitchen from the common room. It was engulfed in flames.

Drenan drew Energy from the dagger in his hand and, using Synthesis, shattered the door. He stepped closer to the doorjamb and peered into the burning tavern.

His eyes locked on a blackened body slumped by the stone hearth, clothes burning.

Danavin.

A long object lay on the floor next to Danavin, untouched by the fire.

His sword.

Drenan reached out with a thread of Energy and lifted the sword, drawing it through the flames toward himself. He grabbed it by the black, bone blade, avoiding the steel threads woven around the hilt to form a decorative cross-guard. He gasped at the beckoning force in the bone.

The bone blade felt cool in the surrounding heat. He held it up and inspected it. Light from the flames reflected from ribbons woven throughout the black bone. He knew that in sunlight those ribbons would be yellow.

Prize in hand, Drenan tucked his dagger into his belt and surveyed the damaged wall. It was imperative that no one suspect their involvement here. Time was short. "Get rid of the bodies outside," he said. "Quickly."

The Overseer stepped through the hole in the wall and called for the others. With help from the other soldiers, they gathered the corpses into a pile, and the Overseers used Energy to burn the bodies, reducing them to ash.

While the Overseers worked outside, Drenan picked up the woman and tossed her into the tavern. He scanned the room and found a body protruding from underneath a burning table. Nearby were two thin swords. *One of the failed assassins.* He retrieved the swords in the same manner as he'd retrieved Danavin's, then searched the room for their throwing knives. He found them embedded in the wall near the stairs. After he'd collected them, he siphoned more Energy from Danavin's sword and burned away the table and body hidden underneath. *Where's the other one?* He didn't want there to be more than two sets of remains found in the building on the morrow. *Maybe upstairs?* But searching up there was impossible.

"Draego's Fire," he swore through clenched teeth.

He was running out of time. With one more quick scan of the tavern, he decided it didn't matter. *It'll be unrecognizable by time the fire's out; an unlucky patron.*

Drenan turned from the room and burned away the blood pooled on the stone floor where the woman had died. He frowned when he looked up at the hole in the stone wall. He hated the idea of leaving evidence behind, but the locals were on their way. He walked through the rubble, cursing Danavin for the mess, and signaled to the others that it was time to leave.

Drenan gave the assassins' weapons to an Overseer, then led the group back to the sea of grass. At the top of a small rise, he stopped and turned around. Several torches floated down the road from the town toward the burning tavern.

A smile crept onto Drenan's face. Finally, his wife and daughter were avenged.

He turned, sword in hand, and followed the others into the night.

CHAPTER 1

410 United Era

An arc of light inched over the Mindon Mountains and pushed back the darkness. It climbed higher, forcing the starlit sky to cede its ground. As the arc advanced above, the sleeping valley awoke below. The shadowy silhouette of a large oak, its thick arms stretching into the sky and reaching down to the ground, gained definition. Its leaves became visible, transitioning from grays to greens, and began shining as the sun crested the distant mountains to the east.

By the time the transition from night to day was complete, the town square surrounding the oak bustled with activity. Proprietors opened the shuttered windows of their shops and unlocked their doors. Merchants opened the sides of their wagons lined up along the waist-high fence surrounding the tree and set out their wares. Locals moved from shop to shop, running their daily errands, and gave a wide berth to the armored horses tethered to the fence.

On the opposite end of the growing town, across a creek flowing low from another winter of poor mountain snow, Yolken Thornhill filled a mug with ale. He set it before one of a dozen men hunched over the bar in the tavern he ran with his aunt and younger brother. Patrons occupied every table sandwiched between the bar and hearth on the opposite side of the quaint room. He had barely finished breaking his own fast and taking the chairs down before they'd begun streaming in. He looked over at the stairs with a furrowed brow then gathered an empty plate and mug from the bar top.

"Hey! I wanted another!" complained the scruffy man with dirty hands and clothes.

"Sorry," Yolken said. "I thought you were finished. Another mild, then?"

"Yah."

Yolken set the empty plate on the bar and refilled the mug. He set the mug down before the man then looked over at the stairs again.

The wooden kitchen door swung open and his Aunt Selena, a slender, middle-aged woman, walked out holding two plates of steaming hot food in her hands. "Where's your brother?" she asked as she passed the bar. She deposited the plates at one of the tables and returned to the kitchen.

"Still sleeping," Yolken said as she walked back by. He snatched the dirty plate from the counter, his annoyance at Javen rising to the surface, and followed her into the kitchen.

He set the plate in the sink then stepped out through the back door for a breath of fresh air. He closed his eyes and inhaled deeply, reveling in the tingly feeling that accompanied the warmth of the sun on his skin. The Little Mindon bubbled forlornly as it flowed past the tavern. He let his breath out slowly and visualized himself breathing away his annoyance at Javen. He didn't mind his brother enjoying himself now and then, but Javen was growing increasingly irresponsible.

"It's too early to be angry, Yolken," Selena called through the doorway.

Yolken ignored her and breathed in again.

"It's dying, you know," a raspy voice said.

Yolken opened his eyes and saw Relan, one of the tavern's

regulars, stop in front of him. His clothes, as usual, looked as though he'd been sleeping in them for half a season.

"What is?" Yolken said.

Relan gestured over his shoulder with his thumb. "The sun. Just a matter of time. He knew it, too."

"What? Who knew?"

Relan shook his head and walked away. Before he walked around the side of the tavern Yolken barely heard him mumble, "No cursed scales gonna be sniffing 'round my place."

When Relan was out of sight Yolken went back inside.

"Relan's here," he said. "And I'm not angry at Javen. Just annoyed."

"Angry. Annoyed. What's the difference?" Selena said, turning from the stove to look at Yolken.

"I'm tired of him shirking his responsibilities all the time."

"He just needs a little more time to mat—"

"He's twenty-two years old!" Yolken exclaimed. Feeling oddly warm, he reached up and wiped his brow with the sleeve of his shirt. "If he doesn't want to do his part around here maybe it's time he finds his own way."

"Yelling at me won't help," Selena said. "And neither will threatening him."

"Sorry. I didn't mean to—"

"He's your brother, Yolken. And there's nothing more important in life than family." Selena turned back toward the stove. "I know your brother's not as hard a worker as you," she said over her shoulder, "but the Great Dragon makes each of us different. Forcing him to do something he doesn't want won't help matters. And besides, if anything, *you* could stand to work *less*. How are you ever going to court Kaylan if all you do is work?"

"How did you…" Yolken started, feeling the warmth inside him move to his face.

"I watched you grow up together, and I see how you look at her whenever the two of you are around each other," Selena said.

She turned and placed a plate piled with eggs and pan-fried ham on the table. "It's obvious you've been in love with the lass since you were little."

"I… I didn't think you knew."

"Yolken, dear, I might be your aunt, but I'm also a woman."

Yolken picked up a towel to wipe the sweat beading on his forehead. "How am I supposed to work less if Javen won't do his share?"

"Talk to him."

"I have."

"Talk to him again. Gently. And not in anger. Keep trying until he comes around."

"Can't you talk to him?"

"He's a grown man, same as you. I could talk to him, but it'd be better coming from you. He needs to know you need him. Maybe you show him that by giving him more responsibility."

"I'm not giving him more responsibility until he learns to manage what he already has."

"That's for you to decide. Now, take this to Relan." Selena added a thick slice of buttered bread to the plate. "He'll be cross if his food gets cold."

She turned back to the stove, and Yolken knew she was done with the conversation. He picked up the plate—then dropped it back onto the table with a yelp when it became scorching hot.

Selena turned around at the sound of the ham and eggs beginning to sizzle. "What happened?"

"I don't know," Yolken said. "The plate got really hot when I picked it up."

"Did it burn you?"

"I don't think so," Yolken said, looking at his hand. When he looked up, he locked eyes with his aunt and sensed her displeasure. With a shake of her head, Selena turned back to the stove. Yolken used the towel to pick up the plate and hurried out of the kitchen. He set the plate in front of Relan and said,

"What would you like to wash that down with?"

"Mild," Relan said. "My head's pounding this morning, lad. You weren't kidding about the strong being strong."

"I warned you, didn't I?" Yolken grabbed a clean mug and asked, "You sure you don't want water instead?"

"Nah. Once I get this fine cookin' of Selena's in me I'll be good."

Yolken turned around and pulled the stopper on one of the six barrels lining the wall until the mug was full. He never understood how Relan could wake so early each morning, considering that he spent every evening sitting at the bar—and never with an empty mug—until Yolken closed the tavern for the night.

The moment Yolken set the mug down, Relan picked it up and drank deeply from it. "Where's Javen?"

The stairs creaked before Yolken had a chance to respond, and he looked up. Javen was slowly descending them, rubbing his eyes with the heels of his hands. He still wore the clothes he'd had on the day before; his damp shirt clung to his body, and his light brown hair stuck out haphazardly.

"Late night?" Yolken said when Javen plopped onto the last open bar stool. The question was rhetorical. He knew Javen hadn't come home until it was getting light out; Yolken had already been awake, thinking about the coming day, when Javen had stumbled down the hallway and not so quietly shut his bedroom door.

Javen grunted.

Using a metal hand pump, Yolken filled a mug with water and set it in front of Javen. He watched Javen pick it up and take a sip, then said, "Norin came by last night and told me our shipment came in, so I need you to pick it up."

Javen looked up at him with bloodshot eyes. "Do I *have* to?"

"Yes, you *have* to," Yolken said. He turned and called into the kitchen through the window, "Javen's awake!" then began attending to the other patrons sitting at the bar. Selena emerged with a plate of food. He watched intently, hoping she would say something, but she just set the plate in front of Javen and went back into the kitchen. He could still sense her displeasure.

A few minutes later Selena reemerged and set a list on the bar next to Javen's plate. "Finish your breakfast and then see to your errands," she said. "You've slept half the morning away, and there are things that need doing."

"Yes, ma'am," Javen said.

Yolken gave his aunt a nod of approval.

"You and I need to talk about what happened in the kitchen," she said. She made her way through the tavern, gathered a few plates and mugs, then shouldered the kitchen door open.

When the door swung closed behind her, Javen said, "What happened in the kitchen?"

"Nothing," Yolken said. "I also need to brew today, so when you get back, I'll need you to tend the bar."

"Again?" Javen exclaimed.

"Yes, again," Yolken replied. "It's been busier than normal with all these southerners passing through. And for once I wish you'd be willing to help around here."

"I help."

"Barely."

"If it's so busy then maybe you should hire someone."

"The lad's right," Relan said. "Your father was the same."

"What do you mean?" Yolken said.

"He kept himself so busy here he never got around to building that house of his."

"I have help," Yolken retorted. He knew Relan was right, though. Their father had bought a plot of land by a maple grove east of town, situated on the Little Mindon, where he'd intended to build a home for their family. "If Javen put as much effort into helping me as he does chasing girls, we wouldn't have a problem."

Javen shoveled food into his mouth and mumbled, "I help."

"Just finish your breakfast."

Yolken tended the bar while Selena moved between the kitchen and the tavern, filling orders and taking empty plates and mugs back. When Javen finished his food, he snatched the list from the bar and shuffled back to the stairs. He came back down several minutes later with clean clothes and washed hair.

"Hurry back, Javen!" Yolken called before Javen disappeared through the door. When the door closed behind him, Yolken watched Relan mumble into his mug. He typically ignored Relan's half-crazed remarks about the Regency, but his curiosity got the better of him. "What were you talking about earlier, Relan?" he asked.

"Huh?"

"Why would the Regency sniff around your place?"

"Not gonna let them."

"But why would they?"

"Dunno, but I saw them scales sniffing round the backside of Brall's place on my way here."

"What for?"

Relan shrugged.

"Huh," Yolken said. Whenever Dalia, the regent of the Croff province, came down from Croff, Brall hosted her at his inn, so Yolken wondered what interest the Regency would have in him. He'd heard the stories whispered by ale-loosened tongues about people going missing, but they were always stories from faraway places. Relan claimed to have known people that went missing, but Yolken had long ago learned to ignore the tales he spun. "And what about the sun?"

"What about it?"

"You said—"

"Haven't you learned yet not to pay any mind to what old Relan says?" Relan said.

He had a point. Relan did talk a lot of nonsense. How could the sun possibly be dying? The Great Dragon sustained the sun by breathing its power into it. It was probably the most nonsensical thing Relan had ever said.

The front door swung inward and slammed against the wall. Brall, a rotund, bald, and sweaty man, barged into the tavern. "Yolken!" he shouted, swabbing his glistening forehead with a soiled handkerchief. "I need your help! The chancellor of the south is coming to the Oak!"

CHAPTER 2

B rall scurried over to where Yolken stood behind the bar.

"The chancellor of the south?" Yolken said when Brall stopped in front of him. His caravan passed through Lonely Oak periodically, but he had never stayed before.

"First thing this morning soldiers came traipsing in the front door and informed me His Highness will be staying at the Oak tonight!" Brall said. "They haven't stopped scouring the place over since."

"How can I possibly help?"

"I need all the ale you have."

"What?"

"Your ale. I need all of it."

"I can't sell you all my ale." Yolken's was the only place that didn't import its ale from other cities—such as Croff. He took pride in that.

Brall wiped his forehead with a shaky hand. He reached into a vest pocket and pulled out a large golden coin. It was twice the size of a regular drake but didn't have any monetary value—the possessor of such a coin would never dare sell or trade it. It signified that Brall was a Suit, a class of people the Regency elevated because they generated more tax revenue than the other commoners. He was the only person in Lonely Oak who possessed one. Although it wasn't really one of his goals, Yolken sometimes imagined growing his tavern to the point that Dalia one day gave him one of those coins. Such recognition from the regency garnered respect within your community, and with the respect came a certain amount of sway. But Yolken knew for a fact that Brall had received his coin less than a month ago. He didn't even have a suit yet.

"Put that away," Yolken said. "You don't want to establish that reputation for yourself, do you?"

"What reputation?"

"Brall, that *Suit* who pushes everyone around with his *special* coin."

Brall hesitated, then shoved the coin back into his pocket. "All right, Yolken, but please. His Highness will expect nothing but the best at the festival!"

"There's going to be a festival?"

"Yes. To honor the chancellor!"

"That's the first I've heard of one. I didn't even know the chancellor was coming."

"Nobody did until this morning. I have people scrambling all over town trying to put together the things I'll need to transform the Oak into an establishment worthy of his presence. On top of that, the chancellor's guards have been poking their noses into every inch of my establishment—they're even interviewing my guests!"

Yolken looked at the nervous proprietor a moment. Then, sighing, he said, "Just a moment." He left Brall dabbing at his forehead with the handkerchief and walked down to the end of the bar. He poked his head through the window into the kitchen and said, "Auntie, can you watch the front for a bit? I need to help Brall with something."

"Yes, dear. Let me get these orders out first," Selena answered.

"It'll be just a few minutes," Yolken said, walking back over to Brall.

"I usually spend weeks preparing for the moon festivals, and they expect me to put one together *tonight*," Brall said. He dabbed at his brow and added, "And with no forewarning!"

Yolken collected empty mugs and plates and refilled drink orders. His mind raced with thoughts of Kaylan as he worked. He had wanted to start courting her for as long as he could remember, and festivals were customarily when a man asked a woman's parents for permission. But the thought made his stomach churn; he spent most festivals feeling ill.

"Cursed scales," Relan slurred as Yolken passed his hunched form.

"I can't believe the chancellor will be spending the night here tonight," Yolken said.

"Here?" Relan looked over both his shoulders. "Why ya gonna share that flea-infested lump you call a bed with the scale?"

"Not here," Yolken retorted. "In Lonely Oak. And unlike you, Relan, neither I nor my tavern is flea infested. At least not until after your daily visits. Do you know how much time I spend every day rounding up your little friends after you leave?"

"Hah!" Relan guffawed. "Another mug, lad!"

Yolken refilled Relan's mug, then moved on to other customers, all the while wondering what it would be like to have the Blessed stay in his tavern. He would be beside himself. Selena wouldn't be pleased though, he knew. Her attitude toward the Blessed had been one of cool reserve at best. She hid it well, but he could tell that deep down she didn't trust them, let alone revere them as they were raised in the Dragon Shrine to do. He paced the bar, checking on the needs of those sitting on either side of Relan.

"That must've been why them scales was poking around Brall's. Can't imagine the Blessed deigning to stay in this lowly town," Relan said.

Yolken knew Relan was right. Despite how his aunt felt

about them, the Blessed were chosen by Draego, the Great Dragon, to rule over Dradonia. They bore Draego's Gift, lived long, opulent lives, and had no reason to ever want to visit Lonely Oak. Dalia made an appearance only on the rarest of occasions, such as to bestow Brall with his coin. Most of the time they were just passing through on their way to more important places.

"We should count ourselves blessed by the Great Dragon," Jed, the man sitting to Relan's left, chimed in.

"Hah!" Relan guffawed again. "S'long as they don't go burning no more'a our fine establishments."

"There you go again with your crazed ideas," Jed said. "You know there's no proof they caused the fire that took Yolken's folks. And I'm sure he'd appreciate you not reminding him every time your tongue loosens."

"Sorry, lad," Relan said.

"It's fine," Yolken said. It didn't happen every day—just when Relan got to talking about the Regency. He'd never understood why Relan hated them so much. He went on and on about it but never talked about why. When Yolken asked, Relan would bury his nose in his mug.

He stole a glance at Brall, waiting in the corner by the door dabbing his forehead, and thought about how many barrels he could afford to sell. He recognized Brall's plight, but he knew he would have a hard time catching back up, especially since any chance of him brewing today was likely gone. He filled a few more orders, then the kitchen door swung open and Selena emerged, two plates on her left arm and one in her right hand. She nodded in his direction and moved around the tavern, delivering the steaming plates of food to hungry patrons.

Yolken met Brall at the end of the bar and said, "Sorry to keep you waiting so long. As you can tell, it's a bit hectic right now." He had been hesitant to help Brall at first, but he was starting to realize what an opportunity this was—the Chancellor of the Southern Realm would be drinking his ale. "Did you bring a wagon?"

Brall nodded.

"Out front?"

Brall nodded again.

Yolken took off his apron and together they walked to the front entrance. Brall had his horse and wagon tethered to the railing of the bridge spanning the Little Mindon, and it blocked half the bridge. It was barely wide enough for two wagons to pass abreast, so several wagons were lined up, waiting their turn to cross. A few disgruntled men heckled Brall about blocking the road while he unwrapped the reins from the rail. He led the horse down the path between the creek and the tavern, then Yolken helped Brall maneuver the horse and wagon so that the back of the wagon faced the back door.

"Come on," Yolken said, leading Brall down the stairs to the cellar.

Two of the four walls contained floor-to-ceiling racks filled with barrels. Brall walked along the two walls and counted them. "I'll take them all," he said.

"You can't possibly think you'll go through fifteen barrels in one night."

"I don't wanna take the chance."

"I'm sorry, you can't have them all." Yolken considered the barrels and ran his hands through his short-cut hair, interlocking his fingers across the back of his head. "You can have these," he said, gesturing to the rack along the back wall. It contained eight barrels, half milds and the other half bitters.

"That won't be enough, though!" Brall exclaimed.

"Sorry, Brall, but that's all I'm willing to sell."

"Please, Yolken. Your ale is better than anything else served in town, and I'm prepared to pay good money for all of it."

"Thank you for the compliment, but if I sell you everything I have, then I won't even be able to keep the tavern supplied. This festival caught us all off-guard, and I haven't brewed anything that can replace it if I sell it all to you."

"Draego's Fire," Brall said, shaking his head. His jowls still moved after his head stopped, but he acquiesced. "Sell me all you can, lad."

Yolken used the pulley system installed next to the staircase to move the barrels out of the cellar. Brall's grunting accompanied his thoughts about the festival. His stomach was already expressing its disagreement, but the opportunity was perfect. Unexpected. He needed to convince Javen to watch the tavern, but he knew the Great Dragon blessing him was more likely than Javen willingly missing out on a chance to charm some unsuspecting southern girl.

"How much?" Brall asked when they were done.

Yolken looked at the eight barrels. They represented half of his remaining supply. He considered this extraordinary occasion, as well as Brall's compliment, and came up with what he thought was a fair value. "One hundred eighty drakes," he said.

"Blessed Dragon!" Brall exclaimed, dabbing his forehead. "You must be mad! Maybe—just maybe—the whole lot of what you have down there would be worth that amount, but not eight barrels!"

"The pulley carries the barrels down as easily as it lifts them up, Brall," Yolken said. "I'll have to brew nonstop for two weeks to replace all this. Besides, rumor has it my ale is better than anything else served in town."

"You're shrewd, lad. Shrewd." Brall took a purse out of his coat and dropped it into Yolken's hand.

Yolken felt its weight and raised an eyebrow.

"I'll have the rest sent over to you later. I don't usually make a habit of carrying that much gold around."

As Brall led his horse and wagon full of barrels away, Yolken considered the task before him. *I'm definitely going to need help now, even if Javen suddenly decides to be useful.* Once Brall's wagon was out of sight, he returned to the tavern through the kitchen and retrieved his apron.

"Another mug!" Relan called when Yolken pushed the kitchen door open.

Yolken took the empty mug from Relan and filled it anew. He set it down in front of his most loyal patron and said, "You wouldn't happen to be looking for work, would you?"

CHAPTER 3

Javen squinted at the brightness that greeted him outside the tavern. *This certainly doesn't help,* he thought, shielding his eyes with his hand. He crossed the wooden bridge spanning the Little Mindon and worked his way toward the Haven. He hated the days he had to get Kena and the cart out because it took so much longer to complete his errands. He also hated that Yolken got on him every time he needed him to do it.

He dodged locals carrying baskets of produce or leading horses pulling wagons filled with a variety of goods to sell at the market. There were also many unfamiliar faces of men, women, and children; some traveled on foot or on horse-drawn wagons laden with personal belongings. Their increasing presence resulted in a mix of vexation and welcome from the locals. Those who felt vexed hated the unwanted growth, while those with open arms saw the opportunity that came with it.

Most were passing through, which meant more inns, pubs, and a variety of other shops to accommodate their needs. But some chose to make Lonely Oak their new home, which even the opportunistic didn't approve of. Southerners brought with them change. Nobody liked change. Javen didn't mind, though—he loved the never-ending stream of new girls to flirt with. When he talked with them in the pubs, they all told the same story—they were fleeing the growing troubles in the south.

As he approached the Haven, he stepped aside to make room for Brall, who was holding the reins of a horse, which was pulling a wagon. He followed the overweight man with his eyes, wondering what he was doing, but turned back around when he heard a female voice shout "Hi Javen!" He looked up through squinted eyes and saw a blond-haired girl sitting on the horse post in front of the inn coyly waving at him.

He wanted to turn around and go the other way but forced himself to continue. "Hello, Astora," he said as he approached the girl he'd spent the night drinking, dancing, and rolling around in a hayloft with.

"G'morning," Astora said. She hopped off the post and hugged him.

He stepped back and said, "Your pa didn't see me this morning when I left, did he?"

"I don't think so."

"Did he say anything?"

She shook her head, then looked up into his eyes. "You know, we wouldn't have to sneak around anymore if you'd just talk to him."

"Where would the fun be in that?" He enjoyed the nights he spent with Astora—and the other girls, both locals and southerners passing through—but there was only one girl he wanted to marry.

"For one, you'd be all mine."

He didn't have a response. So, after an awkward silence, he said, "I really better get going. I have a lot to do yet this morning." He stepped forward and gave her a quick hug and kiss on the cheek. "I'll think about it," he lied. He didn't want to marry her, or even to court her. But he got the desired effect. He left her blushing and walked around the side of the inn to the stable in the rear.

Every stall contained a horse. It wasn't that long ago that Astora's father had eagerly stabled Kena for them—he stabled several horses for locals without room to do it themselves—but now the stable was so busy he kept increasing the fee. They were almost to the point of needing their own stable, and Javen was sure that, if they ever built one, taking care of Kena would be another thing Yolken made him do.

The roan that had belonged to their parents greeted him with a nuzzle when he opened her stall. Even though it was expensive to feed and stable her, she was invaluable to their family. Not only did they use her to move goods from Norin's warehouse to the tavern, but Yolken's ales were so popular they often used Kena to transport barrels of ale to wedding celebrations, barn raisings, the moon festivals, and any number of other celebrations. Despite her old age, she still faithfully hauled the goods they needed.

Javen led Kena around to the back of the stable where the carts and wagons were stored. A few of them were laden down with household goods, furniture, cooking implements, and locked chests. Some had canopies and places to sit. Their own wagon was small and simple. Javen hitched Kena to it and led her out onto the road. As he passed the front of the building, he glanced over to the horse post, and a sense of relief flooded through him. Astora was gone.

Javen led Kena through the town square. He passed merchant wagons lining the southern side of the fence surrounding the oak tree at the center of the square. The wagons hid the tree's lower branches, which curved down close to the ground. Armored horses tethered to the east side of the fence came into view as he passed the merchants. He kept his distance, but eyed the armor, which he thought looked like some sort of scale—fish scales were what came to mind. Small, overlapping, oval-shaped pieces covered the horses' heads and necks, and large plates covered their chests and haunches. Children sat in the grass under the tree, just out of reach of the muzzles craning over the fence to nibble the grass, watching them. A group of armored soldiers milled around on the boardwalk outside the front door of the Oak. *Is Dalia here?* he wondered as he led Kena past them.

The Dragon Shrine, a large stone structure with a steep yellow roof made with slate tiles resembling the armor the horses and guards wore, stood alone, set back from the road on the other side of the square in stark contrast to the square's tightly spaced buildings. A wrought iron fence with staked tops encircled it. The gate, which was twice as tall as the fence, had two dragons facing each other with heads tilted up. The fire spewing from their mouths arched up and met in the middle. A small wooden pushcart sat outside the gate. It had been several months since he had been to the shrine, but Kristana brought Issa daily to petition to Draego to heal Issa's crippled legs.

On the north end of town, Javen pulled Kena to a stop in front of Norin's Goods. The barrel-chested proprietor stood outside the front door smoking a pipe. "Morning, Norin," Javen said.

"G'morning to you, Javen!" Norin replied. "Pull Kena round the back, and we'll get ya loaded."

Javen led Kena around to the back where Norin waited by a large bay door. He wrapped the reins around the hitching post and followed Norin into the warehouse. There were goods stacked along every wall of the spacious brick building, up to the ceiling in some areas and organized into piles in the middle. Norin led Javen to a stack of grain bags and several new oak barrels.

"What news did your teamster bring?" Javen asked as he heaved a sack of grain onto his shoulder.

"Mostly the typical: who the emperor is bedding, which regents are feuding with each other," Norin said as he picked up a sack. They made their way back to the rear of the warehouse. "Although I've heard from a couple different sources now that the emperor may be taking a wife."

"Really? Who?"

"Dunno."

"It's about time, I suppose," Javen said, setting the sack of grain in the wagon. "Auntie said his last wife died over three hundred and fifty years ago." He'd always thought it strange considering the Blessed practically lived forever.

"When you're Blessed, I suppose there's no rush in doing anything." Norin set his bag in the wagon, then they turned from the cart and headed back inside.

"What else?"

"Well, let me see… Ah, yes—the talk of the town when Tad left Croff was that the mayor had been apprehended by the Regency. And that's not a rumor. He really was arrested."

"What were the allegations?"

"That he was a rebel."

"A rebel?"

"That's the rumor." Norin and Javen each retrieved their second round of grain sacks and made their way back to the cart. "How are things down at the tavern?"

"Pretty good, I suppose. I just wish Yolken would hire someone to help out."

"Why, so you have more time to chase girls around?"

"No," Javen replied with a cross look. "We really *could* use some help."

"Well, if your brother wants to make his tavern shine, he might get his chance."

"What do you mean?"

"Several days ago, Tad passed Dorlan's caravan on its way back to Hantlo."

Javen nodded, remembering when the caravan had passed through Lonely Oak several months ago on its way north.

"Well, a few nights ago, while lodging in Edis for the night, he shared a few drinks with a particular guard who turned out to be a part of the chancellor's forward guard. He was securing the chancellor's lodgings in the towns he would be staying at on his way back to Hantlo. As it turns out, His Highness will spend the night here, in lowly old Lonely Oak."

"Dorlan will be staying here?" Javen replied, the pitch of his voice elevated. The Blessed often passed through Lonely Oak, but except for Dalia, the provincial regent in charge of Lonely Oak, they never stopped.

"Yep."

"Wow! Any idea where he'll be staying?"

"Sorry, lad. Tad couldn't get the guy to say any more, no matter how many drinks he bought him," Norin answered. "I'm told that quite the festival is planned tonight, so be sure to tell your brother if he ever wants to make more of that brewing operation of his, this is his chance. And if he starts exporting that stuff, he's going to need a means of distribution. That and a steady flow of supplies. And I happen to know the perfect person to meet both of these requirements!"

They both chuckled, then worked silently loading the remainder of the sacks of grain and the new oak barrels.

"Wait, I almost forgot the best news of all!" Norin exclaimed as they loaded the last of the barrels.

"What?" Javen asked with a raised eyebrow.

"Rumor has it that a strapping young lad was seen sneaking out of a certain hayloft early this morn."

A twinge of fear shot through Javen.

"And," Norin continued, "rumor also has it that a certain father is not pleased."

Javen shook his head as he grabbed Kena's reins. Astora hadn't indicated that her father was upset with her. She would have said something if he was. It was probably one of the stable boys, and her father didn't know… yet. He would need to talk to her and let her know. "And where did you hear this?"

"You know what they say, Master Thornhill."

Javen knew exactly what Norin was going to say. So when Norin spoke, he spoke in unison with him, "The only things that fly faster than the emperor's condors are rumors!"

CHAPTER 4

Kristana's cart was no longer outside the Dragon Shrine when Javen passed the shrine on his way back to the town square. Instead, he found the pushcart inside the shop on the corner as he entered the square. Issa was sitting in it, looking bored.

He wrapped Kena's reins around one of the many hitching posts lining the square, slung a couple of large burlap sacks over his shoulder, then went from shop to shop gathering the things on his aunt's list. He saved his favorite stop of the day, the Browning Bakery, for last.

Deborah Browning's bakery, built from reddish-brown bricks, sat snugly between an herbalist and a little shop hawking trinkets on the west side of the square. Nothing differentiated it from the other shops in the square except for the wooden sign with a loaf of bread hanging over the door. Javen pushed the door open and a little mechanical arm at the top of the door rang a bell.

The aroma of fresh baked bread greeted him. He stepped up to the counter dividing the room in half and looked at the assortment of bread stacked on it. He gravitated toward the left end to look at the sweet bread while he waited for someone to come help him. After a moment, the door on the right side of the back wall swung open, and a young woman wearing a flour-covered apron emerged.

"Good morning, Javen," the young woman said.

"Morning, Kaylan," Javen said with a smile.

"What'll it be today?"

Javen handed Kaylan the burlap sack and his aunt's list.

He watched her as she worked. Until recently, he'd always thought of her as a sister. He had grown up with her, her mother, and her uncle, whenever he was around, often spending the evenings with his family at the tavern. Lately, though, he couldn't help but admire her for the beautiful woman she had blossomed into. She was slender and wore her long, light-brown hair in a single braid extending down to the middle of her back. The combination of her vivid green eyes, narrow nose, and large smile combined to form a comely face that was hard to look away from.

When she looked up at him, he looked directly into her eyes and said, "How are you today?"

"Fine, thank you," Kaylan answered, looking down. She loaded a few more loaves and said, "How's your brother?"

"You know Yolken… nothing but work, as usual," Javen replied. Of all the girls he'd ever shown an interest in, she was the only one who never returned his attention. All she ever wanted to talk about with him was his brother. And he hated talking about his brother with her. He wanted her to show an interest in him. "Did you hear that the Chancellor of the Southern Realm will be staying in Lonely Oak tonight?"

"I did. My uncle arrived last night and told us."

"He's back?" Javen asked. It had been a while since her uncle's last visit. A couple years at least.

Kaylan nodded.

"I heard there's going to be a festival," Javen said.

Kaylan placed a couple more loaves in the sack and said, "Me too."

"Have you made any plans for it yet?"

Kaylan shook her head.

"I was wondering if you'd like to spend the evening with me?" Javen said.

"Umm…" Kaylan started. "Maybe."

"Well… good. I'll check back in with you later today if I get the chance," Javen said. Even though he enjoyed kissing on different girls, what he really wanted was the opportunity to talk with Kaylan without the display case between them. Kaylan handed Javen the sack of bread, and he gave her some copper coins. "I'll see you later," he said.

"Bye, Javen."

When Javen turned to leave, Kaylan's uncle, Jorgan, came out of the kitchen. His face was more age-lined and his beard had turned partially gray since the last time Javen had seen him. He waved at Kaylan and said, "Why, hello Javen!" Javen didn't even get the chance to reply before Jorgan ducked out the front door.

Javen turned back to Kaylan and said, "I really do hope to see you later tonight."

She blushed and walked back through the door leading to the kitchen.

Javen smiled and followed her uncle out of the bakery.

He was finished with all his errands, but he still had one thing he wanted to do before returning to the tavern. He placed the sack of baked goods into the cart and walked around the oak tree to the other side of the square, keeping his distance from the armored horses, and entered another little shop. He exited a moment later with a small brown bag, then looked around the square. He found Issa sitting in her cart under the sign with a meat cleaver carved into it.

Javen walked over to the little girl, who looked longingly at the children playing under the oak tree. He stepped between her and the tree, blocking her view. At first, she tried looking around him, but her eyes lit up, and she grinned when she saw it was him. Javen smiled back. He swallowed a lump in his throat when he looked down from her smiling face to her crooked legs. Every day his heart broke at the thought of her living her life being carted around, unable to run and play with the other children.

"Morning, Issa," Javen said. "How's my lily today?"

"Good," Issa answered, her face turning red.

Javen knelt beside her and kissed her on the forehead. He handed her the brown bag.

Issa dug her hand into the bag and pulled out a sweet. Without hesitation, it disappeared into her mouth. "Will you promise to still buy me these when we're married?"

"Have a good day, my beautiful lily," Javen said with a wink. He stood back up, retrieved Kena, and proceeded back to the tavern. After guiding Kena around to the back, he grabbed the burlap sacks and went into the stone annex. Selena was busy preparing plates. He set the burlap sacks on the large woodblock table in the middle of the kitchen and hollered through the small window, "Yolken!"

Yolken entered through the swinging door. As it swung in the opposite direction, Selena slid through with plates in both hands. Yolken followed Javen out the back door and greeted Kena with a rub on her muzzle. "How are you, old girl?" Kena returned his affection with a gentle nuzzle. He rubbed her some more then inspected the new barrels. "That cooper in Croff really does good work," he said.

The two brothers worked together to unload the barrels from the cart. They carried them into the brewing shed affixed to the back of the tavern. As they worked, Javen reported the news he'd gathered about the chancellor and the festival while he was out on his errands. "And I'm hoping to spend the evening with Kaylan," he said as they walked out of the shed for another load.

"Kaylan?" Yolken said.

Javen prepared to lift another barrel out of the wagon, but Yolken wasn't there. He looked over his shoulder and saw him standing in the shed staring blankly out. "Yolken?"

Yolken shook his head and joined Javen. "You want to spend the festival with Kaylan?"

"I thought it'd be the perfect chance to let her know how I feel."

"How you feel? What do you mean?"

"The last few months I've felt different about her."

"Different?"

"Yeah. I don't really see Kaylan as a sister anymore. Help me with this," Javen said, grabbing a barrel.

Yolken helped Javen lift the barrel out of the wagon. "What do you see her as?"

"A woman."

"But what about Astora?"

"What about her?"

"I thought… weren't you just with her last night?"

"Does everybody know about that?" Javen said as they set the barrel down with the others.

"I heard it from—"

"It doesn't matter," Javen said. "I like her, but I don't feel what I feel for Kaylan."

"Which is what?"

"I don't know. But I know it's her I want to spend tonight with. Why?" Javen asked, stopping at the wagon.

Yolken shook his head. "What about the tavern?"

"You won't need me the whole night, will you?"

"I don't know."

"Not this again," Javen said with a sigh.

"Just help me finish unloading," Yolken said.

The two brothers finished moving the barrels then the grain bags in silence. When they finished, Javen followed his brother into the kitchen, kicking the dirt with his foot. Whatever happened, he was *not* going to spend the whole night working while the town celebrated.

CHAPTER 5

The tavern didn't let up, and Yolken kept Javen busy. He gladly went out with another list from Selena; if he couldn't get out of working, at least he could see what was happening. The square was being transformed with decorations, and Brall's men were erecting the dance floor.

"How goes it, Gordy?" Javen said, walking up alongside Issa's father on his way back to the tavern.

"Fool woman," Gordy huffed.

"What?"

"She's planning on taking Issa out to stand with the beggars, hoping that Dragon-cursed scale does something miraculous for her. It's bad enough she carts her to the shrine every cursed morn, but I especially hate seeing the lass's disappointment every time one of them passes through."

Javen stepped ahead of Gordy and opened the tavern door for him.

Gordy entered and plopped the jug he was carrying onto the bar. "'This'll be different,' she says, 'because one of them has never stayed here before.' 'You and every other poor or infirm will be hoping for the same thing,' I said, but she's determined. 'Go,' I said, 'but I won't stand in no beggars' line with you.'"

"Hello, Gordy," Yolken said.

"Bitter, please," Gordy replied.

Yolken took the jug and started filling it.

"I'm sorry," Javen said. "You know we adore Issa and wish the best for her."

"Thanks," Gordy said.

Javen carried the burlap sacks into the kitchen.

"That's it?" Selena said after looking through them.

"It's crazy out there, Auntie," Javen said. "Everybody was really busy. The square is packed, and every shop you sent me to was either running low on supplies or completely out."

"It'll have to do," Selena said. She returned to her tasks, muttering to herself.

The afternoon wore on and evening set in. Javen shuffled around the tavern delivering food and clearing vacated tables, disappointed he had missed the arrival of the chancellor's caravan. He listened to the patrons talking about it. He'd seen the caravan pass through town before, but he was sore he'd missed today's fanfare.

As Javen cleared off a table in the corner of the tavern by the unlit hearth, he looked around the room; more than half the tables were now empty. He carted the dishes and mugs off to the kitchen then seized the opportunity to try to make a break for it. "Yolken," he said, approaching his brother behind the bar, "I think it's finally beginning to slow down. You think I could leave?"

"I don't know, Javen," Yolken answered. "It's hardly let up all day and your help today has been invaluable."

"But it's let up now!"

Yolken looked around the tavern then said, "Fine. Go."

"Thanks, Yolken!" Javen said as he ran for the stairs. He went up to his room on the second floor and picked out the cleanest shirt he could find. That wasn't an easy task, since every shirt he owned lay on the floor in a pile. He sniffed each one in turn to find the one he thought best, went to the washroom, and quickly washed the day off. He changed shirts, bolted down the stairs, and crossed the tavern toward the front door before Yolken could change his mind.

"Javen!" Selena called.

Javen stopped by the door and waited anxiously as she approached him.

"Javen, dear," Selena said, giving Yolken a quick look, "I don't want you getting yourself into trouble."

"I hadn't planned on it," he said, looking over at his brother wiping the bar.

"Yes, dear, I know. But with the Blessed in town, you can be sure everyone will be extra sensitive to… rabble-rousing. So just be careful, all right?"

"Yes, Auntie," Javen said. He waited while she kissed him on the forehead, then disappeared through the door.

He ran across the wooden bridge toward the square but had to slow down when the road became crowded. He made his way as quickly as he could and thought about his two goals for the night: to see the chancellor up close, and to spend the night with Kaylan. As he followed the crowds toward the square, he scanned the passing faces, hoping to find her.

Hundreds of decorative oil lamps illuminated garlands and streamers wrapped around poles and signs along the fronts of buildings. Javen stopped in front of the Weary Traveler Inn when he saw the silhouette of a person lurking on an unlit balcony. People bumped into Javen as they tried to go around him. The shadowy figure's eyes reflected the light of the street below. *A Watcher,* he thought. They always accompanied regents, wearing those things over their eyes. He wondered what they were for. The flow of people jostled Javen from his thoughts and back into motion.

When he entered the town square, Javen froze, amazed by the scene before him. Ribbons tied into bows, streamers, and flickering oil lamps adorned the oak tree. It wasn't a new sight, but it invoked in him a feeling he only got during festivals. To

the right of the oak was the inn that was its namesake, the Oak—
the largest building in town, and where he had heard the
chancellor was staying. A barricade blocked off the portion of
the road between the tree and the inn, and a large wooden floor
had been set up for dancing. He turned left and moved through
the crowd toward the Browning Bakery.

Kaylan's mother, Deborah, leaned on the doorpost by the
door. The light made some of the gray in her hair sparkle. She
smiled at him as he approached. "Good evening, Javen," she
said. "Enjoying the festivities?"

"Haven't had a chance yet."

"Oh?"

"I just got here."

"Ah."

"Deb… I mean, Missus Browning," Javen stammered.

"Yes?"

"I was wondering if Kaylan was here?"

Deborah shook her head. "Sorry, Javen. When we finished
baking for the day, I sent her out to enjoy herself."

"Do you know where she is?"

The door to the bakery opened and Kaylan's uncle Jorgan
came out, drawing Deborah's attention. "Where're you going?"
she asked him.

"I thought I'd go pay this lad's aunt a visit," Jorgan said,
nodding toward Javen.

Javen watched Jorgan survey the crowd as he stroked his
bristly beard.

"I'm sure she'll be glad to see you," Deborah said.

Jorgan smiled at Deborah, patted Javen on the shoulder,
then disappeared into the crowd.

"Sorry," Deborah said, turning back to Javen. "What were
we saying?"

"I was wondering if you knew where Kaylan was."

"You do know how she likes to dance. Maybe you'll find her

on the floor."

"Thanks, Missus Browning."

"Mmm-hmm."

Javen wove his way through the crowd as he crossed to the other side of the square. He didn't have his brother's height—Yolken was over a head taller than he was—so he knew it would be difficult to find Kaylan in the crowd. Halfway around the square, he arrived at the barricade encircling the large wooden floor. He climbed up onto the temporary fence to get a better view. On a platform standing on the far side of the floor, musicians plucked away at their instruments, creating an upbeat tune. He scanned the floor but didn't find Kaylan.

The far end of the floor abutted the boardwalk outside the Oak, and he saw several soldiers standing around the entrance. Their armor shimmered in the artificial light of the many lanterns illuminating the square.

He scanned the dance floor again. He saw Astora dancing with a boy he recognized from an outlying farm, but he did not see Kaylan. He hopped over the permanent fence separating the tree from the roadway and used the empty space surrounding the tree to walk around the dance floor. On the other side of the floor, he hopped back over the fence and continued his way around the square, scanning the crowds for Kaylan. He returned to the bakery without success. When he locked eyes with Missus Browning, she shrugged her shoulders.

Javen sighed. Not wanting to miss a perfect opportunity to make his interest in Kaylan known, he made his way around the square again. He moved slowly, afraid he would walk past her without seeing her. He arrived a second time at the dance floor and climbed on the barricade to scan the dancers. Not finding her, he hopped down, feeling dejected. The square was unbelievably crowded—more so than during any of Lonely Oak's usual festivals; he knew he could spend the entire night looking for her and not find her.

"Hello!" a voice shouted next to him.

Javen looked up, hoping the voice he barely heard over the din belonged to Kaylan. It didn't. Instead, he looked into the eyes of a thin, black-haired girl sitting on the fence. Her hair bobbed down to just below the ears and curled near the ends. Her thin, light-blue silk blouse and brown silk pants identified her as a southerner. She had her right leg crossed over her left, and her right foot swung in and out. She sat straight with her arms tucked in at her sides, hands gripping the fence rail. "Hi," he said, looking up at her before climbing up on the fence himself. He scoured the dance floor again for Kaylan.

"Looking for someone in particular?"

"Huh? Oh. Yeah."

"Who?"

"Um… a friend," Javen said, continuing his search. After convincing himself she wasn't on the dance floor, he scanned the crowd on the other side of the square and thought about whether he wanted to keep searching. He climbed off the fence, not wanting to waste the entire night, and looked up at the girl. "You dance?"

"Yes!" she exclaimed with a grin. "Just waiting for someone to ask."

Javen held his hand out, and she placed her hand in his. She hopped off the fence, and he led her to the opening in the barrier. The musicians were in between songs so some dancers were leaving the wooden floor and others were entering. Javen and the girl joined the others entering the floor and took up position opposite each other.

The fiddles took up their music. Javen gave a quick bow to the girl and she curtsied in return, then they started spinning and twirling in time to the music. The tempo was upbeat, so they moved quickly on the floor. By the time Javen thought about asking the girl her name, he had to spin her off to the man to his left, and another girl took her place. He was familiar with this dance, so he knew that after four more women passed through his arms, she would be dancing with him once again.

"What's your name?" he shouted at her over the music when she finally twirled into his arms.

"Hadie!" she shouted. "Yours?"

"Javen!"

Hadie smiled up at Javen, then he spun her again to the next man in line. They danced through three more songs—he was thankful Astora wasn't dancing anymore—and at the end of the fourth song, they were both sweaty and breathing hard. Hadie's silk shirt was damp and clung to her curves. Were it not for her eyes continuously drawing his attention, Javen would have had a hard time not staring. In the short rest between songs, Javen took Hadie by the hand and they bowed to the partners on either side of them, signaling to them they were done.

"Are you hungry?" Javen said.

"Famished."

"Good, 'cause I haven't eaten supper yet and I'm starving, too." Javen led Hadie by the hand through the crowd toward a pub a few buildings to the right of the Oak.

The Tankard was bustling. Javen scanned the establishment and found an empty table in the back corner. He weaved around tables, leading Hadie through the crowded room. They sat down, and after a few minutes a barmaid greeted them. Her low-cut dress was laced up the back, cinching the material tightly around her torso. The resulting effect was what made the Tankard so popular.

"What'll it be?" the barmaid asked with a forward dip.

"We'll take two ales and whatever's cooking," Javen answered. Even though Javen was a regular here, the barmaid gave no indication she had ever laid eyes on him before. The truth was, though, they were intimately familiar with each other. Although he ignored her overt display now, he did no such thing when he came here alone. With his smooth hands and generous money, he was her favorite customer.

"Geena!" A voice hollered through the small window

separating the kitchen from the pub as some steaming plates appeared on the sill. Geena nodded in acknowledgment of his order, then left with another curtsy. She delivered the steaming plates from the sill to a table across the room then returned with two tankards.

"To the chancellor!" Javen toasted, holding up his tankard.

Hadie hesitated, then said, "To new beginnings." She knocked her tankard against his. After taking a drink, she said, "You from around here?"

"Yeah. Lived here my whole life."

"Seems like a nice enough place."

"It is," Javen said, taking a drink. "Though I've never known anything different."

"What do you do?"

"My family has a tavern."

"Your own tavern, eh? So what are we doing here?"

"It's on the other side of town, away from the festivities," Javen said. "And I know that if I step foot back there tonight, my brother won't let me leave again."

Geena returned to their table with two steaming plates. She set one down in front of Hadie first, then set the other in front of Javen. She also handed each of them a cloth napkin with utensils rolled up inside. "Another ale?"

Javen looked at Hadie and raised his eyebrows. She nodded. "Yes, please," he said.

"So," Hadie said when Geena had left, "you run the tavern with your brother?"

Javen nodded, his mouth full of food. When he swallowed, he said, "My brother's pretty much in charge, and our aunt runs the kitchen. I just do what they tell me to."

"How'd that arrangement come to be? Seems like she should be the one in charge."

Geena returned with two more tankards.

"Thanks!" Hadie said.

Geena nodded then left.

Her first tankard empty, Hadie gripped the new one by the handle and took a long drink. "So?"

"Originally the tavern belonged to our parents," Javen explained. "There was a fire when my brother and I were little, and they both died."

"I'm so sorry," Hadie said. She reached across the table and stroked Javen's arm gently.

"Thanks."

"What were their names?"

"Orwyn and Elen."

"Mmm. Those are nice names. Again, I'm sorry."

"Truth is, we were really young when it happened, and I don't even remember it. Our aunt moved here and raised us. She used money our parents had saved to rebuild the tavern, and when my brother was old enough, she let him take control."

"Still, it must have been hard growing up without your parents."

"She's all we've ever known."

"Well, here's to Orwyn and Elen." Hadie held her tankard up.

Javen tapped his against Hadie's and took a drink. "What's your story?"

"Like a lot of people these days, I'm heading north."

"With your family?"

"Just me," Hadie said. "Despite how bad things are getting in the south, my parents refused to leave. We had a lot of land on the outskirts of Hantlo and lived in a mansion in the city big enough for ten families. My father believes whatever the Regency tells him and refused to leave—though if you ask me, he just couldn't fathom leaving his wealth behind. So I left. I wanted to be long gone before the Regency lost control."

"Are things really that bad in the south?"

"Bad enough. Regents might be able to clean their cities up after a cyclone blows through, but they're powerless to stop the droughts causing crops to fail and lakes to dry up. Even Hantlo took a beating this last season. And most people south of Baytown have already fled their homes. Those provinces are all but abandoned."

"What about your mother?"

"She wanted to go, but she would never leave without my father."

"Where you headed?"

"Dunno. North. I stayed in Matis for a few months, but the time came to move on."

"How long have you been in Lonely Oak?"

"Got here the day before yesterday. I was intending on leaving today, but when I heard Dorlan was going to be here tonight, I figured I'd stay another day. He is the Chancellor of the Southern Realm, after all."

Javen took another drink and smiled at Hadie, looking her in the eyes. They were mostly green with a little brown mixed in. They pulled his gaze toward them like reins pulling a horse in the direction it should go. He said, "I'm sorry if I'm being forward, but…"

"What?"

"You're absolutely captivating."

"Thanks," Hadie said quickly. She tried hiding behind her tankard, but Javen could tell she was blushing.

Javen took a drink then said, "Where're you staying?"

"The Oak."

"*You* have a room at the Oak?"

"I do. The chancellor's guards said I could keep my room if I let them interview me. You know, to make sure I'm not secretly plotting to kill him or anything. Since I have nothing to hide, I agreed."

"Have you ever seen him before?"

"My father is wealthy, remember."

"So?"

"So that means I've attended my fair share of galas at his palace."

"So you've seen the chancellor? That's amazing!"

Hadie nodded. "You haven't?"

"I've seen his caravan pass through a few times, but he's never stopped here before. This is definitely a first for our town, hence the festival." He lifted his tankard to his mouth then, lowering it a little, said, "I was kind of hoping to catch a glimpse of him."

"Let's go then!" Hadie upended her drink and downed the rest of her ale.

Javen followed suit, then stood, leaving a generous amount of money on the table. As he followed Hadie out of the Tankard, he was grinning from ear to ear.

CHAPTER 6

Yolken worried that the tavern would get busy again the moment Javen walked out the door. But as the evening wore on, it only got slower. The evening meal was over, and except for Relan and one other bar-mate, the tavern was empty. The late evening rush wouldn't come for a few more hours—there were always those wanting one or two more mugs of ale before returning to their lodgings for the night—so taking advantage of the lull, he worked at getting the place back in order.

When he finished, he returned to the bar to tend to Relan and the other man, who sat hunched with his elbows on the bar, mug clasped in both hands. The front door swung in, and Kaylan's uncle entered. He clapped Relan on the shoulder and sat next to him. Yolken smiled at the sight of Jorgan and walked over to where he sat at the bar.

"Long time no see," he said.

"Indeed, lad," Jorgan said.

"And what a festival they threw for your arrival!"

"I sure pick the right times to show up, don't I?" Jorgan said with a laugh. "The Chancellor of the Southern Realm, eh? How'd you convince him to stay in this cesspool of yours?"

"I promised him world class ale, that's how!"

"It's good to see you, lad," Jorgan said, reaching out and squeezing Yolken on the forearm. "Nice painting, by the way."

Yolken looked over his shoulder at the painting of the Mindon Falls hanging over the barrels. The Mindon Mountain range ended abruptly on its north side in huge cliffs that stretched for nearly a hundred leagues. It was said to be one of the largest waterfalls in all of Dradonia. "Thanks. Got it from a merchant a while back."

"I never had an eye for art," Jorgan said. "Now, give me one of those famous ales before I have to climb over this bar and beat it out of you."

Selena emerged from the kitchen and, with a broad smile, said, "I thought I heard a familiar voice."

"Hello, Selena," Jorgan said.

"Hello, Jorgan."

"Why don't you take a break, lad?" Jorgan said after Yolken set a mug in front of him. "Looks like you've been working yourself near to death. Your aunt and I can manage well enough for a while."

"I don't know," Selena said, looking from Jorgan to Yolken.

"What's the harm?" Jorgan said. "The lad deserves a break now and then."

Yolken looked at Selena, his eyes pleading with her. "A break would be nice. You *did* say I needed to work less…"

"Go on, lad. Have some fun!" Jorgan said.

"Fine," Selena acquiesced. "Just be careful. And don't think I've forgotten about this morning. We're still gonna have that talk."

Yolken's smile faded. He took his apron off and said, "I won't be gone long."

He stepped out of the tavern and took a deep breath of the fresh night air. Excitedly, he crossed the wooden bridge and stopped when he saw Kaylan walking in his direction.

"Hi there," Kaylan said, stopping in front of him.

"Hi, Kaylan," Yolken stammered. He ran his hand through

his hair and grabbed the back of his neck.

"How're you this evening?"

"Tired. It's been really busy all day, but it's slowed down, so Auntie said she'd watch things so I could take a break."

"That's sweet of her."

"What about you?"

"Excellent," Kaylan said with a smile.

"That's good," Yolken said. Then, pointing back toward the tavern, he added, "Your uncle stopped in."

"I figured," Kaylan said. "He always manages to find his way down here before he's been in town for long."

"It's been a while since I saw him last."

"You know him, always traveling the empire," Kaylan said. "You're not too tired to dance, are you?"

The question caught Yolken by surprise. "Here?"

"No, silly. In the square. On the dance floor."

"I'm not much of a dancer, Kaylan. You know that."

"I don't care. Tonight's a rare celebration. Everyone from leagues around is here, and I want to dance. With you." Kaylan reached out and grabbed Yolken's hand and pulled him toward the square. "Just don't break all my toes, all right?"

* * *

Selena refilled Jorgan's mug, and Jorgan scooped it up. He breathed in the floral aroma, then walked over to a table next to the fireless hearth, sat down, and put his feet up. Relan got up as well and followed him unsteadily.

"How are you, old friend?" Jorgan said, watching Selena tend to the sole remaining patron out of the corner of his eye.

Relan held up his mug in a mock toast. "Where you in from?"

"Oh, you know, here and there."

"Not at liberty to speak of it, eh?"

Selena sat at the table. "It's been a few years, Jorgan. Where've you been?"

"He can't say," Relan said.

Selena pursed her lips. "Relan, do you mind if I have a private word with Jorgan?"

Relan drained his mug then said, "I suppose I could call it a night. Good seeing ya, Jorgan."

"You too," Jorgan said. After Relan had stumbled out the door, Jorgan looked at Selena and said, "I miss your cooking, you know."

"Are the rumors true?" Selena asked in a hushed voice.

"They are," Jorgan replied in a whisper.

"What happened?"

"One of the mayor's servants talked to Dalia."

"Should we be concerned?"

Jorgan shook his head. "Not about that."

"What do you mean?"

"We have bigger concerns."

"What?"

Jorgan stared into his mug then took a drink. "The older the lad gets, the more he reminds me of his father."

"Jax…"

Jorgan looked up at Selena when he heard her use his real name. "Is he still using his gift?"

Selena nodded. "Just this morning, right after he came in from outside, he transferred Energy into a plate. He yelped when he picked the plate up because it was so hot."

"What about his brother?"

"I don't know," Selena said. "I haven't noticed anything with him yet."

Jorgan sipped his ale. "Does Yolken know what's happening?"

"Not yet," Selena said. "But he'll figure it out soon enough."

"Has anyone else noticed?"

"I don't think so, but it's only a matter of time until someone does. I'd be lying if I said I wasn't worried about Yolken being out while Dorlan is here in town."

"It's dark out."

"True."

"It's a moot point anyhow."

"Meaning?"

"Meaning the Council has approved the plan."

"You can't possibly think he'll succeed where Orwyn failed, can you?" Selena said.

"We have to try. Conditions are getting worse in the south and the emperor still refuses to do anything."

"What *can* he do?"

"I don't know." Jorgan took another sip of ale. "But we've further refined the astronomer's report."

"And?"

Jorgan looked directly at Selena and shook his head. "We're running out of time, Selena, and Drakonias doesn't seem to care."

"How much time do we have?"

"A year. Maybe five. Does it matter?"

A look of fear crossed Selena's face as she shook her head.

"We have to do something, Selena."

"What about Javen?"

"Our chances will be better if they both go."

"This is not what Orwyn wanted—his children becoming pawns of the Order."

"We don't have a choice, Selena," Jorgan said, his voice stern.

"So that's it? We just uproot them?"

"They're dead if we don't. We all are."

Selena stared past Jorgan and absentmindedly toyed with her hair bun, which he noticed was now peppered with gray. They were all showing signs they were aging. While she was avoiding eye contact with him, he studied her face, remembering. He pushed back against the memories, knowing now was not the time to dredge up the past.

"We're out of options," Jorgan said.

"I know," Selena said tersely. "What's the plan, then?"

"For now, remain here. I need to return to Croff and finalize a few things. But be ready. I'll return quickly and then we'll all leave together."

Selena shook her head. "All of this, their entire lives, gone, just like that."

Jorgan upended his mug and drained it of ale. "You knew as well as I that this is exactly how this was going to end."

* * *

Hadie led Javen along the edge of the square from the Tankard to the Oak. Their footsteps wove on and off the wooden boardwalk to get through the crowd. They were stopped at the front door of the Oak by guards.

"Key," one of them demanded.

While Hadie dug the key from her pocket, Javen gawked at the soldiers' glistening armor. Although he knew it was gray, it looked black in the light of the lanterns. Even after growing up watching soldiers and regents ride through town, their scale-like armor continued to amaze him. One large oval-shaped piece, wider at the top than the bottom, covered the man's chest and torso. There were matching oval plates on his shoulders. The arms and sides were filled in with much smaller, overlapping scale-shaped pieces. He bent forward to get a closer look.

The soldier looked down his nose at Javen but let him be.

Hadie produced the key, made of metal and cast in the shape of an oak tree, and the soldier waved her in. But he held his hand up to block Javen when he attempted to pass.

"We're together," Hadie said.

The soldier kept his hand up.

"We were interviewed earlier today in our room," Hadie lied.

The soldier looked at Javen again, then lowered his arm and let him pass.

Inside the Oak it was just as crowded as outside. People ate and drank at every table. Standing at the base of the stairs were more soldiers like the guards posted at the entrance, and another group of them in the back corner, furthest from the door, positioned around two men wearing blue armor. Their armor resembled the guards' except for the muscled chest pattern on their fronts. One of them wore scaled gloves matching his armor. *Regents,* Javen thought with awe. They were the Blessed of the Dragon, revered around Dradonia as the agents of the Great Dragon's will. His eyes stopped with interest on a honey-skinned woman sitting with the regents. Her thin blue dress was low cut and revealed much of her cleavage. He felt his face getting flushed.

"That's Devin and Karina," Hadie whispered. "I wonder what they're doing with Dorlan."

"*That's* Karina Drake?" Javen said. He knew from his boyhood lessons that Devin was the Regent of Onta in the Western Realm and his wife was the envy of most women, a renowned beauty.

"You know her?"

"Doesn't everybody? Girls talk about her all the time—the greatest lover in all of the United Realms."

"I've always wanted to meet her. I saw her from afar once at a gala back home, but by the time I made it over to where she was, she had gone."

"Well, go introduce yourself."

"No."

"Why not?"

"Because... I can't. What would I say to her? 'Hi, I'm Hadie. I enjoy reading about your exploits in *Lovers of Onta.*'?"

He watched as a couple walked over to the regents and bowed. Karina held her hand out, and the woman kissed the back of it. Elbowing Hadie, he said, "See, she doesn't seem to mind meeting new people."

"I just... they're with Drenan," Hadie said. Her face reflected her dislike.

"What do you have against him?"

"He's vile."

"Really?" Except for old Relan, he'd never heard anyone talk about the Blessed in such a way.

"Let me put it this way: He's someone you do *not* want to cross. Come on," Hadie said, pulling him farther into the inn.

They found a spot next to the bar where they could stand and drink while they waited to see if the chancellor would make an appearance. Javen ordered two tankards of ale from the bar, then noticed a group of people huddling in the corner by the door. Kristana stood in their midst, and Issa sat on the ground at her feet. She looked up at him and waved with a smile. He winked at her, causing her smile to grow.

"I hope he comes down from his room," Javen said.

"He will," Hadie answered.

He took a drink of his ale and, tasting a familiar product, said, "This is my brother's. It's his bitter ale."

"Is it? It's good."

"How do you know?" Javen asked.

"How do I know what?"

"That he'll come down. Maybe he's tired from his travels."

"What, you mean tired from reclining in his carriage, eating, and drinking wine all day? The Blessed are all about show, Javen. All we have to do is wait."

Javen drank his brother's ale and wondered how Hadie could be so disrespectful, but he didn't want to say anything for fear of ruining the evening. Instead, he looked over at Issa and made faces at her. She made a face back.

"Who's that?" Hadie said.

"Issa."

"She seems to like you."

Issa made another face at Javen, and he returned it. "We're getting married," he said.

"Really? Does she know you've been ogling me all night?"

"I have not."

"Maybe I should go over and tell her."

"And break her heart?"

"So you admit it?" Javen bent over to kiss Hadie, but she put her hand over his mouth and said, "And break her heart?"

"Later?"

Hadie lifted her tankard, but not before Javen saw her impish smile. His pulse skipped a beat.

A disturbance behind Javen caused him to turn. The soldiers at the base of the stairs had formed up into a half-circle. As people realized what was happening, silence spread across the large room. Javen locked his eyes on the stairs, about to realize one of his goals for the night.

Elaborate orange boots, made of the same material as the soldiers' armor, came into view and started down the steps. Following the boots, next into view were orange-scaled leggings, then a breastplate with six medium scales over the abdomen and two large scales covering the chest. An orange cloak flowed out behind the man, and a long dagger with a black hilt was cinched into his belt. Then Javen saw his face. *Dorlan Drake,* he thought in wonder. *The Chancellor of the Southern Realm.* He could hardly believe he was standing in the same room as three of the Blessed of the Dragon—one of whom was second only to the emperor.

When the chancellor reached the bottom of the staircase, the other two regents stood, and a wave spread across the room as people fell to their knees. Hadie knelt beside Javen then tugged on his arm, pulling him down with her.

The soldiers formed around Dorlan, making a protective gray-armored circle. A sweaty and anxious Brall met the chancellor and followed him as he strode across the room toward the exit. Javen could hear Brall asking about every aspect of the chancellor's stay, wondering if everything met his approval.

As Dorlan approached the door, cries of "Have mercy on us!" and "Please help!" and "Heal my baby!" chorused from the downtrodden group gathered in the corner. The chancellor stopped and turned toward them. The ring of soldiers parted, making an opening for the chancellor. He looked the group over then gestured for Kristana, who was now holding Issa in her arms, to come forward.

"Oh Blessed of the Dragon, please heal my baby!" Kristana said.

"Lay her on the ground," the chancellor said.

Kristana lowered herself to her knees and gently put her daughter down.

Dorlan knelt near Issa and placed his right hand on the hilt of the dagger at his belt. Then he placed his left hand on Issa's head.

At his touch, Issa began writhing in pain. A tortured shriek pierced the hushed room. Her legs flailed about. Her arms twitched violently. With fear in her eyes, Kristana cradled Issa's head. But then Issa quit screaming, and her legs stopped moving. She lay in her mother's lap, completely still.

Dorlan stood and said, "Help her to her feet."

Kristana hesitated, but when Dorlan nodded, she took Issa by the hands and helped her stand.

Issa wobbled on her feet. She lost her balance and reached out for her mother's arm to steady herself.

Javen stared, amazed. Issa had been crippled her whole life but now she was completely healed.

The inn erupted in applause and shouts of praise to the chancellor and Great Dragon.

The chancellor smiled benevolently at Issa, who beamed up at him. He turned from the group of clamoring beggars, the soldiers closed the gap around him, and he made his way out of the inn.

Kristana followed behind, pulling Issa unsteadily along, shouting, "Thank you! Thank you! Thank you!"

* * *

Yolken collapsed in the grass surrounding the oak tree. Kaylan sat down beside him. They were both breathing hard.

"You… sure… can… move," Yolken said between heavy breaths. "I can barely keep up with you."

"You're getting better," Kaylan reassured him.

"Hardly. After tonight, I'll surely have the reputation of the man who broke the toes of every girl in town."

"It wasn't that bad! Besides, it doesn't really matter how good you are. What matters is that you're having fun, just like everyone else out there."

"I suppose. Though I have a hard enough time looking one girl in the eye, let alone a different girl every couple of minutes."

"That's the beauty of the dance; it forces you to do things you're not comfortable with."

"Yeah, well, I don't like being uncomfortable."

"Oh yeah? How does this make you feel?" Kaylan said shyly, sliding her hand into his.

Yolken felt his face and ears warm. He looked over at Kaylan but then averted his eyes. He looked up at the night sky. The tail of the Great Dragon constellation was visible beyond the edge of the tree's leaves. There was a noticeable gap in the string of stars. It was taught in the Dragon Shrine that the missing star had come down to Dradonia and created the Blessed.

"People of Lonely Oak!" a voice boomed. It was unnaturally loud, distracting Yolken and Kaylan from their moment. They stood and looked in the direction of the Oak, where the sound came from. "I present to you His Highness, Dorlan Drakonias Irigwin Drake, Chancellor of the Southern Realm, and Blessed of the Dragon!"

A procession of armored soldiers exited the Oak, a man wearing orange armor in the middle of them.

"Look!" Yolken said, pointing, "There's the chancellor!" He was filled with a sense of reverence he hadn't felt for a while.

"I can't see," Kaylan said, straining on tiptoe.

"Come on," Yolken said, tugging her hand. He led her over

to the fence and hoisted her up onto the top rung.

The procession slowly made its way around the square. The crowd knelt as the chancellor approached and rose to their feet as he passed.

"Dorlan," Yolken said in a whisper.

Kaylan looked in his direction, but then returned her gaze to the procession passing in front of them. Yolken helped Kaylan off the fence, and they both knelt in the grass.

The chancellor completed his solemn trip around the square then returned to the Oak. Revelry once again overtook the square. Yolken and Kaylan returned to the tree and sat at its base, side by side.

"You wanna dance again?" Kaylan said.

"Not really," Yolken said. "I gotta get back to the tavern soon, so I just want to sit here with you."

Kaylan smiled and snuggled close.

They talked and listened to the music, enjoying their time together, but eventually Yolken started feeling the tug of the tavern.

"I gotta be getting back," he said. He stood and offered his hand to Kaylan, who took it. He helped her to her feet and gathered her into his arms. He pulled back and looked down into her eyes. The desire to kiss her welled within him, but he abandoned the idea at the last moment. Instead he said, "See you tomorrow?"

Kaylan nodded.

Yolken hugged her again then let go.

Kaylan remained standing at the base of the tree while he hopped the fence and disappeared into the crowd.

* * *

Patrons streamed out of the Oak behind the chancellor. Javen figured most people in this area were like him—it was a rare opportunity to see a chancellor, so they wanted to catch every glimpse of him they could.

Hadie downed her ale and grabbed Javen by the hand.

"Come on," she said, glancing out toward the festivities.

He resisted her pull while he gulped down the rest of his brother's ale and set his tankard on the bar along with a few coins. Then he gave into Hadie's urging and followed.

She led him out of the inn to the makeshift dance floor. The music had stopped while everyone was watching the procession. He watched the chancellor make his way around the square and knelt again when he drew near. When the chancellor disappeared back into the Oak, the music started up again.

Javen lost himself to the music and let the dance carry him across the floor from woman to woman. Each time he found himself back with Hadie, their eyes connected—not in the same way they did with the other women he spun around, but in a deeper, more intimate way. He knew their evening wouldn't end with dancing.

Something by the oak tree caught Javen's eye as he received a new dance partner from the man next to him. He completed a half spin, turned his head away from the woman he held hands with and looked toward the tree.

Yolken was sitting against the trunk. Kaylan sat next to him.

Javen turned his gaze back to the woman he danced with, the smile evaporating from his face. He woodenly completed the sequence of steps and twirls and, as he handed her off to the next man in line, he cursed through clenched teeth, "Draego's Fire."

Javen continued the dance, stealing a look toward the oak when he could, looking left here, or right there. He didn't even notice when he was once again dancing with Hadie.

"Hey!" Hadie shouted.

Javen broke his gaze away from the tree and looked down at Hadie.

"What's the matter?"

"Nothing," Javen said, shaking his head.

"You wanna call it a night? Maybe head back to my room?"

Javen broke from custom and stopped mid-dance. He

reached down and kissed Hadie deeply. As the dancers twirled around them, she kissed him back. Finally, she ended the kiss, took Javen by the hand, and guided him between dancers and off the dance platform. Without another word, she led him back to the Oak and up to her room.

When Hadie locked the door and turned to face him, Javen completely forgot about his second goal.

CHAPTER 7

The smile Yolken had awoken with was now gone, replaced with a frown of agitation. On a morning when he really needed Javen's help, Javen was nowhere to be found. Unable to wait any longer for Javen to show up, he found himself having to run Javen's morning errands for him while Selena tended the tavern and kitchen alone.

"I'm going to give him an ultimatum," he'd said as he rushed about the tavern.

"I'm just as disappointed, Yolken, but try not to be harsh," Selena answered. "Remember that he *is* your brother."

"I know, Auntie. But we're having a hard enough time running this place as it is. And after yesterday, I need his help more than ever. If he isn't willing to do that, then I need to find someone who is."

"Just don't be harsh is all."

"I won't. I'm just going to tell him what I expect from here on out and leave it to him to decide if he's willing to do it."

He clutched Selena's list in his hand as he made his way toward the square. He had thought for sure Selena would use the quiet moment they shared each morning while they broke their fasts to talk about whatever she'd said she needed to talk to him about. But she didn't. The previous day had been busy with the chancellor and festivities, and he had fallen asleep with Kaylan filling his mind, so that he'd barely had the chance to think about it. The hot plate was definitely bizarre, and his aunt seemed to think it was his fault. But how in Draego's Fire could he have caused it?

Passing the Haven, Yolken heard someone call his name. He stopped as Astora's father walked over to him.

"Have you seen my daughter?"

"No, sir," Yolken said.

"I know she was with that brother of yours night before last."

"Honest, sir. I haven't seen him since last night."

"If you see her, will you send her home?"

"Yes, sir."

Astora's father turned back to the Haven, grumbling to himself, and Yolken moved on.

The morning bustle of the town was getting off to a slower-than-normal start. Yolken passed through the mostly vacant square littered with the evidence of a glorious celebration. Selena had told him she'd seen the chancellor's caravan leave town before dawn. If a crowd had gathered to bid him farewell, it had long since dispersed. He walked to the left around the great oak because the wooden dance floor still barricaded the road to the right. When he passed the floor, he saw a dozen men working diligently to dismantle it. The only other activity in the square was a handful of children climbing in the tree and hanging from its branches.

Yolken pushed open the door to Norin's and went in.

"Greetings, Master Thornhill!" Norin bellowed. "Lemme guess, the younger of the Thornhill boys didn't make it home last night?"

"How'd you know?"

"A lucky guess, lad. That, and by the looks of the lass your brother was with last night, I figured he wouldn't be waking before noon—at the earliest."

Yolken shook his head. "I was hoping your team hadn't left yet."

"Not yet, lad."

"Good," Yolken said, breathing a sigh of relief. "After last night, I have a lot to order."

"You and everyone else. I figured as much, so I held the team longer than usual so all you proprietors could get your orders in." Norin's eyes widened when Yolken handed him his list. "Blessed Dragon! That's quite the order, Master Thornhill."

"Yesterday saw more ale roll out of the cellar than usually does in an entire month, Norin. When do you think it'll be in?"

"It shouldn't be more than six or seven days."

Yolken thought about what he had left down in his cellar and did the math in his head. He had gone through an entire barrel of both mild and bitter last night. Seven days to get supplies, plus the time it would take for his ale to ferment and age, against the number of barrels he had left... "That'll be cutting it close, especially if any more regents decide to stop over in town in the next two weeks," he said.

"Anything else, lad?"

Yolken thought for a moment then said, "You'd better add ten barrels of the finest you can get in Croff. I hate doing it, but I don't want to risk running out entirely."

"Sure thing, Master Thornhill."

His business with Norin completed, Yolken bid him a good day and turned to leave.

"Aren't you interested in what news I might have?"

"News?" Yolken said. "Or rumors?"

Norin laughed his booming laugh. "Ah, well, you know the ancient saying, 'all news starts as rumors, but not all rumors turn out to be news!'"

"So... which is it?"

"I'll let you be the judge. A reliable source has it that a certain Blessed who graced our humble town last night took a real liking to locally crafted ales."

"The chancellor liked my ale?"

"So much so that he took a barrel off of Brall's hands and took it with him—compliments of the Oak, or so the rumors say."

"Huh," Yolken said, thinking.

"The purveyor of said ale *might* want to consider permanently ramping up his production, as said purveyor might not know when large-quantity orders might start rolling in."

"I suppose that that purveyor will need to start looking for a good, quality supplier, then."

"That smarts, Master Thornhill!"

"See you later, Norin."

With his order placed, Yolken made his way back to the square—which was now filling with its usual morning crowd—and began gathering the goods on Selena's list. When he finally entered the Browning Bakery, the fresh aroma of baked bread and Kaylan's beaming smile greeted him.

"I was hoping to see you again today," Kaylan said, still smiling.

"Me too," Yolken said, returning her gaze. He handed her Selena's list, letting their hands touch briefly, and passed her a burlap sack. "I woke this morning thinking yesterday was just a dream. But then, seeing the aftermath in the square told me that at least the part about the chancellor actually happened. I've spent the morning hoping the rest did too."

Kaylan's face reddened, then she turned to fill Yolken's order. Yolken watched her graceful movements as she filled the burlap sack.

A piercing scream from outside the bakery caused him to look over his shoulder. He stepped over to the window and looked out. People were hopping the fence surrounding the oak tree and gathering at its base. When another scream filled the square, Kaylan ran around the counter and looked out the window as well. The screaming turned hysterical.

"I'll be right back," Yolken said. Kaylan nodded then followed him outside. She stood by the door as he crossed the street toward the tree. He sprang over the fence, approached the group of people crowding under the tree's thick branches, and asked a bystander, "What's going on?"

"A little girl fell from the tree."

Yolken felt compelled to push his way toward the center of the crowd. He moved forward until he saw Issa laying on the ground, her body oddly contorted, with Kristana kneeling over her. "Kristana, what happened?" he asked, kneeling beside her.

"Sh-she fell out of the t-tree," Kristana sobbed.

The rumors were true, Yolken thought. As the late-night patrons had started filtering through the tavern, he'd heard rumors that the chancellor had healed a crippled girl. He couldn't substantiate it, though, because no one had actually seen it happen. However, with so many people reporting the same thing, he figured it had some modicum of credibility. *All news starts as rumors.*

"The chancellor—" Kristana stopped and sniffed. "He fixed her legs and so she—" She sniffed again. "She wanted to play with the other children while I shopped. I heard her scream and I came running. The other children… they said she fell from the tree. Oh, Issa!"

Yolken looked down at Issa. Her head was bent unnaturally to the side, and her left leg had a protruding bone just below the knee. "Has anyone gone to get help?" he asked, looking up at the crowd.

"Yes," someone replied.

Her leg could be set, he knew, but her neck…

She wasn't moving.

Yolken watched helplessly as she labored for breath. He looked up at Kristana and saw the despair in her eyes. She silently pleaded with him to do something for Issa. His heart ached for both Kristana and Gordy at the thought of them losing their daughter.

He reached down and placed his hand on Issa's forehead. If something wasn't done, she was going to die. He wanted desperately to help this innocent little girl, whom the whole town adored. But he knew, looking at her, that her neck was broken. There was nothing that *could* be done.

Yolken looked back up at Kristana. Her eyes continued to plead with him. The desperation on her face begged him to do *something*. He looked down at Issa again and felt helpless. He wasn't like the Blessed, whom the Great Dragon had given the ability to perform miracles. He thought about sending someone after the chancellor to beg him to come back. But he didn't know if Issa would last that long—her breathing was growing weaker by the moment. Kristana's desperation crept into him. He knew Issa was about to die.

Yolken reached up, wiped his brow with the sleeve of his shirt. With his forehead tucked into the crook of his shoulder and arm, he paused—suddenly becoming acutely aware of the heat on his skin. He looked up at the sun standing above the buildings lining the square.

The source of life.

The ultimate source of the life slipping away from Issa.

Yolken stared at the sun with squinted eyes, feeling its warmth on his face.

He acted. He didn't know how—or why—but he drew the sun's warmth in.

The heat of the sun flowed into him. It concentrated in his chest. It grew. He didn't know what to do with the growing warmth, but he knew he needed more.

He wanted more.

It felt amazing.

So he drew more of the sun's warmth in. He drew it in until he felt hot, full.

The sun's heat began percolating through his body, making beads of sweat collect on his skin.

The moment stretched out. Yolken felt as though he'd been staring down at Issa's body for an eternity. He didn't know what he was doing but knew he needed more of the sun's warmth. He felt full, but he drew more in. Somehow, he *knew* he needed to. As he continued to draw in more heat, sweat started flowing from his pores in torrents, stinging his eyes. He used a sleeve to wipe them.

He stopped pulling the sun's heat in when he felt an internal strain. He knew he couldn't hold any more.

It was time to use the life source—the power—he held.

He moved his hand down to Issa's wrenched neck and instinctively reached through his hand and into her neck with the sun's warmth. He directed this new extension of himself through Issa's tissues and into her spine. He probed the bones until he felt the location of the break. Using the sun's warmth, he guided the bone back into place. At the same time, he used his hands to straighten her neck. He felt around with the power until he was confident all the pieces of bone were where they were supposed to be, then he began fusing them back together.

As Yolken worked, he felt the pool in his chest emptying. With more work to do, he began absorbing more heat from the sun. He kept a steady stream coming in as he directed it into Issa.

When Issa's neck was healed, she gasped and opened her eyes. They were filled with terror. She let out a scream and tried sitting up.

"Shh," Yolken said, holding her back. "You took a fall, but you're all right."

Issa tried squirming away but cried out again when she moved her leg.

"Issa, Issa, Issa," Yolken said, cupping her chin and turning it up, so she looked directly at him. He wiped sweat from his forehead with his other arm and said, "If you hold still, I'll fix your leg. Understand?"

The fear in Issa's eyes remained, but she nodded. She laid

back into Kristana's lap, and Yolken directed his attention to her broken leg.

He followed the same process he used on her neck. He straightened her leg and set the bones. Issa screamed. When the bones were in place, he repeated the process of using the power of the sun to mend the bones back together.

After finishing with Issa's leg, Yolken scanned her body for other injuries. Finding none, he withdrew the sun's heat from her.

Issa moved her leg then turned to her mother, who embraced her in a hug.

"Oh, Issa!" Kristana exclaimed, tears streaming from her eyes.

A murmur rose in the gathered crowd.

"She's going to be all right, Kristana," Yolken said.

"I don't know what to say. How can I ever repay you?"

Yolken held up his hand and shook his head.

Sweat still drained from his pores, and he started feeling feverish. He needed to get rid of the heat still inside him, but he didn't know how. He sat back, feeling nauseated. One of his hands brushed the grass, and he felt some of the heat drain away. He looked down then placed his hand on the ground. The rest of the sun's heat drained from him, blackening the grass under his hand. The nausea abated, but fatigue washed over him.

One of the bystanders knelt beside Yolken and asked him, "Are you okay?"

"Yeah, I'm just… tired."

"How did you do that?"

"I don't know," Yolken said.

Individuals in the crowd surrounding him began talking to those standing nearby, looking and pointing at him. Their voices blended together, but occasionally individual voices broke through: "He healed the girl." "He's just like them." "How's that possible? One minute her neck is broken, and the next it's not?"

None of it mattered. The desire to sleep pulled relentlessly at Yolken, causing the voices around him to fade to a dull buzz. It was all he could do not to succumb.

Yolken forced himself to his feet and pushed his way through the cheering and clapping crowd. He stumbled back toward the tavern. When he saw Kaylan running to him, he stopped. As she reached him, he leaned heavily on her.

"Yolken? What happened?" Kaylan said.

"I don't know," he said sleepily. "Issa... her neck—she broke her neck."

"You're soaked."

"The sun—I..."

"Let's get you back to the tavern."

With Yolken's arm over her shoulder, Kaylan helped him to walk. Their progress was slow and clumsy. When they entered the tavern, she called out, "Selena!"

Yolken stumbled into his room and collapsed onto his bed, drenched with sweat. "Thanks," he said with eyes closed, then at last he gave in to the fatigue.

CHAPTER 8

Yolken woke to someone shaking him by the shoulder. When his vision came into focus, he saw his aunt sitting next to him.

"Yolken," Selena said with a quaver in her voice.

He fought the overpowering urge to close his eyes and return to sleep. He looked around, confused, and realized he was in his room. His gaze shifted. Kaylan's uncle stood behind his aunt, wearing a long, travel-worn, brown leather coat. "How did I... Kaylan?" he said. His mind felt muddled and exhausted.

"Can you stand?" Jorgan said.

Yolken tried to sit up, but his body protested against his effort. Every inch of him ached. Selena helped him to a sitting position and propped him against his pillow. He looked sharply from his aunt to Jorgan and back again. "What's going on?"

"Yolken, you're in a lot of danger, and we need to get you to safety," Selena said, her voice still shaky. She looked at the door then back at Yolken. "Jorgan is here to help."

"Danger?" Yolken said, thoroughly confused.

"Do you remember the plate?"

"We don't have time for this right now, Selena," Jorgan said. "Watchers are sure to have seen him Synthesize, and Drenan is traveling with Dorlan. We don't want to be here when he arrives.

You know he's coming."

Synthesize? Drenan? Yolken wondered to himself. His mouth felt dry.

"You're right," Selena said. "Yolken, we'll explain everything later, but right now we need to get you and Javen to safety." There was an urgency in her voice that Yolken had never heard before.

Selena opened Yolken's cedar chest and pulled out the satchel he used when he hiked up into the Mindons. She stuffed a pair of pants and a couple of shirts into it, then grabbed his cloak from the wall where it hung.

"Can you walk?" Jorgan said.

Yolken tried to stand, but his muscles refused to obey. He shook his head.

"Take my hand," Jorgan said. His coat opened as he held his hand out, revealing a sword hanging at his side.

Yolken stared at the sword, then reached out to take Jorgan's hand. Lifting his arm took all his strength. He felt a warmth flow into him and pulled his hand away.

"For this to work, you're going to need to hold my hand," Jorgan said.

Yolken reached out, tentatively, and took Jorgan's hand again. He felt the warmth rushing in again, then his fatigue melted away.

"Stand up."

Yolken stood easily.

"Let's get going," Jorgan said. He moved over to the door, his left hand clutching the cuff of his coat, his right pulling Yolken.

"Where are we going?" Yolken said.

"Up into the Mindons."

"The Mindons?" Selena said, looking at Jorgan. "I thought we were supposed to—"

"It's the safest place, for now."

Selena nodded.

"What about Javen?" Yolken said, looking at Selena.

"He still hasn't returned since he left last night, so I'll wait here for him," Selena said.

"It's foolish for you to stay," Jorgan said. "You should come with us."

"No."

"It's too dangerous here. We can return for Javen once we know it's safe."

"I will *not* leave Javen behind."

Jorgan looked at Selena, shifting his stance.

"Can't we all wait for him, then go together?" Yolken said.

"No!" Selena shouted. Her face betrayed her fear. "We don't have time. Yolken, if Drenan or any of their guards catch you, they'll kill you."

Kill me? Yolken thought. "What's going on?"

"Please—go," Selena said. "Javen and I will be right behind you."

Jorgan stared intently at Selena. "I don't want to leave you behind, Lael."

Lael? Yolken thought, looking at them both through narrowed eyes. *Who's Lael?*

"Please," Selena said. She stepped close to Jorgan and placed her hand on his cheek. "Get him to safety."

Jorgan hesitated, but then stuck his head through the doorway and looked down the hall. "Let's go," he said, and pulled Yolken through the door.

"What about Kaylan?" Yolken said. "I don't want to leave her."

"She's safe," Jorgan said.

"We're coming back, though. Right?"

"I don't know." Jorgan's expression was dark and troubled.

None of this made sense. Just like that, he was leaving? Yolken could hardly believe he and Kaylan had finally—after a lifetime of missed opportunities—realized their mutual interest and now he was leaving?

Hopelessly confused, Yolken followed Jorgan down the stairs. They stopped in the kitchen. Yolken looked hesitantly back at his aunt. She stepped close and hugged him.

"Remember, I love you. Javen and I will be right behind you," Selena said. She placed both of her hands behind Yolken's head, pulled him down, and kissed him on the forehead. Then she exchanged a look with Jorgan and said, "I know you will keep him safe. If you don't, I'll…" Her voice faltered. "I'll…" she started again. Jorgan stepped close to her, and she buried her face into his chest.

"Please come with us," Jorgan said.

"I can't," Selena said, pulling away.

"You know you're in as much danger as the lad."

"I know," Selena said. "But Elen would never forgive me if I left Javen behind. Promise you'll keep Yolken safe."

"He'll be safe," Jorgan promised. He peered out the back door, looking in both directions, then stepped out, pulling Yolken along.

Yolken looked over his shoulder at his aunt standing in the doorway as Jorgan led him away.

Jorgan made his way from the tavern. His steps were swift but measured, so as not to draw attention. He followed the Little Mindon until it curved north, then picked his way around scattered buildings and homes. They passed the last of the new homes behind the tavern and moved through an open field of wild grass. After skirting a few farms, they encountered the Little Mindon again as it curved back to the south. They followed the creek as it wound its way to a modest grove of maple trees, the plot of land their family owned.

The sight of the trees made Yolken think of his parents. They'd bought this land when they moved to Lonely Oak, and his father had intended to build a home here. He'd looked forward to the day he could build the home his father had intended for his family, but for now, the grove stood guard over their graves. He visited when he could, enjoying the sound of the flowing water while sitting in the shade of a sturdy maple.

Jorgan led him into the grove and stopped in front of a gravestone. He let go of Yolken's hand and said, "Sit."

Fatigue rushed into Yolken's body, and he sat heavily on the ground.

Jorgan swept his coat back, pulled a black dagger from his belt, and handed it to Yolken.

Yolken took it from him and looked it over. The blade wasn't made of steel. Instead, it was an unusual black material with little streaks of blue woven through it.

"What's the last thing you remember?" Jorgan said.

"I was watching Kaylan as she gathered the bread my aunt needed for the day, and…"

"And what?"

"I heard screaming." The image of Issa lying on the ground, her neck contorted, flashed into his mind. "She wasn't moving."

"Is that it?"

"I don't know," Yolken said. "It's all kind of foggy."

"Think. When you saw Issa lying there, what did you do?" Jorgan was watching his face intently.

"I… healed her," Yolken said, not believing the words as they came out of his mouth.

"How?"

Yolken struggled, trying to understand what it was he had done. He recalled feeling the warmth of the sun. "I did something with the sun."

"What?" Jorgan pressed. "You haven't slept much yet; the memory should still be there."

"I don't know!" Yolken said. "What does it matter, anyway?" The effort of trying to remember was exhausting.

"It matters because it's not practical for you to hold my hand all the way to where we're going, and you'll be asleep soon if you don't use your gift."

"What gift?"

"Think. What did you do with the sun?"

Yolken thought about it more. Then, as a question more than a statement, he said, "I drew it in somehow."

"Good," Jorgan said. "Now, what you need to know now is that my dagger contains Energy from the sun."

Yolken looked at Jorgan, confused.

Jorgan sighed and explained with forced patience, "When you healed Issa, you drew Energy from the sun into yourself. This dagger is filled with that same Energy. Can you feel it?"

Yolken turned the black dagger over in his hand. He didn't feel anything. "No," he said.

"Close your eyes," Jorgan instructed, "and imagine that the heat of the sun is shining on you."

Yolken did as he was told. They were sitting in the shade of the maples, but he imagined he was standing in direct sunlight. At first, he didn't feel anything except the urge to lie down and go to sleep, but then the dagger grew warm in his hand.

"I feel it," he said.

"Good. Now draw it in, just like you did with the sun, only do it slowly."

Now that Yolken felt the warmth in the dagger, it felt like it wanted to rush into him. Not knowing how, he let the warmth trickle in. His fatigue lessened. He allowed a little more of the warmth in and felt revitalized. He drew a big breath and slowly let it out as his strength returned.

"Good," Jorgan said, seeing the change come over Yolken. "As long as you continue drawing Energy from this dagger, your strength will remain. But when it's gone, your fatigue will return. Draw only as much as you require to stay mobile. And under no circumstances are you to draw Energy directly from the sun. Do you understand?"

"Why not?"

"Because *they* will be able to see it."

"Who?"

"Watchers. But they can't see you using Energy if you take it from the dagger. Understand?"

Jorgan held eye contact with Yolken until Yolken nodded.

"Good. Let's go."

Yolken pushed himself to his feet. He stared at his parents' gravestones while thoughts swirled in his mind. He was confused, not grasping what was happening. He looked back down at his parents' grave again. The epitaph read 'O and E.' He turned back and looked in the direction of Lonely Oak. His brother and aunt were still there, supposedly in danger.

"Yolken!" Jorgan called.

Yolken looked up at Jorgan, who stood several paces away.

"Let's go."

There were too many questions. Yolken stood his ground. "Tell me what's going on."

"Yolken," Jorgan said, walking back toward him. "Now isn't the time."

"No. Tell me what's going on, or I'm going back."

He'd known Jorgan his whole life yet knew surprisingly little about him other than that he traveled a lot and was full of stories. Yolken had grown up sitting around the hearth with Javen and Kaylan, listening to Jorgan spin tale after tale of adventure.

"When the Regency arrives back in Lonely Oak—which they will—and they don't find you there, they *will* go looking for you," Jorgan said. "And if they catch you, they will kill you."

Yolken stared at Jorgan's grim face. Fear enveloped him. But he didn't move. He needed more.

He crossed his arms over his chest. "Why?"

Jorgan looked past Yolken, toward Lonely Oak, then directly at Yolken. "Only the Blessed of the Dragon are supposed to possess Synthesis."

"Synthesis?"

"It's their gift. It's what allows them to rule Dradonia." He turned and strode off, adding over his shoulder, "And you used

Synthesis to heal little Issa."

Yolken watched him walk away and tried to make sense of his words. *He* had used the gift of the Blessed? How could he possibly have done that? Was it connected to what happened with the plate the day before? If so, why now? He was twenty-five years old, and nothing like that had ever happened before. And now, the very morning after he'd finally made some promising progress with the woman he'd loved his whole life, he was being told he had to leave his home because the Blessed wanted to kill him. Was this mad escape effort permanent? He still held to his dream of building a home here in the grove, a home he hoped one day to share with Kaylan. Had he ruined the dream by doing whatever it was he did to Issa?

Jorgan turned and saw that Yolken remained rooted to the ground. He stopped and said, "Do you understand why we need to go?"

Yolken had heard the stories; old Relan was full of them. His hatred of the Regency—"the scales", as he referred to them—was well known. He hated Drenan in particular. But no one ever took him seriously. His rants were just the ramblings of a drunkard.

"I promise I'll explain everything once you're safe."

His aunt knew Jorgan, in fact the idea of leaving Selena behind has distressed Jorgan greatly, so Yolken decided to trust him. "I am going to hold you to that promise."

"Yes, yes, now let's get moving."

Yolken stepped around his parents' grave, and Jorgan nodded. He turned and continued out of the grove to the east. Yolken reluctantly followed.

As the grove dropped out of sight behind them, the Mindon Mountains loomed ahead. He sometimes hunted deer and elk along those slopes, and knew why they were going in that direction—unlike the plains to the north, south, and west, the Mindons were a vast mountain range that would be difficult to find someone in.

They walked for several hours, primarily following the Little Mindon upstream as it wound through the steadily rising terrain. They arrived at a familiar bluff which offered a clear view of the valley and plains behind them. Yolken looked out in the distance at the small town. The sun was descending into the western sky, darkening in color as it approached the horizon. He stared at Lonely Oak for a few minutes before Jorgan came up alongside him.

"Everything will work out as it should, lad," Jorgan said.

"Should we wait here for Selena and Javen?"

"No. They'll catch up soon enough."

They drank from the creek then continued east, through a mixture of sage and juniper. As they continued climbing, the sage and juniper gave way to pine and aspen.

Yolken plodded along behind Jorgan in the fading light. The sky grew darker, and stars appeared overhead. From Lonely Oak, they could see the Great Dragon constellation greet the night as it climbed over the horizon in the east while the sun set in the west, but from their current position the mountains and trees blocked it from view.

They continued walking by the light of the moon. After another hour, the flow of warmth from the dagger dissipated. Yolken could still feel it deep in the dagger, but instead of it flowing into him, effort was needed to draw it out. Soon it ran out altogether. His fatigue crashed over him, and he stumbled to the ground with a groan.

Jorgan looked over his shoulder, then stopped and turned around. "What happened?"

"The warmth from the dagger is gone." Yolken struggled to speak above a whisper.

"It should have lasted longer than this. You must have used more Energy healing Issa than I thought." Jorgan pulled his cloak back and unbuckled his belt. He slid the sword from his belt and held it in front of Yolken. "This sword is just like that dagger, only with much greater capacity. The dagger is to the Little Mindon as this sword is to the Mindon River. If you're not careful, it'll burn you from the inside out."

The painting of the Mindon Falls hanging on the wall behind the bar in the tavern came to Yolken's mind. The power of the river dwarfed that of the creek running by the tavern. He took the sword from Jorgan, wrapping his hand around the hilt. Unlike common sword hilts, this one was made from steel threads woven around the underlying black material. The force within Jorgan's sword immediately pressed at him like a torrent of water slamming against a dam. The power was enticing. He fought the urge to break the dam and free the torrent. Instead, he heeded Jorgan's warning and drew the warmth in slowly. His fatigue once again melted away.

"Get up," Jorgan said. "We have a long way yet to go."

Yolken stood, buckled the sword around his waist, and followed.

CHAPTER 9

Javen woke to someone straddling him and kissing his bare chest. He opened his eyes and could see disheveled black curls tickling him as the tips lightly brushed against his skin. Contentedly, he closed his eyes again as Hadie kissed her way up his neck to his mouth. Their lips met, and they exchanged a passionate kiss.

"G'morning, Javen," Hadie said, breaking the kiss. "Or rather, afternoon."

"Mmm," Javen said. He looked up into Hadie's green and brown eyes. "What time is it?"

"Kissing time." Hadie locked her lips with Javen's again.

Javen returned the kiss, then grabbed her by the arms and rolled her over on the bed until he was straddling her. Sitting astride her, he realized he wasn't wearing any clothes.

"How is it you are clad and I'm not?" he asked.

"Because, sleepyhead, unlike you, I wasn't able to sleep the entire day away without food. I was hungry, so I went downstairs and got something to eat. But I assure you," Hadie said, pausing to kiss Javen, "when I woke, I was as natural as you."

Javen kissed Hadie again and, feeling his stomach growl, rolled to the side and sat on the edge of the bed. He gathered the sheets around his waist and said, "I'm hungry, too."

"After last night, you should be."

Javen felt Hadie kiss him on the back.

"So, what time *is* it?" Javen said, looking out the window to try to gauge the time by the light and shadows. "Looks late."

"Suppertime," Hadie said. She tried to pull Javen back into bed and get the sheets off him, but he resisted.

"As much as I want to stay and get those clothes off of you again, I really need to get going."

"Then why don't you?" Hadie smiled slyly as she unbuttoned the top button of her blouse.

"How am I supposed to leave when you entice me like that?"

"Do you want me to stop?" She unbuttoned another button.

"No. But my brother is going to kill me as it is. If I don't show up at the tavern at all today, he'll never forgive me."

"So what?" Hadie said with a furrowed brow.

"Now, Hadie," Javen said, kissing her in an attempt to remove her pouty face, "if I don't help him, he'll have no reason to continue giving me the small amount of money he does. And how can I properly court a fine lass such as yourself with no money?"

"Court me?"

"Would you rather I said, 'How can I properly get a fine lass such as yourself intoxicated and shirtless again with no money?'"

Hadie slapped him playfully on the back. "Let me show you just how much money it takes for you to get my shirt off," she said. Hadie grabbed the hem at the bottom of her silk blouse with both hands and lifted her hands high over her head, taking the shirt with it. She continued pulling the shirt until her head popped out the top.

Javen gave in to her beauty. "I don't suppose another hour will make much of a difference at this point."

* * *

It was dark when Javen approached the tavern full of apprehension. He hesitated at the front door, preparing himself for the verbal lashing he was about to get from Yolken, and probably Selena too—she sided with Yolken on practically everything, and always had.

He took a deep breath and pushed on the front door. The locks on the inside rattled against their stops. "What the…" He pushed again, then called out, "Yolken!"

He heard the locks slide back and the door opened. Selena grabbed him by the arm and pulled him in, then swiftly slid the bolts back into place.

"Why's the door locked?" Javen said.

"Where have you been?" Selena enclosed him in a big hug with tears streaming from her eyes.

He looked around the empty tavern and said, "Auntie, what's going on?"

"We need to go!"

"Go? Where?"

"I don't have time to explain." She dried her eyes with the sleeves of her blouse, then grabbed Javen by the arm and pulled him toward the kitchen.

Javen pulled his arm free. "Auntie, *what* is going on?"

Selena faced Javen but hesitated. She looked at the door then back at Javen. "Listen carefully," she said, her voice low and clear. "We don't have much time."

"Time for what?"

"Have you heard anything about what happened today?"

Javen shook his head. "I haven't been out much. I came straight here after I woke—"

"It doesn't matter," Selena said. "Something happened with Yolken today."

"What?"

"He…" she started, then paused. "He Synthesized."

"He what?"

"I'll explain it to you later. What's important right now is that you understand we're all in a lot of danger because of what happened with Yolken. We have very little time."

"Danger?"

"I know you're confused. There'll be time to explain everything once we're safe." She retrieved a bag from the bar and thrusted it into Javen's hands. "Now, will you *please* just come with me?"

Javen looked down at the bag and said, "Where are we going?"

"Up into the Mindons. It'll be safe there."

Javen hesitated. What she was saying made no sense, but it was obvious she was afraid of something. "Can I at least change my clothes?"

Selena looked at the door again. "We don't have time for that. I've packed clothes for you. You can change once we're well away from the Regency's reach."

Selena grabbed him by the hand and pulled him toward the kitchen.

The kitchen door swung open, and a man wearing gray armor stepped through.

Selena stopped.

Two more armored men followed the first.

Selena backed away from them, keeping Javen behind her. She pulled a black figurine from her apron pocket—the lucky horse statue she carried around with her—and pointed at the nearest table.

It lifted off the ground and hovered.

Javen stared at it, wide-eyed.

"Don't do anything foolish," one of the men said. He took a step toward them.

The table flew toward the men.

They all ducked, and it crashed into the wall behind them.

Another table lifted off the ground. This time it hovered between Javen and Selena, pivoting on its side, so its legs faced the armored men.

Selena held her free arm behind her and guided Javen toward

the front door. The table moved with them, staying between them and the men.

The bolts on the front door slid back, and Selena pivoted. The table spun with her. The armored men took another step toward them, and she swung the table back in their direction.

"This is the last place I thought I'd find myself," a refined voice from the front door said coolly.

The table crashed to the floor.

Javen recognized the man from the lobby of the Oak—the Regent of Hantlo. Drenan. He wore blue armor, and those strange eyepieces usually worn by the guards known as Watchers.

The front door closed behind Drenan, moving as if pushed by an invisible hand. All the bolts slid back into place.

Drenan stepped farther into the tavern and said, "This is quite the interesting gathering. I came for the boy healer, and here I've found someone *else* with the gift as well." He pulled off his blue scaled gloves, revealing extremely scarred hands. "How very interesting, indeed."

The blood drained from Javen's face as he recognized Drenan anew. Kaylan's uncle Jorgan used to frighten them with stories around the hearth about the scarred man.

He was real.

"Go upstairs Javen, this doesn't concern you," Selena quietly urged over her shoulder. She kept her black figurine tightly clasped in her hand.

"Stay right where you are," Drenan commanded.

Javen wanted to obey his aunt, but he didn't move.

"And you," Drenan said, directing his gaze at Selena, "put the bone down."

Selena shifted her stance but kept hold of the horse figurine.

Drenan stepped toward her, and Selena backed up, keeping herself between Drenan and Javen.

"Is this him?" Drenan said.

"Who?" Selena said.

"The boy who healed the cripple." Drenan looked at Javen, sending a chill down Javen's spine.

"I don't know what you're talking about."

"We tracked the source of today's miraculous event to this tavern. The *Thornhill* tavern." Drenan looked around the room and ran his scarred hand over the polished bar. "Didn't the proprietor of this tavern die when it burned down?"

How does he know about that? Javen wondered.

"You know," Drenan said, "I'd be lying if I said I wasn't surprised when I first saw that this place had been rebuilt. It really was a shame such a fine estab—"

"You're too late," Selena said. "He's already gone, and safely beyond your reach."

Agitation covered Drenan's face. "No one is *ever* beyond our reach."

"Maybe not, but for now, he's where you can't harm him."

"If you think he's safe, then you're as blind as his father was."

"Auntie? What is he talking about?" Javen said.

"Yes, *Auntie,* what *am* I talking about?" Drenan said.

Selena stood rigid.

"Auntie?"

"Did your auntie forget to mention your father was a rebel? Or that she, apparently, is also one?" Drenan said. He placed his right hand on the black hilt of a dagger sheathed on his belt.

"A rebel?" Javen said. He looked at his aunt's back. His father? She was…? *They execute rebels.*

"How can using a gift we are born with—a gift from the Great Dragon—be wrong?" Selena said. "The Order is simply trying to undo the damage—"

"Enough!" Drenan shouted. He slammed his fist on the bar with such force the wood cracked.

Javen and Selena both flinched.

"As I said, I don't know where he is," Selena calmly repeated.

"My patience has grown thin," Drenan said, stepping toward

them.

"I'm sorry, I don—" The horse figurine flew from Selena's hand, and she fell to her knees with a groan.

"This is your last opportunity, fool woman," Drenan hissed.

"Burn in Draego's—" Selena choked. She gasped for breath, her hands groping at an invisible, intangible force at her neck. "—Fire," she managed to choke out.

Selena's body lifted into the air and flew across the room. She smashed into the corner of the hearth and fell to the ground.

"Auntie!" Javen screamed.

He shoved his way between tables and chairs and fell to his knees beside her. She was on her side, facing the hearth. He reached down to check on her but stopped at the sight of the blood pooling under her head.

"Auntie?" he said, gently shaking her by the shoulder. He rolled her onto her back and stared in horror when he saw her crushed skull.

"Auntie!" Javen screamed again.

CHAPTER 10

Yolken trudged along in the dark behind Jorgan. They were following a game trail he used while hunting with his brother. They had been walking for several hours and were now deep into the forest. The moon was out and provided them some light by which to see. Silhouetted pines loomed overhead. By the light of the moon, Yolken could barely see Jorgan or the trail ahead. Fortunately, he was familiar enough with the trail to proceed without much risk of injuring himself. Apparently, Jorgan was also familiar with it, given the ease with which he loped along.

They walked without speaking. As they moved higher into the mountains, Yolken kept looking over his shoulder, hoping to see Selena and Javen catching up with them, but each time he was disappointed. He continued in silence, trying to find some calm in the peacefulness of the woods.

They had been traveling roughly to the north. When the terrain grew steeper, the trail began weaving back and forth, following the shallowest gradient up each slope. Yolken knew that after a few more turns they would reach a point where the trail leveled out for a while, turn to the east and pass through a grassy meadow.

The odd black sword Jorgan had given him hung on his left

hip. He kept his hand on the hilt as they walked, continuously drawing on the heat stored within. A few hours back, he'd tried repeating his questions to try and find out what was going on, but since leaving the maple grove, Jorgan had refused to answer him.

He broke the long silence. "I keep wondering," Yolken said, "why I should believe any of what you've told me. All I did was help Issa. Could that have really been so wrong?"

"Yes!" Jorgan said, turning to face Yolken. "To the Regency, what you did back there *is* so wrong."

"But why?"

"Look, Yolken, I've known your aunt for a long time, and she has put her trust in me to keep you safe. So, for the time being, can you trust me too?"

"I want to, but I'm having a hard time believing you, since you won't tell me what's going on."

Jorgan sighed. "I will. But not right now."

"Why?"

His wry smile was hard to make out in the moonlight, but Yolken could hear the amusement in his voice. "Because you won't remember any of what I've already told you as it is, let alone anything else I might say."

Yolken looked at Jorgan, confused. "Why wouldn't I remember what you tell me?"

"Do you remember healing the lass?"

"Only bits and pieces."

"There's a reason why you can't remember what happened earlier today. Your body is in a state of extreme exhaustion. The only reason you are standing right now is because of the sword," Jorgan said, pointing at Yolken's hip. "Without it, you would collapse in a heap at my feet. And when you do finally rest, everything that has happened today will seem like it was just a dream once you wake. That's why you're only able to remember pieces of what happened today. Believe me when I tell you that I *will* tell you everything, but I don't want to have to tell you everything twice."

"Oh."

"I'm taking you to a cabin where you can rest—safely—for as long as your body requires."

"A cabin?"

"Yes. A safehouse, actually. I knew this day would come eventually, so I prepared."

They continued again in silence. The trail made several more switchbacks, then sharply veered to the right, from north to east. The gradient leveled out. *We're approaching the meadow,* Yolken thought, even though he couldn't see it in the dark yet. "Will you at least tell me why the Regency would have a problem with me helping Issa?"

"It's not because you helped Issa, Yolken. It's how you did it."

"You mean I used their gift."

"Exactly."

As they continued walking, the canopy of trees thinned and then eventually gave way to a clear sky. They were now walking in the meadow. "If they're looking for me, then what's to stop them from following us here?" Yolken asked.

"Nothing, really," Jorgan answered. "Except that they presently lack the resources."

"How do you know that?"

"Because I pay attention. The attachment of soldiers they had with them in Lonely Oak were there to protect the chancellor. Protocol would prevent them from pulling more than a few men away from the unit to go hunting for a single boy. So, unless they were able to determine precisely which direction we went, they simply don't have the resources necessary to launch a search of this entire valley. Even if they were smart enough to eliminate north and south as likely directions we would choose to flee, that would still leave vast reaches to the west and east. Both directions present an immense amount of terrain they would need to search."

"I've heard about their legendary trackers. Couldn't they have just followed our tracks out of town?"

"Yes, they very well could have," Jorgan said. "Which is why we needed to get you and your brother out of Lonely Oak as quickly as we could. We wanted to put as much distance between the Regency and us as we possibly could. If there's not a clear trail"—Jorgan veered left off the trail and started walking north, through the middle of the meadow—"darkness will slow them down, but we'll need plenty of luck as well."

Yolken followed Jorgan across the meadow and thought about their current location. The meadow was in the middle of a long, narrow valley—one of many that existed in the Mindons. If they continued traveling north, in the direction Jorgan was headed, the terrain would start rising sharply again when they left the meadow and were once again under the cover of trees. It would be perilous for them to try scaling those peaks at night, so he was relieved when, after leaving the meadow and traveling a few hundred paces into the trees, Jorgan turned back to the east and paralleled the sharply rising terrain instead. The going was much slower now, since they were no longer on a trail and had to pick their way through the foliage by the light of the moon.

"Can't we stop for the night and continue tomorrow?" Yolken said. "It would be foolish if we hurt ourselves in the dark."

"No," Jorgan replied. "We must reach our destination before you consume all the Energy in the sword. I don't want to have to carry you."

They continued walking through the night. As the hours passed, Yolken became hopelessly confused about where they were. He knew this valley eventually curved south, but another one merged with it from the north. He couldn't tell if they were still following the valley south or if they had veered north. The moon had finished its march across the sky, and he was trying his best to remain oriented by the stars, but it was proving hard to do because the trees blocked most of them from view. He suspected they might have turned north but would have to wait until sunrise before he knew for sure. For now, he had no choice but to continue trusting Jorgan. Then, just as the first hints of dawn appeared overhead, Jorgan again veered left, and the terrain started descending steeply into a ravine. At the bottom, Jorgan turned right and began following a creek.

A small log cabin came into view through the foliage. It had one window, a roughly shingled roof, and a small porch.

Jorgan proceeded up its wooden steps onto the small porch, past a modest bench. He unlatched the door and stepped inside.

After stopping to look at the cabin, Yolken followed Jorgan inside where Jorgan was lighting several lanterns hanging on sconces in the one-room building. Then he fiddled with a large chest at the foot of the bed in the corner. There was a table in the middle of the room and a kitchen stove to the left. Yolken ducked his head under a support log that divided the cabin in half from front to back.

Jorgan turned from the chest with his arms full of blankets. "I know it's quaint, but it'll keep us safe for the duration of your training."

"My training?"

"Yes. After you've rested, I'm going to teach you how to use your gift."

"Wait. You can… you have the gift, too?"

Yolken looked at Jorgan in shock. "Yes. Now, if you'll kindly hand me the sword."

Yolken still had his hand resting on the hilt of the sword. He hadn't lost contact with it since Jorgan had given it to him. Now he drew the sword from its sheath and looked at it. In the light, he admired its wire-bound steel handle. The metal was sunk deeply enough into the black material that when he gripped it, his hand touched the material. He turned the long sword over in his hands. The lantern light illuminated yellow ribbons woven throughout the black. *That's strange.*

"What's it made of?" Yolken said.

"Bone."

Yolken looked at Jorgan then back at the sword. He'd never seen black bone before.

"What kind of bone?" Yolken said.

Jorgan held a hand out and Yolken gave him the sword.

"You wouldn't believe me if I told you," Jorgan said.

The moment the sword left his hand, Yolken collapsed to the ground.

CHAPTER 11

Y ou killed her!" Javen shouted at Drenan.

"And if you try to run," Drenan said, his face impassive, "the same thing will happen to you."

Javen stood in the tavern, frozen. Terrified. He felt as though he could not draw a deep breath. Every instinct told him to run, but he was unable to coax his body to move.

He watched helplessly as two of Drenan's men posted at the kitchen door approached, summoned with a single glance from the regent. They picked up his aunt's body and carried it across the tavern and through the kitchen door. The third man followed them.

When the door swung shut behind them, one of the overturned tables lifted into the air and righted itself. Two chairs slid across the floor and positioned themselves at the table. Drenan walked behind the bar and drew two mugs of ale from one of the barrels. Walking back around the bar, he offered one of the mugs out toward Javen and said, "Come. Sit."

Drenan settled into a chair at the uprighted table. He removed his eyepieces and drank from his mug.

Woodenly, Javen obeyed. He crossed the room and sat in the empty chair.

"I understand that you might be upset right now," Drenan

said with a calm and comforting voice, "but your aunt was an enemy of the Regency."

Javen didn't say anything. He held his mug in his hand and stared blankly, blinking tears away as they formed. He wanted to ask about what they'd said about his father being a rebel, but he was afraid.

Drenan sat silently and drank his ale. When the three armored men returned through the kitchen door, he set his mug down and stood up. He walked over to the hearth and examined the spot where Selena had fallen. Smoke began to curl up where the bloodstain was on the wooden boards. He walked back past Javen and said, "Time to go."

Drenan slipped his eyepieces back on, then led Javen through the kitchen and out the tavern's back door. Six horses were waiting. Javen's eyes widened when he saw Hadie sitting on one of them, her hands tied to the pommel.

"Get up," one of the armored men said, gesturing to a horse.

Javen placed his foot in the stirrup without argument and hoisted himself into the saddle. A guard reached up to tie his hands to the pommel. Javen didn't resist. Drenan and the other men mounted their horses, and two of the armored men held Javen and Hadie's horses by the reins.

"Crin," Drenan said, looking at one of the armored men, "find the other Thornhill boy and bring him to me."

"Yes, Your Majesty," Crin said.

Javen watched as the man Crin started shedding his armor. He handed his breast-piece to one of the mounted soldiers, then removed his leggings. After handing the leggings up to the soldier, Crin pulled folded clothes from a satchel on his horse, put them on, and mounted his horse.

They rode the horses between the tavern and the Little Mindon. At the road, Crin turned right and trotted across the bridge toward the center of town. The remaining riders turned left and rode out of town. Javen held desperately to his pommel as he bounced unceremoniously on his mount. His horse's reins were held by the guard riding on his right. He was doing his utmost to keep his seat. Hadie was doing the same. They rode late into the night, not stopping until they encountered a circle of wagons and long, ornate carriages big enough to be small homes.

They turned off the road and into the encircled campsite. They rode through a perimeter guard. The armored men led Javen and Hadie's horses to one of the carriages, untied them from the pommels, and ushered them up the steps and into the carriage. They entered a warmly lit room lined on each side with couches.

"Sit down, and don't move," one of the men said.

Javen and Hadie obeyed, sitting on opposite sides of the long room. The two men left the carriage, pulling the door closed with an audible click. They exchanged a look, the fear in Hadie's eyes reflecting his own, then Hadie averted her eyes. They sat, neither of them moving, in silence.

* * *

Drenan seethed as they rode into camp. He hated loose ends—and the boy riding behind him *was* a loose end. How could Nera have missed that Danavin had children? She's the head of the Synod; it's her job to know these things. Danavin's wife she'd known about, but not his children?

He rode to Dorlan's carriage and slid out of the saddle. The guard outside bowed and opened the door. Dorlan's servant Sethlan stood in the corner of the sitting room. "Let His Highness know I've returned."

"Yes, Your Majesty," Sethlan said with a bow. He slipped through the door leading farther into the carriage. He came back a moment later and said, "He'll see you in his bedchamber."

Drenan strode through the dining room and into the last room of the carriage. Dorlan lounged on a couch, a glass of ale in his hand and his light-blue silk robe open. The local girl he had brought with him lay opposite him, naked, fondling

Dorlan's manhood with her foot.

"Your Highness," Drenan said with a bow.

Dorlan sat up and closed his robe. "I've learned so much from… what was your name, lass?"

"Astora," the girl said.

Drenan looked at her, and she crossed her arms across her chest.

"Go ahead, Astora," Dorlan said, "tell Drenan what you just told me—about the man who made this ale."

"His name is Yolken," Astora said. "He runs the tavern with his brother and aunt."

"What was it you said about his parents?"

"Oh, it was a tragedy. There was a horrible fire when we were young, and they both died."

"That *is* tragic," Dorlan said dryly. He rose from the couch and tied his robe's silk sash. He walked into the dining room, Drenan two steps behind, and refilled his glass with ale from the barrel in the corner. "And what have you discovered?"

"The cripple girl you healed last night was climbing in the oak tree in the center of the town and she fell. She broke her neck. Word reached us that a local boy healed her."

"And who exactly was that?"

"Danavin's son."

"How was this missed?" Dorlan said.

"I don't know. But I intend on finding out."

"You know how the emperor feels about loose ends."

"Yes, Your Highness."

Dorlan took a drink of ale. "Please tell me you apprehended him."

Drenan looked down at the table.

"What happened?"

"By the time I traced him to the tavern, he was already gone. There are rebels helping him, I'm sure of it."

"And the brother?"

"Is in my carriage," Drenan said.

"Good." Dorlan upended his glass then filled it anew.

"Shall I send him to meet his father?"

"No."

"He's a rebel, Your Highness. He deserves—"

"I said no. I'll deal with him. What *you* need to do is find the other one—the healer. We cannot permit a son of Danavin to be on the loose in the empire."

"I agree, Your Highness," Drenan said. "I have Crin looking for him. He has the best tracking skills in our regiment."

"Good," Dorlan said. He took a drink then called, "Sethlan!" His servant entered and Dorlan said, "Bring me parchment and a pen, and ready a condor. I need to send a message to the emperor."

Drenan stared at the chancellor, hatred for Danavin boiling within him. "Your Highness, I suggest we tie off this loose—"

"That's for the emperor to decide."

"Yes, Your Highness." Drenan bowed then left the carriage, regretting that he had not killed the boy when he had the chance.

* * *

After what felt like an eternity, the lock slid back and the door opened. Drenan stepped up into the carriage. He walked between Javen and Hadie and went through the other door without acknowledging their presence. The door slammed shut and both doors simultaneously locked without the touch of a human hand.

The captives continued to sit on their couches. Javen waited in dread for whatever was coming next. Drenan didn't return. Hadie eventually lay down on the couch and fell asleep. When Hadie started snoring, Javen also lay down, but sleep eluded him. He stared at the dark ceiling, the gruesome scene from the tavern replaying over and over in his mind. Questions swirled around in his thoughts; questions about his aunt, his father, Yolken, and himself.

Sleep eventually came.

The next morning, Drenan emerged from his chamber dressed in a light-blue tailored suit with a dark blue shirt. The suit was finely embroidered to resemble the scales of his armor, and he wore white gloves over his hands. He exited the carriage without a glance at Javen or Hadie.

When Drenan was gone, Javen's befuddled mind began to clear, and he felt compelled to leap into action. He checked the door even though he'd heard the lock slide into place. He went to the door at the other end of the room and checked it too. It was also locked. With no way out of the carriage, he returned to his couch and looked over at Hadie. She sat with her knees pulled up to her chest, fidgeting with her fingernails.

"What are you doing here?" he asked, breaking the silence between them.

"I don't know. A guard just burst into my room at the inn yesterday and hauled me out," Hadie said. She looked searchingly at him. "Javen, what's going on? What does the Regency want with us?"

"I don't know. Something to do with my brother."

"What could they possibly want with a tavern keeper from the countryside?"

Javen was as puzzled as she was. "All I know is, we had a fantastic night together after the festival, and when I got back to the tavern, my aunt met me. She was frantic. She told me that Yolken…"

"Yolken what?"

"She said he… Synthesized."

"Synthesized?" Hadie repeated blankly.

"I really don't know what that means but she said we were all in danger," Javen continued. "Though I don't know what it has to do with you."

"I don't know either," Hadie said. "But whatever they want from us, we have to give it to them, all right?"

Javen nodded, then rose from his seat and sat next to Hadie. He wrapped his arm around her and squeezed her tightly.

CHAPTER 12

Yolken woke to voices conversing nearby. He opened his eyes and stared up at an unfamiliar ceiling. After rubbing his eyes, he turned his head toward the voices and saw two people sitting at a table in the center of a large room. He recognized Deborah Browning and Kaylan's uncle Jorgan.

Deborah saw him looking at them and came to sit beside him on the bed. She placed a hand on his forehead. "Yolken, dear, how do you feel?"

"Hungry."

"Can you sit up?"

Yolken pushed himself to a sitting position. His body felt sore but rested. He looked around the room and asked, "Where are we? I don't recognize this place."

"We're in a cabin deep in the Mindons," Deborah said. "A safehouse."

Her answer brought on more puzzlement than clarity. His stomach growled audibly. "Where's Javen? Is Auntie here?"

"Yolken, come sit at the table and eat. When your stomach is full, we can fill you in on what's occurred these past few days."

Deborah helped Yolken to his feet and supported him as he walked to the table. Once he was sitting, she crossed to a large stove in the corner of the cabin and returned with a bowl of soup and a hunk of bread. He ate the food ravenously. When his bowl was empty, Deborah refilled it.

"Is Kaylan here?" Yolken said, halfway through his second helping.

"Yes, dear. She's out for a walk."

"You've been sleeping for three days," Jorgan said.

"Three days!" Yolken exclaimed. "What happened?"

"Eat, dear," Deborah said, "and then we'll talk."

No one said anything else until Yolken's bowl was empty and he pushed it aside.

"Have you had enough?" Deborah said.

Yolken nodded.

"Over the next day or so you'll be quite hungry, so please eat as much as you want. I'll ensure there's always hot food available."

"What happened? And where's Javen and Auntie?"

Silence hung in the air.

Yolken looked from Jorgan to Deborah, suddenly feeling uneasy. "What happened?"

"Javen is missing," Jorgan said. "And your aunt…" Jorgan's eyes glistened, and he reached up to swipe at them as tears spilled over.

Deborah walked over and placed a hand on Jorgan's shoulder.

"My aunt? What?" Yolken said with increased urgency.

"Yolken, Selena was…" Deborah started.

"Murdered," Jorgan finished.

"Murdered?" Yolken said. A feeling inside crushed him like a barrel in the cellar had fallen off the rack and pinned him to the ground. He couldn't breathe. He was barely able to remember his parents; Selena was his mother—his father, too. She'd given up her own life in Tieger to come to Lonely Oak and raise them. And now she was… dead. Murdered? Tears welled in his eyes. He took a shuddering breath and said, "Who? Why?"

Jorgan wiped his eyes and said, "Three days ago, the Regency paid a visit to your tavern."

"The Regency?" In all the times Dalia had come to Lonely Oak, neither she nor any other regent had ever set foot in the tavern. Yolken could not make sense of Jorgan's words.

"They were looking for you."

"Me?"

"Yes," Jorgan said.

"Why would they be looking for me?"

Jorgan held Yolken's gaze and spoke very clearly, "Because the morning the chancellor left Lonely Oak, you used Draego's Gift to heal Issa."

"I did what?"

"Issa fell from the oak tree and broke her neck. And you healed her."

Yolken stared at Jorgan and Deborah in shock.

"Your safety was compromised," Jorgan continued, "so I took you away as quickly as I could. By the time the Regency arrived at the tavern, you and I were already on our way here. However, your aunt…" His voice faltered, but he continued, forcing out each word, "Your aunt insisted on staying behind to wait for Javen. None of us could locate him that morning. Knowing the danger she was in, Selena still refused to leave him behind."

Yolken felt lost. He tried to remember what Jorgan was talking about. The last thing he remembered was being angry because Javen hadn't returned to the tavern the night the chancellor stayed in Lonely Oak and he had had to run Javen's errands for him the next morning. "If you weren't there, how do you know she's dead?"

"Yolken, we don't know exactly what happened after you and Jorgan left for the safehouse," Deborah said. "Kaylan came rushing into the bakery and told me what happened with Issa and Selena came looking for Javen not long after. We searched for him but couldn't find him. She returned to the tavern and I readied things on my end. When I went to the tavern to check in with her, I found her in the cellar."

Yolken sat in disbelief. How could she be dead? He had just gone to the square to get her supplies for the day. He had been mad at Javen, but she'd steadfastly urged him to be patient. Patience and gentleness was her nature.

"I was able to track down where Javen spent the night, and spoke with Brall," Deborah said. "He said the girl Javen spent the night with came down the next morning and paid for another day, and Javen didn't leave the room until close to sundown. We can assume that when he left he went back to the tavern, but he wasn't there, and nobody else has seen him.

"I also heard from numerous people that a group rode out of town on horses, but since it was dark, no one could positively identify if Javen was with them. As near as we can guess, the group was somehow associated with the Regency and he was with them."

His brother was missing.

His brother was missing, and his aunt was dead.

Yolken pushed his chair back and stood. He paced the small room, feeling the soreness in his muscles, trying to process what he'd just learned.

How did this happen?

"Please sit down, Yolken," Jorgan said, gesturing toward his seat. "I know exactly how you're feeling, but we have much to discuss."

Yolken looked at his seat but didn't move. Instead, he closed his eyes and forced himself to take deep breaths.

A door opened.

Yolken opened his eyes and saw Kaylan standing in the doorway. Tears streamed from his eyes as she stepped toward him and embraced him in a hug.

"I'm so sorry," Kaylan whispered into his chest. "When Mammy told me, I couldn't believe it."

The weight he felt inside finally burst out and overflowed. He cried into Kaylan's hair. She squeezed him tighter, which made the tears flow faster.

Arms wrapped around him from the side and Deborah said, "She was a selfless woman, and we all loved her."

Yolken reached an arm around her as well. They stood together in silence for a moment, supporting one another, tears streaming.

Deborah stepped back and said, "We do have a lot to discuss, but take as much time as you need."

"Thanks," Yolken said, wiping his eyes, "but I think I'd like to hear what you have to say." He returned to his seat and Kaylan sat next to him.

"Can I get you some tea?" Deborah asked.

Yolken nodded, wiping more tears from his eyes. His breath came in ragged shudders as he calmed himself down.

"I guess now is as good a time as any to properly introduce ourselves," Jorgan said.

Yolken looked at them, confused—he'd known them his entire life. "What do you mean?"

"My name isn't really Jorgan."

"It's not?"

"Well, it is, but it's not who I really am. It's a… cover of sorts. I—well, *we* have almost as many covers as there are cities in the empire. But my real name is Jax Karven."

"And I am Acca Hindred," Deborah said, setting a tea tray on the table. She passed cups out to everyone and then, as she filled Kaylan's cup, she said, "But I prefer Deborah."

"I don't understand," Yolken said. He looked over at Kaylan.

She placed her hand on his arm and said, "I was just as confused when they told me."

"You and your brother—Kaylan as well—know us as Deborah and Jorgan, because that is who we are to you."

"So you're in hiding?"

"In a manner of speaking." Jorgan—*No*, Yolken reminded himself. His name is Jax—sipped his tea.

"Why?"

"Because names can be dangerous," Jax said. "For instance, they've been looking for Acca—"

"They?"

"The Regency. They've been looking for her in most of the northern provinces in the Western Realm for several decades. And me—well, let's just say that if the Regent of Hantlo had known I was in Lonely Oak, the festival would have been much more exciting."

"Why?"

"Because those names represent who we really are. But our names are nothing compared to yours."

Yolken stared at them, confused.

"Your father had a very dangerous name," Jax said.

Thornhill? What's so dangerous about that name?

"Just as we aren't who you think we are, neither was your father. His real name was Danavin Hippolyte Drake."

"Drake?" Yolken said, softly.

"Which means *you* are also a Drake," Jax said.

Yolken furrowed his brow. "But the Drakes are the Blessed of the…"

"Dragon," Jax said. "How do you think you were able to heal Issa? And because you have Draego's Gift, you are a threat to Drakonias's rule. You are a Drake, Yolken. And, as much as any of the regents or chancellors, or the emperor himself, you are Blessed of the Dragon."

CHAPTER 13

Yolken sat back in his chair in shock, his mind spinning. His whole life he revered the Blessed, and now he was being told he *was* one? Impossible. But how else could he have done what they say he did? He couldn't believe it. There was no way; he was a nobody who had lived his whole life in the same small town, a place no one thought twice about.

"The look on your face tells me you don't believe me," Jax said.

"It's just…" he started. "They're the *Blessed*."

"And you have Draego's Gift."

"How is that possible?"

"It's possible because your father is a descendant of the Dragon King," Jax said.

"Dragon King? But I thought—"

"And your father didn't just die in a fire. He was murdered. Your mother, too."

"What?" Yolken said, his train of thought interrupted. "Murdered? By who?"

"A team of skilled assassins known as the Black Sodality."

Yolken leaned forward just enough to pick up his teacup but didn't drink any. Instead he asked, "Why weren't we told about any of this?"

"Everything was done to protect you and Javen from the Regency," Jax said.

"I don't understand," Yolken said, setting his cup back on the table. "If my father was Blessed of the Dragon, and I'm Blessed of the Dragon, then why would we need protecting from the Regency? And why would they murder my parents?"

"That question is not easily answered. For it to make any sense you have to understand that the past has a way of favoring those in power. It has been manipulated to favor His Blessed Highness, Drakonias Draeko Irigwin Drake."

"Meaning the past isn't true?"

"Some of it; but not all of it." Jax sipped his tea and said, "We all know how it started on that fateful night fifteen hundred years ago: The Great Dragon constellation descended from the sky and searched all of Dradonia to find one worthy of bearing Draego's Gift. It found Draeko, a man worthy in every regard, and bestowed on him the ability to bring peace to humanity, whose history was written by the blood of endless wars. The Great Dragon blessed Draeko with a spark of his own power, making him the Dragon King."

"The missing star in the dragon's tail," Yolken said.

"The story is retold every day in every Dragon Shrine throughout the empire. Mothers and fathers teach their children the story of how Draeko's rule in the Dragon King Era turned out to be one of merciless tyranny, and how our blessed emperor was duty-bound to free Dradonia of that tyrant. Drakonias successfully removed his father from power and for four centuries we have at last lived peacefully. Not everything is perfect—it is in our nature to do ill to one another, and there are always those who want to rebel against their rulers. But under Drakonias's rule, the Regency executes the Great Dragon's vision for humanity. And I have to admit, the peace Dradonia has had *seems* real. The problem is, much of what the shrines teach is a lie."

Yolken exchanged looks with Kaylan. Jax was actually calling everything he had grown up believing a lie. Yolken wasn't as ardent a worshipper as some people were, like Kristana—really, he simply didn't have time to go to the shrine every day—but he was still thankful for the blessings of the Great Dragon.

Jax pressed on, "The truth is, Draeko wasn't a tyrant. Drakonias is the tyrant. Draeko succeeded in bringing peace to Dradonia for the first time.

"The Dragon King Era was an era of peace, and not of tyranny as we are taught in the shrines. Draeko passed Draego's Gift on to his children, and they their children, from generation to generation. This created an elite class that ruled with power unchallengeable. His rule was absolute, but it was peaceful. Or at least it was until Drakonias decided he wanted to seize the empire from his father.

"Drakonias rebelled, splitting the family between those who wanted to join him and those who remained loyal to Draeko. Those who joined him plunged the world once again into war. Armed with Draego's Gift, the Blessed started a war such as the world had never seen. The war lasted for thirty-one years. Millions upon millions died. In the end, Draeko surrendered. Drakonias crowned himself emperor and then, in a ruthless display of his newfound power, executed his father. He established the Regency, then proceeded to round up and execute his brothers and sisters who had remained loyal to Draeko throughout the war. Much to his displeasure, some of them managed to escape. They went into hiding for a time but were all eventually caught and subsequently executed.

"It took the Regency several decades to round up those of Drakonias's siblings who remained loyal to their father and, in the meantime, many of them had had children. As the centuries passed, those children also had children and so forth. These descendants united in opposition to Drakonias and the Regency. In the hopes of returning the rightful heir to the Dragon Throne, they formed an opposition group known as the Order of the

Dragon."

"You're talking about rebels," Yolken said, hesitantly. Even here, in an isolated cabin, it felt dangerous to converse about rebels.

"Naturally, Drakonias would want you to believe the Order was nothing more than a band of rebels, but in truth, it's the other way around. Drakonias ruthlessly hunts and kills anyone associated with the Order lest they challenge his illegitimate rule. Draeko's descendants—the emperor's own relatives—are the only ones with the power to hold him accountable for what he's done."

"And my father was one of these… rebels?" Yolken said. He was familiar with the Order of the Dragon. Rumors abounded about the Order, but it was dangerous to mention them, so most people avoided it.

"He was."

"And that's why they murdered him?" He phrased it as a question, even though he knew the answer.

"Yes. In their eyes, he could not be allowed to live."

Yolken was beginning to form a clearer picture of the situation, but he still had questions. "Was my mother a rebel, too?"

"No," Jax said. "She was not a rebel. Much as your aunt stayed with Javen amidst great danger…" His voice wavered as he cleared his throat, "…your mother refused to leave the one she loved even though she knew the Regency was coming for them."

Yolken vigorously rubbed his tear stained face and rested his elbows on the table. "So the Regency is after me and killed my aunt because they think I'm a rebel?"

"Their laws are strict and simple: Anyone who isn't a part of the Regency and uses Draego's Gift *is* a rebel."

"But I'm not," Yolken said. It was dangerous even to talk about the rebels, let alone *be* one. He had never thought he had a reason to rebel against the emperor. Why would he? But he'd heard the stories. As much as Yolken discouraged it, old Relan often talked negatively about the Regency after ale loosened his tongue. But what he said never really made sense.

"Maybe you're not," Jax said wryly. "But your father was."

He could hardly believe what Jax was saying. It didn't make sense. But if his father really was a rebel, a member of the despised Order of the Dragon, then…

"Everything you've said—he believed it was true," Yolken said. "As crazy as this all sounds, my father believed it, didn't he?"

"Yes. Your father was an integral part of the Order of the Dragon."

"And if you two are helping me, then…"

"Deborah and I are members of the Order as well," Jax said. "Which is why we needed to hide our real identities from you. The Regency knows who we are, and it wouldn't have been safe for you to be associated with known members of the Order."

"Do you have Draego's Gift?"

Both Jax and Deborah nodded.

"Not every member of the Order has the gift, but Deborah and I do. So did Selena," Jax said.

Yolken looked over at Kaylan, putting the pieces together. Then he said, "Which means we're all related?"

"Technically speaking, yes," Deborah said, setting her teacup down. "But only distantly. The children of Draeko were born well over a thousand years ago. Since then, hundreds of generations have divided our bloodlines. You needn't worry about any… improprieties."

Yolken and Kaylan both went red in the face. Jax laughed, which made Kaylan's face redden even more.

CHAPTER 14

Now, about what happened four days ago," Jax said. "What do you remember?"

"The last thing I remember clearly is that I was out running Javen's errands and was talking with Kaylan in the bakery," Yolken said. "Everything after that is really hazy—like a distant memory that slips away whenever I try to draw near."

"What you're experiencing is a common phenomenon after someone first starts using their gift," Jax said. "The extent to which one experiences this is directly related to the amount of Energy they use. I'm guessing you don't remember our trip here?"

"Vaguely," Yolken said.

Jax raised his teacup to his lips and snickered.

"What?"

"While we were traveling, you were quite insistent on getting answers out of me. I told you to wait because you wouldn't remember what I said," Jax said with a smile.

"I fail to see why that's funny."

"Relax, lad. It happens to everyone to one degree or another. Now, about what happened. It's not uncommon for the Regency to display their power to the people with acts of mercy, earning the worship and devotion of those they rule. They do this in many ways: They clean up after the devastating cyclones plaguing the south, they dig cities in the north out from under mountains of snow by melting it away, and when they are feeling especially benevolent, they heal the sick. When Dorlan stayed in Lonely Oak, he did that very thing."

"He healed Issa," Yolken said, remembering the words Issa's mother had said to him as he'd looked down at her broken neck. She'd said that the chancellor had fixed Issa's legs.

"Yes," Jax affirmed. "Dorlan healed her legs. For the first time in her life, she could run and play. The next morning, she did what every other lass does when her parents are running errands in the square—she played in the oak tree. For years, I'm sure, she watched from her cart and dreamed about playing with the other children. Unfortunately, on her first foray into the tree, she fell."

Yolken looked down at his cup, trying to piece together what they were saying.

"Do you remember? We were in the bakery, and I was filling your order. When we heard the screaming, you ran outside to see what happened," Kaylan said. "I couldn't see what was going on, but after a time the screaming changed into cheering."

"Issa's mother said you knelt down beside her daughter and healed her," Deborah said.

"She had a broken neck and leg, Yolken," Jax said.

"You emerged from the crowd looking like you hadn't slept in a month," Kaylan said. "I helped you back to the tavern, and you fell asleep the moment you laid in your bed. Your aunt met me at the top of the stairs, and I told her what happened. She said I did the right thing by bringing you back to the tavern, then asked me to go tell my mother."

"As a safety precaution, one we established long ago," Jax said, "we woke you up and brought you here. Those Watchers traveling with Dorlan's entourage detected you healing Issa. A team returned to Lonely Oak and tracked you as far as the tavern. They had a run-in with Selena. We think she was protecting Javen." There was a hint of pride in his tone.

"When I found her body, I searched the entire tavern but couldn't find her horse figurine," Deborah said.

"Her horse figurine?" Yolken said. "She carried that with her everywhere she went. Said it was a good-luck charm her mother gave her when she was young."

"It was no luck charm," Jax said. "It was a weapon."

The fleeting thought of a sword entered Yolken's mind. "Where's the sword?"

"You remember the sword?" Jax said.

"I dreamed I was walking around with a sword on my hip. It kept banging against my leg."

Jax went over to the chest in the corner and pulled out a long, black sword. He brought it over and laid it on the table. "It's known as the Harachin sword. It's a powerful weapon; extremely valuable to the Order."

Yolken looked at it intently.

"Go ahead," Jax said.

Yolken traced his fingers over the twining steel hilt, admiring the intricacy of the metalwork. He picked it up by the sheath and drew the sword out. The blade was made from an odd black material with yellow streaks ribboning through it. The streaks shimmered in the light. It was the strangest looking sword he'd ever seen.

"It's made from dragon bone," Jax said.

Yolken looked up, his eyes wide. "*Dragon bone?*"

Dragons were just creatures of legend. He remembered the wild tales Jorgan had told them around the hearth when they were younger. They were both fascinating and frightening. Draego's fabled offspring.

Yolken looked the sword over once more.

"You're probably thinking they're just creatures of fiction," Jax said.

"You told us so many stories about dragons when we were

young, but I never once thought they might be real." Yolken looked over at Kaylan.

"I always thought they were just stories, too," Kaylan said.

"They were very much real," Jax said.

"Were? What happened to them?" Yolken said.

"That I'll explain at the proper time. But essentially, they were driven to extinction during Drakonias' war. Turn it over."

Yolken turned the sword over and saw the inscription on it. "Drae Draeko Harachin Drake," he said.

"The original owner," Jax said. "He was one of nine of Drakonias's siblings who remained loyal the Dragon King. Your father is a descendant of Drae, and he was the last owner of this sword." He paused, then said, "Now it belongs to you."

Yolken looked up at Jax, his mouth agape. "Me?"

Jax nodded. "It's very special, so guard it closely."

Yolken studied the sword, turning it over and over. *Dragon bone,* he thought incredulously. He rubbed his hand over the inscription and said, "So, what exactly is the Order?"

"As I said, the Order is the remnant of those loyal to the Dragon King—we who reject the legitimacy of Drakonias's rule. Our primary purpose is to restore the rightful ruler to the Dragon Throne."

"And who's that?"

"A good question, Yolken. The problem is, we don't know. Members of the Order are all descendants of Draeko, of course, but so much time has passed that the genealogical lines have become quite muddled. Should the Order ever be successful in removing Drakonias from the throne, a careful examination of all the records available to us would need to be taken to determine who should rightfully take his place. The trouble is, the records aren't complete, and the point is already hotly contested amongst the Council. Besides, they are nowhere near a point they could successfully move against Drakonias anyway."

"Oh," Yolken said, slightly crestfallen. "And my father was

involved with them?"

"He was vital to the group's existence."

Yolken took a drink of his tea. Then something occurred to him. "If my father was part of the Order, and you two are as well, what about my aunt? Was Selena really my mother's sister?"

"No," Deborah said.

"So who was she?"

"Her real name was Lael Chafer. She wasn't Elen's sister, but they were close friends in Tieger before your mother and father moved to Lonely Oak."

"She was a member of the Order?"

"She was."

"So raising Javen and myself was some sort of rebel assignment?"

"It was your father's plan, should anything happen to him. But yes, Selena and Deborah were sent by the Order to look after you and your brother," Jax said.

"Selena loved your mother and father more than anyone, and moved to Lonely Oak willingly," Deborah said. "As did I. Looking after you boys was more than an assignment; we did it for Orwyn and Elen." She reached out to hold Yolken's hands, but he pulled them away.

"This is all really too much. *Dragons?*" Yolken said, feeling overwhelmed. "Why should I believe any of this?"

Jax and Deborah exchanged understanding looks.

"We realize we've turned your world upside-down," Jax said, "and it is up to you to choose what you will or won't accept."

"Yolken," Deborah said, taking a gentler tone, "we have all pledged our lives to protect you. You meant the world to your father and mother."

"You're telling me everything I grew up knowing is a lie, and you expect me to just accept it?" Yolken said. He stood abruptly and began to pace around the small cabin.

"We couldn't risk teaching you the truth when you were small. Imagine the danger if you accidently let your true identities slip and the wrong person heard," Jax said. "Your father lived his whole life fighting the Regency. He wanted, if at all possible, to spare you the violent and shadowy life he lived. Not everyone uses their gift, Yolken. And so long as your gift remained dormant, your mother and father wanted you and Javen to live normal lives. Had you known the truth, regardless of whether you could use your gift or not, your lives wouldn't have been normal."

"And now that you have used it, we must tell you the whole truth," Deborah said.

"What about Javen?" Yolken said, still pacing like a caged animal.

"That depends on whether or not you believe what we've told you. But I know you've heard whispers about the darker side of the Regency. Despite our best efforts, Relan couldn't keep his mouth shut."

"I always assumed he was just a drunk who was out of his mind."

"He *has* become quite the drunk," Jax said. "If Javen was taken by the Regency, they will assume he is a rebel. Guilt by association. He is your brother, and you used your gift to heal Issa."

"But we're not."

"They'll try to pry any information they can get out of him."

Yolken's mind was spinning, but he realized what they were telling him was true. "We have to rescue him, then," he said, pushing his chair under the table and turning toward the door.

"I've sent word to the Order of what has transpired, Yolken," Deborah said, catching him by the elbow.

"We have no intention of leaving Javen in the hands of the Regency. Please sit," Jax said, gesturing for Yolken to return to his seat. "Rest assured, the Order will do their utmost to locate him."

"But what about us?" Yolken said. "We can't just stay here

hiding in the mountains while he's in danger."

"We will act when the time is right. The Order needs to be conv—"

"When the time is right?" Yolken looked down at the sword. He reached down and angrily grabbed it. "No. I'm not just going to sit here while Javen is in danger. Kaylan?" Yolken said, looking at her.

"I agree," Kaylan said. "We have to do something."

Yolken strode toward the door, but then his feet froze in place mid stride.

"And what exactly would you do, Yolken?" Yolken heard Jax's challenge from behind him.

He tried to turn around but couldn't move. *What in Draego's Fire?*

"You are a helpless babe against them; and a fool. Imagine if you were to march yourself into the presence of regents and demand they free your brother. They would laugh in your face and then apprehend you as well. No—for the time being, we will remain here."

The invisible force holding Yolken in place suddenly lifted. In shock, he stumbled then whirled back around to face Jax, Deborah, and Kaylan.

Jax's face was serious as he locked eyes with Yolken. "I promise you, we will not permit Javen to remain in the Regency's clutches longer than is absolutely necessary, but right now we must concentrate on what comes next for you."

"Which is what?" Yolken said, feeling more than a little embarrassed.

"You must learn to use your gift."

CHAPTER 15

Javen spent the next day lying on his back, unable to stop the events in the tavern from replaying in his mind. He stared at the sky through the window of Drenan's carriage, mentally watching his aunt's body smash into the hearth over and over. Other than Yolken, she was the only family he had. The thought of losing her brought tears to his eyes. But whenever he thought of her lying to him about her true identity, *an enemy of the Regency,* he angrily wiped them away.

He waffled between grief and betrayal. He couldn't help but think she had lied to them their entire lives about who she was. And if she'd lied about who she was, had she also lied about his parents? What did Drenan mean about his father? *"Did your auntie forget to mention your father was a rebel?"*

Hadie tried consoling him, but he shrugged her off. If it had been Kaylan, maybe he would have responded to her efforts, but as much as he had enjoyed the night he'd spent with Hadie, he barely knew her. It would be exhausting and painful to explain everything to a stranger. He didn't know her enough to trust her with his heartbreak.

Javen fell asleep alone on the couch but woke the next day with Hadie snuggled against him. She had wedged herself between him and the back of the couch and lay on her side with a leg draped over his. When she woke, instead of pushing her away as he had done the day before, he turned on the cushion and accepted her comfort.

They spent the remainder of the day sitting at opposite ends of the couch, facing each other and talking. The conversation floated between what had happened the night Drenan took them from Lonely Oak to stories from their respective pasts. He was frightened about what was happening to him, but he felt compelled to try and get to know Hadie. By the third day, their talking had gradually faded into silence. Only unanswered questions about their captivity remained. The adjoining dining room had food set out for them, but aside from eating—there was no wine or ale—there was nothing of interest there. The last door, the one leading into Drenan's bedchamber, was kept locked.

As boredom set in, Hadie attempted being physical, but Javen wasn't interested.

"We have to pass the time somehow," Hadie pleaded, kissing his neck.

"As amazing as that night was, I can't think about that right now," Javen said. He stood up to put distance between them.

Days were spent rumbling along on the dirt road, their carriage gently bumping and swaying. Each evening, when the caravan stopped, they were permitted to roam around the encampment with explicit instructions to not venture outside the ring of carriages and wagons—which they obeyed. The one time they lingered too long near the edge, armored soldiers standing at the perimeter quickly confronted them and returned them to Drenan's carriage. They tried to be social, joining several different groups around various fires, but it seemed the entire camp knew who they were and didn't want anything to do with them. Instead, in the evening hours, when the camp was alive with activity, they spent their time walking in circles, alone. They avoided returning to Drenan's carriage for as long as possible because they knew what awaited them there—nothing.

The fourth day after leaving Lonely Oak, Javen fell into a half-sleep induced by the rhythmic motion of the carriage but woke when it came to a stop. He sat up from his position—reclining on the couch with Hadie asleep in his arms—lifted the flap covering the window nearest his head and peered out. They were in a town. *Matis*, he thought. He dropped the flap and turned his attention to the sleeping woman beside him. Shaking Hadie gently, he whispered, "Hey, wake up."

"Mmm," Hadie responded after he shook her again. "What is it?"

"The carriage has stopped. We've arrived in Matis."

Before Hadie had time to rouse from her sleep enough to sit up from where they lay on the couch, the door opened and Drenan, dressed in his scale-embroidered suit, entered. He was attended by his personal servant, whose clothing was thin and left little to the imagination. They walked past without acknowledging Javen or Hadie and entered the adjoining room. Javen and Hadie sat up on the couch and waited.

"His Highness wishes to see you in his carriage," Drenan said when he returned to the sitting room, now clad in his chiseled blue armor.

"He does?" Javen stammered.

"Why he hasn't executed you, I don't know," Drenan said.

Javen stared at Drenan, fear and dread flooding into him.

"Best not keep him waiting."

Javen took Hadie by the hand, and they followed Drenan out of the carriage. Guards formed around them to keep at bay the crowd that had gathered to greet the Blessed. As they walked, the crowd bowed and shouted blessings at Drenan.

"Whatever he wants," Hadie said as they walked behind Drenan, "just give it to him, all right?"

"I will," Javen said.

They stopped in front of a carriage similar to Drenan's, but longer and wider. "You wait here," Drenan said to Hadie.

Drenan gestured toward the door, and Javen hesitantly climbed the steps.

He stepped into a room much like the one he and Hadie had been confined to. The chancellor, dressed in orange armor, sat on the couch opposite the door.

"Please, sit," Dorlan said.

Javen sat opposite the chancellor. His stomach churned, and he felt as though he might lose control of his bowels.

"What's your name, lad?" Dorlan said.

"Javen, Your Highness."

"Javen… what?"

"Thornhill. Javen Thornhill."

Dorlan looked at Javen, tapping his finger on the rim of the glass he held in his hand. "May I offer you something to drink? Perhaps some of your brother's fine ale?"

Javen's eyes widened. "You have Yolken's ale?"

"I do. I was very much impressed by it. Would you like a glass?"

"Sure," Javen said.

Dorlan stood and disappeared through the door leading deeper into the carriage. While he was gone, Javen looked at the other door—the one leading out of the carriage—and thought about running. But then Dorlan returned with a second glass filled with amber-colored ale, ruining any chance he might have had.

"Most ale is undrinkable swill when you compare it to fine wine. There's something about this, though," Dorlan said, holding up his glass and looking at it. "It's… exquisite. What's your brother's secret?"

"I really don't know, Your Highness. I don't brew."

"Well," Dorlan said, taking a drink, "it's a shame events have gone the way they have. Your brother seems to have been onto something." He stopped and took another drink. "Now, to the point, young Thornhill. Do you know why you are sitting here before me?"

"Because my brother Synthesized?" Javen said, remembering the word his aunt had used.

"Yes," Dorlan said, sipping on his ale. "And what can you tell me about this ability of your brother's?"

"Nothing, Your Highness. I just learned that word a few days ago."

"I'm told the little girl I healed in the inn hurt herself the next day, and your brother came to the rescue, preventing her death." Dorlan sipped from his ale and looked at Javen. His eyes were as keen as he was casual.

Javen looked down at the glass he held in his hands. All he could do was shrug.

"What can you tell me about Draego's Gift?" Dorlan said.

Javen looked back up at the chancellor. Then, unable to maintain direct eye contact, he looked down at the glass in the chancellor's hands. "Nothing, Your Highness."

"Your aunt didn't teach you anything about the gift?"

"No, Your Highness."

"And what do you know about the Order of the Dragon?"

Javen considered his answer carefully. He didn't want to lie to Dorlan, but at the same time he knew the Order was a dangerous subject.

"It's okay. You can tell the truth."

"I've heard of them," Javen offered weakly. He hoped that by telling the truth he wouldn't anger the chancellor. "Everybody has."

"Hmm," Dorlan said. He sipped his ale.

The quietness compounded Javen's nervousness. He was trying to heed Hadie's advice and tell the chancellor what he wanted to know, but he honestly didn't know anything and was worried Dorlan wasn't getting the answers he wanted. He shifted his eyes and again stared at the cup in his own hand, then hesitantly took a sip.

"You had no idea your aunt was a rebel?"

Javen shook his head.

"But you understand why Drenan was justified in killing her?"

"She was an enemy of the Regency," Javen parroted Drenan's words from the tavern, hoping they made sense. He sipped nervously on his ale again.

"She was," Dorlan said agreeably. "Now tell me—would you be interested in learning to use Draego's Gift?"

Javen choked on the ale. He coughed and thumped himself on the chest, trying to clear his lungs while, at the same time, trying not to spill the sloshing ale held in the other hand. After he regained a modicum of composure, he said hoarsely, "What?"

"You have inside yourself the same gift as your brother. You can be taught to use it. On the morrow, after we've left Matis, we'll talk more," Dorlan said. He stood abruptly and Javen could tell he was being dismissed.

"I have the gift?"

"Indeed. But for now, go and enjoy yourself. You are no longer a prisoner, though I would strongly caution you about trying to leave our protection."

"Yes, Your Highness," Javen said. He set the glass down on a table at the end of the couch. He stood and bowed toward Dorlan, then turned to leave.

"Javen," Dorlan said, stopping Javen as his hand touched the doorknob.

Javen turned and looked back at the armored ruler.

"You needn't fear the Regency."

"Yes, Your Highness," Javen said. He bowed again and opened the door. When his feet hit the ground, he clumsily caught a bag of coins tossed in his direction. Drenan was waiting for him outside the chancellor's carriage.

"There's a room for you in the Blue Mountain," Drenan said. "And you'd better not try to leave us. You wouldn't want to find out what would happen once we caught you."

Javen stared blankly at the regent as Drenan turned and

strode through the crowd, flanked by his guards.

Hadie stepped up behind him and gave his arm a squeeze. "Did you give him what he wanted?"

Javen looked back at the carriage and nodded. "I think so," he said.

Excitement replaced the fear he felt moments ago. He looked over at Hadie, and for the first time since the night in the tavern, he wanted her.

CHAPTER 16

So what did he want?" Hadie said.

"He wants to teach me to use Draego's Gift," Javen said.

Hadie stopped. "*You* have the gift?"

"I don't know. I only know what they're telling me. Until I saw my aunt lift a table off the ground by pointing at it, I would have said no. But now I'm not sure. And if the chancellor wants to teach me to use the power, then I must, right?"

"I guess," Hadie said. "What do you think? Are you going to do it?"

Javen rubbed his chin thoughtfully. "Do I have a choice? Dorlan sounded… friendly, but at the same time, they said not to try to run. And the way we were taken from Lonely Oak, I don't think he was really giving me a choice."

Hadie's expression was doubtful. "This is really strange."

"I know," Javen said with a grimace.

"We can talk about this later. Right now, I'm hungry," Hadie said. She took Javen by the hand and led him down the road.

"Where are we going?"

"There's this little pub I came to love when I was here."

"Came to love?"

"Yeah. Matis is no Lonely Oak, Javen. It's a city with more to offer than a grimy inn to sleep in."

"That's not fair," Javen said. "You didn't even see our tavern. Auntie would have booted you out on your hind end if she ever heard you call it *grimy*."

"If I recall, Javen, it was *you* who refused to take me. *I* wanted to go there, remember."

"You're right," Javen admitted with a wince. It occurred to him that Hadie would never meet Selena.

Hadie led them down one street after another, and Javen quickly became lost. Most of the buildings they passed were taller than the buildings back home—the tallest was the Oak, which boasted three stories.

Hadie turned right at a cross street and, after following it for a while, made a left turn and then another right a few blocks down. As he took in the many shops they passed, he lost count of how many turns they made or how long they stayed on a particular street before they turned again. If he had to make his way back to the caravan, he was sure it would take him until the morning, if he succeeded at all.

He knew Matis was significant in size compared to Lonely Oak, bigger even than Edis to the north—which he'd been to a few times—but not nearly as big as Croff, which he considered to be the nearest *true* city. "Matis is just a town, you know," he said.

"What?" Hadie said.

"You said Matis is a city, but it's actually a town."

"Why do you say that? It's much larger than the bump in the road I found you in."

"True," Javen admitted, "but Matis isn't a provincial seat."

"What does that have to do with it?"

"My aunt always said the thing dividing a town from a city is that cities are typically provincial seats. Matis is part of the Croff province, and Croff is the seat, making Matis a town."

"Oh yeah?" Hadie said, stopping. "If it's 'just' a town, then I'd like to see you find your own way around." She turned and ran away from him, light on her feet, and disappeared around a corner.

Shocked, Javen stood and watched her go. Then, coming to his senses, he charged after her shouting, "Hadie, wait!"

He turned the corner at the intersection of the next street and stopped. He couldn't see Hadie. He turned and looked in every direction, but she was nowhere to be found. He looked up at the sign hanging over the door of the shop on the corner of the two streets—a bakery. It was the sixth he'd already seen as they walked. Maybe Matis wasn't *technically* a city, but it was far bigger than anything he'd ever experienced.

Javen felt a poke on his back and turned to find Hadie smiling at him.

She reached up, kissed him on the lips, then demanded, "Admit it!"

"Admit what?"

"That Matis is a city."

"Whatever it is, I admit I'm hopelessly lost without you."

"That'll do, I suppose." Hadie took him by the hand again and led him along.

"Come on, we're almost there."

Around the next corner, Hadie pushed open a wooden door coated in a layer of grime. The inside of the pub was dark, smoky, and as greasy as the door.

Javen followed Hadie in as she walked over to the only empty table. When he sat down across from her, he said, "*This* is the place you were talking about?"

"Yeah," Hadie said enthusiastically.

"And you said the Oak was grimy."

"Just wait until you eat before you pass judgment, all right?"

Javen was starving, so he nodded his head and sat back in his chair.

A gruff-looking man with a filthy apron came over to their table and set two steins of black ale before them.

"Hi, Zuri," Hadie said.

"Hadie!" Zuri said in a baritone voice. "I didn't recognize you."

"I was wondering if you'd remember me," Hadie said.

"Remember you? How could I forget you?" He furrowed his brow. "I thought you went north?"

"I did. But for the time being, it seems I'm headed south again."

"I see. Let me get you something to eat."

Javen took a sip of the ale when Zuri walked away. It was bold and strong.

"Go easy on that," Hadie said, pointing to his stein. "At least until after you eat something."

"It's good," Javen said appreciatively.

Zuri returned with two plates of food and set them on the table. "Enjoy," he said.

The food was a mixture of rice and noodles, topped with bits of fried meat and vegetables covered in a dark sauce. Javen poked at the unidentifiable bits of meat on his plate, unsure about it, especially in a place that wasn't very clean.

"Relax, it's just chicken and goat, prepared how they do it where he's from," Hadie said.

"Which is where?"

"Up by Hunig somewhere."

Javen poked at it some more.

"If you intend on going to Hantlo, Javen, you're going to have to get used to eating different things. The whole world doesn't eat food made by your auntie."

Javen tasted the fried meat and the dark sauce and found it to be surprisingly delicious. Before long, his plate was clean.

"Now you know why I like Zuri's place so much," Hadie said.

"How long did you stay here?" Javen asked, taking another drink of the dark ale, which had a hint of spice to it.

"A few months. I'd been on the road for a couple weeks and

wanted to take a break. Zuri had a room to let upstairs, and he let me stay in exchange for helping in the kitchen and running errands for him."

Zuri came over with another plate of food and asked Javen in his baritone voice, "More?"

Javen nodded, and Zuri set the plate before him.

"Will you be staying?" Zuri said. "I'll prepare you a room while you finish eating."

"Thanks, Zuri," Hadie said. "But we actually have accommodations elsewhere."

"Where?"

"At the Blue Mountain."

"Blue Mountain!" Zuri exclaimed. "Expensive!"

"My friend here is paying," Hadie said. She winked at Javen.

Zuri looked down at Javen. "You a Suit or something?"

"No," Javen said.

"Then how can you afford the Blue Mountain?"

"Uh," Javen said, not really knowing what else to say.

Zuri furrowed his brow then said to Hadie, "Where'd you find him?"

"I met him in a little town a few days north of here," Hadie said.

"I see. Well, if you need a place, Hadie," Zuri said with a dismissive glance at Javen, "you are always welcome here."

"Thank you," Hadie said.

Zuri left them to finish their meal.

"What was that all about?" Javen said.

"He was probably just being protective."

"Do I look dangerous or something?"

"I can see how it might have looked a little strange to him. I mean, I left Zuri's vowing never to return to the south only to show up again with a stranger with lots of money."

"Well, you're welcome to stay here if you like," Javen said.

"Don't be like that," Hadie said. "Besides, I don't think Drenan would allow it."

Javen snorted and returned his attention back to his food.

When they were done, Javen reached into the bag Drenan had given him and left an ample amount of money.

When they got up to leave, Zuri shouted from across the pub, "See you next time, Hadie!"

Hadie waved.

It was dark when they exited the pub. The busyness of the day was done; the streets had emptied considerably.

"What now?" Javen said.

"Let's go check out this Blue Mountain," Hadie said.

Hadie led Javen back through town. He knew she was just joking about the 'town or city' thing, but he was nonetheless glad she knew the way back. Even in daylight, he had gotten lost on the way to Zuri's, and the fact it was now dark didn't help matters.

While they were walking down a street Javen didn't recognize, Hadie stopped and looked up at the sign hanging over the door of a shop. Then she pushed the door open and pulled Javen in.

The shop was stuffed full of books, from floor to ceiling. The shelves overflowed, and books were stacked haphazardly on the floor. A tan cat reclined on top of one pile of books near the door.

Hadie moved around, picking books up, flipping through them, then setting them back down. She looked over her shoulder at Javen, still standing by the door, and said, "Come on. We need something to keep us entertained in the carriage."

Javen stepped away from the door and looked around.

An old woman walking half-bent over with the aid of a cane slowly made her way toward them. With a frail voice, she asked, "Can I help you find anything in particular?"

"I was hoping to find some *Lovers of Onta*," Hadie said.

"Ah, yes, yes. A fine choice for a young lass such as yourself," the old woman said. "How many would you like?"

"Two or three, if you have them."

"Oh, lass, I have 'em all," the woman said. "The demand for Karina Drake's bedding escapades is never-ending. Any particular volumes you have in mind?"

Hadie shook her head.

The old woman shuffled over to a shelf near the front door and sifted through a pile of books until she found what she was looking for. Walking slowly in her hunched manner over to Hadie, she handed Hadie three books. "And what about you, lad?"

"Do you have anything on the history of the Southern Realm?" Javen said.

"I do, but it's a bit dry compared to *Lovers of Onta*," the woman said with a wink. "Just a moment," she added before shuffling down a row of shelves toward the back. Javen followed her, and she pointed up to the top shelf with her cane. "Up there. Not exactly front-of-the-shop reading, lad."

"I know, but I like history," Javen said. He reached up for the large book she had pointed out and pulled it off the shelf.

The old woman slowly made her way to the front of the store. Without asking how much they owed, Javen pulled a gold drake out of the bag Drenan had given him and handed it to the woman.

"Oh, my!" she exclaimed. "You'll need to pick a few more if you want change."

"Don't worry about it," Javen said.

The woman hesitantly accepted the coin and said, "Well, then, thank you very much. Please do come back."

Hadie and Javen left the shop, books in hand. Once they made it back to a familiar street, Hadie stopped and asked someone for directions to the Blue Mountain.

They followed the stranger's directions and passed a building with half a dozen women standing outside, wearing fine shifts topped with corsets in various colors. The sign hanging over the door had a naked woman carved on it, and the women called lasciviously at them as they passed. Hadie gripped Javen's hand tightly and pulled him along, hurrying her pace.

Finally, they approached a large building, with a group of about twenty ragged-looking people gathered near the door. Javen counted the windows—it was six stories tall. Twice as big as the Oak! A blue sign with a mountain peak carved into it hung over twin doors intricately decorated with a mountain scene. Javen pushed the right-hand door open and went in.

Inside, Javen's eyes widened in amazement. It was the nicest building he'd ever been in. Two large wooden chandeliers hung from the ceiling at opposite ends of the large room, and dozens of oil lamps lit the room. Blue wallpaper—with the same mountain pattern as the front door—covered all the walls. Servants in matching blue uniforms with white aprons moved about the room transporting food and drinks on large trays. Javen saw Drenan sitting at a table with Devin and Karina Drake on the other side of the room. She was so beautiful Javen had a hard time not staring at her. The regents no longer wore their armor but were dressed in royal blue suits instead.

Javen walked up to the long bar along the front wall. It stretched the length of the room and continued the length of the side wall, too. Several barkeeps worked, serving patrons and filling orders for the servants. An attendant behind the bar greeted them, "Welcome to the Blue Mountain! How may I help you?"

"We'd like a room, please," Hadie said.

"It's two drakes for a room on the second floor, and they go up from there. The sixth floor is unavailable tonight."

"Two drakes?" Hadie exclaimed. "For a second-floor room?"

"Yes, ma'am."

"I didn't imagine it would cost so much for a bed to rest our weary heads," Hadie said with a sigh.

"There *are* other inns that you might find more suitable to your means, ma'am, if you find our rates to be unacceptable," the attendant said.

"Sir, do you have any rooms reserved for Javen Thornhill?" Javen asked, wearying of teasing the attendant.

"Thornhill, you say?"

"Yes."

"Let me see, let me see. Ah, yes. Here we go. There's a room reserved for you on the…" the attendant paused, then continued, "…the sixth floor. Are you… are you with—"

"The chancellor?" Hadie finished for him.

"Yes, yes, the chancellor."

"Yes," Javen said.

"My apologies, sir, my apologies," the attendant said with a quaver in his voice. He bowed, then pulled a blue key off a large pegboard hanging on the wall behind him. He handed Javen the key and said, "Here's your key, sir. Your room number is six-zero-two. Show any server your key, and they'll get you whatever food and drink you desire. You may have it sent to your room if you'd prefer."

"What do you want to do?" Javen asked Hadie.

Hadie smiled at Javen and led him down to the nearest free attendant. "Can we order something for our room?" she said.

"May I see your key?" the barkeep asked.

Javen held up the key. The man looked at it then handed him a menu. Javen offered it to Hadie and said, "What would you like?"

Hadie looked the menu over. Addressing the barkeep, she said, "We'd like truffles and a bottle of your finest wine—whichever of these it is."

"Yes, ma'am. We'll send it up."

Satisfied, Hadie took Javen by the hand and headed toward the staircase.

Drenan intercepted them before they reached the base of the steps. "I hope you have been enjoying your evening thus far," he said.

"We have, thank you," Javen said.

"The women at the brothel next door are on the house as well," Drenan said. "The finest women you'll find for leagues around."

Javen blushed at the suggestion.

"Ah. Never had a prostitute before? Well, keep it in mind should you find each other's company… unsatisfying. As I said, on the house."

"No thanks," Javen said. He bowed slightly then stepped around Drenan.

"He has always creeped me out," Hadie said when they were a couple of flights up.

"Something about him does seem a little… off," Javen agreed quietly.

Soldiers blocked their way when they reached the sixth floor and demanded to see their key. Javen held it up, and the soldiers let them by.

The room amazed them both. It was big and luxurious with a four-poster bed, a large armoire, and a porcelain tub supported by four claw-looking legs.

Hadie went and flopped down on the bed. "It's goose down," she said with a deep sigh.

Javen smiled at her, anxious to get her clothes off her.

"Do you require a bath?" a voice said from behind Javen, startling him.

He turned around, surprised. Hadie sat up on the bed.

A young girl stood at the door.

Neither of them had bathed since they left Lonely Oak. In unison, they said, "Yes!"

Servants immediately streamed in and out, carrying large buckets filled with steaming water. They filled the tub and disappeared as quickly as they had appeared, shutting the door behind them.

Hadie rolled off the bed and ventured over to the steaming

tub. She put her hand in and exclaimed, "It's hot!"

Javen reached for his shirt and Hadie raced him to see who could get their clothes off the fastest. Hadie won and was the first in the water. Javen kicked his pants off and joined her.

"I can't remember the last time I had a hot bath," Javen said, easing himself into the tub.

"It's been entirely too long," Hadie said, sinking until only her head remained above water. She closed her eyes and breathed deeply.

Javen grabbed a bar of soap from a small table on the back side of the tub and lathered himself up. When he finished, he sank down into the water and washed the soap off. He handed the bar to Hadie and watched her hungrily as she washed. When they were clean, they reclined in the tub and enjoyed the feeling of the hot water on their skin. Hadie began exploring Javen's body with her foot.

Someone knocked on the door, and Javen suddenly felt embarrassed. He pushed Hadie's foot away, making her giggle.

"Better get it," Hadie said.

"*You* get it," Javen said, not wanting to get out of the water in his current state.

Hadie stood in the tub, giving Javen a full view of her wet body. She stepped out of the tub and grabbed one of the robes hanging on the wall. She wrapped the robe around herself, then pranced to the door and opened it.

A servant held a tray with a bottle of wine, two glasses, and a bowl of truffles on it. "My apologies for interrupting your bath, ma'am," she said with a bow. "Where would you like this?"

"That's alright," Hadie said. "By the bed, please."

When the servant discreetly departed and closed the door behind her, Hadie removed her robe. She used it to towel herself dry then dropped it to the floor.

Javen watched her fill each glass with wine then climb into the bed.

"What are you waiting for?" Hadie said.

Javen stood up, hastily dried himself, and joined Hadie. She handed him a glass, and he took a sip. "This is really good," he said.

They reclined on the bed as they ate the truffles and drank the wine. When they finished, Javen rolled onto his side to face Hadie, who had snuggled down into the sheets. He said, "I could get used to this."

"Shut up and kiss me," Hadie replied.

CHAPTER 17

Javen woke to knocking. He opened his eyes, feeling disoriented. He stared up at an intricately carved wooden canopy depicting a mountain scene. He turned his head to the side and saw a tub; then, hearing a gentle snore, turned his head the other way and saw Hadie sleeping beside him, her back to him. As his disorientation slowly disappeared, the memory of his whereabouts returned.

The knocking repeated.

Javen looked over at the door. He climbed out of bed, grabbed the robe hanging on the post at the foot of the bed, and put it on.

"Good morning, sir," said the female servant from the previous night when he opened the door. "I apologize if I've woken you. I trust you slept well?"

"Yes, thank you."

"It's the deepest pleasure of the Blue Mountain to serve, sir. May we?" the servant said, gesturing to another servant beside her with a pitcher of steaming water.

Javen nodded.

The servant filled a basin at the foot of the tub, then silently left.

"I wanted to let you know your carriage is ready for you. I

am also to inform you the departure of His Highness's caravan is planned for half an hour from now."

"My carriage?" Javen said, rubbing his eyes.

"Yes, sir. You will find your carriage fourth in line."

"Thank you."

The servant bowed and closed the door.

After washing his face and scrubbing it dry with a luxurious towel, Javen walked over to the large windows and pulled the curtains apart.

Early morning sunlight streamed in. Matis stretched out below, and the Mindon Mountains stood silhouetted in the east. He stared, taking in their beauty. After a few minutes, he felt Hadie's arms wrap around him and squeeze him from behind.

"Last night was fun," Hadie said.

"I agree," Javen said. He turned around and kissed her. "You want the good news or the bad news?"

"Bad, I suppose." Hadie rested her head on his chest.

"We have to go."

"I figured that. And the good news?"

"It seems we won't be sleeping on Drenan's couches anymore."

"Really?"

"It sounds like we have our own carriage now."

"They got you your own carriage?"

"That's what the servant said."

"Javen?" Hadie asked, pulling back to look him in the face.

"What?"

"Are you sure you want to do this?"

"What?"

"I don't know… this all seems wrong. All of a sudden we went from being prisoners to being treated like…"

"Like what?" Javen said, stepping back.

"Like one of them."

"What's wrong with that?"

"You're *not* one of them."

"Do you *want* to stay in Drenan's carriage, sleeping on his couch?"

"No. It's just… they killed your aunt. Aren't you the least bit worried?"

"I am. But…" He had spent the whole first day in the carriage wrestling with what had happened. He loved his aunt, but he was having a hard time accepting the fact she had lied to him about who she was. "To be honest, I don't really know what to think. What am I supposed to do?"

"I don't know, Javen. But what I *do* know is that you shouldn't get yourself involved with them."

"They're the Blessed of the Dragon!"

"You don't know them like I do. I grew up around them, remember."

"What do you want me to do? Turn down the carriage?"

"No, Javen. It's just… you need to figure out what it is *you* want. I have no idea where all this is leading, but in the end, whatever it is that you decide is in *your* best interest, you need to be prepared to tell them. The more stuff they throw at you—like this room, or the carriage—the tighter the noose around your neck will become."

Javen didn't know exactly what he wanted, but he liked the idea of being out from under Yolken's control. He liked the idea of being involved with the Regency even more, and maybe this room and the carriage were their way of showing him that was what they wanted, too. That and Dorlan's invitation to teach him to use Draego's Gift.

"Come on," he said, "we gotta get going. We're supposed to be downstairs in half an hour. There's hot water in the basin there to wash up with."

Hadie reached up and kissed Javen. Then she went over to the basin and washed. Another knock came at the door, and Javen answered it. A different servant handed him a platter of fruit, hard-boiled eggs, and bread, which he brought in and set on the table by the tub. Once Hadie finished washing, they got dressed, ate the food in silence, and left the room.

Outside the inn, the carriages once again lined the street. They walked down the line, and Dorlan greeted them at the fourth carriage. He was wearing his orange armor, and guards flanked him.

"I trust you will find your new accommodations much more suitable," Dorlan said as they approached.

Javen looked at the wagon in amazement. "Your Highness… I—"

"We have a long way yet to go before we arrive in Hantlo and there's no sense in you crowding Drenan."

"Thank you, Your Highness," Javen said.

Dorlan left, followed by his gray-armored guards, and Javen watched until the crowd of worshippers hid him from view. Then he climbed up into his carriage.

It wasn't as big as Drenan's—instead of three separate rooms, it had only two. The first was a small sitting room with couches lining both sides, just like the other carriages, and the second was the bedroom. The bedroom had a table in the corner for meals, a little built-in armoire, and a bed.

Hadie followed him into the carriage and stood at the door dividing the two rooms. "Javen, are you sure about this?"

"Shh," he said. Even if he wasn't sure, he didn't think he had a choice. "Come here."

Hadie walked over to the bed, and Javen pulled her down on top of him and kissed her.

CHAPTER 18

Fingers traced the scars on Drenan's stomach. The woman resting her head on his chest smiled up at him. Two more women lay curled up together on his other side. "Get off me," he said. He used his arm to push the naked woman aside. She pulled herself up and sat at the head of the bed, drawing her legs up and out of his way. After he rolled off the bed and stood up, she snuck back under the blankets with the other two sleeping women.

Naked, Drenan walked over to the windows and pulled the curtains open. He looked down at the street. The carriages and wagons were lined up, ready for the day's journey. He hated these trips back and forth between Hantlo and Kyinth. He had long wished the emperor would come to Hantlo now and then.

"Your carriage is ready, Your Majesty," Drenan's servant said from behind him.

"I see that."

"May I dress you, Your Majesty?"

Drenan held his arms straight out to his side signaling his assent. The petite servant walked up behind him with smallclothes in hand. As he stepped into them, he admired her heavy breasts, visible through the sheer material of her servants' garb.

While his servant dressed him in his leggings, Drenan stared out the window. Guards began lining up near the door directly below him. He saw Dorlan emerge from the inn wearing his orange armor. Dorlan walked into the street and passed his own carriage, which was waiting in the middle of the cobbled road right outside the door. Drenan watched with curious eyes as Dorlan passed both his and Devin's carriage, then stopped at a carriage in line behind Devin's. Drenan furrowed his brow, wondering what Dorlan was doing.

His servant buckled the belt on his leggings then went to retrieve the breast-piece. He continued watching the carriage hiding Dorlan as she strapped the breast-piece in place. His eyes darted left at the sight of someone walking toward the carriage. *Danavin's get.* When the Thornhill boy stopped behind the carriage, Drenan stepped closer to the window and said, "Draego's Fire."

Drenan turned from the window and stormed toward the door. He passed the end table, which held a platter of food, and swiped a glass ewer full of water onto the floor. It shattered, making the three whores curled up on the bed sit up in fear. He snatched his gloves from the post supporting his armor then yanked the door open.

As he walked down the candlelit hallway, his gloves tucked under his arm, Drenan worked at buckling the side of his armor. When he finished slipping the buckles into place, he slid the gloves over his hands. Ignoring the servants of the Blue Mountain who greeted him at the bottom of the stairs, he strode across the common room. A servant scrambled to the front door and opened it just before he stormed through it.

Drenan caught sight of Dorlan walking toward his carriage, so he hastened his step to intercept him. "What are you doing?" he said, stepping in front of the chancellor.

"Excuse me?" Dorlan said.

"You're giving him his own carriage?"

"It's fitting, don't you think?"

"Since when did we start treating prisoners so well?"

"He's not a prisoner, Drenan," Dorlan said.

Drenan stepped aside when Dorlan started walking again. He walked alongside the chancellor and said, "What do you mean he isn't a prisoner? Of course he is. He's Danavin's get."

"He *was* a prisoner, but he's not anymore." Dorlan stopped outside his carriage and waited for a guard to open the door. "Now, if you'll excuse me, I'd like to break my fast before my food is cold." Dorlan stepped up into his carriage and the guard shut the door, leaving Drenan staring, dumbfounded.

Drenan turned toward his own carriage and climbed into it, filled with anger. When he saw Devin sitting on the couch in the entry room, clad in the same blue armor he wore, he sighed and said, "What are you doing here?"

"I knew you wouldn't take the news well, so I thought I'd come and console you," Devin said.

"Console me? If you wanted to console me, you'd have sent Karina over instead."

"You know she's not interested in you, Drenan."

"Don't give her a choice, then."

"We don't operate that way."

Drenan shook his head and sat heavily on the couch. The door opened, and his servant climbed into the carriage, her face betraying her fright. She quickly moved into the corner on the opposite side of the room and waited.

The carriage lurched into motion. As the metal-framed wooden wheels rolled down the cobbled streets, Drenan swayed on the couch and worked at removing the scaled gloves he wore. "Why is Dorlan treating this boy like he's one of us?" he asked as he pulled the first glove off.

"I don't know," Devin mused. "Perhaps he's hoping to glean information from him."

Drenan pulled the second glove off. He set them on the cushion next to him then stood. His servant left the corner and began working at unclasping the buckles on his wool-lined breast-piece. When she had the buckles undone, she removed it and set it next to the gloves, then unbuckled his belt and helped him step out of his leggings. He sat back down, wearing only his smallclothes, and said, "This isn't how it's done, and you know it."

"I'm aware of how things are done, Drenan. Don't you think I might be a little suspicious of Dorlan's motives, too?"

"What is he up to, I wonder? He said the boy is no longer a prisoner."

"I heard," Devin said. "And I don't know. Perhaps he's received word from Drakonias about how to proceed. Unless we ask him, we'll never know."

Drenan scowled at his older brother. "I just talked to him. He doesn't seem to be interested in discussing it right now."

"He never has liked having his authority questioned," Devin looked down at Drenan's chest and said. "Why do you insist on keeping those ugly things? I can get rid of them for you, you know."

Drenan looked down at his scar-covered chest and stomach. The marks covered his shoulders, arms, and hands also. Devin was skilled in healing, and he didn't need the scars to remember the fire that had nearly burned him to death in his own room— the attack was still clear in his mind. He'd decided to keep them until he got his revenge on the man who gave them to him. And now his hatred burned even stronger. "You know why," he said, standing.

He gestured toward his servant, then walked back to his bedchamber. She meekly scuttled after him and shut the door behind her.

CHAPTER 19

Yolken sat on the bench on the covered porch of the cabin, leaning back against the rough-hewn log walls. Everyone else was still asleep. He and Kaylan had spent most of the previous day walking along the creek and resting, talking about all the new information they had had thrust upon them. Even still, he had no clue how to process everything that Jorgan—no Jax—and Deborah had revealed, so he closed his eyes and listened to the sounds of the dense forest instead. Birds chattered to each other in nearby trees. Squirrels scurried about on the forest floor looking for food. The towering trees rustled overhead in the gentle breeze, swaying back and forth.

He listened for a while, trying to quiet his mind, then opened his eyes. He plucked a nut from the bag sitting beside him on the bench and tossed it out onto the ground. Three blue jays flew down from their perches and landed nearby. They all slowly hopped closer until one of them was close enough to pick the nut up with its beak. It flew away, leaving the other two behind. He tossed out two more, and the remaining blue jays hopped over to them and picked them up.

Squirrels skittered around, replacing the jays. After tossing a few nuts to them and watching them store them in their cheeks before running off, Yolken decided to play a game. He waited patiently, and the squirrels returned. He tossed a few more out, this time a little closer to the porch. The squirrels quickly picked them up as well. He continued this process, drawing the squirrels closer to the porch until only one was daring enough to come within reach.

The solitary squirrel waited at the base of the wooden steps. Yolken tossed a few nuts out onto the porch. The squirrel hesitated at first, but eventually skittered up the side of the porch and stuffed its cheeks. It ran away with its prize but returned a couple minutes later—and this time it climbed right up onto the porch and waited.

Yolken dropped a couple of nuts by his feet. The squirrel ran over, picked them up, and put them in his mouth. However, it didn't run off. Yolken held another nut in his hand near the porch. The squirrel looked at it and flicked its tail back and forth. Then, it inched closer to Yolken's outstretched hand. When its nose was only an inch from the treat, the squirrel snatched it and ran away.

While the squirrel was away, Yolken stretched his legs out and waited for it to return. When it again appeared on the porch, he held a nut down by his legs. The squirrel again inched forward. However, this time when the squirrel approached the nut, Yolken slowly pulled the nut back, drawing it along his legs, bringing it closer to his waist. The squirrel jumped onto his outstretched legs and climbed toward its prize. When the squirrel reached his waist, he permitted it to grasp the nut from his hand. Instead of running off, the squirrel shelled it right there.

The front door of the cabin opened and startled the squirrel. It leaped off Yolken's stomach and disappeared. Yolken looked up and saw Kaylan standing in the door holding a steaming cup in each hand. She handed one to him then settled next to him on the bench.

"Wanna go for a walk?" Kaylan said after they finished

drinking their tea in silence. "It's a while yet before it's time to eat."

"I'd love to," Yolken said.

Kaylan took Yolken by the hand and led him off the porch. They walked along quietly, holding each other's hand, just as they'd spent the previous day doing. They took the trail along the creek and followed it as it wound its way gently through the ravine.

The foliage and dense forest quickly hid the cabin from their view. After walking around a bit, Yolken began to understand why Jax had built the cabin where he did.

They continued strolling alongside the creek until Kaylan stopped at an outcropping of rock that hung out over the flowing water. She stepped onto it and sat down, letting her feet dangle off the side. Yolken joined her, then leaned forward to look down at the clear water peacefully trickling by beneath their feet. His aunt would have loved this spot. Tears formed when he thought about her. He wiped them away with his shoulder.

Kaylan rubbed his back and asked, "How are you feeling today?"

"I still can't believe she's dead. And because of me."

"It's not your fault, Yolken. You can't blame yourself for what happened."

Yolken shook his head, both agreeing and disagreeing with her. "I feel responsible, though. If I hadn't healed Issa, my aunt would still be alive."

"If you hadn't healed Issa, then *Issa* would be dead."

"I know," Yolken said. He didn't feel any better.

Kaylan scooted closer to Yolken and wrapped her arm around him.

"And what am I supposed to do with… everything else?" Yolken said after a while.

Kaylan shook her head with a gentle sigh. "That I do not know. This is all new for me too; I didn't know about any of it until we came here. Mammy told me to pack a bag, then we left the bakery so suddenly—I was so confused. My Mammy's not really my Mammy—I mean, she *is*, but she's not who I thought she was. And uncle Jorgan—I mean Jax… You have to believe me when I say I was just as surprised as you about all this. None of us are who we grew up thinking we were."

"At least your mother's really your mother," Yolken said. "And now I'm supposed to believe everything they've said about the Regency and yet just sit up here while Javen's out there missing?"

"I know, but Mammy said she sent a message to people in Croff who can help," Kaylan said, trying to reassure him.

"The Order…" Yolken said. "I can't believe everything we've been taught our whole lives has been a lie."

"They said it was for our protection."

"I know, I get that. But it's still hard to believe," Yolken said. "We grew up revering the Regency. They're the Blessed of the Dragon! And now I find out they murdered my parents. What am I supposed to do with that? And now they have Javen…"

Their conversation trailed off, and Yolken stared into the water. After a while, Kaylan said, "Yolken?"

"Yeah?" Yolken said, without looking up.

"Can I talk to you about something?"

He looked over at her. "Anything."

"I think it's safe to say there's something between us," Kaylan said with a shy smile.

"Yeah, I feel—"

"If we're going to move forward with whatever this is," Kaylan said, gesturing from her to him and back, "then there's something you need to know."

"What?"

"For a while now, Javen has been expressing an interest in me."

Yolken nodded.

"You know?"

"He said something about it the day of the festival. Said he was hoping to spend it with you. It surprised me because I always thought he liked flirting with every girl he could… while I've loved only you—"

"Me too!" Kaylan exclaimed.

Yolken looked at her, surprised by her boldness. *Did she just admit…*

"Which is why I never returned any of his flirtation. He certainly is persistent though." She was blushing all the way up to her ears.

He leaned over and kissed her. Years of nervousness and uncertainty melted away. The matter was settled. They belonged to each other. The kiss continued to deepen as certainty and joy flowed between them.

"I've read enough tales and heard enough stories from my uncle to know how it can be between brothers who want the same woman," Kaylan said when their kiss ended. "It troubles me that I might become a wedge between you."

"Let's not worry about that," Yolken said. "If there's a problem, we'll deal with it then."

"I just don't want anything to come between you and your brother."

"It won't."

"Promise?"

Yolken nodded. "How long have you…"

"Do you remember listening to my uncle's… I mean Jax's… stories in your tavern?"

"Yeah," Yolken said with a nod.

"Well, toward the end, before he stopped telling the stories altogether, you quit coming."

"I remember."

"You were too old for stories, you said," Kaylan said.

"I was practically an adult. Besides—"

"It was then that I realized that I missed you being there."

"You did?"

"Mmm-hmm."

"I… was… you couldn't have been more than…"

"I was old enough to notice you weren't there," Kaylan said decidedly. She kissed Yolken then said, "What about you? How long have you…"

"Well, according to Auntie, I've loved you my whole life."

"Have you?"

Yolken looked out over the rippling water, trying to collect his thoughts, then said, "I suppose it's true that I liked you coming over for stories more than I enjoyed the actual stories themselves. I mean, don't get me wrong, Jax is definitely a talented storyteller, but…"

"What was your favorite?"

"Story?" Kaylan nodded. "What was yours?"

"I always liked the stories about Anivera," Kaylan said.

"The mysterious woman who inhabits the Island of Kvorga," Yolken said. "What a creepy place."

"Yes. I've always thought it would be fascinating to visit there."

"Nobody visits there," Yolken said, shivering slightly. "Not even the Blessed."

Kaylan's face was skeptical. "Well, according to my uncle… I mean, Jax. What was your favorite?"

"I always liked the stories about the scarred man."

"Now *those* were creepy," Kaylan said.

"Which is exactly why I liked them," Yolken said. "If they were intended to keep me out of trouble, they worked."

"And to think, now he is telling us dragons were real. I have a hard time believing that."

"Me either."

The conversation lulled and Yolken thought about what it would have been like to see a dragon. He imagined that if they were *anything* like what Jax described in his stories that such an encounter would have been truly terrifying.

They enjoyed a few more minutes by the creek before Kaylan eventually said, "We'd better be getting back."

CHAPTER 20

Yolken sat on a rock ledge high above the cabin, legs aching and breath labored from the strenuous climb. As nearly as he could estimate, he and Jax had climbed at least three hundred paces up the steep slope of the northern side of the ravine. They'd set out that morning after breaking their fasts, and by the time they arrived at the ledge, the sun was high in the sky and shone warmly down upon them.

Jax pulled a pipe and a small wooden box from his coat. He opened the box, pinched out some tobacco, then tamped it into the pipe. The tobacco started to smoke when he put the pipe in his mouth.

Yolken looked at him in surprise. "How... did... you do... that?" he said through breaths.

"With Synthesis," Jax said through teeth clenched on the pipe.

"Synthesis?"

"Draego's Gift." Jax puffed on his pipe until Yolken's breath returned to normal, then he said, "Making fire will be but one thing you learn to do with Synthesis. But first, we need to talk about what happened back in Lonely Oak."

"All right," Yolken said.

"Issa's fall from the tree left her with a broken neck. One of the first things you need to know about using your gift is that its use is limited by your own knowledge. I know you probably can't remember what you did to Issa, but you wouldn't have been able to do it if you didn't first possess in-depth knowledge about our bodies."

"Auntie taught…" Yolken began. *Not my aunt.* "It was one of the many things Selena made us learn. Jax?"

"Mmm?"

"If Selena wasn't our aunt, then who was she?"

"More like a…" Jax said, pausing to think, "a cousin."

"Cousin?"

"We don't have the records to determine what your exact relation to her would be, but as we discussed yesterday, everyone with the gift is at least distantly related."

Yolken looked down at his hands.

"What is it?" Jax said.

"Kaylan and I are… Are you sure our being together isn't wrong?"

"The law only prevents first-generation relatives from marrying and the two of you are only very distantly related."

"Marry?" Yolken exclaimed.

Jax allowed a puff of smoke to rise and drift away. He looked Yolken in the eye. "That is your intention, is it not?"

"I have loved her all my life Jax," Yolken said, returning his gaze.

"I'm not a fool, Yolken. I'm a man, and was young once," Jax said. "Though I must warn you that if you do marry, you will have some difficult decisions to make in the future. The Order has… rules. But let's not concern ourselves with this presently. The education you got from—"

Yolken let out an exasperated groan. "We always hated those lessons."

"You hated learning?" Jax bit on the end of his pipe.

"No, we hated not being able to go out and play with the

other children."

"Selena was just following your father's wishes. And as you will learn, what you can do with Synthesis is limited by the knowledge you possess." Jax paused to puff his pipe back to life. "Now, let's talk about the source of our gift."

"The sun," Yolken said thoughtfully.

The story was sung every day at sunrise in every Dragon Shrine throughout Dradonia: In the beginning, Draego floated in the ether with the ribbon of time twirling all around. Draego breathed his power into the ribbon and gave birth to the sun. The sun, in turn, gave the spark of life to the world. Yolken—and every other citizen of Dradonia, young or old—knew this story by heart.

Jax continued. "Yes. Draego's Power is the gift. And the gift is called Synthesis. Originally, Draego only gave the gift to plants and to dragons." He puffed on his pipe and said, "Plants sustain life by drawing in Draego's Power—or Energy—and converting it to something useful in a process known as Synthesis. By healing Issa, you demonstrated that, like plants, you also have the ability to Synthesize Energy from the sun."

"How did I do it?" Yolken asked, fascinated.

"Do you still remember anything at all from when you healed her?"

Yolken shook his head. "Not really."

"That's a shame. You still had faint recollections when Selena and I woke you back at the tavern, but I'm not surprised the memory's gone now. Doesn't really matter, though," Jax said. He puffed on his pipe a few times then continued, "Energy from the sun streams out in all directions and is always bombarding Dradonia. We aren't able to directly see it. Instead, we experience it as light. We can't see light, per se, but we can see because it *is* light. However, the same isn't true of our enemies."

"What do you mean?"

"With the aid of Glasses, regents can see Energy," Jax said.

"Glasses?"

"You're familiar with Watchers?"

"Is *that* what those things over their eyes are?"

"Exactly. They're called Glasses, and they're called Watchers because that's what they do—they watch. Glasses enable them to see Energy, so we must exercise extreme caution when we Synthesize."

Yolken nodded.

Jax turned his pipe over and tapped it on the rock, emptying out the spent tobacco, then opened the wooden box again. He pinched new tobacco from the box and packed the pipe anew.

Yolken watched intently as, for the second time, the tobacco ignited.

After taking a few puffs, Jax continued, "When you Synthesize, you're drawing Energy into yourself, and it disrupts Energy's natural flow. Glasses enable them to see these disruptions. It's a method they developed to protect the Regency from attacks, and it's fairly accurate."

"How do they work?"

"We don't know. Nor have we ever managed to obtain a pair of Glasses to study. They keep them carefully guarded. The one time someone from the Order managed to get a hold of a pair, the Regency took extreme measures to get them back. This is an edge over the Order they don't want to lose, and they defend it at all costs. Now," Jax said, puffing on his pipe, "let's talk specifically about the process of Synthesizing.

"Synthesis, simply put, is the conversion of Energy for another purpose. As we sit here on this ledge, we can feel the heat of the sun beating down on us. That is Energy. Plants begin the process of Synthesis by first absorbing Energy into themselves. As Energy flows down onto plants, they continuously absorb it. The same, however, isn't true for you and me. What plants do naturally, we must do intentionally.

"You are only able to absorb the sun's Energy when you are in direct sunlight. But before you attempt to Synthesize you must understand what happens to Energy when you absorb it into yourself." Jax puffed on his pipe. "Inside of you is something called your Core. The confusing thing, when you begin to ponder it, is the Core is at the same time a physical part of you and *not* a physical part of you. One cannot cut open a body and find the Core. However, when you Synthesize, it's there. The Core is where you temporarily store Energy when you draw it in."

The briefest memory flashed into Yolken's mind, of looking down at Issa's twisted neck.

"Now, the best way for you to understand this is to experience it. Close your eyes," Jax instructed.

Yolken obeyed.

"Feel the heat of the sun on your face."

Yolken tilted back his head and felt it.

"Concentrate on the warmth."

Yolken pushed away the troubling truth about how his father and mother died, the guilt he felt for his aunt's death, and the thought that his brother was a captive of the Regency. In their place, he focused on the pleasant feeling on his skin and the light that made the backs of his eyelids glow red. He concentrated on the warmth.

The memory of Issa grew. Kristana was pleading with him, and he became acutely aware of the sun.

"Now, draw that warmth—that Energy—into yourself."

"How?"

"Don't think about how," Jax said. "Simply do it. Just as you cannot see Energy, I cannot tell you how to draw it in. But just because you can't see it doesn't mean it's not there. And, just because I can't tell you how to do it, doesn't mean it can't be done."

Yolken tried again. Nothing happened. He didn't feel anything other than the heat of the sun on his skin.

"Clear your mind," Jax instructed.

Yolken pushed away all the thoughts crowding his mind. He

remembered looking up at the sun rising over the buildings of Lonely Oak.

"Your Core is empty. Fill it with Energy."

Yolken tried drawing the warmth of the sun into himself once more, but again, he didn't have any success. Although he knew it was there—that it was Energy from the sun warming him—nothing happened.

"Empty your mind. Think only about Energy."

Only one recurring thought remained: Kaylan. Despite all the information he was trying to process, his thoughts of her refused to be shoved away. Whenever he tried to sort through the many revelations, his mind inevitably returned to her. She was a force acting upon him, stronger than everything else combined. He fought to keep her out of his mind because he knew it was important for him to learn to Synthesize. But the thought of Kaylan always found a way back. He wanted her. He needed her. He loved her. His eyes popped open with the strength of his ardor. Jax was watching him placidly.

Yolken knew he needed to clear his mind. He closed his eyes again and fought against the emotion swirling around inside of him. To help, he promised himself it was only temporary, and he would allow the feelings to return and consume him wholly.

Yolken pictured an image of Kaylan, hair over one shoulder and gazing at him with a smile. Then he imagined guiding her toward a door and shutting the door firmly. There. She was gone from his mind. He resettled himself and focused everything in him solely on the sun. He remembered kneeling next to Issa, drawing the heat of the sun inside until he felt full.

Energy came rushing in. He gasped at the onslaught and fell backward.

"Slowly!" Jax shouted.

Yolken lay on his back and pushed back against the sudden flow of Energy. He reduced the influx to a manageable level, but by this time, he felt full. He pushed back completely, cutting the flow off. As he sat up, the perspiration already glistening on his face started flowing freely.

Jax pointed to Yolken's sweat-soaked clothing. "What you are experiencing right now is what happens when you hold Energy in your Core and don't use it. Energy is many things, but most importantly, it is heat. When you draw Energy into yourself, you must either use it or let it go," he instructed.

"How do I do that?"

"The simplest method is to release it into the ground. But to do so, your skin must be in direct contact with it."

Yolken placed his hand on the rock beneath him and, without being able to explain how he did it, he released the Energy from his Core. He felt it begin to flow through his hand and into the ground.

"It doesn't matter what portion of your body is in contact with the ground; it could be a hand, or a foot—it doesn't matter."

As the Energy flowed out of Yolken, he felt his body temperature reducing. He let it all flow out through his arm and hand into the rock. He felt a tiny jolt of recognition. "Is *this* what happened the other day in the tavern with the plate?"

"Yes. There needs to be a catalyst for someone with the gift to fully come into their ability, but it's not uncommon to start using it unconsciously and gradually at first, which is what you had been doing. You had been showing these signs." Jax shook his head.

Yolken was puzzled. "What?"

Jax tamped his pipe out. "I should have gotten you out of there the moment Selena told me you were using your gift. Instead, I..."

"You what?"

"I was going to follow protocol. The Council would have been furious if I'd acted without authorization."

"And Issa was the catalyst," Yolken said thoughtfully.

"Yes. The catalyst is different for everyone. It's small for some and for others it takes real trauma."

"What was it for you?"

"A fever. I thought I was going to die. I was chilled and weak. I managed to get the window open in my room to let in the sun. When I felt its warmth, I clung to it. Now," he said as he put his tobacco box away, "If you hold Energy in your Core without using it, your body temperature will increase as you just experienced. The more Energy you're holding, the faster this occurs."

Yolken nodded, but he was confused. He wanted to ask about the Council, but he held back since he didn't want to miss what Jax was saying.

"The best technique to avoid this is to create a continuous stream passing through you by releasing it at the same rate you draw it in. Try it. Draw it in, fill your Core, then keep it moving. Don't let it sit idle. However, if you're on the move and can't remain in contact with the ground, you will need to find another means of dissipating Energy from yourself. Make sense?"

"I think so," Yolken said.

"Good," Jax said. "I want you to practice this, but start slowly. If you start a long race sprinting, you will tire quickly and not be able to finish."

Now that Yolken knew what to expect, he sensed the sea of Energy continuously flowing past him. He opened himself ever so slightly and allowed Energy to once again flow into his Core. Like the floodgates of a dam, he could control the flow of Energy by how much he opened the gates.

As the Energy entered him, he began letting it out. It took a little practice, but eventually, he could adjust the rate it was leaving to match the rate it entered. As he got used to the process, he started playing with the rate at which he let the Energy enter while simultaneously adjusting the rate as it left, keeping them in balance.

"Now," Jax said, "The next thing you must understand is that Synthesizing is much like any other form of physical exertion. This is why you felt drained after you healed Issa. You essentially ran ten leagues without ever before having run even one. So, for the next few days, you're going to practice running. You need to condition your Core."

CHAPTER 21

Yolken woke to the smell of warm bread. He opened his eyes and groaned as he pushed himself to a sitting position. His whole body ached. He stretched his sore muscles a little at a time.

"I bet you hurt in places you've never hurt before," Jax said from the table. He smiled at Yolken over a cup of tea.

Yolken groaned. He stood and joined Jax and Kaylan at the table. Deborah bustled around in the kitchen area.

"This should give you a little perspective on just how much Energy you used when you healed Issa," Jax said. "What we did yesterday was only a fraction of what you did in Lonely Oak and look at the result."

"I ache all over," Yolken said.

"As I told you yesterday, Synthesizing is no different than any other form of physical exertion."

Deborah placed steaming plates heaped with biscuits and battered fish, as well as a bowl filled with thick gravy, on the table. Jax placed a couple of biscuits and some fish onto Kaylan's plate first, then onto Yolken's. Yolken reached out and ladled gravy onto Kaylan's biscuits then more for himself, groaning in the process.

"You can have the morning to yourself to do as you wish,"

Jax said, "though I suggest that whatever it is you chose to do involves moving around to work out some of your soreness. After our midday meal, we'll resume your conditioning."

Deborah returned to the table with more fish and a loaf of fresh, hot bread. Jax cut the bread into pieces and slathered each slice with butter before placing a slice on each plate. Deborah pulled up her own chair and sat before the plate Jax had already prepared for her.

"How long will we continue conditioning?" Yolken said.

"However long it takes for you to not wake up feeling like you presently feel," Jax said.

"It will take some time," Deborah added. "One does not build up endurance overnight."

They ate the rest of their meal in silence, then Yolken helped Kaylan clear the table and clean the dishes. Jax and Deborah rose from the table and went outside. After they had finished in the kitchen, Yolken and Kaylan followed them outside, joining them on the porch. Puffs of smoke rose into the air from the pipe jutting from Jax's mouth.

"Let's go for a walk," Kaylan suggested. She went back into the cabin and returned with a leather flask slung over her shoulder. She held her hand out for Yolken then led the way down the steps. He hobbled stiffly to join her.

They walked together to the rock that hung out over the creek. Yolken knew Kaylan liked to sit on the edge and dangle her feet over the water. As he walked, some of the aches in his muscles lessened.

"How did it go yesterday?" Kaylan said.

"Good," Yolken said. "Feeling Energy flowing through me is unlike anything I've ever felt before."

"What does it feel like?"

Yolken thought about an accurate descriptor and finally came up with the only thing he felt could describe it. "Powerful. I felt powerful. Like I could do anything."

"I wish I could do it," Kaylan said. "Mammy said the ability is in me because of who I am, but that not everyone can use it."

"Maybe it will happen eventually. I just did it for the first time, and I'm a bit older than you."

"Do you think I'd be better off if I don't ever use it?" Kaylan said.

"I don't know. But apparently that's what my parents were hoping would happen with Javen and me. Else why would they have gone through such elaborate efforts to create a fictional life for us?" Yolken said. They sat for a while then he said, "Kaylan…"

"Yes?"

"I have a somewhat awkward question to ask."

"What?"

"We've been learning a lot these past few days that people aren't who we always thought they were. If people aren't necessarily who they say they are, then how do I know who *you* really are?"

"What do you mean?"

"I mean, my aunt turned out to not really be my aunt, but what about your mother? They admitted she was in Lonely Oak on assignment, so how do we know she is really your mother?"

Kaylan laughed.

"What's so funny? I think it's a valid question."

"You think my Mammy would lie about that?"

"I don't know. Everything else they told us was a lie. How do you know you weren't placed under her care to add credibility to her cover story?"

"She's my Mammy, Yolken," Kaylan said. "You have to remember that you aren't the only one who's had people in their lives who weren't who they said they were. I truly thought Jax was my uncle, then I learned he wasn't, just like you learned Selena wasn't your aunt. I mean, until two days ago, I thought he was my pappy's brother. Turns out that isn't so. However, what I do know is that Mammy is truly my mammy."

"But how do you know?"

"I guess at some level we all have to trust each other. I know they hid things from us, but I have to believe they had our best interests in mind. Besides, I think it's one thing to pretend to be someone's aunt and another to pretend to be someone's mother. And it's obvious just by looking at us that we're related."

"I suppose," Yolken said. "I hope you don't mind my asking, but I can't help but wonder about your father. All these years I've just assumed he died when you were young like my father did, but now I'm not so sure. Do you remember anything about him? Did your mother ever talk about him?"

"Yes, she talked about him, but there wasn't much to say, really. This was something she never hid from me. She admitted that in a moment of weakness during a spring moon festival, she gave in to the romantic advances of a traveler. They spent one night together and then he was gone. That one night was all it took for her to become with child. She told me, while you and Jor—I mean *Jax*—were out yesterday, that the Order was furious. They'd sent her to Lonely Oak after your parents married as another set of eyes and they felt having a child would interfere with her duty. She wasn't permitted to marry either, you know. They demanded she give me up into their care while she was on assignment in Lonely Oak, but she refused. She volunteered to be relieved of duty if they felt she would be distracted, but they couldn't afford to remove her. So they let her keep me."

"When you say it like that it sounds ludicrous."

"How so?"

"They *let* her keep you."

"Yeah, it's a little weird when you think about," Kaylan agreed.

Yolken stood up and said, "Let's walk some more."

He held out his hand and helped Kaylan to her feet. Holding hands, they followed the creek as it meandered through the valley.

The trail alongside the creek was shaded. As they walked along, Yolken decided to test the limitations of Synthesis Jax had talked about. He opened himself to allow Energy to flow into his Core, but nothing happened. When they were once again walking in direct sunlight, he tried again, and felt Energy flow in. *Definitely something I will have to remember,* he thought. He reached down to brush his hand on the ground and released the Energy.

They continued following the trail as it made a sharp turn to the south and began winding its way up the ridge. Yolken's muscles protested but he pushed through the pain. They passed several small waterfalls as the creek descended the mountain and stopped when they had climbed high enough to have a view of the valley below. They couldn't see the creek at the bottom of the ravine because it was enshrouded beneath the trees, but they did have a beautiful view of the ridgeline forming the northern border of the valley. From their position on the southern slope, they were shaded and cool. They were both breathing hard from the exertion of climbing the steep trail, and since they weren't in a hurry to return to the cabin, they looked for a place to rest. Yolken found a fallen log off the trail slightly below them. He pointed it out to Kaylan, and she nodded. He led her by the hand to the log, and they both sat.

The view was majestic. By Yolken's estimation, the valley floor was about a quarter of a league wide, so the sharp-rising mountain forming the northern wall of the valley looked close enough that he could reach out and almost touch it. He scanned the mountain to see if he could find the rock outcropping Jax had taken him to yesterday. The mountain rose so steeply there wasn't a lot of vegetation growing on it. It took him a while to locate where they had been, but he eventually found the rock, by first locating the zigzagging wash they had used to ascend the mountain. Once he found it, it was easy enough to follow it up until he ran into the outcropping. He tried his best to describe what he was looking at so Kaylan could see, but the entire mountain was a conglomeration of rocks and washes, and he wasn't able to express himself clearly enough.

Kaylan opened the leather flask, took a drink, then handed it to Yolken. When he took a drink, he focused on the enjoyable feeling of the refreshing water descend into his stomach. When he'd had enough, he handed the flask back to Kaylan. She set it beside her on the log, then lifted his right arm and slid under it, nestling herself against his warm body. He took the cue, wrapped his arm around her shoulder, and hugged her tightly.

There was so much to talk about, but Yolken didn't really know where to begin. Instead of speaking, he looked down at Kaylan. She had her head resting on his shoulder with her eyes closed. Instead of trying to verbalize how he was feeling or what he was thinking, he decided to simply enjoy the view and the company he most desired. He didn't know what the future held, or how many perfect quiet moments they would have.

CHAPTER 22

Javen left Hadie asleep in his bed and stepped out of his carriage. The pre-dawn light was just beginning to illuminate the camp. Even though he had failed in his first attempt at accessing the gift Dorlan assured him he possessed, he brimmed with excitement about today's lesson. Dorlan had said that it sometimes took time to Synthesize for the first time, and he believed him. With a spring in his step, he made his way across the camp, feeling confident that today would be different.

Fires burned in a dozen different pits around the camp and grease crackled on hot skillets. The smell tempted Javen to ignore his lesson and instead gorge himself on the savory sausages being prepared. But he knew food would be waiting for him when he returned to his carriage—delivered by a servant—so he ignored his hunger pangs and marched toward Dorlan's carriage.

Javen heard a loud hissing sound just as something huge appeared over his head, startling him so that he fell to the ground and covered his head with his arms. Looking up, he saw the largest bird he'd ever seen—black with large white patches on the underside of its wings—gliding across the camp at low level. It was a condor.

Peals of laughter drew Javen's attention away from the bird.

He looked around and saw people pointing at him and laughing. His racing heart didn't agree with whatever it was they found to be so funny.

Scowling, Javen ignored the laughter, stood back up, and dusted off his clothes. Then he turned to watch as the giant bird flapped its huge wings and, stretching out its spindly legs, landed on a post at the front of a boxy covered wagon parked near Dorlan's.

Javen watched a man approach the condor, which sat with its wings folded. The man untied a small black tube from around the bird's leg and walked over to Dorlan's carriage. He handed the tube to the guard standing at the foot of the steps. The guard disappeared inside the carriage while the man returned to the perched bird. Javen watched as the man pulled what looked like raw meat from behind the railing on the wagon and tossed it to the bald bird, who nimbly snatched it out of the air.

Javen resumed his walk across the camp toward Dorlan's carriage, keeping a wary eye on the giant bird. Just before he arrived at the carriage steps, the door opened. Dorlan's guard emerged and walked past him without acknowledgment. Javen watched as he went over to the man attending the bird and handed him the small black tube. While the guard returned to the carriage, Javen continued watching as the man tied the little tube back to the bird's leg.

"His Highness will see you now," the guard said to Javen.

Enthralled, Javen continued watching as the condor flapped its wings vigorously and lumbered into the air. As it beat its wings, it transitioned to a rapid increase in height over the camp, and Javen watched as it shrank in the distance, flying south.

"Sir," the guard prompted.

"Huh?" Javen replied, taking his eyes off the bird and turning to look at the guard.

"His Highness will see you now," the guard repeated.

"Sorry," Javen said, sheepish. "It's just, I've never seen a condor before."

"Kvorgan condor. The biggest and fastest birds in all of Dradonia. Messengers of the Regency."

"Kvorgan?" Javen said, thinking of the stories Kaylan's uncle used to tell them about the island when they were younger.

"Yes sir," the guard replied.

He hadn't thought about the fireside stories in years. Animals from Kvorga were *different*—dangerous to anyone foolish enough to step foot on the island; at least that's what Jorgan had always said. He wanted to go talk to the bird keeper but knew it would have to wait.

Javen climbed the steps and opened the door. When he stepped inside, Dorlan's chamber servant, Sethlan, was raising the blinds covering the windows. Not wanting to get in his way, Javen sat on the couch opposite of where Sethlan was working.

"Good morning, Master Javen," Sethlan said over his shoulder. "His Highness will be out shortly."

"Morning, Sethlan."

"Master Javen," Sethlan said, turning to look at Javen, "it isn't necessary for you to address me in return."

"I know, you've told me," Javen said. He didn't feel comfortable with the servant-to-master relationship and couldn't help but be friendly to Sethlan. He hadn't even learned the man's name until yesterday, and that was only because he couldn't stand not knowing and finally asked him. The man had hesitantly responded, but only after Javen's repeated requests— and after ensuring Dorlan wasn't in the room. "I'm just trying to be nice."

"I don't consider your lack of response to be unkind, Master Javen."

Sethlan resumed his work of raising the blinds. When the door separating the sitting room from the dining room opened, he stopped again and turned to bow as Dorlan—dressed in his night robe and holding a glass of wine—walked in.

"Care for some wine?" Dorlan asked.

"No thank you, Your Highness," Javen said, rising to his feet to greet the chancellor. He had nowhere near the tolerance for strong drink that Dorlan seemed to possess. A mild ale this early in the morning, perhaps—if he ate right away—but nothing as strong as wine. "I haven't eaten anything yet, so it'll just go right to my head."

"I trust your night was pleasant?" Dorlan asked.

"Yes, thank you, Your Highness," Javen replied. "It's been much more comfortable having a little privacy."

Dorlan nodded. He took a sip of wine and said, "I always enjoy these early mornings."

"Not me," Javen said. He much preferred to stay up late. He had developed the habit of going to bed as the sky began to grow light, but he usually regretted it, especially when he had to get Kena out.

Dorlan sat on the couch opposite the open windows.

Javen joined him and directed his attention out the windows. The arrival of the sun was imminent, heralded by the pink clouds reflecting the sun's light. He kept thinking about the condor, so he decided to ask Dorlan about it. "Your Highness, may I ask a question?"

"Go ahead," Dorlan said.

"I've always known the emperor's messenger birds were condors, but I never knew they were *Kvorgan* condors."

"Yes. And what is your question?"

"How did you manage to tame an animal from Kvorga?"

"Why do you ask?"

"It's just… I thought the island was enchanted. I mean, everybody's heard the stories."

"And what stories have you heard?"

"That there's something strange about the island; that it's uninhabited by people and that those living nearby refuse to set foot there; that terrifying creatures live there. My friend's uncle used to scare us as children with tales about it."

"Although it's true the island is mysterious, you shouldn't believe every tale you hear," Dorlan said. "They're nothing more than glorified rumors."

Javen snorted slightly as a small smile grew on his face.

"What?"

"I was just thinking about something someone back in Lonely Oak used to say."

"Enlighten me."

"'All news starts out as rumors, but not all rumors turn out to be news,' Norin would always say. I never thought about tales that way before."

"This Norin sounds like a smart man," Dorlan said.

"Can I ask you something else?"

"Of course," Dorlan said. He took a drink of his wine.

Javen opened his mouth, but suddenly felt afraid to ask his question. He didn't know if he really wanted to know the answer.

"What is it?"

"Drenan said something back at the tavern that has been bothering me. Something about my father."

"And what was that?"

"My aunt was killed because she was a rebel, but Drenan said my father was a rebel, too."

"Ah," Dorlan said, taking a sip of his wine. "I was wondering when that would come up."

"Was he?" Javen asked.

"Yes."

"And the fire? Did that have something to do with it?" Drenan had seemed to know about it, and he couldn't think of any other reason why the Regent of Hantlo would know about a simple tavern fire in the Croff province.

Dorlan frowned thoughtfully. His voice was pained. "Your father was powerful and inflicted much harm on the Regency. The emperor made every effort he could to convince your father to pledge his loyalty to him, but he refused. In the end, the emperor did what he had to do."

Javen looked down at his hands. Finding out his aunt was a rebel had been devastating. It had left him wondering whether anything she'd ever told them was true. And now… his father? He felt utterly crushed. Everything his aunt had told him about his father was a lie. And he was the son of a rebel. "Then why are you treating me this way?" he asked.

"Because it is what the emperor wishes. Now, let us not distract ourselves anymore. Instead, let us direct our attention to waking your gift."

Then, as if responding to Dorlan's cue, the tip of the sun crested the flat and treeless horizon. Javen put thoughts of his rebel father and the giant bird out of his mind and focused on the sun inching its way higher into the sky.

CHAPTER 23

Javen stepped out of Dorlan's carriage full of frustration. For the second day in a row, he'd sat beside the chancellor on the couch, watching the sun rise above the horizon. He'd listened to the chancellor describe their gift and how to access it, but again he had failed. The lesson had lasted until messengers demanding the chancellor's attention had interrupted them. When Dorlan ushered Javen out of the carriage, a line of people seeking an audience with Dorlan had formed outside.

Javen trudged across the circle of carriages and wagons with his head down, paying no attention to the busy workers breaking down the camp and preparing the caravan for the day's travel. Sullenly, he made his way back to the carriage he now shared with Hadie.

He approached the new carriage, still in disbelief that Dorlan had given it to him. He should be feeling elated, but he couldn't shake the frustration growing within him. It was true that, growing up, he'd had the tendency to be lazy, especially when it came to his responsibilities at the tavern, but it wasn't because he couldn't do the job; it was because he didn't really *want* to. This was different. When Dorlan offered to teach him to Synthesize, it had made him think he might have a future with the Regency. Now, having failed for the second time, he wondered what would happen if he proved to be unable to use his gift. What use would Dorlan have for him if he couldn't Synthesize? He had the tendency to be lazy, he knew, but he absolutely hated failing.

When Javen got back to his carriage—modest in comparison to Dorlan's—he climbed the steps and slammed the door behind him. He knew he was just beginning his lessons, but he couldn't understand how his brother could accidentally Synthesize without even trying, yet he himself was unable to do it even with the guidance of a chancellor—one of the strongest in the gift. Typical. It had been this way his whole life—Yolken effortlessly bested him at everything, and it annoyed him. Yolken was the better climber and could always get the highest in the oak tree; he always understood their lessons with their aunt better. And when they became adults, it was Yolken who had gained control of the tavern passed down to them from their parents, and he had somehow become his brother's errand boy instead of his partner. He thought about Issa—she had looked up to him and mentioned almost every day her desire to marry him, yet it was Yolken who had saved her life. The only thing he was better at than his brother was flirting with girls but seeing Yolken sitting under the oak with Kaylan had made him realize Yolken even bested him there.

"How'd it go?" Hadie said, greeting him with a smile as he stepped up into the carriage.

"Not very well." He sat heavily on the couch opposite Hadie.

Hadie set down the book she was reading and joined Javen. She slid her arms around him in a welcoming hug.

He wrapped his arm around her neck and returned the embrace. He couldn't help but think about Yolken besting him with Kaylan. He was enjoying his time with Hadie, and she was incredibly beautiful, but he didn't feel the same way about her as he did about Kaylan. He broke off the hug, went into the bedroom, and flopped himself onto the bed. With frustration brimming inside, both with himself and with his brother, he stared at the ceiling.

Hadie followed Javen into the room and lay down beside him. She snuggled up to his side and wiggled in under his arm, resting her head on his shoulder. She pulled her knee up over his legs then she slid her hand up under his shirt and lightly stroked his firm stomach and chest with the tips of her fingers.

Pushing his training and thoughts of his brother with Kaylan out of his mind, Javen redirected his attention to the warmth of Hadie snuggled against him. He closed his eyes and enjoyed the tingling of her fingers as they lightly stroked his skin. As he relaxed, his thoughts wandered aimlessly until the frustration he felt once again pushed its way back. "Dorlan says I simply need to accept the gift within me. That with time and practice it will eventually come to me naturally," he said, verbalizing his thoughts in an effort to release the building tension.

"It'll happen," Hadie said. Her fingers made their way lower.

"I suppose. But all I've done is sit and stare at the sun as it rises. I can't feel the Energy Dorlan says is there, let alone allow it to flow into me."

"He hasn't been able to help?"

"He says there isn't anything he can do to help me use it. Apparently, it has to be something I do on my own. Once I finally do draw Energy in, he says he can teach me how to use it, but until then, I'm on my own. He keeps saying that using Synthesis is as simple and natural as breathing, but I'm beginning to feel that isn't necessarily true."

"If there isn't anything he can do, then why aren't you allowed to practice on your own? All we do is sit around all day. Seems to me you're missing a lot of opportunities to practice."

"Because it's important for him to be present when it finally happens," Javen said.

She twirled her finger lightly around his navel. "Maybe all you need is a little help clearing your mind."

"Like what?"

"I can't *tell* you so much as show you," Hadie said with a sly look on her face. She climbed on top of Javen and pulled his shirt over his head, then moved on to his pants.

When Hadie lifted her shirt over her head, Javen forgot about everything else.

* * *

Javen lay on the sweaty sheets with Hadie once again curled up beside him, her head on his chest. It didn't take long for him to start thinking about his brother again. He didn't hate Yolken—their situation wasn't really Yolken's fault. Except for Kaylan. *He knew how I felt about her and then chose to ignore my feelings.* He shook his head, allowing the resentment he felt toward his brother to grow.

"What?" Hadie said, turning her head to look up at him.

"Nothing," Javen lied.

"No. I can tell you're upset again."

Javen didn't really want to discuss what had happened that night with Hadie, so he shifted to the other thing bugging him. "Truth is, I'm beginning to worry about what might happen if I'm unable to use my gift. Dorlan's told me a lot about who I am, who my father was, and I'm afraid that if I'm unable to please him—"

"Javen, I realize we haven't known each other for very long, but I hope you don't mind my saying that ever since I was taken from the Oak, I've known we were in trouble. And just because they aren't treating us like prisoners anymore, that doesn't mean we aren't. Try to remember that, all right? The fancy room at the Blue Mountain, the bag of drakes, this carriage—they're all a façade. You have to believe me when I say you're getting yourself mixed up with the wrong people."

"They're the Blessed of the Dragon, Hadie!" Javen said, sitting up. "How can I possibly be getting mixed up with the wrong people?"

Hadie sat up beside Javen and said, "What are you worried

about, then?"

"I'm worried because I'm still the son of a traitor. If I'm unable to help them, then they'll have no use for me. And, as silly as this might sound, I think I might've finally found a way to make something of myself—to be successful."

"I get that, Javen. They're doing an excellent job at making you feel important right now by throwing all this wonderful stuff at you and encouraging you. But I don't think any of it's real. You've lived your entire life practically free of the influence of the Regency, but I haven't. I grew up in Hantlo, under their shadow, attending their galas with my parents. Let me tell you: Dorlan isn't who you think he is! And as bad as Dorlan is, Drenan is ten times worse. Part of the reason I left Hantlo in the first place is that, over time, I realized who and what the Regency really was. Despite what you may think or what they might be telling you, the Regency is truly dangerous."

CHAPTER 24

Yolken followed Jax as they climbed back up to the rock outcropping for a second training session. His muscles ached with every step he took. A groan escaped from his mouth when he looked up and saw how much farther they still had to climb. When they finally arrived, he fell onto the rock in exhaustion. "Are we… going to… come here… every day?" he asked between heavy breaths.

"Yes," Jax said. "At least, *you* will be for the next several days."

"Me?"

"You have many days of conditioning ahead of you before I can actually start teaching you how to Synthesize. Our time will be wasted if you collapse in exhaustion every time you use your gift. So, starting tomorrow, you will make this ascent twice a day."

"Twice a day!" Yolken exclaimed.

"After you break your fast in the morning, you will climb up here, condition yourself, and then return to the cabin for your mid-day meal. Then you will again ascend the mountain and remain here until the sun sets."

"Can't I just bring food with me and not have to do this climb twice?" Yolken said.

"You could, but it's evident you need the physical exercise as well. Your days of standing behind a bar all day are gone."

For the first time, Yolken noticed that Jax wasn't winded like he was and realized there must be some truth to what Jax said. It was true that he didn't get out to exercise much anymore. Except for the rare occasion he had been able to convince Javen to tend bar, he'd been confined to the tavern from the time he woke in the morning until he closed for the night. On an even rarer occasion, he was able to escape to the mountains with Javen, but that hadn't occurred enough for him to maintain any semblance of physical fitness. He wasn't a sloth, by any means, but hiking up and down a mountain twice a day definitely required a higher level of fitness than what he was accustomed to. He accepted the fate that was his foreseeable future, and when his breathing returned to normal, he decided to ask Jax about something he'd been afraid to mention.

"So I'm never going back, am I?"

"Not likely. That life is a thing of the past now. It was foolish to raise you in Lonely Oak, if you ask me, but to return there now would be even more so."

"So what am I supposed to do after we rescue Javen?"

Jax took his pipe and tobacco box out and prepared a smoke. "That will be for you to decide when the time comes," he said after the tobacco was lit.

Yolken stared pensively down at the trees while Jax smoked, then said, "Kaylan tells me she and Deborah are leaving for Croff soon."

Jax nodded, his pipe in his mouth.

"When?"

"In six days or so," Jax said through clenched teeth.

"Can't we all go together?"

"It'd be dangerous for you to practice while we traveled. Remember what I told you about one of the dangers of Synthesizing? As you condition yourself, the rate you absorb Energy will increase, and so will the capacity of your Core, dramatically increasing the chances someone will see you. Synthesizing must always be done with discretion—you never know where there might be a Watcher. Remember, streams of Energy bend in your direction when you draw it in, and the more you draw in, the farther away that disruption can be detected. I intend to make you as strong as possible, and in doing so, you will be a beacon to anyone looking.

"Now, let's begin. Just like yesterday, I want you to draw Energy in until you feel like your Core is full, and then let it drain out at the same rate."

Feeling the warmth of the sun on his face, Yolken opened himself to the flood of Energy and began absorbing it, letting it fill him. He closed his eyes and reveled in the feeling of power now within him. He didn't know what to do with it—Jax had yet to say anything about it—but he could feel it within him nonetheless. As he felt his Core becoming full, he felt the flow rate of Energy begin to slow down. Sweat began to pour from his skin. He placed his hand on the rock on which he sat and let the Energy flow from his Core, down his arm, and through his hand into the ground. As Energy flowed out of him, the Energy flowing into his Core began once again.

"Remember to practice adjusting the flow of Energy you draw in and then match it with the flow you release," Jax said. "Get used to the process. As you begin to feel more comfortable, play around with it a little. Decrease the amount you're drawing in in relation to the amount you're letting out and feel your Core begin to drain. Then when your Core is empty, reverse the process and bring in more than you let out. Don't try stretching your Core just yet. Let's give it a few days of gentle conditioning before we see what you can really do."

"Gentle conditioning?" Yolken said. "This morning I felt like I'd been dragged behind a horse all day!"

"Which is nothing compared to the result after you healed Issa."

Thinking about what Jax said, Yolken asked, "What do you mean by 'seeing what I can really do'?"

"The more you Synthesize, the stronger you'll grow. Once you're a little more conditioned, we'll talk about increasing your strength. Now, I'm going back down to the cabin."

"You're leaving me up here?" Yolken exclaimed, feeling the floodgate slam closed.

"You don't need me for this part." Jax tamped out his pipe, slipped it and his tobacco box back into his coat, then stood up. "Come down just before the sun sets behind the mountains to ensure you're back to the cabin before it gets dark."

Yolken watched as Jax stepped off the rock outcropping and down onto the trail. Yolken called after him, "Can I ask you a question before you leave?"

"Sure," Jax said, turning back to look up at Yolken.

"It's not about Synthesis."

"Oh?"

"You said the Order has rules about marriage. What rules?"

"Mainly, they do not allow members to marry someone from the outside."

"Why wouldn't they allow that?"

"Becoming intimately involved with someone outside of the Order creates all sorts of secrecy problems. Not to mention it presents ample opportunities for the Regency to exploit."

Yolken was bewildered. "Exploit? Like what?"

"Well, for instance, if the Regency is after a particular rebel, how much simpler would it be if they could coerce them by apprehending a helpless loved one?"

"Makes sense, I guess," Yolken said. "But I thought you said my mother wasn't a member. Why did the Order let my father marry her?"

Jax chuckled. "Your father had a… proclivity to not follow the rules. But unlike myself, or anyone else for that matter, he could get away with it."

"Why?"

"Because he had leverage, and he knew it. The Council needed him, and he threatened to leave the Order if they wouldn't agree to his demand. They couldn't afford to let that happen, so they allowed it.

"Your father dedicated many years of service to the Order, but then he met your mother and fell in love. He went against the Order's rules and then, much to their chagrin, he quit the Order altogether.

"Eventually the Council was forced to practically beg him for help. Before he agreed to work again, he made them promise that if anything ever happened to him, they would look after and protect his wife and children. He was specific about what that meant, and, in the end, the Order had to commit valuable resources to look after you and your brother. Now, don't get me wrong—most of the members of the Order loved your father and understood his desire to live a different life. It was the Council who had an issue with his decision and demands."

"What exactly is the Council?" Yolken said.

Jax shifted his footing. "They are the leaders of the Order. I know I promised you that the Order would do everything it can to rescue your brother, but the truth is if we want help from the Order, we must convince the Council. That's why Deborah and Kaylan are leaving; Deborah is going ahead to lay some groundwork for our formal request to get help finding Javen."

"What reasons would they have for not wanting to help?" Yolken asked, astonished.

"It's complicated, Yolken. Let's not trouble ourselves with the inner workings of the Order, but rather, for the time being, let's focus on learning to use your newfound gift."

"When *are* you going to teach me how to use it?"

"I already am," Jax said, turning once again to go. "Now, get back at it and come down just before sunset."

Jax descended the steep path and left Yolken sitting alone on the rock high above the valley floor. Yolken watched him go then turned his attention back to the sun.

CHAPTER 25

Yolken lay on the familiar rock outcropping with his eyes closed and his shirt off, absorbing the heat of the sun. He clasped his hands behind his head, resting them on his folded shirt. A sheen of sweat covered his face, arms, and chest as his Core stretched against the Energy that would burn him up if he let it. The amount of Energy he could safely contain now dwarfed what he had been able to hold in his Core two weeks ago when he first began his conditioning.

"Today, I want you to begin stretching your Core," Jax had said several days ago.

"How do I do that?"

"The process is similar to stretching a muscle. Have you felt the resistance when your Core becomes full?"

"Yes."

"Just as if you were trying to increase the flexibility of your legs, say, by slowly, diligently, pushing against the resistance you feel, you will gradually stretch your Core and increase its capacity."

"How much can I stretch it?" Yolken said.

"In the same way that there are limits to the flexibility of your legs, there are limits to how much you may stretch your Core. Everybody's limits are different."

"How will I know when I've reached mine?"

"It will take some time for you to achieve that, longer than I intend on staying hidden here in the Mindons, but as you continue to condition yourself, the time will come when you'll know you've reached it."

Before that conversation, Yolken's daily routine had been the same: Wake, break his fast, hike up the mountain, condition, hike down for a mid-day meal, and repeat the process. Now, a half month after he had first begun to use his gift, he was much more fit—both his Core and his body. The physical effort required by the steep incline of the mountainside, and the effort required to continuously allow Energy to flow through him, no longer put the strain on him it once had. Possessing a firm grip on the process of drawing Energy in and releasing it into the ground, his mind began to drift to other concerns as he sat for hours, building his endurance and stretching his Core.

Although he thought a lot about his many unanswered questions about his aunt, the Order, where Javen might be, and the mysteries of dragons, he usually gravitated back to the same persistent, irresistible thought—Kaylan. She'd been gone for seven days now. He often thought about the time they'd spent together walking alone through the woods, especially their last afternoon together.

"How did you manage to convince Jax to give you the afternoon off from your training?" Kaylan had asked.

"It was his idea, actually," Yolken said. "He knew you'd be leaving in the morning, so he thought it would be nice for us to have a little time together."

"That was thoughtful of him. He's really been pushing you hard."

"He says we don't have the time to go about training leisurely, so he's pushing me. He wants to leave these mountains as quickly as possible."

"Yolken…" Kaylan said, her feet dangling over the ledge of

their rock, occasionally letting them dip into the frigid water.

"Yeah?"

"I really wish I didn't have to go tomorrow."

"Me either."

"Every bit of me wants to stay here with you."

"I wish you could, but Jax said you need to go speak to the Council about what's happened."

"You mean *Mammy* has to go speak to the Council," Kaylan said. "I don't have anything to do with it, which is why I think I should just stay here. I tried explaining that to her, but she said I'm a distraction." Her eyebrows betrayed her distaste for the word.

"Distraction?" Yolken said. "What kind of distraction?"

Kaylan scooted closer to Yolken and leaned over to kiss him. He wrapped his arms around her and lowered her until she was lying on the rock, cradling her head in his arm, and returned her kiss.

"I guess I can see the logic in that," Yolken said, breaking off the kiss. "You might be a *bit* of a distraction."

"I'm going to miss you," Kaylan said, a hitch in her voice. She looked up at him. Her eyes glistened. When a tear formed and slid toward her ear, Yolken wiped it away with the back of a finger.

"I'm going to miss you, too," he said. He leaned down and kissed her again, then kissed each of her closed eyes and hugged her tightly.

"How long will you be up here?" Her voice was muffled from their embrace.

He leaned back and took a deep breath. "Jax says another month at most."

"It's such a long time."

"I agree. But let's enjoy the afternoon and not think about tomorrow."

The next morning Yolken stepped out onto the porch behind Deborah and Jax, holding Kaylan's hand. With their fasts broken on Deborah's delicious cooking and travel bags packed, it was time for them to leave. Deborah and Jax continued down the steps, but Yolken held back, wishing for one last moment alone with Kaylan.

As Jax and Deborah stepped off the porch, Yolken overheard Jax tell her, "Do whatever's necessary to convince them that, despite what's happened, we must continue as planned."

"I will," Deborah said. "But it'll ultimately be up to Yolken."

Deborah and Jax walked around the side of the cabin, and Yolken turned and pulled Kaylan close. He hugged her tight, wishing he never had to let her go.

Kaylan buried her head against Yolken's chest and began sobbing.

Yolken placed his nose in her hair and breathed her in. Tears welled in his eyes. "Everything is wrong," he said. "I wish… I wish everything was the way it was before: that none of this had happened, that my aunt…"

Yolken felt Kaylan squeeze her arms tighter around him. "Yolken," she said, pulling back just enough to look up at him.

Yolken looked down into her beautiful green eyes.

Kaylan hesitated, looking up at him, and said, "I—"

"Love you," Yolken finished for her.

"I know this… us… is new, but—"

"Not new for me; I've loved you for as long as I can remember," Yolken admitted with a smile.

"Me too," Kaylan said, returning his smile. Then her face grew serious. "I just want to… I want to go home. With you."

Yolken pulled her close, and she started sobbing again. Both of them knew that returning to Lonely Oak was likely not possible.

"Make it go away," she said into his chest.

Yolken held Kaylan until Jax reappeared around the side of the cabin. Yolken looked over at him, knowing goodbyes couldn't last forever. He forced himself to let Kaylan go—but she didn't let go of him. He reached around his back, took hold of Kaylan's hands, and pulled them free. Holding both her hands up by his chest, he looked down into her eyes and said, "I love you, Kaylan Browning. Whatever the future holds, this will always be true."

She drew a deep, shuddering breath and composed herself. "I love you, too, Yolken Thornhill." She stood up on her toes and kissed him.

Yolken led Kaylan by the hand down the steps to Jax, who waited patiently, eyes averted discreetly.

"Will you be going back through Lonely Oak on your way to Croff?" Yolken asked.

"No, we'll follow the creek down toward the Mindon River, where we'll head north out of the mountains," Deborah said. Then turning to Jax, she urged, "Don't tarry here longer than absolutely necessary. We must move forward quickly."

"We won't be far behind," Jax said, confident.

"Come, Kaylan, we'd best be on our way," Deborah said.

Kaylan turned and gave Yolken another hug, squeezing him tight, then broke their embrace.

Yolken watched as she and Deborah started walking down the middle of the creek. When they were out of sight, he turned to find that Jax was already on his way back toward the cabin. He caught up to him and said, "Do you think it's safe for them? Traveling on their own?"

"Deborah is a capable Synthesizer," Jax said gruffly.

Satisfied, Yolken asked, "What were you saying to her?"

"What do you mean?"

"Something about continuing as planned."

"Deborah must lay the groundwork necessary to convince the Council to rescue your brother."

Yolken felt a niggling worry. "So there's a chance they won't help?"

"We've discussed this, Yolken. There is a chance, yes. Which is why she's going ahead to Croff," Jax said.

"And what do I have to do with it?"

Jax looked at him sharply. "What do you mean?"

"She said it'll ultimately be up to me."

"The Council can be stubborn, Yolken. If Deborah is unable to convince them, then you and I will have to try our hand."

"How? If Deborah can't sway them, then what more can we contribute?"

"Well," Jax said, walking up the steps leading to the cabin porch, "to be perfectly blunt… I'll show them you."

Yolken stopped, one foot on the ground and the other on the first step, looking up at Jax.

"You have proven to truly be your father's son. The Council will find that simple fact to be *most* valuable. A fact that might be enough to convince them."

CHAPTER 26

Each day that passed became another day in which Javen failed to Synthesize. He became accustomed to the disappointment awaiting him each time he stepped out of Dorlan's carriage. Dorlan showed patience with his repeated failures, so each day he woke with a renewed sense of confidence and hope that this would be the day. *"If you don't believe in yourself, then you'll continue to fail,"* Dorlan often said.

As the chancellor's caravan continued to work its way south, the countryside gradually changed. The Mindon Mountains guarding the eastern horizon gave way to level ground, the grassy plains gave way to dense forests, and the dry heat dominating the days gave way to wet air, making Javen's clothes cling uncomfortably to his body. The farther south they traveled, the more frequently he saw the giant messenger birds flying to and from the caravan. One thing, however—the thing Javen wanted most to change—remained the same; he found himself day after day stepping down out of Dorlan's carriage having failed to Synthesize.

The day was once again new. Javen made his usual walk through the encampment way toward Dorlan's carriage for his daily lesson. He waved as he heard people wish him a happy morning. After their stay in Matis, the camp's attitude toward

Javen and Hadie had thawed. The camp no longer shunned them at night; they were welcome around any fire. This was a relief. It decreased the monotony of the journey. They enjoyed the time they had together during the days: Javen read his book on the history of the Southern Realm—he learned that the Regent of Hantlo wasn't originally Drenan, but Sheal, the emperor's brother, who was now the Chancellor of the Western Realm— and Hadie read her *Lovers* books. They talked, and often engaged in vigorous beddings. When the caravan stopped for the night, they emerged from their seclusion and socialized.

"Mornin', Master Javen," said a voice off to Javen's left.

He looked and waved to the red-haired, freckled teamster who tended Dorlan's horse teams. "Good morning, Lyoll," he said.

The teamsters proved friendly to Javen, especially Ganip, a gangly boy with wild hair who had a fondness for flowers. Javen learned a lot about the caravan by talking with the teamsters over a campfire and drink, and it turned out Hadie wasn't the only one who thought Drenan creepy.

Just as Javen passed Lyoll by, he caught a glimpse of a girl he thought he recognized. She rushed by him in the opposite direction. He turned to get a better look. In disbelief, he watched as the petite blonde from Lonely Oak moved farther away. "Astora!" he shouted.

The girl didn't respond and continued walking away with a hurried step.

"Astora!" Javen shouted again. Either she didn't hear him, or she was ignoring him. He hesitated for a moment, then jogged after her. Catching up to her, he placed his hand on her shoulder, and said, "Astora?"

She turned toward him, head down, looking at her feet.

Javen lifted her face with a nudge under her chin to get a better look at her familiar face. They'd spent the evening together the night before Dorlan arrived in Lonely Oak. Her blue eyes were puffy and red; tears streamed down her freckled cheeks. "What's the matter?" he asked with concern.

"Nothing," Astora said quickly, sniffing. She reached up to wipe her eyes with the heels of her hands.

"What in Draego's Fire are you doing here?" He was surprised to see someone else from Lonely Oak in Dorlan's caravan.

"He cast me off!" Astora sobbed. "Told me to go away, that he was done with me!"

"Cast you off?" Javen asked, confused. "Who cast you off?"

"I don't want to talk about it," Astora said. She shrugged Javen's hand from her shoulder and ran off.

Javen looked at Astora as she fled. He felt conflicted, wanting to chase after her, but at the same time fearful about being late for his lesson. He took a few hesitant steps in the direction she had run but then turned back toward Dorlan's carriage.

As he crossed the remainder of the camp, his mind jumped between trying to figure out what Astora could possibly be doing in the camp and fearing what would happen if Hadie ran into her.

He glanced at the box-shaped wagon parked next to Dorlan's carriage but didn't go over there today. Kole, the bird-keeper, stood at the front of the wagon. Javen found the mysterious birds intriguing. Each morning he stopped and talked to the bird-keeper, who gave him a little piece of raw meat to feed to the enormous bald-headed birds while he asked his questions.

"Hey, Javen!" Kole shouted. He held his arms out to his sides. "No questions today?"

Javen's mind was on Astora and he didn't feel like talking to Kole. He shook his head and waved.

He walked past the guard at the door—wearing his standard gray, scaled armor—and climbed into the carriage. Unfamiliar people sat on the couch opposite Dorlan, who was looking down at a piece of parchment. Javen looked at the strangers, wondering what they were doing here. Previously, every training session had involved just him and the chancellor.

"Yes, Your Highness," one of the individuals sitting on the couch said, "both Yarin and Wrenda."

"Why am I just learning of this now?" Dorlan said testily, without looking up from the parchment.

"There were no condors, Your Highness."

"And Venan?"

"As of when I left Hantlo, Your Highness, there had yet to be word from Venan."

"Draego's Fire. The Dragon cursed cyclones aren't even in season yet." Dorlan finally looked up. His brow furrowed when he saw Javen. "I don't have time today, Javen. See Drenan tomorrow. He'll supervise your training until we reach Hantlo."

Javen's stomach suddenly felt as though he had drunk one too many mugs of ale. Drenan? He stared at Dorlan, whose relaxed attitude, he noticed, was gone. He wore his regal orange-trimmed attire instead of his silken bed robes.

The sudden change worried him.

Hadie had warned him about the Regency from the day they'd left Lonely Oak—which he had largely ignored because Dorlan consistently treated him with patience and respect—but what his new camp friends said about Drenan confirmed her warnings. None of them knew the stories he had grown up hearing about the scarred man, but if half of what they told him were true, then the stories couldn't have been entirely made up only to scare children.

He swallowed a lump of fear and said, "Drenan, Your Highness?"

"Yes," Dorlan said. "As you can see, I'm very busy."

Javen turned to leave, dejected. Before he stepped out of Dorlan's carriage he turned back. "Your Highness?"

Dorlan looked back up from the parchment he was reading.

"Hmm?"

"Can I ask you something?"

"Yes, yes—what is it?"

"I just saw a girl from Lonely Oak, and was wondering—"

Dorlan turned his attention back to his parchments. "Astora. Yes. She was keeping me company."

Javen stared at Dorlan.

He glanced up. "Was there something else?"

Javen shook his head.

"Then report to Drenan's carriage on the morrow. Same time."

"Yes, Your Highness," Javen said.

He left Dorlan's carriage with plenty of time to look for Astora before the caravan got under way. He didn't know what she was doing with Dorlan—he had an idea but couldn't believe it; even though they'd bedded each other, she wasn't a whore—but he intended to find her and make sure she was all right.

CHAPTER 27

D on't look so comfortable," Jax said.

Yolken's mind jerked back to the present at the sound of Jax's voice. He opened his eyes, shielded from the sun by his right arm, and saw Jax standing over him with the Harachin sword hanging at his hip. Jax opened a leather flask of water and handed it to him. Yolken sat up and accepted it. After drinking deeply of the refreshing creek water, he gave it back and said, "Sorry, I've developed a bit of a rhythm, and sometimes my mind wanders. Energy in Energy out became monotonous after a while."

"Come, let's take a break and talk," Jax said.

Yolken stood up, grabbing the shirt he had used as a cushion for his head, and followed as Jax led him around the large boulder sitting on the flat outcropping. Jax stopped on the lee side of the boulder, sheltered from the sun, and removed his coat. As he pulled the coat from his shoulders and shrugged his arms out of the sleeves, Yolken saw that Jax also had a black dagger tucked underneath the belt on his back. Jax lay the coat on the ground next to the boulder, pulled the dagger from under the belt, and set it down on the coat. Next, he unbuckled the belt, wrapped the belt around the sword, and sat, resting his back against the boulder.

"Sit," Jax said, then took a drink from the flask. When Yolken sat opposite him, he held the sword out to Yolken and said, "Let's talk about dragons."

Yolken took the sword by the sheath. He laid it across his lap and gripped the hilt with his right hand. The moment his hand contacted the black bone, visible through the woven steel threads of the hilt, a flood of Energy beckoned to him. "It's full of Energy!" he exclaimed.

"It is," Jax said. "Dragons had the unique ability to store Energy in their bones."

Yolken looked confused. "How come I didn't feel it the other day in the cabin?"

"Because at the time you couldn't remember Synthesizing. Just as you've lived your entire life without feeling the presence of the Energy from the sun, you wouldn't have been aware of the Energy in the sword. But now that you *are* aware, you feel its presence. And as a Synthesizer, these are more valuable to you than a trunk full of gold drakes. Dragon bones provide a means to Synthesize when you don't have access to the sun."

"Because they store Energy," Yolken said, thinking aloud.

"Exactly. As you now know, you can't store Energy in your Core to use at your convenience. Which means you can't Synthesize at night or when you aren't in direct view of the sun."

"How does Energy get into the bones?" Yolken said.

"You put it there," Jax said, handing Yolken the dagger.

Taking it from him, Yolken didn't feel any Energy in it. "It's empty."

"You drained it the night we fled from Lonely Oak."

"I did? How?"

"You used it, as well as a significant amount from the sword, to give your body the strength to come here," Jax said. He reached into his coat and removed his wooden pipe and tobacco box. After stuffing the pipe, he put it in his mouth and grabbed the frayed cuff of his coat. Smoke began to rise from his pipe, even though they were sitting in the shade.

Yolken looked at Jax, amazed, "That's why you always wear that thing."

Jax puffed on his pipe quietly, a grin growing on his face. "I wove bones in parts of it for emergencies. The bones are small, so it doesn't store a lot of Energy, but it's gotten me out of several jams."

"I always thought it was because you were a little crazy," Yolken said. Despite the simplicity of what Jax had just done, he was still amazed. He was now accustomed to the presence of Energy, but he had yet to *do* anything with it. Each time Jax lit his pipe, Yolken wondered how he did it. Moving past the amazement, he asked, "What did I do with the Energy?"

Jax puffed on the pipe enough to ensure it wouldn't go out before he removed it from his mouth. He said, "When Selena and I found you in your bed that day, you were extremely fatigued from healing Issa. So much so that you were unable to rise from your bed. Had we not woken you, you would have slept for several days. However, the Regency was on the hunt. We needed to get you out of there, and I couldn't carry you all the way up into the Mindons. As I've said, if you permit Energy to sit idly in your Core it will heat your body. Too much will cause you to burn up. Energy is heat, and heat is Energy. Typically, you get the Energy your body needs through the food you eat, but those of us with the gift can give it to our body directly, in small doses.

"Were it not for the heat in our bodies, we would be no more active than the rocks upon which we walk. When you have synthesized Energy inside you, your body seeks to use it. By drawing from the dagger and sword, you were able to artificially boost the Energy level of your body, which temporarily replenished what you spent healing Issa. With their aid, you were able to remain awake and mobile. With practice, you can direct the Energy to the specific part of your body you wish to be strengthened: your legs, for instance, to run faster, or your arms, to lift something you normally wouldn't be able to budge. However, using Energy in this manner has its consequences. Physical exertion, whether under your own capacities or aided by Energy, tires your body and will demand its requisite period of recuperation. If you use a large amount of Energy in this fashion, expect your body to tire accordingly."

Yolken took a minute to let Jax's words sink in. He drank from the flask again. "So what happened to them?"

"Dragons? As I previously said, they were slaughtered into extinction during Drakonias' war."

"Why?"

"Because, unlike us, they were designed to Synthesize, much like plants. When we Synthesize, we have many limitations. However, the same was not true with dragons. They weren't given the gift as an afterthought, like us; it was a part of them from the beginning. And once we learned what they could do, we exploited them."

Yolken frowned. "How so?"

"Well, for one, their bones can somehow store Energy," Jax said, pointing at the sword and dagger. "Drakonias fought to overthrow his father for fifteen years, but neither side was able to gain the upper hand. Until, that is, Drakonias's son Donlin made a discovery which would change the direction and momentum of the war." Jax took a puff on his pipe. "He discovered that a dragon's scales protected them from attacks of Energy."

"Is *that* what their armor's made from?" Yolken asked.

"Yes. So far as is known, dragons never took part in the affairs of humans. Through observation—always from a distance—we knew they were intelligent beings. Although humans had developed various levels of relationship with other creatures, there is no record of dragons ever interacting with us. Despite the efforts of those who came before us, it would seem they went out of their way to avoid contact. This remained true even during Drakonias' war. As in all past human wars, the dragons kept their distance while we relentlessly killed each other.

"Donlin died trying to capture the first dragon, but it didn't take long for Drakonias to figure out how to do it successfully. After that, they were systematically butchered for their scales and bones. As their scales were turned into armor and their bones into weapons, the war turned dramatically in Drakonias's favor. Facing defeat, Draeko was forced to start killing dragons himself."

"Were the dragons actually the color of the armor they wear?" Yolken said.

"Yes. The color is the natural color of the scales," Jax said. "Gray and brown were by far the most common colors for dragons, which is why you see so many of the soldiers wearing gray. The other colors were rarer, and if you're familiar with the colors and the hierarchy of the Regency, you know the color of their armor identifies their rank."

Fascinated, Yolken asked, "How did they find out that dragon bones stored Energy?"

"After they harvested the dragon carcasses, the remains were burned on giant pyres. But only the flesh burned away—the bones didn't. They might as well have been made of granite for all the effect fire had on them. Naturally, Drakonias was curious, and it didn't take long for them to figure it out. But unlike our Cores, their bones could store Energy indefinitely. Instantly recognizing the advantage of this, they cut the bones into manageable shapes and sizes and introduced an entirely new element to the war—Machines."

"What's a Machine?" Yolken said, not liking the tone Jax had used for that word.

"Weapons of war powered by dragon bones," Jax said. "I don't know all that they did, or could do, but I've heard stories—they had huge Energy-powered carriages which moved large numbers of soldiers quickly over vast distances, and Machines

that used Energy to hurl projectiles—or even blasts of Energy—
at deadly speeds.

"With the advent of these weapons of war, the pace of the
war increased—and so did the casualties. They created entire
armies which fought with these powerful weapons. Synthesizers
became war leaders, generals, and captains who organized these
armies and ensured their dragon bones remained charged."

"What happened to all the bones and Machines after the
war?" Yolken asked.

"When the war ended four hundred and ten years ago, and
Drakonias solidified his rule, the Regency developed new
Machines for peaceful purposes. An entire civilization was built
around these Machines. The transports that had carried soldiers
during the war now carried citizens from place to place in a
quarter of the time it took a galloping horse; buildings had
artificial light, making candles and lanterns obsolete. Machines
did just about everything. There were divisions within the
Regency whose sole purpose was to ensure the dragon bones
remained charged for all their many uses. The Regency made
great leaps in technological advances. But it all came to an end
around the year 295."

"What happened?"

"For some reason, Drakonias issued an edict banning the use
of dragon bones. The Regency systematically collected and
removed them from circulation. Within a few months, three
hundred years of advancement were lost, and the entirety of
civilization reverted to pre-Machine conditions and has
remained in such a state ever since."

"Why have I never heard of Machines before?" Yolken said.

"Because the Regency has ways of scrubbing inconvenient
truths from the annals," Jax said. "And anyone who so much as
whispered about days past inevitably disappeared. As it stands,
the Order is in possession of precious few dragon bones." Jax
puffed on his pipe a few times then said, "There's another
advantage to dragon bones other than permitting us to

Synthesize when out of sight of the sun."

"What?"

"Remember that I said we have to use caution when Synthesizing because Watchers can detect disturbances in the natural flow of Energy from the sun?"

Yolken nodded.

"Well, if you draw Energy from a dragon bone, it has no effect on the flow of Energy from the sun. Once it's in your Core, you can break down what you do with it into two categories: inward expressions and outward expressions."

Yolken looked confused.

"Inward expressions are things you do without the Energy ever leaving your body. For instance, you can draw Energy from the sword and use it to stave off fatigue, or help you lift a heavy rock. That Energy doesn't leave your body and Watchers can't detect it. However, they *can* detect when I use Energy I draw from the bones in my coat to light my pipe. In this instance, I'm Synthesizing outwardly. Make sense?"

Yolken nodded. "I think so."

"Good," Jax said, rising to his feet. He walked around the boulder, back out onto the ledge.

Yolken stood and followed him, holding the sword by the sheath in his right hand and the dagger in his left, to where the heat of the sun once again beat down on them. "How do I use them?" he asked.

"You draw Energy into your Core from a dragon bone just as you would draw from the sun on your skin. But first they need to be charged," Jax said. "The process is relatively simple. Open yourself to the Energy flowing from the sun." Jax paused, giving Yolken the chance to obey. "As Energy flows into you, transfer it into the bone in the same manner as you transfer it into the ground."

Yolken allowed Energy to flow into his Core then directed it into the dagger. "How do I know when it's full?"

"When no more Energy will go in," Jax said. "Since you seem to have the knack of it, I'll leave you with your task."

"Which is?"

"Fill the sword and dagger. It will take some time, especially on the sword. When you're done, come down, and we'll see about moving on to the next phase of your training."

Yolken nodded his agreement. He watched as Jax retrieved his coat and made his way down the mountain, leaving the flask of water behind. When Jax was out of sight, Yolken directed his attention back to the dagger and settled into a pace that wouldn't tire him quickly.

Determining when the dagger was full turned out to be as simple as observing that Energy stopped flowing down his arm. No matter how hard he pushed, he couldn't get any more to go into the dagger. He set it down and picked up the sword, and Energy resumed flowing.

As he worked to fill the sword, Yolken drew it out of its sheath and held it up. The light from the sun made the yellow ribbons running throughout the black bone shimmer. He wondered why the dagger had blue ribbons and the sword had yellow.

He thought he could make quick work of this seemingly easy task, but filling the sword turned out to take much longer than the dagger. By the time the sword was full, the sun had noticeably transited the sky. He stood, his tanned body covered in a sheen of sweat, and made his way down the mountain.

By the time he reached the bottom of the ravine and walked into the shade of the trees, he felt unusually tired. As he walked, he remembered what Jax had told him and gripped the hilt of the sword, opening himself to the Energy he felt inside. He allowed it to trickle into him, and his fatigue vanished. *Excellent*, he thought. Actually, now that he was thinking about it, he couldn't remember ever being tired while he Synthesized. It was only at the end of the day, when he no longer had Energy flowing through him, that he felt the toll of his day's work.

Remembering what Jax had said about the fatiguing effects of Synthesizing, he closed himself off from the flow of Energy, not wanting to tire himself further.

Despite being tired, he brimmed with excitement about the progress he was making in his training and the new things he had learned. Walking up to the cabin, he found Jax sitting on the porch bench smoking his pipe. He sat down next to Jax, overflowing with anticipation.

Jax pulled the pipe from his mouth and said, "Draego's Fire is not ordinary fire. It burns hotter than any fire you've ever known. Dragons breathed it out, melting everything it touched. We aren't capable of anything near what dragons could do, but you have in you the ability to wreak a destructive force no man should have the capability of. It was this force that swept through the tavern the day your parents died." Jax puffed on his pipe. "Because of its destructive nature, it is one of the Regency's favorite methods of attacking us. Defending against it is not easy. And if you hope to rescue your brother, you will need to know how."

Yolken nodded.

"It's much easier to make a fire than it is to stop it, so we'll start there. Tomorrow," Jax said with a wink, "I'll teach you to breathe fire."

CHAPTER 28

Crin sat in the shade of a tall pine, his back resting against its rough bark, intently watching the northern side of the deep ravine. His Glasses turned everything gray of various shades. Everything except for Energy. Energy fell like a torrential downpour of every color imaginable. But instead of falling straight to the ground, massive amounts of it was converging to a point on the far side of the ravine. It had taken him two weeks to find his target, but at last, he had achieved the first of the tasks assigned to him.

When he found the boy, he couldn't help but feel excited. He hoped that if he succeeded with this assignment, his father would finally place him in a more esteemed position. Serving as captain of the chancellor's guard, or even as a Watcher, was beneath him. He refused to accept that he was somehow less blessed simply because his father was not married to his mother.

Not only had he lived his entire life without the blessings of a Drake, his half siblings looked down on him just as their father did. Except for Cara—she always loved him like the brother he was and didn't blame him for something that wasn't his fault. But the way his other siblings—or even his father—treated him was nothing compared to how Therese had treated him. Until her death, she made sure he knew he was a pariah, reminding him almost daily that he was not her son.

Interviewing the Lonely Oak locals had been an excruciatingly slow process—sending a solitary soldier to track someone down was not the way to do it, but he knew Dorlan wouldn't approve anyone else. And the town had been very tight-lipped with regard to the Thornhills. His first lead didn't come until his third night of interrogations, and it was razor thin. He didn't know what relevance it was that the boys occasionally hunted in the mountains to the east of town—the Mindons—but that was all he'd learned. No one saw the Thornhill boy leave town; the merchants passing through on their way either north or south had seen no one matching the boy's description. So, with no other leads and already three days behind, he went with it.

At first, the Mindons proved to be a dead end. He crisscrossed his way up the gentle slopes, looking for some sign of recent human passage. As the terrain became steeper, he found an animal trail to follow, but there was no evidence that other humans had recently used it.

Crin spent several chilly nights in the mountains, staring up at Draego as it slowly passed overhead. He intentionally avoided lighting a fire, not wanting to accidentally alert the boy of his presence. Instead, he used small amounts of Energy from the hilt of the dagger he carried to stave off the chill.

Because of the vastness of the mountains, he almost gave up his search. But then, with Draego's luck, he crested the southern top of the ravine and saw disruptions in the streams of Energy. As he rested with his back against the pine, he realized how perfect this ravine was for a Synthesizer to hide—the Energy disruptions were invisible to anyone not in the ravine themselves.

The display of strength was astounding. It confirmed for Crin that he'd succeeded in finding the boy—no one in the Order was this strong. However, his excitement quickly gave way to worry because he knew the boy's strength greatly surpassed his own. If he was going to have any hope of apprehending him, Crin would need to be at full strength. Even then, the odds were not going to be in his favor. He considered turning back for reinforcement, but he would be lucky to catch up with Dorlan's caravan before they reached Hantlo and by then it would be too late—the boy would likely be gone before he returned. He gritted his teeth, knowing his only hope of apprehending him was doing it alone.

Crin settled in against the rough pine and gnawed on some dried meat. While he watched the display below, he toyed with the bone hilt of the dagger tucked into his belt. All he had ever wanted—even more than being acknowledged as a Drake—was for his father to love him. For several years it seemed like his faithful work was being rewarded with affection, but all the progress he'd made had been wiped out when Therese died. How *that* was his fault, he didn't know. His hand went to his throat, remembering how his father had almost killed him when Cara later died in a botched attempt to capture Danavin, the man responsible for Therese's death. None of it was Crin's fault— not the fact that Drenan had fathered a bastard nor that Therese and Cara had both died at the hands of the same rebel—but that didn't change the fact that he'd been futilely trying to gain his father's favor ever since. Until now.

Looking down into the ravine, he knew this was his chance. He doubted Drenan would ever love him, but if he could hand him Danavin's son—if he could deliver the son of the man responsible for the deaths of those his father truly loved—he knew he would at least gain the recognition he deserved.

CHAPTER 29

Javen held his hands over the fire, palms out, as if they needed warming. He wasn't cold—the night was hot and the air was wet—but it felt like the natural thing to do when sitting before a fire on a starry night. The crackling of fires around the camp, the sounds of the dozens of horses up and down the picket line, and the voices chattering around him combined to form a din of distraction.

He'd searched the camp for Astora before the caravan got under way, but he didn't find her and no one seemed to know who he was talking about. Hadie tried bedding him the moment the caravan lumbered into motion—she said mornings were the best time for bedding in the south, because it wasn't oppressively hot yet—but he couldn't be physical with her while he was thinking about Astora. Disgruntled, she left him alone on the bed, where he spent the majority of the time thinking about Astora and his coming lesson with Drenan.

"Javen? Hey, Javen!" Lyoll said.

"I don't think he's heard a word of what you said, Lyoll," Ganip said.

"Well, Draego's Fire if I'll repeat any of it."

"Were it not for the flower sitting beside him, I'd say he was thinking about a girl he wants to bed."

"Why should my sitting here stop him?" Hadie said. "Besides, he's been this way all day." Sitting close to Javen, she nudged him with her shoulder. "Hey."

"Huh? Sorry," Javen said. He picked up the tin cup sitting next to him and took a sip of the whiskey it held. It burned his throat going down and he had to suppress a cough.

"You don't seem yourself, lad," Lyoll said. He tossed back a gulp of the whiskey without batting an eye.

Javen looked up at Lyoll and wondered how Lyoll did it. "I got a lot on my mind."

"Such as?"

He looked over at Hadie.

"What?" she said.

"I saw a girl I know in the camp. A friend from Lonely Oak."

"That's it?" Lyoll said. "All this moroseness over a lass?"

Javen's cheeks flushed.

"Now, lad, it's hard to tell by the firelight, but I think you might be blushing."

Javen looked up at Lyoll, then quickly averted his eyes.

"Ah… I understand. This lass is a former lover of yours."

"No," Javen said, looking hesitantly over at Hadie.

"You don't have to lie," Hadie said, amused.

"I… when I saw her, I thought you'd be mad."

"Why would I be mad?"

"I don't know. I just thought…"

"So that's it? All that today was because you were worried I'd be mad at you if I found out about this girl?"

"That was part of it."

"What else, then?" Hadie said.

"My training isn't going well," he said.

"Hasn't that been the case for a while now, though?"

Javen nodded.

"What's changed?"

Javen's shoulders slumped. He muttered into his cup, "Dorlan canceled my lesson today."

"He's a busy man," Ganip said. "I've heard tell of diplomats waiting for weeks at a time just for an audience with him, so I'm not surprised he doesn't have time for lessons anymore."

"I get that," Javen said.

"What is it, then?" Hadie said.

"He said starting tomorrow my lessons will be with Drenan."

"Ah," Lyoll said. He stood up from his rickety wooden seat, picked up the glass jug, then stepped around the fire and held it out before Javen. "Here."

Javen accepted some of Lyoll's whiskey. He put the full cup to his lips and took a large gulp. He attempted to emulate the ease with which Lyoll drank the stuff, but instead, he gagged on it and coughed violently, spraying it from his mouth.

"Hey, now, I know it's not the finest," Lyoll said with a boisterous laugh, "but don't go wasting it, lad."

"I don't know how you do it," Javen said after regaining some composure.

"I've had years of practice."

Javen sat quietly and stared into the fire, sipping from the cup while listening to Ganip and Lyoll banter with each other about horses, the repairs needed on the carriages and wagons, and women. Hadie stroked his back, causing his mind to wander again. She drank from a tin cup also but seemed to handle the whiskey better than he did. He kept thinking of Astora, so he finally asked, "What would she be doing here?"

"You talking about the blond girl?" Ganip said.

"Yeah. You've seen her?"

"I have. She has the back side of a—"

"Ganip…" Lyoll said, a tone of warning in his voice.

"What? She reminds me of a particular lily I saw growing once up near Tieger—tall, thin, but with plenty a—"

"Ganip!" Lyoll shouted.

"All I'm trying to say is she's probably with one of the regents," Ganip said.

"Dorlan said she was with him," Javen said.

"That's not uncommon," Lyoll said. "They often invite women to warm their beds while they're on the road."

"She said something about being cast off."

"Sounds about right. It doesn't take long for them to grow bored with their… toys," Ganip said. "Earlier today I saw her going around the camp looking for someone to take her home."

"Do you know what happened to her or where she might be now?" Javen asked. He still couldn't believe she would leave her home and turn to whoring—even for one of the Blessed.

Ganip shook his head.

"Unless she's willing to go it alone, she'll be stuck in the caravan until we pass a merchant wagon or maybe a family traveling north," Lyoll said. "Though, if you ask me, she'd be better off finding another bed to warm in this caravan than joining up with a merchant wagon. The regents may take advantage of the vulnerability of local girls, but at least they mostly treat them decent enough. Can't say the same to be true with merchants. Drenan may leave them bruised from time to time, but with merchants, she'd as likely to end up dead on the side of the road as not."

Javen had known Astora most of his life. As children, they'd played together around the oak while her mother and his aunt ran errands, and when they were older, they'd occasionally shared a night in the hayloft together. He'd most recently bedded her the night before he met Hadie. He didn't hold any deep romantic feelings for her, but he felt a certain level of responsibility for her wellbeing—she was a part of his community. He certainly hoped she hadn't left the caravan on her own. He took a sip from his cup and said, "I wish there were something I could do."

"Why don't we go look for her," Hadie suggested.

Javen looked over at Hadie. "Then what?"

Hadie shrugged. "She could stay with us."

Javen opened his mouth to speak, but he didn't know what

to say. His initial thought was that he didn't want two women he'd bedded sleeping in the same place. That might end in disaster. But he didn't want her to try to go back home unprotected either.

"Where else is she going to go?" Hadie said, mildly exasperated.

"You're right." Javen upended his cup and coughed when the liquid burned his throat.

Javen and Hadie spent the next hour going from fire to fire asking after Astora. Some recognized her description, thinking they'd seen her at some point, and others looked at them like they had no clue who they were talking about. A few were annoyed he was asking them again when they'd already told him no once before. Whether they recognized her or not, their answers were all the same: They didn't know where she was.

"We can look again tomorrow," Hadie said as they walked back toward their own fire.

"Yeah," Javen said.

"No luck?" Lyoll asked when they walked back into the light of the fire.

Javen shook his head.

"Ah, you'll find her, I'm sure. She's around somewhere."

Not knowing Astora's whereabouts made Javen worry about her safety. He wanted to make sure she was all right.

"Another drink, lad?" Lyoll said.

"No, thanks," he said. His stomach felt upset. "I think I'm going to turn in."

"Yeah, I think we'll call it a night," Hadie said.

When they moved toward their carriage, Lyoll said, "Don't worry, lad. She'll turn up."

Javen hoped he was right.

CHAPTER 30

G'luck!" Ganip called out as Javen walked by.

Javen waved absentmindedly to the gangly boy stoking a fire pit back to life. He wasn't interested in engaging in banter. As he made his way across the camp, he held a hand over his unsettled stomach. The whiskey Lyoll had provided last night and the stress he felt about this morning's lesson were doing a number on his innards.

For the first time since leaving Matis, he wasn't looking forward to his lesson. After Dorlan had handed him off to Drenan yesterday, he had become apprehensive about continuing. He fought the urge to run away and not stop until he was back home.

Despite Hadie's and Ganip's misgivings toward the regents, Javen had actually come to admire Dorlan. The chancellor continued to exercise patience with him in his continued failures. However, he didn't feel the same way about Drenan. The stories he heard night after night about Drenan's ruthlessness made him worry. Lyoll said comparing Drenan's cruelty to Dorlan was like comparing a ravenous lion with a kitten who still suckled at its mother's teat. Consequently, he feared that if he failed his lesson, Drenan wouldn't exercise the same patience with him Dorlan had.

Astora added to his worries. He couldn't help but worry about her safety. As he crossed the camp, he looked around, hoping to see her. If Drenan didn't keep him at his lesson any longer than Dorlan usually did, he would have time to search the camp for her before it was time for the caravan to begin its day's journey.

The guard standing at the door of Drenan's carriage nodded at Javen as he approached and permitted him to climb the steps. The door was locked, so he knocked. After a brief moment, the door opened. He stood face to face with a disheveled girl wearing a sheer, light blue silk robe.

"*Astora?*" he said. His pulse raced. She looked away from him, and he averted his eyes from her slender body, visible through the thin material.

She stepped aside, permitting Javen to enter, then closed the door behind him. She went and opened all the shades on the eastern-facing side of the carriage. When she finished, she sat on the couch on the opposite end of the carriage from Drenan, who stood by the door leading into the dining room. Drenan held a glass of wine in his hand and wore a silk robe similar to the one Astora wore, as well as white gloves. His scarred chest was visible through the thin material.

Drenan gestured to the couch opposite the open windows and said, "Sit."

Javen sat hesitantly as instructed, glancing quickly over at Astora. *What's she doing here?* He turned his attention to Drenan, sitting opposite him.

After taking a sip of wine, Drenan said, "Dorlan tells me you are having trouble Synthesizing."

Javen looked at Drenan and nodded.

"Then there's really no point in having you try when the sun rises because, given your continued failure, it is evident to me you will be unable to do so."

"So what am I doing here?" Javen asked.

"Don't get me wrong: If you truly are who we think you are, then you have the gift within you. The problem you face is, I believe, that you lack the proper motivation to use it. And unless you are properly motivated, you will continue to fail." Drenan's voice was steady and calm.

"What sort of motivation am I lacking?"

Drenan took a drink of his wine then said, "It isn't entirely uncommon for those with the gift to struggle to use it for the first time. I admit I, too, struggled to Synthesize when I was young."

"You?" As apprehensive as he was about Drenan, he was still Blessed. For them to struggle…

"My father took me up into the mountains north of Kyinth, away from the safety of the city in which I grew up, and told me there are a few things that work wonders to help motivate someone: fear, anger, and desperation. To help me, he put me in a situation which perfectly blended them together. Far from any city or town, he beat me until I was near death then left me there to die. While I lay in the snow seething with rage at what he had done, a pack of wolves circled me. When they moved in for the kill, I was forced to fight for my survival. I lay battered in the snow, angry and fearing my imminent death. So, in an act of desperation, I reached out to the sun beckoning overhead." His voice was detached, as if it had happened to a different person.

"What does this have to do with me?" Javen said. His pulse quickened, half expecting Drenan to beat him. He'd been in fistfights before but knew those would be nothing compared to what Drenan described. But… Dorlan wouldn't let him do that, would he?

The sun crested the horizon, and Javen squinted as it streamed in through the carriage window.

Drenan set his wineglass down on the end table to his right and removed his white gloves, revealing scar-covered hands. "Did I ever tell you how I got these scars?"

Javen shook his head. He glanced over at Astora, who clutched her knees to her chest and rocked back and forth.

"They're quite extensive, actually," Drenan continued. He untied the blue silk robe, revealing the scars on his chest and stomach.

The scarred man. The scars were just as gruesome as they were in the stories. "What happened?"

"An act of retribution."

"For what?"

"For killing your father."

Javen's gaze leaped from Drenan's scars to his face. His vision narrowed and blood pounded in his ears. "You killed…"

"When the message arrived from Nera asking me to lead the mission, I gladly accepted."

Pieces fell into place. Drenan somehow knew about the fire, and after talking with Dorlan, Javen knew his parents' deaths were no accident. "*You're* responsible for the fire…"

Astora gasped.

"It wasn't the original plan," Drenan said. "However, when our assassins failed to kill your father, I started the fire to finish the assignment."

"You—you killed… my parents?" Javen stammered. He rose to his feet.

"I trapped your father inside that tavern, which was nothing more than a façade—an attempt to hide from who he really was. I trapped him so that he couldn't escape."

Javen lunged toward Drenan but was frozen mid-step.

"I don't know what you think you're doing but assaulting a regent will guarantee you hang by sundown," Drenan said.

Javen slid backward against his will. An invisible force pushed him back onto the couch. He looked over at Astora. He wanted to grab her hand and flee from the carriage.

"Now, where was I?" Drenan took a drink of wine. "Ah yes; my scars. After I killed your father, I confiscated his most prized possession—the Harachin sword. I didn't think the Order had it in them, but they sent someone—Jax, I believe he is called—to kill me and steal the sword back. He managed to get away with the sword, but due to the quick response of the woman I was about to bed, I'm still alive."

Javen was shaking. He wanted to strangle Drenan. He didn't care what happened after.

"I tell you this not out of cruelty or to hurt you," Drenan said as he wrapped the two sides of the robe back across his scarred body, "but because I knew it would incite within you certain emotions. You see, I already know you fear me—you betray your feelings the same as this whore."

"She's not a whore," Javen said through clenched teeth, still held immobile by Drenan's power. He looked over at Astora. She was looking at him with obvious fear in her eyes.

"And now, correct me if I'm wrong—though, by the way you keep burning holes in me with your eyes, I suspect I am not wrong—now you're angry. Perhaps furious?"

He was right. Right now, Javen wanted nothing more than to see Drenan burn the way he had made his mother and father burn.

"Furious. Excellent," Drenan confirmed with satisfaction. "The only piece of my father's equation still missing is desperation." Drenan took another drink of wine and smiled. "Which is where our mutual friend here comes in."

Javen glanced over at Astora again. "What do you mean?" he said, looking back at Drenan.

"Seeing as how the chancellor no longer requires her services, I thought she might be of use to our purpose," Drenan said. With the white gloves again hiding the scars on his hands, Drenan looked Astora up and down. "I must say though, I see now why His Highness kept her around for so long."

"You monster!" Javen shouted. He tried standing again, but the force held him on the couch. He couldn't stand the idea of Drenan touching her, let alone bedding her.

"She's rather timid and quiet, but I managed to... persuade her to cooperate. Imagine my delight to find that the two of you are familiar with each other!"

Javen looked over at Astora.

"I'm so sorry," Astora whispered. "The chancellor told me that if I came with him, he'd make my family rich."

"So you *do* know each other?" Drenan said.

"We grew up together," Javen said. He regretted the words as soon as he said them.

"Did you enjoy bedding her as much as I did?"

Javen glared at Drenan, then shut his eyes. He refused to continue participating in this.

"Answer the question!" Drenan commanded. "I am not the chancellor, and I will not tolerate insolence. I expect answers when I ask questions."

Javen looked over at Astora apologetically, then turned back toward Drenan. "I don't see what relevance it has to my lesson."

"It isn't your place to question the purpose or reason behind any question I ask of you, only to answer them when I do. But, if you must know," Drenan said, taking another drink of wine, "I said that I thought she might be of use to us."

"How?"

"It's simple, really." Drenan set his wineglass on the end table again and stood up.

Javen watched him walk through the door leading deeper into the carriage, still unable to move.

Drenan returned, gripping a long knife in his right hand. He strode over to where Astora huddled on the couch and grabbed her by the hair, pulling her up onto her knees. He tilted her head back and said, "All we need to complete my father's equation"—with a quick, smooth motion, he drew the knife across Astora's throat—"is desperation."

CHAPTER 31

"You know, I haven't been enjoying the meals as much since Deborah left," Yolken said. He rose from the table and took his plate to the sink.

"You're right," Jax said. "Deborah has a gift. Selena as well. If there's one good thing that came out of what happened with your parents, it's that Selena was forced out of retirement."

"What do you mean?"

"Before she joined the Order, she was quite well known in Tieger for her culinary aptitude."

"You knew her before the Order?"

"I did. But once she joined the Order, she put her former life behind her. Stomachs around the city mourned the loss," Jax said. "At any rate, you're welcome to take over the kitchen duties if you're unsatisfied with my cooking."

Yolken was excited to begin his lesson. Finally, he was actually going to learn to *do something* with Synthesis. He spent the whole night dreaming he was a fire-breathing dragon.

After Yolken put his plate in the sink, Jax said, "You know what we could use around here?"

"What?"

"Ale."

"Ale?"

"You know, to make up for the poor quality of food."

"I thought you were going to teach me how to breathe fire," Yolken said.

"I am," Jax said. "Though that was more a figure of speech. But if you really want to breathe fire, you're welcome to give it a go." Jax went to the door and said, "Come on."

Yolken followed Jax, eager to get started. They circled around to the back of the cabin, where a shed sat situated several paces behind it. He'd wondered about the shed since they had arrived, but it was always locked. Every time he'd asked Jax about it, Jax had just smiled and changed the subject.

The shed was about half the size of the cabin and, instead of the rough-hewn logs the cabin was made from, it was made of milled planks. A metal stovepipe with a conical cap stuck out of the roof. Jax unlatched the two wide wooden doors and swung the right one open.

Yolken walked up to the open door and peered in. Inside, he found a setup similar to his brewing shed back home. There were three matching iron kettles, each twice the size of the oak barrels along the back side of the shed. They sat elevated above the ground on an iron frame built in three tiers. The kettle on the left was the highest, sitting so the bottom of it was about a hand higher than the top of the next kettle. The same relation existed between the second and the third. The third sat a barrel's height off the ground. A valve and pipe connected the first kettle to the second, and the second to the third.

When he had swallowed some of his shock, Yolken managed to ask, "You have brewing equipment? Up here?"

"The finest Croff had to offer," Jax said, beaming.

"How in the world did you get it all up here?"

"Let's just say it involved a very unhappy mule."

"And you want me to brew?"

"I don't know about you," Jax said. "but I could sure use some ale. Go on, have a look."

Yolken walked into the shed and inspected the setup more closely. He noticed right away the main difference between what was here and what he had back at his tavern: There was no fireplace. The kettles in his shed back home sat on top of a tier of three fireplaces he could control individually, but these kettles rested on an iron frame. "How am I supposed to heat these?"

"With fire," Jax said.

"But how am I supposed to make a fire with no—" Yolken said, cutting himself off. He turned around to face Jax, only to find Jax smugly looking at him. "You want me to Synthesize?"

"Exactly," Jax said. "Now, come back outside so I can show you how it's done. Then I'll leave you to your work."

Jax led Yolken to a spot about ten paces from the shed, where a small ray of sunlight pierced through the thick canopy of trees and reached the ground. "Remember earlier when I said using Synthesis required knowledge of whatever it was you wished to do?"

Yolken nodded.

"The reason you were able to heal Issa was because you possessed the requisite knowledge about anatomy," Jax said. "The same is true in all areas of Synthesis—except for fire. Anyone who can Synthesize can make fire. It's the most basic expression of Draego's Gift."

Yolken was ready. "How do I do it?"

"Like this," Jax said. He held out his hand, palm up, and a small fire burst to life, hovering an inch over his hand.

Yolken looked curiously at the flame, and a thought occurred to him. "I thought you said we could only release Energy into the ground?"

"What I said was that the *simplest* method of discharging unused Energy in your Core is to release it into the ground. You can release it into anything you want—including the air. However, you must remember that Energy is heat, and when you release what you hold in your Core, you risk setting things on fire or burning those around you. The ground absorbs more

Energy than you could ever put into it, so it's the safest choice for beginners," Jax said. "Now, you try."

"Okay," Yolken said, confused. "Are you going to explain how you did that?"

"Hold your hand out like this," Jax said, holding his hand extended, "and draw a little Energy in. Then let it flow out of your hand the same as if you're dispersing it."

Yolken did. As the Energy left his fingertips, he felt it scatter in all directions. It felt odd—it tickled. It was different from when he let Energy flow from him directly into the ground; that didn't feel like anything.

"Reduce your flow to a trickle, and turn your hand over," Jax said.

When Yolken did, he felt waves of heat rising from his hand. The air shimmered around his palm.

"The Energy leaving your hand is yours to control. Take hold of it and concentrate it. Focus it to a point over your hand. As Energy builds on the focal point, it'll naturally ignite. But be careful—use only a small stream of Energy. The more you use, the bigger the flame. You don't want to accidentally singe all the hair off your body—or worse. I know Kaylan says she loves you, but she might think twice if you come down off this mountain without any hair."

Yolken looked at Jax crossly.

Jax cleared his throat to cover a laugh. "Anyway, once your fire's going, you can add Energy to the flame to make it bigger if you need to."

Yolken concentrated on the Energy as it left his fingertips. With a little experimentation, he found he *could* control which direction it flowed. He picked a point above his hand and began focusing on it. A flame considerably bigger than Jax's example ignited. The size and heat startled him.

"Careful," Jax said calmly. "Ease up on the Energy."

Yolken did, and the flame decreased in size.

"Keep in mind that fire made with Energy—Draego's Fire—burns much hotter than other forms of fire," Jax said. "If you aren't careful, you'll melt those kettles. So, there you have it, your first Synthesis skill." He clapped Yolken on the back. "Now, how's about you busy yourself with that other skill of yours?" Jax started back toward the cabin but stopped after several steps and turned back. "Oh yeah, I almost forgot—you'll find those flowers you use in your brewing growing on the back side of the shed."

"And what are you going to do?" Yolken said, letting the fire over his hand disappear. "This is going to take me all day."

"I think I'll go for a hike," Jax said.

Yolken stood in the small beam of sunlight breaking through the trees and watched as Jax walked around the side of the cabin. As much as he enjoyed his trade, he wasn't interested in spending the rest of the day brewing. He would much rather spend his time practicing his Synthesizing. The sooner he finished his lessons, the sooner he could start looking for his brother. Heating water seemed like such a menial task. There had to be more practical things he could do. With every passing day, he felt as though his brother was slipping farther away.

On the other hand, Jax was a fan of his ale—every time he visited Lonely Oak, he drank the night away in his tavern, conversing with Selena. If Jax was intending to stay isolated up here for a while, then having ale *would* be nice. He resigned himself to the task—menial as it was—and turned back to the shed.

Before getting started, he needed to inspect the equipment to determine what he had to work with. He walked into the shed and over to the iron structure supporting the three kettles. He still couldn't believe Jax had the foresight and means to get this equipment way up here into the middle of the mountains. Inspecting the kettles carefully, he found they bore the same maker's stamp as his kettles in Lonely Oak—DM. The whole system—the kettles, valves, and pipes connecting the kettles together—was identical to his system in Lonely Oak. *The man is very sly,* he thought. He could hardly believe Jax had taken the time to find out which of the blacksmiths in Croff had made his equipment. As he continued his inspection, he shook his head, trying to imagine Jax sneaking around to set up this system.

Each of the kettles had a thin metal lid fitted snugly to cover its top. Yolken went over to the lowest kettle, unclasped the clamp, and removed the lid. He peered inside and was pleased to find the kettle was clean. He could just reach the top of the middle kettle from the ground, so he took its lid off also. Then he climbed up the metal steps built next to the top kettle and checked it. He stacked the lids out of the way, then inspected the building further.

A grain mill sat in the corner next to several barrels and sacks of grain. Two large wooden paddles and two wooden buckets hung on the wall next to the doors. A ladder sat propped in the corner next to the buckets. Yolken looked at the paddles curiously and, walking up to get a closer look, saw that one of them had his family name engraved on it. *How did he—?* he thought. It was his father's paddle, which had gone missing a few years ago. *Draego's Fire. So* that's *where it went.* He felt a twinge of regret because he had blamed Javen, despite Javen's insistence otherwise.

Satisfied with what he had to work with, Yolken took the two buckets off the hooks and walked over to the creek. He filled them both, then walked slowly back to the shed. With the weight of the two buckets straining his arms and shoulders, he climbed the metal steps as smoothly as he could to prevent sloshing. He stopped next to the highest kettle and gently set one of the buckets down. He poured the water from the second bucket into the cavernous kettle, then emptied the second one. *Ugh,* he thought as he realized how many trips it was going to take him to fill the first two kettles with water. *The sot could have at least helped haul water.* He picked up both buckets and carefully made his way down the iron steps. He set the buckets on the ground and reached up to turn the valve at the bottom of the highest kettle. The water trickled through the pipe and drained into the middle kettle.

Yolken worked for the next hour filling the kettles with water. He mentally cursed Jax as his shoulders ached each trip from the creek. After emptying one final bucket into the highest kettle and realizing he had sufficient water, he let out a sigh of relief. He set the buckets down and rubbed his aching shoulders.

When he turned his attention to the next task—heating the water—it dawned on him that the kettles were inside and he didn't have access to Energy from the sun. With arms and shoulders aching, he looked down at the kettle full of water— then he thought of the sword propped against his bed. He rubbed his shoulders on the way to the cabin and retrieved the Harachin sword.

He returned to the shed and stopped in front of the middle kettle. He placed his hand on the hilt of the Harachin sword and drew Energy into his Core. Then, he held up his right hand, let a small stream of Energy flow from his first finger, and concentrated it a foot underneath the kettle. Almost instantly, the heat built up and a flame appeared.

He needed to heat the water in the highest kettle as well so, feeling complete control over the Energy flowing from him—as if the Energy was just a natural extension of himself—he split the stream as it left his finger into two. He directed the second stream to the base of the highest kettle, creating a fire underneath it, too. It took longer for the fire to appear, though, and he noticed when the stream split into two the fire under the middle kettle shrunk. He compensated by increasing the total flow of Energy, and both fires increased in size.

Once the streams of Energy were flowing, the flames under each kettle didn't require any effort to maintain. He lowered his hand and the two streams of Energy shifted from his fingertip to his chest. He felt two little pinpricks tickling his skin where the Energy exited his body. They danced around, but never strayed far from his sternum.

While he waited for the water to heat, Yolken ground grain, then went around to the back of the shed where Jax had said he would find the flowers he used in his brewing. He found lattices nailed to the back of the shed, covered in vines that were unseasonably mature. They were tall and heavy with small cone-shaped flowers. Their fragrant smell triggered in Yolken a feeling of deep connection to his father, even though he could barely remember him. He always wished he'd had the same opportunity to grow up with a father like the other boys in Lonely Oak, and somehow Yolken felt connected to him every time he brewed.

Yolken went back into the shed, retrieved one of the water buckets, and returned to the vines. Harvesting the little cones, he lost himself in the joy he felt when he plied his father's craft. With the sun shining warmly on his back, he had no need to draw Energy from the Harachin sword to maintain the fires burning within the shed.

A clap of thunder overhead brought Yolken's mind back to the present. He looked up at the sky but didn't see any clouds. *Must be a ways off*, he thought. It hadn't rained since they had been up here, but thunderstorms were common over the Mindons. He'd spent many a night looking out the windows of his bedroom watching the storms light up the skies over the distant mountains. A second clap of thunder sounded. By the time the storm arrived, if it was moving in this direction, he would be done picking flowers, so he didn't worry—he would remain dry inside the shed. But just as a precaution, he picked up his pace to ensure he collected enough flower cones should the storm arrive swiftly.

"Yolken!" he heard someone yell.

Yolken dropped the few flowers he held in his hands into the bucket and looked up. *Jax? But he was hiking. By now he shouldn't be anywhere near the cabin.* In the time it had taken him to haul all the water and grind the grain, Jax could be halfway up the mountain. But there was nobody else for leagues around.

"Yolken!" the yell came again.

Yolken put his hand on the Harachin sword and walked around the shed. He saw Jax on the opposite side of the creek, bare-chested and bloody, running frantically in his direction

CHAPTER 32

Astora's eyes opened wide as blood spurted from her throat. Javen gasped as Drenan let go of Astora's hair and her body slumped over on the couch. Her hands clutched desperately at the wound in her neck. Blood quickly soaked her robe and the couch cushions. The sight made Javen gag. He fought against the force holding him on the couch, and it lifted. His stomach, unsettled from his night of worry and drinking, forced him off the couch and onto his knees.

He vomited.

"If you don't heal her, *Master* Javen, then she will die," Drenan said. "If you truly *are* Blessed, do something."

Javen looked up at Astora as she struggled for breath. He wanted to do something but was frozen with terror.

"Astora," Drenan said, "did you know *Master* Javen here possesses within him the ability to heal you? Yet, for some reason, he won't do it. It's a shame, really. I thought after all those nights you spent together in the hayloft you might mean something to him. Guess I was wrong."

Drenan walked over to the table where he had set his wine, picked up a white cloth folded next to the glass, and wiped the blade of the knife with it. Then he picked up the glass of wine with his free hand and took a sip.

"Drenan!" Javen yelled. "She's dying!"

"Yes," Drenan said. "You must do something quickly."

Javen crawled over to Astora as her hands fell away from her throat. Her glassy eyes shifted to look at him. They screamed for help. Javen pulled his shirt over his head and tried to stem the flow of blood.

"That will do nothing for her," Drenan said, standing idly by drinking his wine. "You must heal her!"

Javen looked over at Drenan when he spoke and, seeing that he didn't intend to help, turned his attention back to Astora. Her eyes continued to plead with him. Tears filled his own eyes. He blinked them away and stood up to get a view of the sun. He looked out the window and felt its heat on his face. However, just like every other day since his lessons with Dorlan had begun, that was all he felt. He couldn't draw the Energy into himself as he'd been instructed so many times to do. He imagined the empty Core within himself, then pictured Energy rushing in to fill it.

But nothing happened.

"Your brother, when confronted with a dying girl, used the gift that was his birthright and healed her. Are you telling me *he* is better than *you*?"

"No!" Javen shouted. He looked out at the sun and pleaded with it to fill him with Energy. When nothing happened, he looked down at Astora. Her glazed eyes stared lifelessly at the ceiling, but her chest still struggled, weakly, to bring in breath. Realizing the futility of what he needed to do, he gave up. He knelt beside her, hoping to at least provide her a little comfort— to let her know she was not alone in her last moments. Javen placed his bloodied hand over her forehead and looked up at Drenan one last time, hoping he would intervene. "Heal her, please!"

Drenan sipped his wine.

Javen looked back down into Astora's blank stare and whispered, "I'm so sorry."

Her shuddering breath stopped.

"Perhaps tomorrow we'll invite that whore who has been warming your bed," Drenan said.

"No!" Javen screamed. He crawled toward Drenan, but Drenan stepped through the door to the dining room before Javen reached him and it clicked shut behind him.

Retching, Javen vomited again and again. He wiped his mouth, smearing blood across his face, and sat back on his heels. He looked over at Astora's lifeless body then crawled over to her. The tears streaming from his eyes blurred the gruesome wound in her neck.

CHAPTER 33

Crin woke with his back against the rough bark of a pine. His body ached from spending the night in such an uncomfortable position. Cursing the tightness of his muscles, he pushed himself to his feet and placed his hand on the sturdy pine to balance himself while he stomped feeling back into his numb legs. He shivered slightly in the cold air.

The long shadows cast by the rising sun still surrounded him, so Crin gripped the black hilt of the dagger to take off the chill, but it was empty. When feeling returned to his legs, he moved down to a spot where sunlight broke through the tree canopy.

He drew Energy in from the sun and divided it between warming himself and recharging the bone hilt. The task was completed entirely too quickly so, with nothing else to do until nightfall, he sat against another pine. He pulled the dagger out of its sheath and closely inspected the steel blade he'd spent the previous day honing. He wanted to ensure the blade would easily slice through anything he needed it to, in case he was not successful in remaining undetected.

Satisfied with his work, Crin held the blade by the tip then deftly tossed it into the air. He watched carefully as it pivoted on its way up then back down, catching the blade by the tip. His time in the guard had taught him this simple and entertaining game, but it was usually played over drinks. And unlike many of the other guards who played, he had never needed a regent to heal him after catching the dagger wrong. Over the years, it had garnered him a fair amount of money.

As entertaining as this little game could be, without the drink or exchanging of money, it would soon grow boring. For now, however, it gave him something to do to help pass the time. It would be a long day of waiting as the sun made its daily journey across the sky. He slipped his Glasses on and settled in to enjoy his game for as long as it would last.

* * *

Jax enjoyed the burn in his legs with each step he took. He stopped, wiped sweat from his brow, and assessed how much farther he still had to climb. With Yolken occupied for the remainder of the day, he decided he wanted to climb to the top of the northern ridge—something he hadn't done since he had originally surveyed this valley. It didn't take him long to start sweating, so he'd removed his shirt and tied it to his belt.

Breathing heavily, he looked around for some shade to rest, but didn't find any. Instead, he sat on a smooth and relatively flat ledge. He unscrewed the cap on the leather flask and drank the cool water. It felt immensely refreshing as it hit his lips and cooled his parched throat. He wanted to reach the top of the ridge but wasn't in any particular hurry. There was plenty of daylight left.

The valley really was the most ideal place he had ever come across to safely train someone in Synthesis. Even from this high-up spot, he was still well hidden below the northern and southern ridges of the valley. It must have been fifty years ago— long before he'd agreed to look after Orwyn Thornhill's family—when he had first come across this ravine. He had been smuggling dragon bones from Hantlo to Tieger. The Order didn't want to risk any chance of the bones being intercepted by the Regency, so he had needed to avoid the highways connecting the two cities as much as possible. Going through the mountains added considerable time to the trip, but he wouldn't have discovered this valley otherwise.

Looking down at the valley, his thoughts turned to the boy. Thus far, he had been impressed with Yolken's progress. It was time to start assessing his strength. Healing Issa was no small feat, but if he was going to move forward with his plan he needed to know exactly what Yolken could do.

Jax took another drink of water and admired the southern boundary. It was steep, but not nearly as steep as the northern ridge upon which he perched. Its more gradual grade resulted in a dramatically different landscape. Rather than being mostly barren and rocky like the northern ridge, it was covered in the same tall pines densely concealing the valley floor. A few of the waterfalls cascading down the slopes where the creek entered the valley were visible through the trees. He looked down toward where he knew the cabin was—he couldn't see it through the trees—and wished he had a pair of Glasses. With them, he would be able to directly see Yolken's strength.

A glint of light flashed in the corner of his eye, drawing his attention back to the cascading water. An uneasy feeling washed over him. *It was just the sun reflecting on the water.* He stared down, waiting to see if it would repeat. Exposed as he was, he grew anxious.

Light glinted again.

He was staring right at it.

It was *not* light reflecting off the waterfalls.

It was about three-quarters of the way up the southern slope, near where he knew the trail leading down into the ravine was located, and he knew exactly what it was—the sun reflecting off metal.

Jax fought back panic. It was possible that whoever was down there was just a random wanderer, but for the sake of his oath to Orwyn, he had to assume the worst—the Regency had somehow found them.

Up on this ledge, he was separated from the boy he had sworn an oath to protect. He stared at the spot where he'd seen the flash and considered his options.

Light flashed again.

He made his choice. He allowed Energy from the sun to flow into his Core and filled it to the brim. He waited, letting the Energy flow through him into the rock on which he perched. If it was the Regency down there, then he was a beacon beckoning to them. But if they showed their hand it would be worth—

* * *

Each time Crin tossed the blade, he focused intently on every twist and turn of the sharp edge as it spun up and down, ensuring he caught it on the flat sides. A sudden change in the flow of Energy descending from the sun caused him look away from the blade when it was at the top of its arcing path, so he let it fall and land point first into the ground. He stood, leaving the blade where it fell, and studied the location of the disturbance.

The boy was much higher on the ridge than he had been yesterday and the day before. Because he'd spent so much time in one spot the last two days, Crin figured he must have been conditioning himself, which meant he was a new Synthesizer. It also meant he wasn't alone. If the boy knew enough to know he needed to condition, someone had to be teaching him. And if he wasn't alone, then Crin's plan was useless.

His primary mission was to apprehend the boy and take him to Hantlo. However, he knew he was authorized to do what was necessary, should the need arise. His father would rather him return having eliminated the boy than fail in his mission completely. Moreover, he'd had the benefit of the better part of two days to conclude that he was in no way a capable enough Synthesizer to be of any real threat to this boy. Even untrained, the boy was dangerous, but now he knew the boy wasn't alone. He couldn't help but feel that his father had acted hastily in choosing him for this mission—how could he possibly have thought that sending a single soldier to apprehend a known powerful Synthesizer was a good idea? However, Crin had obeyed, like every good soldier—that, and he wanted to finally do something to prove his worth to his father.

As Crin stared at the Energy bending to a point on the opposite ridge, his new plan coalesced in his mind. He would obey his order and accomplish his mission, but in his own way. As the weaker Synthesizer, Crin had to use the advantage he had. Killing the boy would be much easier than trying to apprehend him then transport him all the way to Hantlo. Alone in the middle of a vast mountain range, his father would know only what Crin told him. With his mind made up, he drew Energy into himself. Then, holding up a hand, he reached out with Energy.

While attending court in Kyinth, Crin had learned that his grandfather was a fan of the summer storms that towered over the mountains north of the capital. "The power that these storms exhibit reminds me that those in positions of authority must occasionally demonstrate their power to those beneath them," the emperor had said. Crin had learned that day that a different type of energy existed in the air, and that this energy displayed itself magnificently during thunderstorms. It was this force that he reached out to and gathered with the Energy streaming from his hand. As he collected it, he funneled it to a single spot high over the boy. When the electrifying force reached a critical point, he pointed down to the boy with his other hand and connected the boy and the gathered force above with a single small thread of Energy.

Lightning erupted between the two points.

* * *

A bolt of lightning struck the rock to Jax's right, and he dove to his left. Thunder crashed around him as he landed hard. His side erupted in pain, and his ears rang loudly. *Draego's Fire*, he thought, his mind racing. *They found us.*

Jax knew he had to get off the mountain fast. He could take

no chances now. He had to beat them to Yolken. Pushing himself to his feet, Jax reestablished his connection to the sun. Another bolt of lightning struck behind him, and thunder reverberated around him, but he held onto his connection. After taking a deep breath, he looked at the valley stretching out below him and took a running jump off the ledge.

* * *

The flow of Energy streaming down from the sun returned to normal, no longer converging to a point. Crin smiled. He held his position and prepared for another strike. He waited. If he was lucky, the single strike would be all he needed. His brow furrowed when Energy began to gather again in the same location. He was not lucky; the boy lived. Crin quickly let loose with another bolt. However, this time, Energy continued to bend to a point. He waited anxiously for enough of the electrical force to gather for another strike, but he stared helplessly as the point of Energy convergence dropped suddenly off the mountain. *He jumped,* Crin thought. *The fool boy jumped!*

Crin watched helplessly as color exploded out around the boy. He took his Glasses off and saw the tiny figure falling quickly. With angst-filled amazement, he watched the figure slowly move across the valley then disappear into the forest below.

"Draego's Fire!" Crin swore aloud. His father would not be pleased if he let the boy get away. In a panic, he gathered his things and made his way down the trail leading into the valley.

Dread filled him as he realized his sole advantage was now gone. He wanted to turn around and leave, but he knew had no choice but to pursue the boy—and without the protection of his armor. He understood the reasons behind armor being prohibited on missions such as this, but that didn't change his desire to have it. The absolute worst possible thing would be if he returned empty-handed. He knew his father well; it would be a kinder fate if he died trying to capture the boy than if he returned to his father a failure.

* * *

Air rushed around Jax as he fell toward the ledge where Yolken had trained. It took only seconds to descend back down to the ledge even though it had been an hour's hard hike since he'd climbed past it. As the ledge loomed before his focused eyes, Jax reached out with every bit of Energy in his Core and used it to gather air around him. The pressure around him increased, and the sound of the rushing air decreased. He fell in near silence for a split second before he moved all the air gathered over his back. His body moved away from the rocks and out over the valley floor, narrowly avoiding the rock outcropping.

Bits and pieces of the creek were visible through sporadic breaks in the tree canopy below. Jax searched for a place to land, wishing for the first time that the trees weren't quite so thick. He scanned the canopy and found a small clearing on the north side of the creek. It wasn't directly below him, so he increased the pressure along his entire front side, which pushed against his body, moving him in the direction of the clearing. When his body was over it, he balanced the pressure around himself and fell straight down.

As he approached the ground, Jax manipulated the air pressure surrounding him to pivot end over end. When his feet were pointing at the ground, he equalized the pressure over his entire body and stabilized his fall.

Not wanting to lose one second of lead time on those encroaching on the valley, he let himself freefall until the very last second. Then, with all his might, and with every ounce of the Energy that threatened to burn him from the inside out, he pushed down with the air gathered around him. His descent slowed quickly then he hit the ground and rolled to a stop.

He picked himself up and ran in the direction of the cabin shouting at the top of his lungs, "Yolken!" Splashing through the creek, he repeated his call. "Yolken!"

CHAPTER 34

The smell of blood filled Javen's nose. He knelt next to Astora, resting his head on her thigh, and cried uncontrollably with deep, lumbering gasps. Overcome with grief and fear, he was unable to bring himself to move. He wanted to flee. He needed to flee. He needed to get Hadie and escape from the caravan.

But he couldn't leave Astora.

How could Drenan be so cruel? How could he so easily murder an innocent girl then walk away as if it was no big deal? As Javen cried, guilt replaced the anger, fear, and desperation that had filled him moments ago.

Astora's death was his fault.

He hadn't killed her, but he should have saved her. She died because of his inability to Synthesize. He knew the gift was in him—Yolken had proven it when he healed Issa. Never before had he been responsible for the life of another. Selena had taught him to respect life. How could Drenan, one of the Blessed, care so little? *They're supposed to protect us, not ruthlessly murder us.*

Hadie.

"I… will make… him pay," Javen whispered between gasping sobs. "I promise you; I will make him pay. I have to."

The door separating the adjoining room in the carriage

opened, and Drenan said, "It's time you returned to your own carriage. I'll see you and your whore on the morrow."

Javen lifted his head off Astora's thigh, his face covered in tears and blood, and looked up at Drenan standing over him. He was wearing his blue armor.

Drenan looked down at Astora and shook his head. "I imagine it will be tricky to clean the blood from the cushions. They'll likely need replacing altogether. Now, be on your way. I have matters elsewhere requiring my attention."

Javen watched Drenan move toward the exit. He wiped the tears from his eyes, his blood-covered hands smearing his face even worse, and pushed himself to his feet. "How could you be so cruel?"

Drenan stopped with his hand on the latch of the door and turned to face Javen, "I have vehemently argued to His Highness that you hang like the rebel you are, but for some reason, the emperor thinks differently. What his plan is, I don't know, but while I'm supervising you you must understand one thing: When I give you an order, you obey it. What unfolded here just now had nothing to do with cruelty. Dorlan ordered me to make you Synthesize, and I obeyed. I, in turn, gave you an order, which you did *not* obey." Finishing, he turned the latch, and before walking out the door, he added, "I look forward to when you make me *pay*."

Javen watched Drenan step out of the carriage, leaving him alone in the room with Astora's corpse. When the door shut behind Drenan, he looked down at his blood-soaked clothes and arms. The light of the sun shining brightly through the windows eerily illuminated his bare arms. He stared helplessly at his hands for what seemed like an eternity, not knowing what to do. He couldn't simply go back to his carriage as if nothing happened. What would he tell Hadie? He had to *do* something. If he didn't, she would be next. But what? He was powerless against Drenan. He thought about going to Dorlan, but he wondered if he would care. Drenan said Dorlan had ordered him to do it. No—if he was going to do something about this brutal murder, and save Hadie, he needed to do it himself.

His emotions boiled over. Fear. Anger. Desperation. Hatred. He glared at the sun, accusing it, as one of his emotions quickly dominated the others—Hatred. He clenched his eyes shut as the hatred within him grew. There were so many things he hated: He hated that he had grown up thinking his parents died accidental deaths only to find out they were murdered; that Selena had lied to him his whole life about their fate; that they were enemies of the Regency; that Selena had lied about being his aunt when in truth she was associated with the same traitorous group as his parents; always being second to his brother; that Yolken had won Kaylan's heart instead of him; that he continued to fail at Synthesizing; Drenan; and now the sun, for failing to help him save Astora.

He looked over at the door the armored regent had just walked through. Staring at it, his body started shaking uncontrollably. The hate was rapidly growing within him, and he let it consume his other emotions: fear, anger, desperation, and even love. When only hate remained, the mixture of emotions no longer clouded his head. Then he finally realized what he wanted most—revenge. And, he would start with the thing he hated most—Drenan. The scarred man was real. He was a terror. He was as evil as Hadie, Lyoll, and Ganip said he was. He had ruthlessly killed Astora. He was threatening Hadie. If he didn't do something, she would die as well.

He couldn't let that happen.

With nothing but hate burning in him, something changed. Javen no longer simply felt the heat of the sun on his face. Instead, it beckoned to him. He finally felt the Energy Dorlan had assured him was there. He felt it pushing to get inside of him. He wanted it in him. He needed it in him. Reveling in the feeling of Energy flowing around him, Javen opened himself to its beckoning call. Energy flooded in. He felt it pooling in his chest, near his heart, in his Core. He pulled in as much as he could, until it threatened to burn him up. When he could hold no more, he closed his eyes and focused on the hate within him.

It was time to do something about it.

Javen stepped over to where Astora slumped on the couch. Reaching down, he closed her glazed eyes, which stared vacantly at the ceiling. Then, with determination, he followed Drenan out the door. When his feet hit the trampled grass, he looked left and saw Drenan walking toward Dorlan's larger and more opulent carriage. His gray-armored guard flanked him on his right. The sight of Drenan turned the hate burning in him into rage.

With sweat seeping from his pores, Javen moved toward Drenan, letting the rage guide his steps. His feet quickened to a jog, and he covered the ground quickly. When less than a dozen paces separated them, he shouted, "Drenan!" He stopped and inhaled deeply when both Drenan and his guard stopped and turned.

"I thought I told you to return to your carriage," Drenan said.

Astora's blood itched on Javen's face as sweat streamed from his pores. He forced his eyes open even though they stung. He would watch Drenan burn. He held up both hands.

"Ah, I see you have finally—"

Javen pushed every ounce of Energy and hate pooled within him toward Drenan. A stream of fire exploded from his hands, burning his flesh. He screamed but kept pushing.

Drenan made no move to avoid the inferno except to lift his arms and shield his face.

Javen stared in disbelief when the flames disappeared the moment they touched Drenan. Drenan and his guard stood in the middle of a scorched circle of grass, unscathed. His rage evaporated, and he cried out as pain shot up his arms.

"Fool boy," Drenan said.

Every ounce of strength within Javen vanished, and he crashed to the ground.

"Pick him up," he heard Drenan say before everything went dark.

CHAPTER 35

Drenan strode across the trampled grass to Dorlan's carriage. His guard walked alongside him, carrying the unconscious boy in his arms. Dorlan's guard hastily pulled the door to Dorlan's carriage open when he saw him approaching. Drenan climbed the steps, telling his guard tersely, "Follow me." His guard climbed the steps sideways to fit the boy through the door.

"Get out!" Drenan shouted at the people lining both couches.

The numerous people seeking an audience with Dorlan stared at him and the blood-soaked boy. When he shouted, "Out!" again they scrambled to their feet and practically climbed over each other attempting to get through the door first.

When the room was empty, Drenan opened the door to the adjoining room and went in.

"What in Draego's Fire," Dorlan said when he saw the guard standing in the doorway holding the lifeless boy in his arms. "Get him out of here."

The guard turned and walked out of the room and dropped Javen onto one of the couches.

Dorlan had been eating. He set his fork down, took a sip of ale, then turned his attention back to Drenan. "Please tell me why Javen is unconscious and covered in blood. And what happened to his arms?"

"He attacked me," Drenan said.

"With Synthesis?"

"He attempted to kill me the same way that rebel did in my palace—which proves they are colluding together."

"It doesn't prove anything, but it does explain why he's unconscious. What about the blood?"

Drenan hesitated.

"Drenan?"

"I used the whore you took from Lonely Oak during our lesson this morning to encourage him to Synthesize."

"Used her? How?"

"Father said you need—"

"Yes," Dorlan said. "I'm aware of what Father said. Just tell me what you did."

"I cut the girl's throat and told the boy to heal her."

"Did he?"

"No," Drenan said. Then, seeing the displeased look on Dorlan's face, he added, "Your Highness."

"You killed an innocent girl to make the boy Synthesize?" Dorlan asked. "On your first lesson with him?"

"Yes. And it worked," Drenan said. "He Synthesized."

Dorlan pursed his lips and stared into the glass of ale sitting next to his plate.

"We need to have a trial immediately and hold him accountable," Drenan said.

"You would have me try an unconscious person?"

"He attacked a regent in front of the entire camp!"

"No," Dorlan said.

"You can't be serious," Drenan said. "He consciously attempted to murder a regent." Drenan waited for a reply, but Dorlan said nothing. "This is now the second time a rebel associated with Danavin has attacked me," he continued. "I barely survived the last assault as it was, and this boy's assault wouldn't have left anything to heal. It was fortunate I was wearing my armor."

"Which is why I must adhere to the emperor's instructions," Dorlan said. "We cannot risk letting him fall back into the hands of the Order."

"He wouldn't fall into the hands of the Order if you would try him, convict him of the crime he has committed, and execute him."

"My realm is crumbling to pieces, Drenan," Dorlan said. He picked up the silver fork and a matching knife and began cutting a slice of meat off the steak he was eating. "Drakonias is more concerned about the woman he's bedding than he is that another realm in his empire is going the way of the east. He continues to remain unmoved in his resolve toward our situation and angering him won't help matters. I simply cannot afford to violate the orders he gave me concerning the boy." He placed the meat in his mouth and, after chewing and swallowing, said, "Besides, it sounds to me like you deserved it."

"You told me to make him Synthesize, so I did what I deemed necessary," Drenan said, defensive. "Besides, the girl was as good as dead anyway. You sealed her fate the moment you took her from her home. What I did was the merciful thing."

"The merciful thing?" Dorlan took a second bite.

"Yes. I spared her months of abuse at the hands of the Dragon knows how many different merchants as they passed her around, abusing her every way imaginable."

"Everyone must follow the orders they have been given. I don't intend to disobey the emperor. If you have a problem with what he has instructed me to do, you are free to take it up with him."

"Your Highness, what sort of an example are we setting if we permit those who assault regents to go unpunished?"

"He *assaulted* you, Drenan, because you butchered an innocent girl!" Dorlan shouted, slamming his fork on the table.

"Now, do as you are instructed. Get the boy off my couch, have Devin heal his arms, then take him back to his carriage."

"Yes, Your Highness," Drenan said. "But I must insis—"

"Do as you are told," Dorlan said, cold finality in his voice. "I wish to finish the rest of my meal in peace."

CHAPTER 36

A scream reverberated across the camp, making Hadie jump to her feet and knock the plate on her knees to the ground. Gravy-covered biscuits spilled onto the trampled grass. She looked in the direction of the scream, thinking of Javen, but couldn't see who it was. She thought she could make out the blue armor of a regent near Dorlan and Drenan's carriages, standing in the middle of a throng of people. She squinted to see if Javen was anywhere near the regent, but she didn't see him.

The buzz that overcame the camp died down as people lost interest and returned to finishing their morning meals. Looking down at her feet, Hadie shook her head at the mess she'd made.

"Never mind it, lass," Lyoll said, picking her plate up for her. He grabbed another biscuit off the hot plate, slathered it with more of the meaty gravy he always seasoned to perfection, and handed it to her.

"Thank you," Hadie said. She sat back down on the stump and resumed her breakfast. As she ate, people stopped as they passed by, telling tales of what had happened: The Regent of Hantlo and the chancellor got into a big argument, and the chancellor burned the regent up with fire; the Regent of Onta fought with the Regent of Hantlo over a camp prostitute, and one attacked the other; a violent dispute between two teamsters forced a regent to intervene; a boy walked into the middle of the camp and somehow threw a fireball at the chancellor; no, it was a regent; the rebels sent him; he acted alone; it wasn't a boy, it was a girl.

"Whatever or whoever it was," Lyoll said, "there's bound to be a hanging. The chancellor doesn't tolerate discord within the camp."

The mention of the boy attacking a regent made Hadie nervous. She knew the truth of Lyoll's words. Anyone who spent any amount of time around the Blessed knew they were swift and unbending in their intolerance toward violence against anybody—especially against the Regency. The Dragon knew she had witnessed her fair share of executions in Hantlo. Her father used to take her to the square in their district as a reminder of what happened to those who stepped out of line. She'd never known them to show mercy.

She decided not to worry until she knew more. She could drive herself crazy over a silly rumor. Whatever it was, it was a bit anticlimactic anyway since no one seemed to have actually seen what happened. It must not have been that spectacular in the first place.

Hadie finished the remainder of her food, then went over to the barrel of water used to wash soiled dishes. She grabbed the greasy rag draped over the edge and used it to scrub what she could from the plate. She looked for soap to help in the process, but there never seemed to be any. Lyoll always swore he put some out, but more often than not, it went missing. She did her best to clean the plate with just water. Mostly, she smeared the grease around with the rag. There was nothing she could do about it, and Lyoll never complained. She took the plate and fork back to the fire and placed them in Lyoll's camp bin. "Thanks again for letting me join you," Hadie said.

"You're welcome anytime," Lyoll said. "Though I can't imagine why you prefer eating our greasy food over what they serve you in your carriage."

"Because I hate pretending to be someone I'm not," Hadie said.

"You aren't going to stick around to see which rumor turns out to be true?" Ganip said.

"No thanks," Hadie said. She made her way back to the carriage she shared with Javen. The sun was well over the horizon now. He would be returning from his lesson soon, and she wanted to be there when he came back, to hear how his first lesson with Drenan had gone.

She couldn't help but worry. Javen had hardly slept last night because he was so nervous. She couldn't blame him—Drenan had a well-deserved reputation in the south for being harsh. She didn't know what it was like in the other realms, but in the south, the people worshiped and respected the regents. Not him, though. Any respect that existed for Drenan was purely a result of fear. And then there were the stories Javen had told her about the scarred man—to Javen, Drenan was literally a childhood nightmare come true. *Maybe it was Javen who attacked Drenan.*

Back in the carriage, she settled in to read the first in the series of *The Lovers of Onta* for probably the sixth time—she couldn't honestly remember how many times she'd read it. After seeing Karina Drake back in Lonely Oak, she couldn't help but imagine she was right there in the stories with Karina. As much as she hated being a part of the caravan, she did secretly hope to catch sight of Karina, to maybe talk to her. But so far, she seemed to be reclusive, oddly opposite of how she was portrayed in *Lovers*.

Hadie found herself looking forward to arriving in Portstown so she could get some new books for the remainder of the journey to Hantlo—that and hopefully get a night or two away from this carriage.

She wasn't excited to be arriving back in the south, though. She'd long ago made her peace with her decision to leave her parents behind, but the closer she drew to her old home, the more she feared she wouldn't be able to leave again.

She wasn't interested in reading the entire book again since she practically knew it by heart, so she flipped to the first of several bent-over pages to read one of the scenes that made Javen blush. She smiled at the thought of reading them to him. He always wanted to know how she could read such stories. She usually replied by asking him how he could read the boring history books he did. When he said it was because he liked them, she always replied pertly, "And so do I."

The door opened, and Hadie looked up over the top of her book. She came to her feet when she saw an armored guard enter the door sideways, carrying a limp and bloody body in his arms. *Javen.*

Drenan, wearing his blue armor, followed the guard into the room. As the guard walked past her and into the bedroom, she saw Javen's face, unconscious and smeared with dried blood. "What happened?" she exclaimed.

"His training was successful," Drenan muttered bitterly.

The guard walked back out of the bedroom empty-handed, then straight out the door.

Before Drenan turned to follow, he looked at her. "Your time with the boy is done when we arrive in Portstown. Keep him fed until then."

Hadie stared helplessly as Drenan walked out the door. She wanted to shout at him, "You can't do that!"—but she knew she was powerless to stop him. Tears welled in her eyes. Knowing there was nothing she could do she went into the bedroom. Javen lay awkwardly on the bed. It looked like the guard had simply dropped him there. She inspected his body for the source of the blood but didn't find any. *What happened?*

She could hear Ganip hitching the horses to the carriage outside. They would be underway soon, so if she wanted to clean him up before the servant came to remove the water from the basin, she needed to start immediately. She put the thoughts of what Drenan had said out of her mind and turned her attention to getting Javen washed and into clean clothes.

"What did Drenan do to you?" she said while she worked at unlacing Javen's boots. She pulled them off then unbuckled his belt, grabbed each pant leg down by his feet, and yanked them off. She tossed them into the corner.

She looked at the blood covering Javen's face, arms, and chest, then retrieved one of the fresh towels from the small wooden table next to the washbasin. She dipped it in the water the servant had brought when Javen left for his lesson. She wrung the excess water out of the towel and started gently wiping the blood from Javen's face. The towel soiled quickly and started smearing the blood—similar to the grease-soaked rag she had tried to clean her plate with—so she went back to the basin and washed it out. The clean water in the basin turned pink. She wrung the towel out again and worked diligently until Javen's face and chest were clean. When she worked at cleaning his arms, she noticed the skin tone of his hands was noticeably lighter; newer, somehow.

She dropped the blood-soaked towel in the basin and wiped her brow with her arm. Observing that the sheets were soiled, she took a deep breath, pulled the sheet out from under Javen, and tossed it into the corner with Javen's pants. Lastly, she straightened him out on the bed and placed a pillow under his head. She collapsed down next to him on the mattress, tired from tugging his dead weight around.

A knock on the door made her glance up. Drenan's servant Rennie stood with her eyes to the ground, holding a large pitcher with fresh towels balanced on top. "Pardon me, ma'am, I—"

"No, no. It's all right," Hadie reassured her, climbing off the bed. "There are some soiled items in the corner. Could you please see to their washing?"

"Yes, ma'am," Rennie said. She moved to the basin and placed the towels down on the table. She looked into the water basin and, seeing the bloody water, looked up questioningly at

Hadie.

"Your guess is as good as mine," Hadie said. "Something's happened to his arms, but I can't find any other sign of injury."

Hadie watched as Rennie lifted the basin and emptied the contents into the pitcher. She picked up the pitcher and the untouched plates of food, and said, "I'll return shortly to clean up the rest of this and bring him something he can eat."

"Do you know what happened this morning?"

Rennie shook her head, eyes still trained on the floor. "His Majesty stopped me outside and told me to come straight here."

"If you hear anything, will you tell me?"

"Yes, ma'am."

"Thanks."

While she waited for Rennie to return, Hadie got a glass from the table and poured some water into it from the small water pitcher Rennie had brought with their morning meal. She went to the bed and sat down next to Javen and pried his mouth open with two fingers. Then she slowly poured a little water into his mouth. He gagged on it at first, spraying it out of his mouth as he coughed, but then his mouth closed, and he swallowed. His mouth opened again on its own and she tried pouring a little more water in; this time he swallowed the water without gagging.

Rennie returned a few minutes later with a bowl of steaming liquid. "Stock, ma'am. His Majesty told me the lad will be unconscious for several days and will need plenty to eat if he is to recover." She set the bowl on the table. "Just spoon it slowly into his mouth."

Hadie went to the table and exchanged the water cup with the bowl. She blew on each spoonful to cool it, then slowly poured the liquid into Javen's mouth. He swallowed. While Hadie fed Javen, Rennie washed out the inside of the water basin and removed the soiled clothing and sheets from the room. By the time the carriage lurched into motion, Hadie had successfully transferred the entire contents of the bowl into Javen's stomach.

With the caravan once again underway and Javen lying

motionless on the bed, Hadie was faced with nothing else to do until they stopped at the end of the day. She kissed Javen on the forehead and went to the other room. She plopped down on the couch and picked up the book from where she had dropped it when Drenan barged into the carriage. However, no matter how hard she tried, she couldn't concentrate on what she read because the words Drenan had spoken echoed incessantly in her mind.

"Your time with the boy is done when we arrive in Portstown."

CHAPTER 37

Yolken let the kettle fires go out when he saw Jax running toward the shed. He kept his hand on the Harachin sword and watched Jax—shirtless and bloody—draw near. "What in Draego's Fire happened to you?" he said when Jax stopped in front of him and doubled over, breathing heavily.

Jax looked up at Yolken and gasped, "We need to go!"

"What do you mean? I'm just getting started on the brewing."

"They found us!" His voice was loud and urgent.

Yolken stood frozen with fear as Jax dashed toward the cabin. *They found us?* When Jax disappeared around the corner, Yolken ran after him.

Jax was digging through the chest at the end of his bed when Yolken arrived in the cabin. Jax pulled out a shirt and pulled it over his head.

"Get your things," Jax said when his head popped out the top.

When Jax reached into his chest again Yolken hurried over to his own. By the time Yolken retrieved his cloak and satchel Jax had his coat on, satchel in place on his shoulder, and was tucking two bone daggers under his belt.

"What happened?" Yolken said.

"I can't hear! Lightning!" Jax said, pointing at his left ear. "Come on, fill your satchel."

They gathered dried food and bread. Jax grabbed two leather water flasks and said, "We need to go! Now!"

Jax dashed for the door and Yolken followed. But he suddenly became acutely aware of the Energy he'd been holding in his Core. Before following Jax outside he bent down and discharged the Energy into the wood flooring, leaving a blackened spot in the shape of his hand where he touched the wood.

Outside, Jax was crouched on the porch with his hand on one of the black daggers. He hopped onto the ground when he saw Yolken and headed for the creek. He stepped in and started jogging down the middle of it.

Yolken followed, jogging awkwardly over the rocky creek bed. He kept his left hand on the hilt of the sword to keep it from banging against his leg. He was tempted to draw Energy from it to have ready in case they were attacked, but then he thought about what Jax had said about discharging unused Energy.

His boots quickly soaked through, and his pants got wet up to the middle of his thighs. The creek was relatively shallow, rarely coming up over the tops of his boots—which came up to mid-calf—but the splashing from his boots sent water cascading up around him. Occasionally the splashes reached up to his shirt, which was still drying from hauling buckets of water. It wouldn't be long before he was completely soaked and, not having brought any spare clothes with him, he was already ruing the approaching evening chill.

The terrain blurred by. Slogging clumsily through the water, they weren't moving fast, but Yolken kept his eyes trained on the creek before him, keeping an eye out for objects that threatened to turn an ankle. Occasionally he looked up to ensure Jax was still ahead of him.

The creek twisted and turned. The trees thinned as they progressed, revealing Yolken's lengthening shadow in front of him. As his shadow lengthened, the creek grew deeper. Before long, the water was consistently above his knees—sometimes deeper—slowing their pace significantly. Instead of jogging, they now moved slowly, one wet, lumbering step at a time. The swift current kept throwing Yolken off balance. He stumbled more than once.

After sloshing down the creek for what felt like about an hour, Jax climbed out of the water onto the left bank and Yolken gladly followed. Jax filled the two leather flasks he had taken from the house and handed one of them to Yolken. He strung the flask over his right shoulder and seated it against his left side—opposite the satchel full of food. Then he followed Jax as Jax made his way up the fern-covered bank.

They picked their way through the woods, moving around thick foliage vying for the light penetrating through the trees. Compared to the noise they had made sloshing down the creek, they now moved in relative silence—the needle-covered forest floor muted their steps.

Jax moved away from the creek but kept it on their right. Yolken couldn't see the stream, but he heard it, so he knew Jax was still following it. As the sky grew darker, the sound of flowing water became louder.

They broke through some brush and Jax turned left. Yolken stopped abruptly at the edge of a small cliff. In what little light remained, he saw the creek plummeting off the rock face down to a large river flowing below. Yolken knew that the Mindon River began in the mountains sharing its name, but this was the first time he'd actually seen it.

The view was breathtaking. Yolken looked down at the wide, fast-moving water about thirty paces below. It looked ominous in the fading light; the top of the water appeared to be black as it flowed by. He could barely make out the trees on the opposite side—they mostly appeared to be tall silhouettes standing guard over the murky waters.

"Make a flame," Jax said, interrupting Yolken's transfixed gaze. "But keep it small! We don't want to give our position away.

Yolken placed his hand on the hilt of the Harachin sword and drew in a tiny thread of Energy. He held his right hand up and let the thread flow out the tip of his finger, focusing the Energy a pace in front of his face. A small flame ignited. Once the flame was burning brightly, he lowered his right hand but kept his left hand on the sword. The Energy continued to flow up his left arm, into his Core, and out of the center of his chest, just as it had when he worked in the shed.

Jax nodded, and they resumed their flight. As he walked close to the ledge with his own flame hovering in front of him, Yolken followed closely behind.

When he saw a dark shape ahead of him on the ground, Yolken raised his hand and held it out toward the object. The stream of Energy sustaining the small fire shifted from his chest back to his hand, which he used to direct the flame. It illuminated a jagged rock protruding from the ground, which he safely stepped over.

As they walked, Yolken looked up at the clear, starry sky visible over the river. The Great Dragon constellation stood directly over them. The trees obscured the stars of its head; however, its body and tail stretched across the sky to his right. The existence of the Great Dragon—and whether it truly was responsible for creating Dradonia and the stars—was always a subject of debate. Most of the town's residents attended the Dragon Shrine regularly. Some, such as Kristana and Issa, went every day. But he also had patrons who vehemently argued against the Great Dragon's existence and refused to accept the emperor and Regency as Blessed. He personally believed in Draego but hadn't been to the shrine in several seasons. He had no reason to doubt where Drakonias got his power. And now *he* had the power. If there had ever been a question in his mind on that matter, it was gone. He felt more connected with the Great Dragon than he ever had when he'd visited the shrine in Lonely Oak. It was said that Draego acted with purpose, and if Draego gave the gift to the Dragon King, Yolken wondered how *he* fit into that purpose.

Yolken stumbled on a root protruding from the ground. He stopped himself from falling and realized he needed to stay focused on the ground and not let his mind wander. He focused on Jax as he wove around countless bushes, thick trunks of tall pines, and boulders and rocky mounds.

Draego moved farther to the west, diving for the horizon. Their cliffside view of the moonlit river slowly faded as the floor of the forest gradually lowered down to the river. Eventually, Yolken lost sight of the dragon's tail as it descended behind the trees. He estimated it was about four hours until dawn.

Jax stopped ahead of Yolken and said, "We'll stop here for the night. I don't want to use up all our Energy in one night."

Jax turned away from the water and headed deeper into the woods until they found a suitable break in the foliage. Jax unslung the water flask from his shoulder and sat with his back against the trunk of a pine on the other side of the clearing.

"Try to get some sleep," Jax said. "I'll keep watch."

Yolken sat down on the bed of needles covering the ground, adjusting the sword's scabbard so it didn't interfere with the process, and began unlacing his boots.

"Keep your boots on," Jax said.

"But they're still damp."

"Use Synthesis to dry them."

"How do I do that?"

"Energy is heat, remember. Use it to your advantage," Jax said. He moved his flame down to his feet, and Yolken saw his boots were completely dry. "Just don't light them on fire."

Yolken thought about it for a moment then split the stream from his fire. He sent the new stream into his left boot. The heat enveloped the leather and began to warm his foot. He watched as steam rose into the air and the color of the leather lightened. After about two minutes, it was dry. He moved the stream into the right boot and repeated the process.

"Now, try to rest," Jax said.

Yolken unhooked the cloak and folded it up. He lay on his back and placed the cloak under his head. He cut off the stream of Energy and let the flame go out. Jax did the same thing, and darkness enveloped them.

The forest wasn't as dense in this small clearing so as Yolken waited for sleep to overcome his tired body, he looked up at the canvas of stars visible overhead. The moon was almost full and moved toward the western horizon with the dragon. During the full moon, it sat directly beneath the dragon's belly, but tonight it sat underneath the dragon's back legs. The light of the moon got him to thinking.

"Jax?"

"Hmm?"

"Where does the moon gets its light?"

"It's reflected from the sun."

"The sun? Then why can't we use it to Synthesize at night?"

"Because the amount reflected back at us is nowhere near enough to be useful. The same goes for the stars. They emit Energy just like the sun, but it's so faint it's practically nonexistent. Now, get some sleep."

Yolken closed his eyes. He tried to sense the Energy from the stars and the moon but couldn't feel anything. Sleep still didn't feel near, so he said, "Jax?"

"Yeah?"

"What happened back at the cabin?"

"When I was up on the ridge, I saw something on the southern side reflecting light. I thought it was the Regency and panicked. I was separated from you and didn't want to risk them getting to you first, so I decided to try and draw them out by filling myself with Energy."

"Did it work?"

"Too well. I wasn't prepared for such an aggressive response. Next thing I knew lightning came out of nowhere."

"I heard the thunder," Yolken said. "How'd you get down so fast? I heard you calling only a couple minutes later."

"I jumped."

Yolken sat up and looked at the dark figure sitting at the base of the tree across the clearing from him. "You jumped?"

"Yeah."

"*Off* the ridge?"

"Don't be so surprised," Jax said. "You can't imagine the abilities you'll eventually learn. Soon, you'll be able to do things you never thought possible. I'm only strong enough to control my descent and glide down, but I wouldn't be surprised if one day you're able to fly like a bird."

"Fly like a bird?" Yolken said, his voice elevated in pitch. "*You* think one day I'll be able to fly?"

"I do," Jax said. "Now, get some sleep."

Yolken lay back down on the cloak and stared up at the moon in wonder. He imagined himself soaring through the skies with the grandest of birds—the hawks and eagles and condors. When sleep finally came over him, he was still in complete disbelief.

CHAPTER 38

Crin followed the trail down to the floor of the ravine, cursing as he went. The boy was a new Synthesizer, he knew from the conditioning, but if he could already do something as complex as diving off the side of a mountain, he was far more dangerous than Crin had originally thought.

When the trail turned and began to follow a creek flowing toward the east, he began to move more cautiously—he didn't want to accidentally blunder into the boy unprepared. Whenever the trail turned a blind corner, he slowed and carefully made his way around. He stopped when a small, cleverly hidden cabin came into view. He ducked behind a thick bush to hide.

Out of sight of anyone who might be in the cabin, Crin waited. With his Glasses on, he watched the single window on the side of the cabin facing him to see if he could see anyone inside. A few rays of Energy broke through the canopy of trees overhead, making it to the ground. After several minutes with no sight of anyone—inside or outside—he slowly made his way around the bush toward the cabin. As he walked, he pulled his dagger from his belt and siphoned Energy from it.

Crin stepped up onto the porch, testing each step before placing his full weight on them, and went up to the door. He placed his ear on the smooth wood and listened. Not hearing anything, he snuck over to the window and looked in. The cabin appeared empty.

Holding the dagger firmly in his right hand and standing back from the door, Crin used Energy to turn the metal knob. He crouched slightly and yanked the door open. No one was in the kitchen area visible through the open door. He moved from the right side of the door to the left, searching the inside of the cabin. Then he listened. Nothing. Crin filled his Core, readying himself for an attack, then stuck his head in and quickly searched both sides of the front wall not visible from the outside. The cabin was empty.

Crin stepped through the door. A burn mark on the ground caught his attention. He knelt on a knee and traced the handprint with a finger. Feeling the effect of the unused Energy within himself, he placed his hand on the floor next to the burn mark and discharged the Energy he held. His own print barely scorched the wood. He stood back up and looked around the single-roomed cabin. Two open trunks at the end of beds told him that whoever was here had left hastily. He turned and walked out the door.

He stepped off the porch and followed the trail, which continued between the creek and the side of the cabin. He stopped at the back corner and peered around. There was a shed on the opposite side of a small clearing. He waited again, watching the shed. The doors were open, and he could see inside, but like the cabin, there appeared to be nobody in it. He refilled his Core, sidled around the corner of the cabin, and followed along the back wall, keeping an eye on the inside of the shed as he made his way to the other corner of the cabin. From there, he crossed the clearing to the nearest corner of the shed, which allowed him to approach it without exposing himself too much to anyone who might be inside. Repeating the same process as he used with the cabin, Crin determined that the shed was empty. He was too late—the boy was already gone.

A sense of both relief and foreboding filled Crin as he looked at the back of the cabin. Draego had spared him from an encounter with the boy, but even though the boy was gone, his problem wasn't. Energy brightly illuminated the far side of the creek, so he quickly crossed it and began replenishing the hilt of his dagger.

He was exposed as he stood in the open, but with his Glasses in place over his eyes he wasn't too worried about being caught off guard—it was the one remaining advantage he had over the boy. As he directed the Energy into the hilt of the dagger, he looked past the distortion in the pattern of Energy caused by his own Synthesizing for any sign someone might be preparing an attack.

While he worked, Crin considered his path forward. There weren't many routes the boy and whoever he was with could have taken from the cabin. He felt certain they hadn't fled in the direction he had just come, though it was possible they could have hidden in the thick undergrowth until Crin passed them by. In fact, they could be hiding anywhere, hoping he wouldn't find them. But if he had to guess, they hadn't stuck around. They were here to hide, and now that their sanctuary was no longer a secret, it wouldn't be safe to remain—even if they managed to stay hidden until Crin left.

Crin looked around for other possible escape routes. The northern ridge was exposed, and the southern ridge was steep enough that it would not be conducive to a rapid escape—and if the boy was desperate enough to jump off the side of the mountain, he didn't think they would choose the slowest route out. Which left only one other direction for him to go—down the creek.

When his dragon bone was full, Crin walked over to the creek. He stepped out into the middle of it and faced east—the direction it was flowing. Both sides were heavily vegetated. He searched both sides for a game trail to follow but didn't find one on either side. If that was indeed the direction the boy went, then he had gone down the creek itself. With no other option but returning to his father in shame, Crin began plodding down the middle of the water. The Dragon's Fortune had led him to the boy's almost-perfect hiding place in the ravine, so he had to trust it would lead him to the boy once more.

CHAPTER 39

Yolken woke to someone shaking his foot. He sat up slowly, his mind feeling groggy. After rubbing his eyes with the heels of his hands to help clear his thoughts, he saw Jax kneeling at his feet. He shivered in the chilly air and briskly rubbed is hands up and down his arms.

"Time to get moving," Jax said.

Yolken looked around at the small clearing, the memory of his surroundings and the previous day's flight slowly returning. He picked up the folded cloak from the ground and, as he unfolded it and put it on, he wished he had used it to stave off the chill instead. He took a drink from the water flask lying on the ground next to him and slung it over his shoulder. With the flask in place, he returned the satchel to its place on the opposite side of his body.

Jax immediately set off again, first returning to the bank of the Mindon, then turning to follow it north.

Yolken followed behind him. He felt the pangs of his night's fast, so he lifted the flap on the satchel and inspected its contents. He pulled out the half-eaten loaf of bread and ravenously ripped pieces off of it, shoveling them one by one into his mouth. "How are your wounds?" he asked after the bread was gone.

"Scratches mostly," Jax said.

"You were bleeding pretty badly in some places, if I recall."

"I tended to them while you were sleeping. There were a couple that were a little more troublesome, but nothing to concern yourself with. If I ever need any of that healing power of yours, I'll let you know."

Jax's mention of healing reminded Yolken that he still didn't know much about what he had done to Issa. He'd spent several hours lying on the rock outcropping thinking about it. He wanted desperately to remember what he had done, or how he did it. "You think I'll be able to repeat what I did?" he asked. "What if healing Issa was an accident?"

"Yes, I think healing people will be one of your stronger gifts," Jax said. "Nothing ever happens on accident."

Yolken reflected on this notion while he followed Jax. Jax didn't seem to be talkative as they made their way north. In fact, Yolken could hear him muttering to himself, but whatever he was saying was inaudible. Hoping to find out what was bothering Jax, he asked, "What now?"

"What do you mean?" Jax said over his shoulder.

"You said the plan was for us to remain at the cabin while I learned to Synthesize. But they found us, so I'm wondering what the plan is. Shouldn't we go back and reclaim it?"

"The whole point of the cabin was that it was supposed to be a safe place for you to learn. Now that the Regency knows about it, the cabin's existence is moot. We won't be returning."

"What then?"

"We make for Croff."

"What about my training?"

"Your training will continue, though we'll have to exercise more care to not attract attention. For now, though, it'll have to wait until we're certain we aren't being pursued. I don't want to risk a confrontation with whatever force might be back in the ravine. With any luck, they'll search the area, assume they lost us, and return to wherever they came from."

"So we're just going to run?"

"Yes," Jax said.

"But what if there are only a few of them? Couldn't we somehow outsmart them? Maybe the cabin doesn't have to be compromised."

"It's not worth the risk."

"I feel like we should do something. Maybe they know where my brother is," Yolken said. "I hate feeling like we're somehow at a disadvantage."

"We *are* at a disadvantage, Yolken—and have been for hundreds of years," Jax said, stopping and turning to face Yolken. "Besides, what would you have us do? I've only just taught you how to make fire. The only thing fighting with fire would accomplish would be to burn the forest down. We have to be smarter. And I'm certainly not interested in facing them alone." He turned and resumed walking. "Which brings up an important point," he continued over his shoulder. "It goes without saying that I'm a fan of your ale, and as much as I was looking forward to having some of it around, I had hoped by having you brew yesterday you would be compelled to Synthesize to aid in the process. I've been around your father enough to know how menial the task can be, and my hope was you'd recognize that and use your new-found gift to your advantage."

"What do you mean?" Yolken said. "I *was* using my gift."

"To do what?"

"I was using it to heat the water in the kettles."

"That's a start. What else could you have used it for?"

"I don't know."

"How did you get the water from the creek to the kettles?"

"I hauled it, two buckets at a time—which you could've helped with."

"That's exactly the point I'm trying to make," Jax continued. "You didn't need my help. You had all the help you needed."

Yolken walked behind Jax, thinking about what he was saying. They continued making their way north, always following the Mindon. The scenery didn't change from what it had been the previous night, but now Yolken could see the river's true enormity. The Little Mindon was minuscule in comparison to it—and yet the Little Mindon had been bigger than any of the creeks he'd ever come across in the mountains, including the creek running by the cabin.

He chuckled at the memory of an argument that had broken out in his tavern one night between locals about whether the Little Mindon was a river or a creek: "It's a river because it has a name!" "Naming a trickle of water doesn't automatically make it as a river." "Yeah? Then what does make a river a river?" "It depends on how big it is." "And how big does it need to be?" "Dunno, but bigger than the Little Mindon for sure!"

As the morning wore on, Yolken couldn't help but look over his shoulder to see if anyone was following them. He didn't expect to see anyone, and he doubted the Regency would simply quietly follow, but he couldn't resist the urge to look. "How will we know if we're being pursued?" Yolken finally asked.

"Unless we see them, we won't," Jax said. "But these woods should make it harder to track us."

"Should I recharge the sword?"

"Best wait for now. They've got Glasses."

The remainder of the day mirrored the morning. They followed the Mindon as it wound its way north, keeping far enough away from the water's edge to remain safely hidden under cover of the forest, and stopping when they needed to rest. Unlike the morning, though, they walked mostly in silence. Yolken could tell Jax's mood had soured again and he resumed muttering to himself, so Yolken followed along silently, looking over his shoulder often.

They walked through a valley much like the ravine the cabin had been in, only much grander in scale. Thanks to the river, Yolken had a picturesque view of the peaks to the east.

Occasionally, when the trees broke enough, the peaks to the west were also visible.

As the day wore on, Yolken alternated between eating food from his satchel and picking wild berries off bushes. He estimated that, if he ate sparingly, he had enough meat and cheese to last a few days. He didn't know if the same was true with Jax's own supply, so he made a mental note to bring it up with Jax once he was in a better mood.

As the sun dipped behind the obscured peaks to the west, they walked into a large meadow. They walked directly across it and passed dozens of grazing white-tailed deer. Some of the closer ones lifted their heads and looked at them as they passed by, then, seemingly unconcerned with their presence, lowered their heads and resumed their evening meals.

A rocky butte rose higher than the trees on the opposite side of the meadow. Jax pointed up at it and said over his shoulder, "We'll spend the night up there."

After reaching the other side of the meadow, they walked only a few more minutes through the trees before they arrived at the base of the butte. Yolken stopped and looked straight up at the steep rocky protrusion.

"It's sheer like this all the way around," Jax said.

"How are we supposed to get up there?"

"This way." Jax turned to his right.

He started walking along the base of the sheer rock toward the river. As the roaring water grew louder, Yolken began wondering where they were going. Peering past Jax, it looked as though the rock wall went all the way to the river.

At the river's edge, Jax turned and followed a path wedged between the wall of the butte and the river. It was only a couple paces wide and dropped sharply to the water. Amazingly, a few pine trees somehow clung to the small pathway. Their roots jutted out where the ground dropped off and hung out over the water. Jax and Yolken had to squeeze between the trunks and the rocky wall as they negotiated the trail.

Jax stopped when the path ended. "This is where we go up."

Yolken looked up. The top was at least six paces over their heads. There were roots sticking out of the rock like they did on the pathway, but they were high over their heads.

"Give me a boost," Jax said.

Yolken looked at him in question.

"If you help lift me, I can get a hold of one of those roots sticking out up there. Then I can pull myself the rest of the way up. This is the only spot around the entire butte that's low enough to climb. If we can't get up here, we'll have to find somewhere else to spend the night."

"All right," Yolken said. He looked up at the roots hanging out over their heads then cupped his hands together. He bent over slightly, holding them out to Jax.

Jax placed his left foot into Yolken's cupped hands and gripped Yolken's left shoulder with his hand. He pushed off the ground with his right foot, and Yolken simultaneously pushed up with his hands, heaving Jax up into the air. Jax reached up with both hands and grabbed onto a thick root sticking out of the side of the rocks.

Yolken watched from below as the wiry man—who was still a few paces from the top of the ledge—pulled himself up using the exposed roots. As he neared the top, he used his feet to step on the thicker roots. Before long, he disappeared over the top. Yolken waited below then saw Jax stick his head back out over the edge. "How am I supposed to get up?" he called.

"I guess I didn't think this through entirely," Jax said. "You'll figure something out, I'm sure." His head disappeared.

A gasp of indignation escaped Yolken's lips as he looked up at the rocky wall. If he was going to join Jax, he needed to be able to jump high enough to grab the first root protruding from the rocks, but they were too high. *Maybe if I have a running start,* he thought.

He backed several paces away from the wall, looked

hesitantly down at the river then up at the lowest protruding root. He took a deep breath, then ran toward the wall. Just before reaching it, he jumped. He reached up and tried to grab hold of the root. Instead, he crashed into the wall and fell back down to the ground.

"It's too high!" he shouted up at the wall. Yolken waited but got no response from Jax.

Yolken looked up at the wall of rock again. The roots were too high for a single person to reach alone. Then he realized something: The roots were too high for an ordinary person to reach alone. He wasn't ordinary, though—he had Draego's Gift. He thought about it for a moment, remembering Jax's warning about Synthesizing. But there was no other way for him to get up on the butte. And it seemed to him Jax knew this.

Jax had said he wanted Yolken to explore how to use his gift while brewing, so he thought about how he might use it to help him reach the roots. Then he remembered the conversation he'd had with Jax about how he had used Energy to boost his strength when they fled from Lonely Oak. *"With practice,"* Jax had said, *"you can direct the Energy to the specific part of your body you wish to be strengthened."* Using the natural strength of his legs, he would never be able to reach the roots. But what if he used Synthesis?

Yolken placed his left hand on the hilt of the Harachin sword. He drew a little Energy into his Core and, letting it sit there unused, he felt it begin to absorb into his body. He started feeling warm, but some of his fatigue from the day's walking also drained away. He drew a little more Energy from the sword and this time, as it slowly transferred from his Core to his body, he took control of it and directed it into his legs. The ache in his legs disappeared completely. He kept the flow going—from the sword to his Core, and from his Core to his legs—and tested the theory Jax had talked about. He squatted down, then jumped straight up. His feet lifted a full three times higher into the air than he'd ever jumped before. When his feet hit the ground, a smile washed over his face.

With determination, Yolken turned and walked away from the wall. He stopped about twice as far from the wall as his first attempt and turned to face the rock. He drew more Energy from the sword, creating a pool of it in his Core, then he ran toward the wall. As he ran, he directed Energy into the muscles of his legs. When he drew near the wall of rock, he jumped.

Soaring into the air, Yolken smacked into the rock at the top of the ledge, high above the roots he had been aiming for. He landed with his arms over the ledge and saw Jax sitting with his back against a pine a few feet away. Yolken scrambled to grasp onto something as the weight of his body pulled him down. He screamed out as he slid back over the edge, thinking for sure he was going to injure himself when he fell back down onto the path.

Then Jax reached down over the edge of the rock and grasped his outstretched arms tightly. With ease, Jax pulled Yolken up and onto the flat surface of the butte. Yolken collapsed onto his back, breathing heavily, and looked up at Jax in amazement.

"Well done," Jax said. "A little ungainly, but, nonetheless, well done." Jax turned and walked away from the edge of the rock.

Yolken pushed himself to a sitting position, then up onto his feet. Standing at the edge of the rock, he looked down at the path below in wonder at how high he had just jumped. He shifted his gaze to his left and looked at the river straight below. From the point where the butte bulged out and blocked the path, it dropped straight down to the water. Feeling a bit of dizziness come over him, he backed away from the ledge and turned to follow Jax, who was walking up the slope toward the top of the butte.

Yolken followed Jax up the relatively steep incline to the top. He reached a point where the grade flattened out and found himself on a large, mostly flat, rocky surface. The only tree on the top of the butte was the solitary pine whose roots Jax had used to climb with. The rest of the butte was bare rock. The center of the butte had another large rocky buildup, adding an additional dozen paces to the butte's overall height, but Yolken saw Jax walking around it to the far side. He continued to follow Jax, only catching up to him when he arrived at the southern edge. He stopped next to Jax and looked down at the meadow. "This is amazing!" he said. When Jax didn't respond, he added, "Did you have that planned?"

"What?"

"Leaving me down on the path with no way up."

"You have to learn how to Synthesize somehow."

"But I thought it was too dangerous to Synthesize right now?"

"Remember what I said about inward expressions of Energy?"

"Yeah."

"There you have it," Jax said. "Nobody would have been able to see you Synthesize because you did it internally." He sat near the ledge and crossed his legs.

Yolken sat next to Jax in the fading light. He watched the deer in the meadow slowly begin to leave, prancing off on their separate ways in search of a place to bed down for the night. "Are you going to sit here all night?" he asked.

"Only until the light's gone," Jax said. "Once it's dark, I doubt our pursuers—if there are any—would be foolish enough to use any sort of light to guide their way. We should be safe up here, but we'll keep watch just in case."

Yolken gathered his cloak around his body as the remaining light of the sun faded. The air was comfortable enough when he fell asleep last night, but he had been stiff with cold by the time Jax had jostled him awake. Tonight, he would definitely use the cloak for warmth rather than as a pillow. "I suppose a fire is out of the question," he said, already knowing the answer. "If I get cold, I could just hold a little Energy in my Core to warm me, right?"

"Yes," Jax said, without taking his eyes from the barely perceptible meadow below. "Just be sure not to give yourself access to Energy from a dragon bone while you sleep. You can't control what happens when you're sleeping, and Synthesizers have been known to burn themselves to death while they slept."

When the stars were visible in the west, Jax stood. "Come, likely we are the only ones left who have yet to find a place to bed down for the night."

Yolken pushed himself to his feet and followed Jax, visible only by the light of the full moon rising in the east, across the top of the bare butte.

There was a slight breeze blowing from the west, so Jax walked until he was on the downwind side of the rocky buildup. He sat down against the rock and said, "Since I haven't slept in two nights, you keep the first watch. If anyone were to find their way up here in the dark, it'd be exactly where we climbed up."

Yolken sat down next to Jax and wrapped the cloak around himself again. The rock shielded them from the breeze, but the air would grow chillier as the night progressed. Within minutes, Yolken heard Jax snoring next to him. *How long's a watch?* he thought, wondering when he should wake Jax. In the end, he decided the easiest thing to do would be to wake Jax when the moon was halfway through its journey across the sky. He looked up at the moon, which was almost directly under Draego's belly. Only the eastern half of the sky was visible from where they sat, so he decided to wake Jax when the moon disappeared behind the rocks they rested against.

He had a few hours to watch and, feeling the fatigue in his body from the day's journey, he knew he needed to keep himself occupied so he wouldn't fall asleep. Immediately he thought of his aunt. Despite what Jax, Kaylan, and Deborah kept telling him, he couldn't help but feel responsible for her death. He wished there had been a way both Issa *and* Selena could have survived. He wished they had told him all along. Why would they agree to keep it from them for all those years? The whole thing seemed like such a waste. *Why would our father not want us involved?* he wondered. In the end, he knew he couldn't change what happened. Instead, he thought about who Selena really was. He knew next to nothing about her life before she came to Lonely Oak, except that she had moved to Lonely Oak from Tieger. What she had done before she joined the Order, and how had Jax known she was such a good cook?

Yolken's thoughts drifted to his parents. He had grown up thinking Selena was his mother's sister, but now he knew they weren't actually related. Even so, Selena had known a lot about their mother and talked a lot about growing up with her. He wondered how much of it was true. As he continued thinking about them, he realized he knew almost nothing about his father before he'd met their mother—Selena usually talked about their lives together. His mother was from Tieger, and that was where their father had met her, but he didn't know anything before that.

The moon continued its slow arc across the sky. Next, he thought about Kaylan. Day after day of training in Synthesis, days of doing nothing except sitting on a rock, he'd spent a lot of time thinking about her. For as long as he could remember, Kaylan was there. He always enjoyed the nights they huddled around the hearth, shoulder to shoulder, listening to her uncle's stories. He didn't know what it was about her, but to him she was perfect. And as they grew older, he found it harder and harder to talk to her. He loved her but was afraid to tell her how he felt. He had convinced himself Kaylan would never settle for anyone such as himself and forced himself to move on before he had even tried. He chuckled at the thought of how much grief he could have saved himself over the years if he had just had the nerve to talk to her. And now that she knew he loved her and he knew she loved him, he worried what Javen would think. He could still hardly believe what Javen had told him while they'd unloaded the goods from Norin's.

The thought of his brother made Yolken worry. He fully intended to marry Kaylan, but he worried how Javen would respond. How deep were Javen's feelings for her? Did he love her, or was it just a passing fancy like all the other girls he chased around?

More importantly, he worried about where the Regency had taken Javen and whether or not he was all right. Were they hurting him? Could he Synthesize as well? How was he ever going to rescue him? They were at a disadvantage. The way Jax reacted made him realize just how weak the Order was. Could the Council even help? Yolken's worried thoughts jumped from place to place like a jackrabbit in an open field.

"Nothing is an accident," Jax had said. He had been talking about Synthesis, but maybe it applied to his brother, too. He didn't know how he was going to rescue Javen, but if him being captured by the Regency wasn't an accident, then he knew it was part of Draego's plan, whatever that was. And *when* he rescued Javen—he knew deep down he *would* somehow figure out how to do it—he didn't want his love for Kaylan to come between his love for his brother.

He only hoped the same was true for Javen.

CHAPTER 40

renan stared into the glass of wine he held with both hands. He sat next to Devin and across from Dorlan in the sitting room of Dorlan's carriage. Dorlan was discussing the upcoming plans for the Thornhill boy, but since they no longer involved him, he wasn't paying attention. He kept thinking about all the trouble Danavin had caused the Regency, and him personally. Even from the grave, Danavin continued to trouble them.

Therese.

It had taken much longer than Drakonias had hoped, but when the Sodality finally managed to kill Drakonias's brother, Drae, it brought to an end the rebellion that lingered after Draeko surrendered. Pockets of resistance still cropped up from time to time, but they were easily squelched—until Danavin appeared. *How was he still alive? I could have sworn he died alongside Drae.*

Cara.

The Sodality had hunted Danavin unsuccessfully for centuries. When they finally called Drenan back to the Black, he was thrilled to have the opportunity to personally rid the world of the man he so despised. But even when he had killed the last real threat to the Regency and taken his revenge on the man responsible for killing his wife and daughter, the man wouldn't go away. His get still lingered.

Drenan took a drink of wine. As the liquid cooled his throat, he stared at the white gloves concealing his scarred hands. He never had figured out how the rebels had infiltrated his palace, and he'd been lucky someone proficient in healing was present; else he'd be dead. He had personally interrogated every servant serving under his roof. Even under the threat of suffering the pain he had just experienced, no one admitted to knowing how the rebel had become his personal servant.

And now this business with his children. Since he could inflict no more pain on Danavin for what Danavin had done to him, he wanted nothing more than to make his children suffer. However, Dorlan seemed intent on preventing him. The idea of having control of Danavin's get brought him pleasure that no whore could match, but he'd just gotten started when Dorlan took him away. He'd had plans for the girl the boy was bedding—plans wherein the boy would see her suffer day after day.

Now his only hope rested in his bastard apprehending the elder of Danavin's get.

Drenan tried turning his attention away from the whole mess, but his thoughts eventually coalesced on the tavern where he had killed Danavin, where he'd thought he put to the grave his own enmity. While Dorlan continued to discuss his plans for Javen, his mind drifted back to the first moment when the tavern—like Danavin—had defied its fiery grave to trouble him.

* * *

The carriage slowed as it pulled into the small town. Their tedious process was slowed further each time a town or city interrupted the carriages' progress. Drenan hated traveling. It was such a waste of time. Ever since Drakonias had issued the edict that strictly limited the use of dragon bones, traveling between Hantlo and Kyinth had become painstakingly slow. At least the trip was bearable in their Energy-powered transports, but then—for reasons still unknown even to those who ran his empire—Drakonias had hurled them centuries into the past with one stroke of his pen. Drenan had somehow avoided making the tedious trip to the capital since he was last due for Regeneration, but it was time once again, so he had resigned himself to the lengthy trip.

Having made the trip hundreds of times over the centuries, he knew exactly where he was, but he pulled the curtain back to look out anyway. A smile grew on his face.

"So His Majesty does remember how to smile," a female voice said.

Drenan dropped the curtain and looked at the two naked women stretched out on the couch opposite him. The younger of the two—black-haired and petite with the dark, honey-colored skin of one from Onta—lay on her side against the back cushions of the couch and supported her head with her fist. With her other hand, she lightly stroked the pale skin of the brunette—and slightly older, more voluptuous—woman lying on her back next to her with the fingers of her other hand. They were his two favorites from Sonja's Brothel in Hantlo, on loan to accompany him on his journey. If he had to spend the better part of a season cooped up in this carriage while he traveled to Kyinth, he could think of no better company to spend it with than these two.

"Excuse me?" he said, indignant at the suggestion. It was true, though; his mood had soured once they'd left the south.

"It has been days since I saw you smile," Franna, the voluptuous one, said. She had goosebumps on her skin from Bree's fingers dancing up and down her torso. "Not even our company seems to bring a smile to your face anymore." She pouted and batted her eyelashes.

Drenan took his eyes off the two beautiful women and lifted the curtain again. He reached down with his left hand and felt the hilt of the sword strapped to his belt. It had been three years since he had visited this town, struck a definitive blow to the rebels, and gotten his revenge. Eagerly, he looked outside as the carriage rumbled through town.

His smile disappeared as his carriage passed the location where Danavin's tavern once stood. The burned structure was gone, and a new building stood in its place. It was only a matter of time, he supposed, before someone tore down the blackened frame and built something new, but it irked him nonetheless. Danavin was no longer a threat, but the presence of the building would only serve to remind him of Danavin every time duty called him north. He would have to see if he could convince Dalia to do something about it.

Not wanting to think about the tavern any longer, Drenan dropped the curtain and returned his attention to the naked women across the carriage from him. "See if you can't bring my smile back," he said.

The two women seductively rose to their feet and joined him on his side of the carriage. Bree unbuckled his belt and Danavin's sword fell to the ground. While Bree worked to undo his pants, Franna worked on his shirt.

* * *

Drenan's thoughts returned to the present. He was angry and fought back the urge to scream out his frustration. It wasn't his brother sitting next to him that invoked the feeling—the fact that the boy was being transferred out of his control and into Devin's wasn't Devin's fault. It was Dorlan. He insisted on continuing with their father's foolish plan. He took another drink of wine, emptying his glass of its contents, to help bury the desire to vent. Already on Dorlan's bad side, he didn't want to make it worse.

"How much farther until we arrive in Portstown?" Dorlan said.

"We should arrive by this evening," Devin said.

"Good," Dorlan said. "I'm ready to be rid of that fool boy. This trip to the capital has caused me to be away far too long, and I can't afford such inconsequential annoyances to distract me from the troubles within my realm any longer."

CHAPTER 41

Yolken carefully felt for a root with his right foot. When he found one that felt substantial enough to support his weight, he tested its strength. Satisfied it would hold, he stepped down on it. He repeated the process with his left foot and gradually lowered himself down the steep wall. When there were no more roots to step down on, he gripped a thick root tightly with his hands and, holding onto it, he let his feet slide down the rock until he was hanging in the air. He looked down at the ground below and, letting go of the root, dropped the remaining distance.

The morning had greeted Yolken more pleasantly than it had the day before, when Jax had had to shake him awake. His eyes opened on their own when the sky was just light enough that he could see details of the surrounding area. Jax was sitting cross-legged on the ledge overlooking the meadow, rather than next to Yolken, guarding the path up onto the butte. Yolken pushed himself to his feet, held his cloak tightly around his body to fend off the chill, and went over to sit next to Jax. The deer that had peppered the meadow the evening before had returned.

"Do you know how much planning went into building a cabin way up here in the mountains and supplying it for months of seclusion?" Jax said when Yolken sat next to him. Continuing as if he didn't expect a reply, he added bitterly, "All of it for naught."

"Is that why you were so cross yesterday?"

"You would be cross too, Yolken, if you'd expended as much time and effort into creating such a reclusive haven. I could've sworn nobody would ever come across that ravine, not even Draego himself."

"*You* came across it," Yolken said.

Jax looked at Yolken with a scowl. "It's your pity I seek, Yolken. Not your logic. How could the cabin sit unnoticed for years only to be discovered less than a month after you arrived?"

Yolken wanted to reply but realized Jax just wanted to vent a little.

Jax rose to his feet. "Come. We best be on our way." His stride was swift. Yolken scrambled to gather his things and follow.

"How long will it take us to reach Croff?" Yolken said when he caught up to Jax on the trail.

"We're getting an early start today," Jax said, his mood brightening. "So, if we press ourselves, we should be able to get to the Mindon Falls in a couple of days. After we descend from the mountain, it'll take another three or four days to reach Croff."

The mention of the Mindon Falls reminded Yolken of the painting hanging on the wall in his tavern. It had not occurred to him that at the end of the river they were following was one of the places he'd most wanted to visit.

Most people didn't have the luxury of traveling around the realm to take in all the majestic wonders of Dradonia, so most folks lived vicariously through the eyes and stories of someone else. Yolken had never imagined he would leave Lonely Oak. Other than Jax, the majority of the people he knew had never traveled more than a few leagues from home—and usually, that was to either Edis to the north or Matis to the south. So he always made every effort to peruse the wares that traveling merchants had to offer and listened to their tales when they stopped in his tavern. He remembered Selena shaking her head when he'd bought the painting—she called it a waste of money—but he had enjoyed it ever since. Anticipation welled within him at the thought of seeing the falls with his own eyes.

It took them only a few minutes to reach the southern end of the butte, at which point Jax turned and followed along its base to the west. They continued to follow the rocky protrusion as it slowly and jaggedly curved to the right. When they reached its northern end, they left the butte behind and continued into the forest. Yolken couldn't see the river to his right, but he heard its roar over the soothing rustling of the wind blowing through the tops of the trees.

As the sun arced overhead, occasionally breaking through the trees and warming their backs, they settled into a routine. Yolken followed slightly behind Jax as they steadily made their way through the woods. Most of the time they walked in silence, which irritated Yolken. There were so many things he wanted to know. However, since Jax was still sore over the debacle that had forced them to flee the cabin, he resolved to leave him alone as much as possible.

The feeling of a sword swinging at his hip was still new. As he walked along, he continuously felt its pull on his belt. The only thing he knew about it was that Jax said it was special and belonged to his father. The sword tugged at his curiosity just as it tugged at his belt. He didn't want to bother Jax but finally decided to break the silence. He gripped the hilt of the sword to hold it in place then increased his pace until he was walking next to Jax. With his hand still resting on the hilt, ignoring the beckoning of the Energy stored within, he said, "What's so special about this sword?"

"It was your father's."

"You already told me that."

"Did I tell you that it was stolen from him the night he was murdered?"

"No."

"Well, it was. And I risked my life to get it back."

"You risked your life for a sword? Why? I mean, I understand it's a dragon bone, but risking your life seems a bit excessive."

"The fact that this sword belonged to your father was reason enough for me to risk my life."

"I admit that it's nice to have something that was of value to my father, but I still don't understand how that was worth risking your life."

"Truth is, Yolken, there were a number of reasons for me to do what I did. But, first and foremost, I loved your father and mother very much. The night they died devastated me. It was the single hardest day of my life. I was dedicated to your father and what he stood for and would have done anything if I thought it might somehow avenge his death. Even if the sword hadn't been stolen, I probably would still have done what I did. I simply couldn't allow your mother and father's murderer to get away with it."

"So the person who killed my parents is dead?"

"Well, no. Although I was successful in returning your father's sword to you, I failed to avenge their deaths."

"But you know who did it?"

"More or less."

"What do you mean?"

"When dragon bones are confiscated, they're supposed to be turned in. However, I had a contact who happened to spot the sword after it was stolen from your father."

"Where was it?"

"The Regent of Hantlo was wearing it as if it belonged to him."

"Drenan?"

"You know your regents?"

Yolken nodded. "Selena made us learn them."

"Good," Jax said. "And yes, Drenan had it."

"So you think he killed my parents?"

"I don't know for sure, but yes, I do."

"What happened?"

"We're getting a little off topic. You said you wanted to know what was special about the sword, right?"

"I do," Yolken said, "but I also want to know more about what happened to my parents and how you got the sword back. I want to know everything."

"I promise to tell you the story, Yolken, but for now let's discuss the sword."

"All right."

"The Harachin sword is priceless not simply because it belonged to your father, or even to Drae. Though, I suppose, the fact that it was originally Drae's contributes indirectly to its specialness."

"What do you mean?"

"As Draeko and Drakonias both learned during the war, not all dragon bones are the same."

"How so?"

"Draw the sword," Jax said.

Yolken drew the blade from its sheath.

"Now, hold it up."

Yolken held the sword up before him. Jax held one of the daggers he had up next to it.

"What do you see?" Jax said.

They were both black, which Yolken still thought was odd every time he looked at them. They both had ribbons of color weaving through them. However, the ribbons in the dagger were a dull blue, and the ribbons in the sword were yellow. The ribbons shimmered when the sun reflected on them.

"They're different colored," Yolken said.

"Exactly."

"I noticed that before, I just didn't realize it was significant."

"The amount of Energy a particular bone can hold depends on the dragon from which it came. Since the dragons had different strengths in Synthesis, their color came to represent one's rank within Draeko and Drakonias's respective armies."

"How many colors were there?" Yolken said. Jax slipped the dagger back into his belt, so he re-sheathed the sword.

"The most common colors are gray and brown."

"Soldiers and guards wear gray," Yolken said. Every guard or soldier he'd ever seen accompanying one of the Blessed had worn that color. "I've never seen brown, though."

"You wouldn't. Gray was the color the soldiers in Drakonias's army wore, and brown was the color Draeko's soldiers wore. After the war ended, brown wasn't used again."

"Why not?"

"I don't really know."

"What happened to it all? There had to have been thousands of pieces of armor."

"Hundreds of thousands. It was most likely cached by the Regency," Jax said. "If I had to guess, it's probably in the same location where they store all the Machines and dragon bones."

"Which is where?"

"Unfortunately, we don't know," Jax said. "But that is a question of great interest to the Order. What other colors are you familiar with?"

"Well," Yolken said, thinking. "I've seen regents wearing green, blue, and violet. And," he said, pausing, "when I saw Dorlan in Lonely Oak, he was wearing orange armor."

"Anything else?"

"I've seen paintings of the emperor that merchants were selling. He's always wearing red in those." Then, excitedly, he added, "I've also seen paintings of him surrounded by guards wearing white!"

"That's the Dragon Guard," Jax said. "Anytime anyone sees the emperor, or he goes out in public, they will be there. Any others?"

"Yellow," Yolken said, remembering the color of the ribbons in the sword.

"Yellow was Draeko's color. His armor is on display in the palace in Kyinth."

"You've seen it?"

"I have," Jax said. "Once. It's rumored when the Dragon King sat upon his throne clad in his golden armor, he looked like the sun itself shone from him. Supposedly, it was the ultimate display of his supreme rule, ordained by Draego himself." Jax paused and drank from his water flask. After screwing the cap back on, he continued, "There's also black. Typically we think of black as mourning, but it's also for—"

"Judgment," Yolken said.

"You're familiar with black armor, then?"

"No. It was something Selena taught us."

"You're correct, though. When it pertains to the Regency, black armor is the color of judgment. It's worn by the Black Sodality."

"The assassins who murdered my parents…"

Jax nodded grimly. "They exist primarily to hunt down and kill members of the Order."

"Wait," Yolken said, putting the pieces together. "So Drenan is a member of the Black Sodality?"

"He had the sword. Does that mean he is a member of the Sodality and killed your parents? I don't know. But it makes the most sense."

"Hmm," Yolken said, looking down at his feet as they walked.

"That's all of them," Jax said. "During the war, Draeko's warlords wore green and violet, and Drakonias' warlords wore orange and blue."

"Were warlords always Drakes?"

"They were. That was essentially how the armies were organized. The soldiers on foot and those operating the

Machines were ordinary people, and those in charge were the Blessed. They planned the battles and ensured the Machines had a steady supply of charged bones.

"Today, a Drake's position is identified by the color of their armor, which we've already discussed," Jax said.

"So, how does all this relate to the specialness of the sword?" Yolken said.

"Except gray and brown, all of the dragons were extremely rare. So the majority of dragon bones still in circulation are from either gray or brown dragons."

"So this sword is made from the bones of a yellow dragon, and this dagger from a blue one?"

"Correct."

"So the sword is special because it is more rare?"

"Not exactly," Jax said. "It didn't take long for Draeko or Drakonias to realize that a dragon's strength in Synthesis varied, similar to our own abilities. The rarer the color, the more powerful the dragon was. This is important for us because the rarer the dragon bone, the larger its capacity to store Energy. If you'll remember, dragon bones were cut into various shapes and sizes. The amount of Energy a particular bone could hold was predicated on both its size and, more importantly, the color of the dragon from which it originated."

"So, if these bones were the same size, the sword would still hold more Energy because it came from a yellow dragon?"

"Exactly," Jax said. He pulled the dagger back out of his belt and handed it to Yolken. "You should be able to feel the difference between the dagger and the sword."

Yolken placed his hand on the hilt of the sword and said, "I do. The Energy push of the sword is much stronger."

"Of all the other rare colors, yellow dragon bones are the most powerful. There was something about the yellow dragons which set them apart from the rest. Draeko had sole possession of both the skin and bones of the yellow dragons," Jax said. "And using those bones, Draeko made a sword for each of his children who remained loyal to him."

"There's more of them?"

"Yes, eight more," Jax said. "For their size, they are the most powerful dragon bones in existence."

They stopped to rest at a creek. Yolken drank what remained in his water flask then dipped it into the frigid water to refill it. He took several swigs then filled it again. After replacing the cap, he felt his stomach growling, so he pulled a piece of dried meat out of his satchel. "What I have in here won't last until we get to Croff," he said. "We can't live solely on berries once my dried meat runs out."

"I have some line and hooks in my coat," Jax said. "If need be, we can fish at the river."

"We'll need to cook it. Won't a fire give away where we are?"

As he filled his own water flask, Jax said, "There is that risk, I suppose. Or we could come up with a quicker way to cook it."

Yolken grinned when he remembered he had the ability within him to do just that.

Jax crossed the small creek, and Yolken followed him. They settled back into their steady journey through the woods, and after a few minutes Yolken asked, "Where are the rest of the swords?"

"One of them is on display along with Draeko's armor in Kyinth. The rest are unaccounted for."

"So, this is the most powerful dragon bone?"

"There are larger bones with overall greater capacity, but of those that can be wielded by hand, yes. With one exception."

"What?"

"When Draeko made the swords for his children, he also made a weapon for himself—the Dragon Scepter."

"I've heard of that," Yolken said. "The emperor is always holding it in paintings."

"The scepter doesn't belong to Drakonias, though, just like that sword didn't belong to Drenan," Jax said. "It belonged to his father, whom he murdered."

Thinking about paintings of the scepter he'd seen, Yolken said, "It isn't black like these bones."

"It's gilded and quite heavy. Although I've never held it, I imagine it would require Synthesizing just to be able to comfortably move around with it."

"What did Draeko do with the rest of the bones from yellow dragons?" Yolken said.

"I don't know."

The conversation waned. Yolken continued walking beside Jax on a game trail they had recently joined. Their pace improved now that they had a clear path to follow rather than having to pick their way through the dense forest. The trail meandered as it went and, for the most part, didn't stray far from the river. Every once in a while, the path took a sharp turn to the left. When that happened, they left the trail, continuing into the woods and joining back up with the trail when it curved back.

As they traveled, Yolken thought about the conversation they'd just had about the sword and what it meant to have it in his possession. If his father had possessed such a powerful weapon, then his place within the Order must have been truly significant. Which made him think about something. "Jax?"

"Yeah?"

"If this sword is so valuable, how is it that *I* have it? I'm not even a member of the Order."

"You're right. And the majority of the Council will disapprove of your possessing it. They would rather hide it away and safeguard it to ensure it doesn't fall into the Regency's hands again. However, there are also those on the Council who know the sword rightfully belongs to you."

"Will they try to take it from me?"

"I don't think they'd be that bold," Jax said. "They know they wouldn't have the sword were it not for me, so, I have a certain amount of leverage in deciding what happens to it. I made the Council agree to my terms before I went after it. I would, however, expect some of them to come down hard on you when we present ourselves before them. Try not to let it bother you, though. No matter what they might say, or how much they might try to belittle you, that sword belongs to you. Don't ever let anyone convince you otherwise."

Yolken's mind turned from the sword swinging at his hip to another subject which had come up the morning after they fled from the cabin. "Why is it that the Order is at such a disadvantage? Aren't we all descended from Draeko?"

"We are," Jax said. "For starters, the Regency has dragon armor and we don't. They also control virtually every dragon bone. However, the most important reason is because the bloodline of the regents is much purer than that of anyone in the Order."

"Which means they are all stronger with Synthesis," Yolken said.

"Yes. Remember, after the war Drakonias executed his father and eventually rounded up those siblings who fought against him, including most of their children and grandchildren. Those of us in the Order today are the descendants of those who managed to hide and survive. Our bloodlines are many generations removed from Draeko. On the other hand, the leaders in the Regency are primarily Draeko's children and grandchildren. This is why the Order operates the way it does."

"What do you mean?"

"The Order doesn't involve itself in open confrontations with the Regency, because we know we would lose. They are stronger and better equipped, and they far outnumber us. Instead, we work underground and behind the scenes in an attempt to undermine them."

"Then what hope does the Order ever have in succeeding?"

"There is always hope, Yolken. If we didn't think we could one day defeat them, we would have given up a long time ago. The answer to your question, though, is what we have been striving toward for centuries. We haven't found the answer yet, which is why we're having this conversation. But we continue to hope that eventually we'll find that answer and be able to place the rightful heir on the Dragon Throne. Until then, we continue to work in other ways which are more effective than open confrontations and accept small victories when they come—such as regaining possession of your father's sword."

The risks Jax had taken to recover the sword were starting to make more sense to Yolken now, even though he still didn't know what those risks were. As he mulled over the latest insights, he looked over at the man walking next to him. His light brown hair was cropped at his shoulders and he wore it tied back in a small tail. He also had a short beard matching the hair on his head, except that his chin had gone mostly gray. His cheeks and forehead were smooth, with a nice coppery complexion. If he had to guess, he would say Jax looked to be in his early fifties.

"Jax?"

"Yes?"

"According to the history of the Regency," Yolken said, thinking back over the lessons he and Javen endured from Selena, "Drakonias is about fifteen hundred years old, right?"

"One thousand six hundred, to be precise."

"And many of the regents and chancellors are just as old?"

"Yes. The chancellors of the north and west are his—"

"Brothers."

"Right. His younger brother Reago is Chancellor of the Western Realm, and Sheal of the north. Reago is close in age to Drakonias, but Sheal is quite a bit younger, though even he is still quite old," Jax said. "What about the Chancellor of the Southern Realm?"

"Dorlan. He's his son."

"Correct. As are many of the regents."

"I already knew all of that," Yolken said.

"Then why did you bring it up?"

"Because I want to know how it works. How do they live so

long?"

"When the Great Dragon blessed Draeko with the gift of Synthesis, it came with knowledge of how to reverse the effects of time on our bodies. It's known as Regeneration."

"So you still age?"

"Yes," Jax said.

Yolken looked pensively over at Jax, studying his features. "Jax?"

"Yes, Yolken?"

"How old are *you*?"

"Ah. We've finally arrived at your *true* question." Jax gave a quick look over at Yolken, rubbed a hand through his beard, and said, "How old do you think I am?"

"I don't know," Yolken said, looking over at Jax again. "Fifty?"

"Hah!" Jax exclaimed. "I'm one hundred and seventeen years old."

Impossible! Jax did *not* look like he was over a hundred years old.

"What about Missus Browning?"

"Three hundred and fifty-six."

Yolken gasped.

"She grew up when Machines were still in wide circulation. You'll have to ask her about them when we see her next. Your aunt was ninety-eight."

"I'm only twenty-five and can't begin to imagine what it must be like to be that old. And my father?"

"He was a little older than me. We keep busy, so it hasn't really seemed like that long."

"So, you know how to do it? Regeneration?"

"No. Besides, it takes a great deal of Energy, and my blood is nowhere near pure enough."

"But someone in the Order must."

"Did."

Yolken looked over at Jax. "My father."

Jax nodded.

"That was the leverage he had, wasn't it?"

"And now that he is gone, the Order is growing old while the Regency is not."

Yolken thought about all Selena's lessons he'd endured growing up, and how he already demonstrated he could heal the body with Issa. "Could I do it?"

"If you're strong enough, it's possible."

"How do I know if I'm strong enough?"

"There are ways of measuring one's strength," Jax said.

"Like what?"

"We test you."

"How?"

"Sorry, Yolken, but I'm not at liberty to say," Jax said. "It's a moot point anyways because your father was the only one in the Order who knew how to do it."

The conversation lagged again, and for a time they walked in silence. Jax eventually looked over his shoulder and said, "I need to teach you how to protect yourself from fire in case someone is following us. As I said, it's one of their favorite ways of fighting."

"All right," Yolken said. He immediately felt excited about the prospect of learning something new.

"What do you know about weather patterns?"

The question caught Yolken off guard. "Not much," he said, wondering what the weather had to do with protecting himself from fire.

"Weather patterns are all the result of the movement of air. If you master how to manipulate the flow of air around you, you'll be able to protect yourself. It's also essentially the same technique that will enable you to fly."

Yolken was exhilarated at the idea of flying. "All right. Tell me how it works."

"It's practically impossible to stop the fire altogether, but you can control where it goes if you control the air around you. When I jumped off the side of the ravine, I simply moved the air and made it do what I wanted it to do.

"The air around us is often experienced as a gentle breeze or sometimes as a stiff wind, but it can also manifest itself as a destructive force. A force which, using Synthesis, we can control," Jax said.

"So," Yolken said, trying to visualize what Jax was talking about, "if I wanted to control the force of the air, I do what?"

"Synthesis is about manipulating the elements around us. We burn oxygen when we make fire. You manipulated Issa's bones when you healed her. You knew what needed to be done and then reached out with Energy and took control of the elements in her body. The same is true if you want to control the air around you." Jax looked behind them again.

Yolken followed his gaze. They had recently crested a small rise and were now walking down the opposite side. Jax stopped and turned toward him.

"Draw a little Energy in," Jax said, "and then reach out with it, similar to when you want to make fire. But instead of concentrating it in a point, use it to feel the air."

"Won't I endanger us?"

Jax looked back toward the slowly rising terrain behind them then said, "Life is not without risk, Yolken. Every time we Synthesize, we put ourselves at risk. However, properly assessed, it can be mitigated. The Order has not existed for so long by never Synthesizing, but by doing so with shrewd wisdom. We're on the downward slope of a rise, so if you don't reach out far with Energy, we should remain unnoticed. If someone is following us, they won't be able to see us Synthesize unless they're right behind us."

"All right," Yolken said, feeling a little more secure.

He drew a small amount of Energy from the sword and reached out with it. He probed around for a minute then said, "I don't feel anything."

"Just because you can't see the air around you doesn't mean

it's not there. Just as your body is composed of elements, so is the air," Jax said. "Close your eyes."

Yolken obeyed.

"What are the different forms in which elements occur?" Jax said.

"Solid, liquid, and gas," Yolken replied, again recalling his lessons with Selena.

"The rocks, trees, and ground are visible to you because their elements are solid. If you tried to feel the ground with Energy, you would undoubtedly succeed because your eyes confirm for you that it is there. The air, however, isn't visible because it is in the form of gas. However, as I said, that doesn't mean it's not there. You know it is every time you draw in a breath, or the wind blows across your skin. If you feel around trying to touch it as if it were a solid or liquid, though, you'll grope blindly. Instead, know that the air around you is as real as the ground upon which you stand, even if you can't see it."

Yolken thought about this concept and, making the connection from his studies so long ago, he reached out again with Energy, understanding that the air physically surrounded him, that it was as real as the ground. This time he felt it. It surrounded him. He felt it touching his skin. He felt it going in and out of him as he breathed. "I feel it."

"Good," Jax said. "Now, reach out around you, take hold of it, and gather it in around you."

Yolken extended his reach, feeling the air all around. He grabbed hold of it and pulled it toward himself. He felt an odd sensation. "What's happening?"

"The pressure around you is building," Jax said. "The great cyclones that have cut the Eastern Realm off from the rest of Dradonia are giant swirling storms. To protect yourself, all you have to do is make the air around you swirl like those storms."

Now that Yolken could control the air, making it move where he wanted it to was relatively easy. Instead of feeling the building pressure, the air started moving around him in a circle. The more he pushed, the faster it moved. His cloak wrapped around his body as the air pulled on it. Jax's coat flew out perpendicular to his body.

"In the center of these storms is an area of great calm. Keep the air swirling around you but create an area of calm by pushing the air away from you."

Yolken followed Jax's instructions, and the wind stopped whipping around him. His cloak unwound itself from his body and hung limply while Jax's coat continued to whip furiously.

"Push it out farther," Jax said.

Yolken pushed until the area of calm included Jax.

"This is how you protect yourself from them," Jax said. "It's not a perfect solution, however. If they throw fire at you, the fire will follow the cyclone you are creating, but it will do nothing about the heat. This technique will keep you from burning up, but you must flee lest the heat kills you. Understand?"

Yolken nodded.

"Good. Let's go."

Yolken let go of the Harachin sword, and the swirling air around them slowly returned to normal.

After a few minutes of walking, Jax said, "It was similar manipulations of air that permitted me to jump from the side of the ravine to the valley floor. When I was attacked, I was twice as high as your training spot. With your safety compromised, I needed to get off the mountain as quickly as possible. So I jumped from the cliffs and used the latent force of the air to both slow my descent and maneuver myself to a safe spot to land. I used the pressure you felt when you gathered the air around yourself to control my fall."

As they continued on under the afternoon sun, Jax shared with him the techniques he had learned to help control the air and how he used it to glide to the clearing.

"It's quite exhilarating," Jax said, "the feeling of falling freely through the air and then moving around as if you were born to defy the ground. Now, on the lee side of rises, I want you to practice the things we've discussed. You never know when you might need to use them."

CHAPTER 42

The next morning, as they continued to follow the Mindon's northward journey, Yolken alternated between manipulating the air and recharging the Harachin sword. After their midday meal, Jax finally decided to tell the story of how he had reclaimed the sword from Drenan.

"But don't let it distract you from practicing," Jax said.

"I won't," Yolken said. His heart started to race in anticipation of hearing the story. He and Javen used to love it when Kaylan's uncle Jorgan was visiting her and Deborah. His fondest memories were of sitting around the tavern hearth while Jorgan spun his elaborate tales of adventure. It had been years since Yolken had heard Jorgan, now Jax, tell a story.

"Remember when I told you that the Order works secretly, in the shadows, to undermine the Regency?"

Yolken nodded.

"Part of what I meant by that is that the Order has been successful in infiltrating the Regency to gather valuable information. And no other member of the Order was more successful at it than me. I'd spent years establishing my network, carefully placing spies within the Regency to gather information for me. And of everyone in my network, no one was more important to me—or to the Order, though at the time, even they didn't know about him—than Dorlan's personal servant."

"Dorlan's servant is a spy for you?"

Jax looked almost smug. "He is. I worked long and hard, and spent a lot of money, to ease my long-time friend Sethlan into the position—though, using the term 'friend' to describe our relationship is a bit of an exaggeration. Even though I'd come to think of Sethlan as a friend, it was all really just about the money.

"Your father's death was deeply tragic to the Order in more ways than one. Not only was he powerful in Synthesis and knew the secret of Regeneration, he also possessed the Harachin sword. Three years after your parents died, long after the Order had resigned ourselves to these losses, I learned who had your father's sword and I knew I had to get it back."

* * *

I was on assignment in Tieger at the time. The details of it were actually quite boring, but while I was there, I got wind that the chancellors of the north, west, and south had all been summoned to Kyinth for a meeting with the emperor. The Council would have been livid if they knew I'd left Tieger for my own meeting at a grimy pub in Kyinth. *Livid.* But corresponding with the servant of such a high-profile individual as Dorlan was painfully slow and tedious, so I simply couldn't pass up the opportunity to meet face to face with Sethlan.

I puffed on some of the finest tobacco found in Kyinth while I waited. I took a deep puff, making the tobacco flare, when I saw a familiar face duck into the smoky pub. The man proceeded straight to the table where I sat in the back corner and sat across from me. Sethlan wore a tailored brown suit instead of his servant's garb. I waved at the barkeep, and the gruff man came and sloshed a mug of ale down before Sethlan.

"What news do you have?" I said. With the din in that particular pub, I never worried about being overheard; besides, ninety-nine out of a hundred conversations in the pub were gossip of some sort or backhanded political maneuverings.

"I believe I have something that might be of interest," Sethlan said, drinking healthily from his mug.

"Such as?"

Sethlan didn't respond. Instead, he took another drink.

Having long worked with Sethlan, I reached into my coat, pulled out a bag filled with gold drakes, and set it on the table.

Sethlan quickly scooped it up.

"New suit?" I said.

"Do you like it?"

"Other than the fine clothes you always seem to turn up in, what do you do with all that gold, anyway?" I said. "I'm guessing in your current position you don't get much personal time."

"I can't very well rendezvous with you wearing servant's clothes, can I?"

"True."

"Let's just say that you're making me very rich."

"Fair enough. The news?"

"I thought you'd be interested in knowing that a certain regent in the south has a particularly extravagant new addition to his accoutrements." He took another healthy swig of his ale.

I puffed on my pipe then said, "Such as?"

Sethlan sat across the table from me and drank his ale with a smug look on his face.

"Do you know how many drakes are in that bag I just gave you?"

"Worry not about the price you pay. I'm confident you'll leave here today fully satisfied with our transaction."

I considered the man sitting across from me, downing his ale and dressed in a suit finer than anything I owned. Then I reached into my coat again and pulled out another bag containing about a third of the gold as I'd just paid. As I placed it on the table, I said, "You mentioned a particular regent's attire?"

"It has been inordinately difficult to extract information from the Synod about who's currently serving as Overseers in the Sodality. However, following the death of a certain individual, an item of interest to you began swinging on the Regent of Hantlo's hip."

Finally, after months of searching, I had the information I so desperately wanted.

Sethlan finished off his ale and rose to his feet.

"Thank you," I said.

Sethlan smiled, and before he walked away, he said, "Like I said, you're making me very rich."

* * *

"Getting to Kyinth without the Council finding out was the easy part," Jax said. "Those I was working with in Tieger knew the importance of my contact with Sethlan and were willing to cover for me."

"So you pay servants to betray their masters?" Yolken said.

"They are our eyes and ears within the Regency," Jax said. "Them, and whores."

"Whores?"

"For being the Blessed of the Dragon, regents and chancellors are surprisingly naïve and speak relatively freely amongst their help. Information we glean from servants comes in waves as new servants replace old ones. It takes time to gain their loyalty and not have to worry about walking into traps. Almost without exception, though, every servant can eventually be bought. We try to fill in some of the holes in our information by buying it from whores—though they are considerably more expensive to bribe. You'd be surprised what you can get a man—or woman—to talk about in bed."

"Where do you get the gold for all of this?"

"Many of the Council members are Suits, positioned within various trades that bring in more gold than we know what to do with. There's a reason the Council is located in Croff, you know. Its location makes it an epicenter of trade. A good portion of the gold they earn is used to maintain their façades, but they filter the rest underground, to the Order."

"What's the Synod?" Yolken said.

"The Synod is the secret court located in Kyinth who investigate the citizens of Dradonia. They are the ones who decide who to send the Sodality after. The emperor's sister Nera is the head of the Synod."

"So, she is the one responsible for giving the order to kill my parents."

"Technically, the Synod as a whole decided, but I don't actually know how many people are in the Synod."

"What about Overseers? What are those?"

"The Sodality is comprised of small units of soldiers led by an Overseer. Overseers are always Synthesizers.

"Now, back to my story. Keeping my trip to Kyinth from the Council was the easy part. The next part would be much harder: Convincing them to go along with my plan."

* * *

"It is uncommon for us to engage in missions of revenge," Enif, the Head Councilman, said.

"I am aware of this," I said, addressing the Council members.

"Then why are you seeking permission to engage in such a mission?" Enif said.

"Because I believe it's the right thing to do."

"We all know the risks of what we do. I don't see why Orwyn's loss, as tragic as it was, is subject to—"

"Because his life was worth more than all of yours combined!" I shouted at the nine individuals sitting behind the raised bench.

"Do not forget to whom it is you are speaking," Enif warned.

"If for no other reason," I began again, more coolly, "let it be an act of contrition. You, all of you, took advantage of Orwyn. You took advantage of him because of his strength, and you know it. You exploited his abilities and now you—*we*—owe it to him… to his memory."

"That is all the same," Enif said. "We do not engage in acts of revenge. That is not our purpose."

"If you aren't willing to avenge his death because it's the right thing to do, then you should agree because of the fact that the Order had never before been in possession of such a powerful weapon as that sword."

"And I suppose you know what has become of the sword?"

"I do," I said with a grin. "You know as well as I that we are at a point where every dragon bone is extremely valuable to our cause—especially one such as that sword. And, for whatever reason, the Overseer responsible for Orwyn's death didn't send the sword to Kyinth as he should have."

"What did he do with it if not send it north?"

"He kept it."

The Council discussed this information amongst themselves, leaving me to stand before them waiting. I knew I would get their approval. If they were willing to approve my request to return to Croff from Tieger, it meant they were amenable to whatever it was I had to say. I was confident that, since they were discussing what I said rather than outright denying me, they weren't going to—not even after they heard my plan.

"And what is it you're proposing?" Enif said.

I spent the next several minutes detailing what it was I intended to do. The Council listened silently, and by the looks on their faces, I knew they were not pleased. However, that didn't matter. I didn't need them to be pleased with the plan, just to approve it.

When I finished, they again conversed amongst themselves, then Enif called for a vote.

It passed five votes to four.

The next thing I knew, I was on my way to Hantlo. And the road to Hantlo went straight through a place I hadn't been in three years.

* * *

"Lonely Oak," Yolken finished for Jax.

"Yes."

"After my parents died you didn't go back to check on us?"

"I couldn't bring myself to. The very idea was too painful. As I made my way south from Croff, I considered going around Lonely Oak altogether, but I forced myself to stay on the road. I knew it would probably be at least another two years before I got another opportunity, so as much as I wanted to avoid it, I made myself go."

* * *

I stepped out of Deborah's bakery, having stopped there first, and admired the three-story building on the other side of the square. The front door swung open and a fat, balding man stepped out and wiped his brow with a grimy handkerchief. I recognized the proprietor of the Oak and waved.

The heavy-set man lifted a hand to shade his eyes from the late afternoon sun casting a red hue on everything. Then, squinting, he waved back and called out, "Greetings, Master Jorgan!"

I crossed the square and shook Brall's hand. "Greetings, Brall. How's business?"

"Couldn't be better. With the increasing travel north, I've had nary a problem filling up the additional rooms. Probably should've added more."

"It's a shame that whoever recommended you expand didn't negotiate a cut of your extra earnings," I said.

Brall chuckled and wiped his brow with his handkerchief.

"Well, I best be on my way," I said. "Take care, Brall."

"You too."

I followed the road around the oak tree and through town. I stopped outside the newly built tavern, hesitating. The sign hanging above the door had the shape of a coned flower on it, painted light green. I took a deep breath and pushed the door open.

My stomach growled as the aroma filled my nose. I closed

my eyes momentarily, as nostalgia washed over me.

I opened my eyes again and looked around. A small fire burned in the hearth and patrons occupied at least half the tables. No one stood behind the bar. It felt wrong to see the tavern rebuilt and operating without Orwyn there.

The kitchen door swung open, and a lanky boy with unkempt hair walked out with a plate of steaming food in both hands. You delivered the plates to a couple sitting at a table then, smiling, walked over to me and said, "Sit anywhere you like."

I wiped a tear from my eye and said, "Hello, Yolken. You've grown."

"Do I know you?"

"I doubt you'd remember me. But I knew your father."

"My father?"

"Could I talk you out of a mug of ale, please?"

You rubbed your hand through your hair then said, "Yeah, sure." You walked around the bar, drew a mug of ale from a barrel, then placed it on the bar in front of me. "Anything to eat?"

"I'll have whatever it is that smells so good."

"Yes, sir. Be right back."

I took a sip of the ale. It tasted surprisingly good. "Who made this?" I said just before you disappeared into the kitchen.

"I did."

"You did?"

"Yessir. Auntie taught me how to use my father's old equipment."

"Did she?"

"Yessir."

"Hmmm," I said. "It's really good."

You smiled.

"Would you let your aunt know I'm here?"

"Sure. What's your name?"

"Right. My name is Jorgan."

You nodded then walked into the kitchen.

I sat at the bar and took a large drink of the ale. Nostalgia swept over me again as the familiar taste filled my mouth. I had drunk half the mug before the kitchen door swung open again and Lael walked through it with a steaming plate of food.

"Ja…" Lael said, stopping herself short. Referring to me by my cover had never been easy for her, I knew. "Jorgan."

"Selena," I said, rising from my stool.

"Sit. Eat."

I obeyed. It had been decades since I had eaten anything she'd made. "You can't imagine how much I missed this," I said, holding up a piece of roast skewered on the fork.

"I miss cooking for you," Lael said.

I looked at Lael just long enough to make the eye contact awkward then shoveled the roast into my mouth.

Lael picked up my half-empty mug and refilled it at one of the barrels lining the wall behind the bar. When she set it down next to my plate, she asked, "Why has it taken you so long to come?"

"I just couldn't bring myself to do it."

"So why now?"

"I wanted to see my niece," I lied.

"She's growing fast," Lael said.

"Aye. Before you know it those nephews of yours will be clambering all over her." I ate a few more bites while Lael idly wiped the counter with a rag. I looked at her intently as she cleaned for a few minutes then said, "Can we have a private word, Selena?"

Lael looked up at me. "Come into the kitchen."

I set the fork down, picked up the mug, and followed Lael through the swinging door. "I'm going to be gone for a while."

"You've already been gone a while Jax," Lael said. "I haven't seen you since I was in Croff."

"I know. I'm sorry. But I'm on my way to Hantlo—"

"For what?"

"I'm going to get Orwyn's sword back."

"You found it?"

I nodded.

"What's it doing there?"

"Drenan has it."

"Drenan?"

"I'm certain he killed Orwyn," I said. "With everything that's happened between them, it makes sense that he was the one to do it. And I can't permit him to keep the sword as some sort of a trophy."

"I don't like this, Jax," Lael said. "He's dangerous."

"They're all dangerous."

"Him especially."

"I know."

"Does it have to be you?"

"The Council doesn't even want me to go."

"Then why are you?"

"Because I have to. It's the right thing to do."

Lael folded her arms across her chest and looked at me. "Just be careful, all right?"

"I will," I promised.

I knew Lael spoke the truth about Drenan. The regents were like lions; they were dangerous to anyone not trained to handle them. However, Drenan was like the lion that killed indiscriminately; the type of lion that would kill even within its own pride if it saw fit to do so. He was just like his father.

Unexpectedly, Lael stepped around the table and wrapped her arms around me. She buried her head into my chest. It was a feeling I had long missed. I looked down at the top of her head and returned the hug. Memories of the past flooded my mind.

* * *

"Wait," Yolken said. "Are you telling me you and—"

"Time to practice," Jax said.

"But..."

"You must take advantage of every opportunity you get."

Yolken could do nothing but oblige. While he practiced his mind swirled. Thinking back to his years growing up in Lonely Oak, he tried remembering every time Jax had visited, looking for clues to answer what he suspected. In truth, though, Jax's refusal to answer was answer enough. Jax wouldn't admit it, but he was almost certain Jax and Selena had loved each other.

When the terrain started to rise again, Jax resumed his story, "The hardest part of my plan was the waiting. Gaining the trust of Drenan's servants—more importantly, his Servant-Master— would take time. For two years I gave up everything and subjected myself to the humiliation of serving the one man I despised more than the emperor."

"I can't believe you did that for so long," Yolken said.

"I had to. I couldn't get the access to Drenan I needed unless I became his personal servant. And that took time. But I still remember clearly the night it happened."

* * *

I was reclining on my less-than-comfortable bed in the servants' quarters in the Regent of Hantlo's palace with my hands clasped behind my head, looking at the ceiling, when I heard a gentle knock on the door. I sat up, took the two steps it required to cross the tiny room, and opened the door. As I expected, it was Orivin, the palace's Servant-Master.

"Vigs is seriously ill and unable to attend to his duties," Orivin said. "On the morrow, you will take his place as His Majesty's servant. By the looks of him, I suspect this change will likely be… permanent."

I went back into my room and pulled a wooden box from under the bed, removed the lid, and took out a heavy bag of gold. I returned to the door and handed it to Orivin. The bag disappeared into Orivin's robe, and without another word, he turned and walked away.

* * *

"So Drenan's Servant-Master was willing to betray him for a bag of gold?" Yolken said.

"Sethlan doubted where Orivin's loyalties truly lay. Being the Servant-Master was the most esteemed position a servant could aspire to, so he would be careful not to do anything to put that at risk. But Sethlan slowly gained Orivin's trust and convinced him to position me as Drenan's servant."

"What happened to the servant you replaced?"

"Orivin didn't ever say, and I didn't ask."

They came across another creek flowing toward the Mindon. Yolken stopped to refill his water flask.

"You hungry?" Jax said.

"Yeah."

"Let's eat then. How about some fish?"

"That'd be great!" Yolken exclaimed.

Jax followed the creek down to where it met the Mindon and pulled fishing line and hooks out of his coat. They found some long sticks to affix the line to, then threw the lines into the fast waters of the river. It didn't take long for either of them to land a trout. They were bigger and more brilliant than anything Yolken had ever caught.

After they had them cleaned, Jax instructed Yolken to use the same process they'd used to dry their boots. Yolken's filet was cooked in less than a minute, and for the first time since fleeing the cabin, he ate a hot meal.

"Now," Jax said when they were on their way again, "where was I?"

* * *

I remember clearly the night I reclined in one of two matching velvet chairs. They were positioned before a large fireplace, and I wore the traditional southern servant's garb: tan silk pants with a matching shirt.

Despite the oppressive heat, a fire burned in the fireplace. I held a crystal glass containing some of the finest wine from the Onta province in my hand. After giving it a swirl and admiring how the wine clung to the sides of the crystal, I took a drink.

That night was the culmination of two years' worth of planning. So, after I finished setting the fire and prepping the wine, I decided that after suffering the humility of serving Drenan, I was going to enjoy my last evening in the palace.

Sitting in Drenan's plush chair and drinking his wine were both serious breaches of servant protocol. As I felt the richness of the velvet with my fingers and tasted the wine, I reveled in the thought that any other servant caught behaving in this manner would likely lose their life. It was forbidden for servants to use their masters' belongings. But unbeknownst to Drenan, I was no ordinary servant. And if things went according to plan tonight, it wouldn't be me who lost my life.

I took a drink of the red wine and closed my eyes. I held it in my mouth, swished it around a little—I preferred your father's ale, but I was no stranger to fine wine—then swallowed it.

With my eyes still closed, I took a deep breath and wished with all my being I didn't have to be there just then. No matter what I accomplished that night, I couldn't shake the fact that I was at least partially to blame for the events that had brought me to that moment.

Before I sat in the chair, I'd searched Drenan's large bedchamber hoping to find the sword. In the moment, I'd hoped to avoid the impending confrontation, but the sword wasn't there. I wasn't surprised, though. Drenan had the annoying habit of wearing the sword everywhere he went. For almost two years, as I maneuvered my way into becoming Drenan's personal servant, I'd watched him wear the sword at every opportunity. Each day I wanted to kill him a little more.

The evening grew late, and I knew the hour was drawing near when Drenan would retire to his chamber. I remember growing anxious and rising from the forbidden velvet chair and walking over to the large double doors that led out onto the balcony. I opened them and went out.

The view from the balcony was incredible. I'd heard that

during the day the Kvorgan Sea was visible on the far side of the city, but I didn't intend on being around when it got light enough to find out. Standing on the precipice that fell sharply to the hiding sea was the only building which exceeded Drenan's in grandeur: the Chancellor of the Southern Realm's palace. Now, in the dark, thousands and thousands of streetlamps illuminated the city below, blotting out all but the brightest of the stars in the sky.

I admired the view, then turned my attention to the palace wall. I reviewed the distance from the wall to the base of the palace in my head. I'd paced it off many times: it was two hundred paces from the palace to the wall. The balcony, according to my best estimates, was one hundred paces tall, and the wall was four paces. Clearing the wall was going to be difficult.

I nervously felt the fringe of my shirt. I had wanted to smuggle a dagger into the palace so I could kill Drenan in a more traditional manner, but I knew the palace guards would search me when I left the servants' quarters to begin my tasks in the regent's chamber. Attempting to get a blade in would have put my entire mission at risk. It would be more satisfying to end the life of a Blessed using Draego's Gift anyway. It always was.

I returned to the bedchamber and closed the door. I cleaned the crystal glass I'd been using—Drenan's glass—and returned it to the tray. Then I stood in the servant's spot—in the corner, out of sight—and waited.

The pieces couldn't have fallen into place on a more perfect day: It was an official court day at the palace, which meant the Silks of the Hantlo province would be gathered in the city and palace. There were also several displaced regents from the abandoned provinces and others from around the realm who had business with Drenan and would also be in attendance. If I succeeded tonight, not only would the Order once again be in possession of the Harachin sword, but I would embarrass the

Regency considerably. I truthfully didn't know which elated me more.

The door to the opulent bedchamber opened, and a tall man with light-brown hair walked into the room—the regent of the Hantlo province. Drenan. He was clad in the attire which would most convey his authority in court—his blue dragon armor. The Harachin sword swung at his hip, perfectly complementing his attire. He led a woman by the hand. Her light blue, low-cut dress clung tightly to her body and left little to the imagination. The amount of cleavage visible through the cut, which extended all the way down to her navel, left me a little taken aback. I had never grown accustomed to the cultural fashions of the south, and the west was even worse. I had to avert my eyes.

Drenan eyed me in the corner—Orivin had personally seen to Drenan's needs in the morning in order to inform him his servant had taken ill and had assured me he would be expecting me this evening. It was my first time serving in this position, but I'd had two years to learn the routine of Drenan's personal servant, and I knew it well. When Drenan brought women to his room to bed, the routine was always the same.

Drenan led the woman to the large tapestry depicting the capital of the empire and some of its outlying areas. I'd heard about this tapestry; it truly was stunning. Drenan removed his dragon-scaled gloves and began pointing out its various features. He started with the stunning mountains dominating the landscape at the top. He pointed out a few of the towns nestled at the base of the steep mountains then described how the Ronin River formed the boundary between the Northern Realm and the Western Realm.

While Drenan explained the tapestry to the woman, I poured wine into each of the crystal glasses then carried the tray over to where they stood. I approached as Drenan was talking about Reelog, the city just visible on the edge of the tapestry. He saw my approach and exchanged his gloves for the glasses. He offered one to the woman, and she gladly accepted it.

As I walked away, Drenan moved on to the thick walls protecting the city. Starting at the perimeter and moving in, he explained the purpose of many of the towering buildings rising behind the walls—including the four towers spaced evenly from the center of the city, which were the homes-away-from-home of the four chancellors. He ended with the epicenter of the city and the empire, the palace where the Emperor of the United Realms ruled and dwelled.

I carried the gloves on the tray over to the wooden stand where Drenan's armor hung. I set the tray down and hung the gloves on their designated pegs. I was amazed at how pliable and supple they were. It was nothing like the rigid, metal armor I'd read about in the few ancient tomes remaining from the Previous Era. After I had hung the gloves on the rack, I returned to my spot in the corner to wait as Drenan's routine continued to play out.

When he finished showing off the elaborate tapestry, Drenan led the woman out onto the balcony where, I'd been told, he praised the beauty of the view. When the women he took out there inevitably agreed, he would say he wasn't talking about the view of the city but the beauty standing next to him.

After about fifteen or twenty minutes, they came back inside, and Drenan led the woman to the velvet chairs next to the fireplace. I moved over to them and refilled their empty wineglasses. Seeing me approaching with a bottle in hand, the woman set her glass down on the gilded side table and began taking her raven-black hair out of its intricately woven bun. I looked up briefly at her as I dabbed the tip of the bottle with a small white towel to prevent any drips and was amazed at how long her hair was. I could hardly believe the number of pins piling up next to her glass.

I left the bottle on the table, returned to my corner, and waited patiently as the two of them conversed and became intoxicated on the finest of wines. When the bottle was empty,

Drenan gestured at me for another.

When the second bottle was empty and the woman drank the last of the wine from her glass, Drenan said, "Take off your dress."

The woman set her glass down on the table and stood up. She swayed as she stood in front of the regent. Drenan watched as she slipped the dress off her shoulders, revealing the portion of her breasts the dress hadn't concealed, and pushed the dress to the ground. Her beauty distracted me from why I was there, so I averted my eyes and stared across the room at the tapestry. Out of the corner of my eye, I saw her saunter over to the elegant four-poster bed, after which Drenan immediately rose to his feet. This was my cue to attend to the regent once again by helping him remove his armor.

The armor was designed such that it could be donned or removed by the individual wearing it, but Drenan believed the Blessed were above the menial task of dressing and undressing themselves. I started the process by unbuckling Drenan's belt. I was careful not to touch any part of the sword—doing so would incur the same wrath as being caught reclining in the velvet chairs or drinking the wine—and took it over to the wooden frame.

As I was strapping the belt to the frame, I considered touching the sword. The Energy stored in the dragon bones woven into the hems of my clothing would be enough to kill Drenan, but not enough to make my escape. I was relying on Drenan keeping the sword charged. At that moment, I decided I needed to risk touching it. If it wasn't charged, my escape was going to be much more challenging.

I chanced a quick glance over at Drenan; he was looking at the naked woman on his bed. I seized the opportunity and brushed my forearm on the hilt of the sword as I finished strapping the buckles of the belt. A torrential amount of Energy beckoned to me in the brief moment my skin contacted the sword. I hid the relief that overwhelmed me, preventing it from translating into any form of outward reaction, and returned to where Drenan stood.

Next was the breast-piece, which consisted of two parts: the larger front piece, which covered the shoulders, chest, stomach, sides, and arms, and the smaller back piece. The two pieces attached on the sides and shoulders with a series of buckles. I unbuckled the straps on the left side. The back piece remained attached only on the right side, and Drenan held his arms out before himself. I slid the breast-piece off Drenan's torso and arms, revealing his muscled frame. I took the armor over to the frame then returned to finish my task.

Now clad in only leggings, Drenan stood half-naked. If I proceeded and removed the leggings, Drenan would go to the woman waiting for him on his bed, and my job would be finished for the night. I would then retire to the servant quarters. But that wasn't my plan.

Drenan stood with his arms at his sides waiting. He was looking over at the woman and didn't see me staring at him. I grabbed the small bone hidden by the frays on the hem of my shirt and drew from the tiny bones woven throughout the hem as much Energy as I could hold. Sweat formed on my brow as the Energy pooled within me. Then, after a moment's hesitation, I broke protocol and spoke.

"Danavin…"

Drenan turned his head and looked down at me. His brow furrowed as he said, "Excuse me?"

"…was my friend," I continued as calmly as I could, staring into Drenan's brilliant blue eyes. "And I am come to avenge his death."

I waited just long enough for Drenan to process what I said. When his narrowed eyes widened in realization, I held up my right hand, keeping hold of the tiny bone with my left, and let loose a torrent of fire.

Drenan screamed in pain and stumbled backward. His hands

went up to shield his face. He stumbled and fell onto his back, then stopped moving.

The smell of burned flesh hit my nose.

I turned to the woman on the bed. She was sitting up, covering her breasts with her arms, and staring at me in horror. "If you move or make a sound, you will be next," I said.

She did not move. She did not scream.

I moved quickly over to the armor, took the sword by its hilt, and pulled it from the scabbard. The torrent of Energy beat against me like a raging river suddenly dammed. Never before had I held your father's sword; I was truly shocked at how much Energy it held.

I looked over at Drenan again—he still wasn't moving—and considered hitting him with a fire magnitudes greater than what I could do with the minuscule amount of Energy I had stored in the bones hidden in my clothing, but when the woman's shock wore off she would inevitably scream, and I didn't want to have to kill her. So I pushed open the balcony doors and gave the woman one last glance. Then I turned to face the open doors.

Taking a deep breath to calm my nerves, I held the sword up and inspected it. The flickering light of the room illuminated the yellow ribbons woven into the black bone. I lowered it to my side and drew deeply from it. I gasped as Energy rushed into me quicker than I expected.

My Core strained. I closed my eyes and took another breath.

I'd never actually done what I knew I needed to do. I never really believed I could. Orwyn had taught me what I needed to know, but knowing how and actually having the nerve to try were two completely different things. But there was no other way of escape; the palace was crawling with regents.

I let my breath out, opened my eyes, and ran for the door.

As I ran, I reached out with Energy and gathered air around me—more than I'd ever gathered in all the times I'd practiced. The curtains hanging at the edges of the door pulled toward me; the wineglasses shattered on the ground; a velvet chair tipped over backward.

I compressed the air, building the pressure around me as much as I could. Just before I reached the edge of the balcony, I pushed Energy into my legs, adding to their strength, and leaped. My right foot landed on the granite railing and, bending my leg, I used the momentum and jumped.

I dove toward the wall, stretching my body out flat, while simultaneously adjusting the air pressure around me. I slowed my fall and accelerated forward. I continuously drew Energy from the sword and gathered more air as I glided toward the wall.

You are a Synthesizer, Jax. Your path is no longer what it once was.

Orwyn's words from so many years ago echoed in my mind; the confidence my one-time teacher and now friend had instilled in me returned and vanquished my self-doubt.

I glided over the wall with several paces to spare. With Drenan and his palace behind me, I concentrated the air pushing against my chest and lessened the air pushing on my waist and legs. My body pivoted upright, and I landed on my feet running.

Feet firmly on the ground, I released the air compressed around me, and focused the excess Energy now available in my Core into my legs. I ran through the streets of Hantlo faster than a galloping horse. I avoided the larger streets, which would be patrolled throughout the night, and kept to the smaller, forgotten ones. My escape from the city zigzagged back and forth, but it was safer than risking the busier streets. As I continued to run, the denseness of the city waned, and the buildings were spaced farther and farther apart. Brown granite structures gave way to decrepit wood, then the city was behind me.

I stayed off the busy highway leading north out of Hantlo and, instead, turned west toward the sea. Hantlo was built on craggy cliffs overlooking the Kvorgan Sea, so I didn't have to run far before I arrived at the cliffs. I turned north and followed them.

I counted my strides as I ran. I drew up short after reaching my predetermined and practiced number and walked until I came upon a crevice. There were many cracks in the cliff-side, few of them negotiable. But this one was one of the exceptions. I knew my body would be weary from the amount of Energy I'd expended, so I continued drawing from the sword as I carefully made my way down the steep and rocky crack.

At the bottom, I lit a flame large enough to illuminate the rocks and sea at my feet. I found a rock protruding from the water and stepped onto it. Then I found another, and another. I stepped from rock to rock, with one hand on the sword and the other on the sheer cliff wall. Two dozen paces down, an opening in the cliffside appeared in my light, and I stepped off a rock and into the opening. I flared my flame and illuminated the passageway I now stood in. I walked deeper into it and entered a large cave.

I inspected the hideaway I'd discovered in preparation for today, wanting to ensure it hadn't been disturbed in the last two years. Everything was as I'd left it. My coat lay folded on top of a small boulder, covered in a fine layer of dust. I lifted it carefully, revealing two black daggers laying underneath it in the shape of an X. I unfolded my coat and changed into my own clothes which I'd hidden within.

Satisfied that the cave hadn't been disturbed, I sat down next to several jugs of water and propped the sword on the wall of the cave. When I broke contact with it fatigue washed over me before I could even pick up one of the jugs. I pushed back against it with what little strength I had left, long enough to satisfy my thirst.

I remember setting the empty jug down and closing my eyes. I listened to the waves crashing on the rocks outside the cave, knowing a manhunt was under way. I thought of the night at the tavern, the night your mother and father died. I had struggled every single day with what happened that day and knew nothing

I did would ever fully vindicate their deaths—not even killing every single member of the Regency. The collective lives of the Blessed were not worth Orwyn's and Elen's. But I knew Orwyn would have wanted his sword in the hands of its rightful owner. And for that, I had been willing to risk my life and subjugate myself for two years to the humiliation of serving the man responsible for his death.

CHAPTER 43

"Wow," Yolken said.

"It might not have seemed like much to you at the time, but the day I gave you Orwyn's sword was an important day for me. Seeing the sword in your hands finally made it possible for me to forgive myself for what happened that day."

Yolken didn't know what else to say, so they just walked together silently. The light was starting to fade, so their pace slowed.

"My father taught you how to do that flying thing?" Yolken said after a while.

"He taught me many things," Jax said.

"And that was the first time you'd ever actually done it?"

"He'd been trying to get me to do it forever, but I could never bring myself to. It was one thing to practice the techniques such as you are, but it's an entirely different thing to actually make yourself jump when you know it could cost you your life."

They continued walking in what remained of the twilight, Yolken appreciating what Jax had done more with every step he took. Eventually, Jax called it a night, and they found a thicket by the river in which to sleep. Yolken wearily fell asleep, thinking about his parents and what might have happened between Jax and Selena.

The next morning, after he finished eating the fish they'd caught, he said, "Were the things Selena told us about our parents true?"

"What do you mean?" Jax said.

"We thought she was our mother's sister, and I now know they weren't actually related. She used to talk about them a lot, so I'm wondering if everything she told us about them was a lie as well."

"It's true that Selena wasn't related to your mother, but she did know her. In fact, it was Selena who introduced your mother to your father."

"Really?" Yolken said with a raised eyebrow.

"Really. Selena had a semi-permanent assignment in Tieger long before she came to Lonely Oak. It was her home before joining the Order, so her knowledge there was invaluable. One day while she was at the market, she met your mother and eventually introduced her to your father."

"So my mother is really from Tieger?"

"Born and raised."

"What about my father?"

"Nobody knows where your father was born. Does it matter?"

"It'd just be nice to know more about him, is all."

"I'll tell you everything you want to know."

"What about Selena?"

"What about her?"

"Did you love her?"

"Let's get moving," Jax said. Before leaving the water's edge, he bent down and filled his flask.

Yolken looked at Jax as he filled his flask. His hesitancy told him everything he needed to know. It was clear Jax didn't want to talk about it, so he decided to let it be.

His flask also needed filling, but right before dipping it into the river, he thought of something. Having spent the last couple of days manipulating the air, he wondered if he could do the same with water. He held the flask out and a stream of water spouted from the river and arced directly into his flask. His face lit up in surprise.

"Yolken," Jax said tersely.

"What? You told me I'd have to figure out most of what I'm going to learn on my own."

"Yes, but did you think about your surroundings?"

Yolken shook his head.

"This thicket may hide us from prying eyes, but it does nothing to inhibit a Watcher's ability to see you Synthesizing."

"Sorry."

"No, it's all right. I'm pleased to see you experimenting with your gift. Just think about your surroundings first next time."

Yolken nodded.

"Let's go," Jax said.

They made their way to the edge of the thicket and studied their surroundings for a couple of minutes before proceeding out. Jax instructed Yolken to practice when the terrain again became conducive to it.

Thinking, Yolken opened his water flask and upended the water onto the ground.

"Why'd you do that?" Jax asked.

"I wanted to try something."

"What?"

"The water flowing in the river is in its liquid state, right?"

"Yeah."

"Well, it also exists in two other states."

"True."

"I didn't think about it until just now, but the whole time I've been manipulating the air, there's been water in it."

"Yolken, you're right, but—"

"Let me try something."

Yolken altered the way he had been using Energy to manipulate the air and water. Instead of using the Energy to draw air or water toward him, he used it to feel the water in the river off to their right. He wanted to know what the elements of water felt like. When he had a grasp on it, he felt the air in the same fashion. He searched it until he felt the water in it. Then, he drew only those elements toward himself and concentrated them above the flask. A small stream of water started falling into the open mouth of the flask. As he continued to pull more and more of the water elements from the air around him, the stream grew in size. Before he knew it, the flask was once again full.

"There," he said.

Jax looked over at him.

"What?" Yolken said, confused by the look on Jax's face. "I thought you wanted me to experiment?"

"I do," Jax said. "I just hadn't thought of doing that before. Quite frankly, Yolken, I'm impressed."

Yolken smiled at the compliment.

Yolken continued to practice the air manipulation techniques throughout the day. He alternated between making a small cyclone around himself and increasing and decreasing the pressure on different parts of his body. He added to that his new method of refilling his flask whenever it became empty.

He looked over at Jax, wondering about the extent of his relationship with Selena. Were they ever together? And if so, what happened? Jax had visited their tavern often while Yolken and Javen were growing up, and the way Jax and Selena had interacted was always friendly, but he'd never once thought they loved each other. They certainly didn't act as though they did. And now Selena was dead. When he first found out she'd died, Yolken had felt… he felt sick. The woman who raised him—his aunt—was gone. If Jax loved her, her death must have been just as hard on him. Maybe that was why he didn't want to talk about her.

As they bedded down for the night again, Jax indicated that on the morrow they would reach the end of the mountain range and begin the steep descent to the valley below. From there, he said, it would be only a few more days until they reached Croff.

Excitement built in Yolken at the thought of embracing Kaylan. He hoped once they were reunited, they wouldn't have to be apart for such a duration again.

He was also excited about arriving at the Mindon Falls. He couldn't count the number of days he had descended the stairs in the tavern first thing in the morning and seen the painting hanging over his barrels of ale and wished he could travel to see them.

The next day, as they inched closer to the falls, Yolken continued to cautiously practice his new skills, always mindful of the terrain. He was becoming adept at the techniques Jax taught him, but he was limited in his practice because Jax limited the amount of Energy he could use to manipulate the air around him. "The farther away you reach, the more you increase your risk of detection. Keep the flows of Energy small and close," Jax kept reminding him. Doing so limited what he could do, though. If he was ever going to do something like Jax had done when he'd jumped off the side of the ravine or jumped out of Drenan's palace, he would need much more air.

* * *

Crin's pulse quickened when he walked around the thick trunk of a pine and saw two figures in the distance. He had been hunting the boy for the last several days without any sign of his passage, hoping he was making the right decisions with regards to the direction the boy might have fled. He quietly thanked Draego for once again bending fortune in his direction.

He'd pressed himself as much as he dared and watched diligently for signs of Synthesizing but had yet to see anything. Now that the boy was in sight, he watched the boy reach out all around himself with streams of Energy flowing close to the ground. The streams circled back toward the boy then swirled around him. The other person walking slightly ahead of him was definitely teaching him techniques established long ago to minimize one's exposure to someone such as himself—someone with Glasses.

Crin followed along cautiously, ducking behind trees or bushes while at the same time trying to close the distance between them. He was fortunate to once again have surprise on his side, so he needed to make his attack count. He knew that if he lost it, he would likely as not be the one who ended up dead. That was why he decided to begin his attack with the method of killing at which he was most adept—steel. If he could kill the boy quickly with his blade, the other would be easier to deal with; members of the Order were laughably weak in Synthesis.

* * *

When the sword ran out of Energy, Yolken recharged it. The first time it needed charging, Jax had explained that it was much safer to charge a dragon bone slowly by only drawing Energy from the sun when the rays were close to the ground. By doing so, a Synthesizer could minimize how much the sun's rays bent in their direction. The more the rays bent toward them, the easier it was for Watcher's to see them. This, however, made the process excruciatingly slow.

Yolken felt as proficient as he was going to get, causing boredom to set in. After walking for a few minutes, he looked over at Jax. A smile spread on his face. He reached out with air and made Jax's coat fly out behind him as though he were walking in a gale. The look on Jax's face indicated he was not amused, though. "I've got to practice somehow," Yolken rationalized.

"Practice on yourself," Jax said.

Yolken continued snickering to himself while he returned his efforts back to moving the air around himself. However, boredom overtook him again, so he directed his attention back to messing with Jax. Instead of making Jax's coat ripple in the wind, he flipped it up and over his head.

Jax scowled at Yolken and grabbed his coat off his head.

Yolken started laughing, but then Jax turned abruptly, and Yolken froze in place, mid-step, unable to move.

"Still think it's funny?" Jax said.

Yolken couldn't even move his jaw.

"Huh?" Jax said, cupping a hand to an ear. Then he started laughing. He turned and began walking away from Yolken, leaving him frozen where he was. Only when Jax had disappeared through the foliage did the air around him return to normal.

Humbled and feeling sheepish, Yolken jogged to catch up. "I'm sorry," he said when he once again walked alongside Jax. "I'm just getting—"

Something flew by Yolken's head and slammed into an aspen just ahead of him. His eyes barely had time to focus on the black object protruding from white bark when he felt immense heat behind him.

"Yolken!" Jax yelled. "Run!"

* * *

Crin crested a rise and saw two men ahead. He ducked down before he could be seen. The man facing toward him had a graying beard and the man facing away looked considerably younger. They were talking. At least, from his vantage, the older man was talking. The older man held a hand up to his ear, started laughing, then turned and walked away.

Crin seized his opportunity.

He drew the bone-hilted dagger from his belt and silently closed the distance between them. He drew Energy into his Core when he stepped out of the shadow of the trees and flipped the dagger in his hand, catching it by the blade, and got ready to throw it. He directed Energy into his arm as Danavin's son started jogging to catch up to the other man. Crin threw the dagger.

The razor-sharp blade flew at the back of Danavin's son at an unnatural speed. At the same time, he focused Energy a few paces ahead of him as he ran, preparing a ball of fire. He cursed when the dagger flew past the boy's head and slammed into a tree, knowing his own life was likely over. But instead of abandoning his attack in the interest of self-preservation, he poured all the Energy within him into the focal point ahead of him, causing it to explode in flame. Then he pushed, sending it hurling forward.

The flames swirled around the two men, igniting the undergrowth and surrounding trees. When the burst of flame passed and only the burning bushes and tree trunks remained, he was staring eye to eye with the boy.

* * *

Flames and their accompanying heat swirled past Yolken as he stared at the black object sticking out of the aspen. Bushes and trees ignited around him. Sweat broke out all over his body as his eyes shifted to the flames moving away like a river being divided in two. He looked back at the black object; it remained unchanged as the aspen burned and its bark blackened. He turned to find the fire's source and locked eyes with a man wearing plain gray clothes. They exchanged looks of fear, then an invisible force tugged at him from behind.

He turned back toward Jax and saw Jax waving for him to follow. Jax turned and ran, and Yolken followed. Jax's coat billowed out behind him as Yolken followed, gripping the hilt of the Harachin sword to keep it from tripping him. He quickly realized he was falling further behind even though he was running as fast as he could. He looked over his shoulder and saw that his purser was not far behind. He tried to coax his legs to move faster, but they were already burning with strain. Then he remembered how he had strengthened his legs so he could jump high enough to grab a root on the side of the butte. He drew Energy from the sword and directed it into his legs. The burning evaporated and his speed increased.

Yolken ran as hard as he could. The trees and bushes moved

by at a dizzying rate, but he wasn't gaining any ground on Jax. As fast as he was moving, he didn't dare turn around and see whether they were still being pursued.

He thought about turning around and confronting the man chasing them, but knew he needed to follow Jax's lead. If Jax wasn't willing to face this person, then what did he think *he* would do? But then he wondered what they were supposed to do—keep running in the hopes of losing him? Even if they did lose him, what then? If that man had followed them this far, he wasn't likely to give up.

They had to do something.

Instead, they ran.

They ran without slowing.

Yolken knew he should be getting tired—*no one can sprint this long*—but he wasn't. Even in the midst of knowing he was in danger he couldn't help but be amazed by this.

"Get ready!" Jax shouted over his shoulder.

"For what?" Yolken said.

The forest around them began to rapidly thin. The ground changed from soft forest floor to rocky shale. Just ahead of them, Yolken saw that the forest gave way altogether.

"Remember what I taught you!" Jax shouted. He increased his pace and pulled farther ahead of Yolken.

They ran out into the clearing, the Mindon River flowing to their right, and Yolken saw the ground abruptly end ahead. He skidded to a stop and watched in horror as Jax continued running and jumped off the cliff.

CHAPTER 44

Hadie watched the sun through the thin fluttering curtains of the carriage. It was just finishing its daily journey and was about to meet the western horizon. For the majority of the day, the breeze passing through the open windows carried with it the fresh smell of the sea. Normally, she enjoyed watching the sunset—its color deepened almost to the color of blood as it inched closer to its daily rest. However, when the air soured with the smell of fish, dread replaced the beauty and joy she normally felt. This change meant one thing: They had arrived in Portstown. She couldn't yet see the familiar rows of docks out the window, but the smell heralded their proximity.

As she'd taken care of Javen these past three days, she had come to realize she'd never felt the way she felt about Javen with anyone before. She'd never felt this burning in her chest with any of the men she'd shared a bed with. Nothing was keeping her in the carriage. She could have left the day Drenan had returned Javen bloody and unconscious to the carriage, and nobody would have cared. Spoon-feeding a grown man, washing his lifeless body, and tending to his other bodily functions wasn't something she had ever envisioned herself doing. Ever. For any man. She had left relationships for things much less unpleasant than tending to an unconscious man while he passed his water.

However, with each day she cared for him, kept him alive, she understood more and more why she was willing to do for this man what she would do for no other—she loved him.

The smell of fish meant she was about to lose the first man she'd ever loved.

Hadie forced her sweaty self from the couch and went to the back of the carriage, where Javen lay unconscious on the bed. She looked down at his naked body, covered from the waist down by a thin sheet, and knew her time with him was ending. The worst part of the whole thing was that she knew there was absolutely nothing she could do about it.

She was powerless to oppose Drenan.

She wanted desperately to stay with Javen and declare her love for him, but she knew that, with their arrival in Portstown, Drenan would come for her. Tears streamed from her eyes when she looked down at his still body covered in a sheen of sweat. She knew Drenan wouldn't have stopped her if she'd left the day Javen attacked him; he had only allowed her to remain this long out of—what? Pity? It wasn't out of compassion; the man had no heart.

Hadie climbed onto the bed and lay down next to Javen. She untied the thin brown silk robe she wore—the customary indoor attire worn in the south to help stave off the heat—and snuggled close to his body, so her skin touched his. She tucked her nose in at the nape of his neck, below his ear, and breathed in deeply. Soon, the only thing she would smell would be the stench of Portstown. But until that time came, she would remain here, next to the man she loved. She closed her eyes and cried, tears streaming down the side of her face and mingling with their sweat.

Hadie dozed off and woke when the lumbering motion of the carriage stopped. The end had come. However, she didn't move. She had promised herself that they would have to pry her away from Javen if they wanted her to leave.

As the minutes passed, she tried to flee from the moment by

remembering the night they had met in Lonely Oak. The first time she'd looked down at Javen as he searched the crowds was clear in her mind. Tears began anew as, in her memory, she watched him turn toward her and look up into her eyes. He'd looked hopeful at first, then disappointed. That hadn't stopped her from talking to him. She didn't know why, but she felt compelled to. She remembered the quickening of her heart when he'd asked her if she wanted to dance.

The carriage door opened in the other room.

Hadie forced herself to be in the present. She opened her eyes and kissed Javen multiple times, first under his ear where her nose had been, then on his cheeks, forehead, and lastly, his mouth. She closed her eyes and saw Javen interacting with the crippled girl looking up at him with unbending adoration. She'd teased him but had known at that moment he was a man with a heart full of unselfish love.

The door dividing the two rooms opened.

She ignored the intruders.

"Get the boy," an uncaring voice said.

* * *

Danavin's son turned and ran. Crin should have stopped him, but he froze, unable to force himself to move. In that brief moment their eyes were locked, the day Cara died replayed in his mind. Even though it had happened a long time ago, the fear of staring eye to eye with Danavin was as acute as it ever had been. He'd frozen then, just like he did now, and it had resulted in Cara's death. If he had acted, Cara would likely still be alive, and his father wouldn't hate him so bitterly. All the way back to Hantlo after that failed mission, he'd thought seriously about lying to his father about what happened, but he knew Drenan would have eventually found out. And when he did, he wouldn't have stopped squeezing.

When the boy and his teacher were nearly out of sight, Crin was finally able to convince himself to move. He reached into the flames with a tendril of Energy and yanked the dagger out of the tree where it was buried to its hilt. He mentally cursed himself for missing. He never missed. He'd spent so much time practicing with his dagger over the centuries that the dagger was essentially an extension of himself.

Surrounded by a growing fire, he filled his Core with Energy and reluctantly started moving. Within seconds, the fire was behind him and the forest passed by in a blur.

* * *

Yolken's heart quickened as he edged closer to the ledge and peered over. His cloak tugged at his neck as it flapped in the wind. "You've got to be joking," he said. *How in the world does he expect me to do that?* Yolken looked over his shoulder to see if the man chasing them had caught up to them yet. When he didn't see anyone in the clearing behind him, he turned back to the cliff. A bout of vertigo overtook him, forcing him to step back.

"There's no way I am doing that," he said.

But what options did he have? The man following them would catch up soon, and he had nowhere to go. He stepped back to the edge and looked over again. It was true he'd spent the last few days moving air around, practicing the techniques Jax had taught him, but he did *not* feel ready to actually jump off a cliff. He knew if he tried, he would fall to his death. He turned back around and studied the forest, considering finding a place to hide. But that was no solution. That man knew he was here and would not leave without thoroughly searching the area.

He turned back again and looked over the cliff. The falls were almost a thousand paces tall. From this vantage, he looked down at the river as it made its way north into the vast northern plains. At any other time, he could have sat here for hours, if not days, admiring what had to be one of the most picturesque views in all of Dradonia. But instead, he knew if he didn't do something quickly, he was going to die.

I could confront him, he thought, but quickly discarded the idea. If Jax, a seasoned Synthesizer, was not willing to risk a confrontation, what could he possibly do?

He looked over at the river and wondered if he'd survive if he jumped in and let the water carry him down. The falls were so high, though, he knew hitting the water at the bottom would probably be no different than if he jumped off and hit the ground instead. No, he realized, his only option was to jump and hope he could remember what Jax had been teaching him about manipulating the air.

But there has to be another way down. He knew Deborah and Kaylan had come this way and that there was no way they'd jumped. Even if Deborah knew the same air manipulation techniques, Kaylan couldn't Synthesize. Then he saw it. A distinct path was cut into the rock to his left.

Yolken moved closer to it to inspect it. Up close, he saw there was definitely a trail zigzagging steeply down the cliff. The idea that there was another path down caused him to breathe a sigh of relief, but he quickly realized that taking it while being pursued would be dangerous. If confronting a skilled Synthesizer was not something Jax wanted to do, how much more dangerous would it be if he did it perched on the side of an enormous cliff?

He looked back at the tree-line again, panic growing in him as he tried to think. He didn't like either option. He closed his eyes and wished they could all be back in Lonely Oak and that none of this had ever happened.

Yolken took a deep breath and felt the warmth of the sun on his back.

A sense of calm washed through him.

He knew the path forward.

He was no longer simply a man who owned a tavern with his brother and aunt. Even though he hadn't chosen it, the path his life would now follow was no longer the path it was before he'd first used Draego's Gift. In his Core, he knew this to be true. He'd long wondered if he could ever return to Lonely Oak, to his tavern, and live the life he dreamed of living with Kaylan. Jax had already told him the answer, but now he knew for himself. The life he once dreamed of was no longer possible. He was a Synthesizer, possessing the gift only the Blessed of the Dragon possessed, and the path of the Synthesizer was not down the trail.

Yolken steeled his nerves and opened himself to the warmth of the sun. He let its Energy rush into him and fill his Core. Filled with the power of the sun, with a spark of the very gift the Great Dragon saw fit to bless the Dragon King with, he reached out all around and pulled air in. He did so without the caution Jax had insisted he exercise these past several days. He pulled air with every element of Energy within his Core.

The pressure around him built quickly.

The sound of the rushing water died, and he stood in the middle of an eerie calm.

He took several steps back from the ledge and readied himself to jump.

* * *

Crin ran into the clearing, dagger in hand, and stopped. The boy stood alone on the edge of the cliffs with thousands of tiny threads of Energy reaching out all around him. He watched as the threads reached out, stopped, then pulled back in. The process repeated itself over and over. Threads extended, retracted, and new threads replaced them. Having seen the boy jump once already, he knew he must be preparing to jump again.

He looked around the clearing, unable to find the other person who had been with the boy. *He must have already jumped,* he figured.

Crin had no idea what the boy was doing that enabled him to control how he flew through the air, so he knew he couldn't allow the boy to jump. If he did, Crin would fail in his mission. From the bottom of the falls, the boy could go in any number of directions. And by the time he made it to the bottom himself, if he could even find a way down without having to turn completely around, the boy would be gone.

The son of the man who had caused him so much grief took several steps backward then crouched, readying himself to make a running start at the cliff. Not wanting to risk missing with the dagger again, Crin opened himself to the Energy streaming down from the sun and filled his Core. He waited for the boy to make his move, sweat beading on his skin as his body temperature shot up. When the boy sprang forward, Crin reached out with a thick tendril of Energy.

* * *

Hadie kissed Javen one last time then looked up. Drenan stood in the door wearing his blue armor, and a guard wearing gray armor accompanied him. He looked like the same man who had delivered Javen to her covered in blood.

She sat up and drew her robe tightly around herself. She knew her robe still revealed much to Drenan and the guard, and normally her southern nature wouldn't have cared, but she felt exposed in front of them, so she crossed her arms over her breasts. Tears itched at her cheeks, and she reached up and wiped them away.

The guard hesitated only a moment, locking eyes with Hadie before he obeyed the command of his master and moved toward the bed.

Hadie willed her nerves to not betray her emotions to the monster standing before her and spoke. "Let me stay with him, please," she said, her voice giving her away.

Both the armored men ignored her. The guard bent down to scoop Javen into his arms.

All desires of modesty fled from her. In a moment of panic, she reached up with both hands and pushed the guard by his shoulders. She didn't actually have any effect on him, but he gave in to her desperation and stood up. She let out a small sigh of relief, but then an invisible force hit her and threw her back on the bed. Her robe flew open, and she couldn't move to cover herself.

"It is foolish to interfere with the business of the Regency, girl," Drenan said coolly.

The guard bent down and scooped Javen into his arms.

Hadie lay pinned to the bed, fully exposed, completely helpless to do anything. When the guard moved toward the door, she struggled, wanting more than anything to stop him. But the invisible force held her pinned to the bed. "Please. Don't. Do. This!" she shouted.

The guard walked out of the room with Javen's naked body slumped in his arms.

Drenan stepped closer to her, his right hand resting on the hilt of a dull, black dagger tucked into the belt of his blue armor.

Hadie's heart raced. She was exposed and alone with the most feared regent in the realm. Fear overflowed when the invisible force pinning her to the bed lifted her into the air. Her robe was ripped from her body, and she hung helpless and naked before the vile man. She turned her head to avoid his eyes.

"Look at me," Drenan said.

Hadie refused, but her head turned against her will.

"Well, well," Drenan said. "I knew you looked familiar."

Hadie looked as far to her right as she could.

"I wonder what your father would think if he knew you were involved with a rebel."

Hadie looked at Drenan, but then averted her eyes again.

"You know, if it weren't for your mother, he'd have let me bed you years ago."

Hadie looked at Drenan again. "I would never—"

A force pushed her jaw shut.

"Tsk. Tsk. I did not take you because I rely on your father's loyalty," Drenan said, staring into her glistening eyes. "But know that I can have you anytime I desire. Including now."

Hadie clamped her eyes closed. She couldn't bear the thought of Drenan looking at her nakedness, let alone touching her.

"You're lucky to be alive," Drenan said, "because you would have been next."

Hadie opened her eyes and looked at Drenan, wondering what he meant.

"Now, go home to your father. If I ever see you again, I promise that I will do more than simply look at you. And neither your father nor your mother will be able to stop me."

Hadie fell to the bed.

Drenan tossed a handful of gold drakes at her, then left.

Hadie curled up on her side and tucked her knees up to her chest.

Javen was gone.

Likely forever.

She fought the urge to run after Drenan and plead with him to let her stay with him. It would do her no good, and probably only cause her more pain.

She fought the urge to scream, her body shaking, but kicked her feet straight down, rolling onto her back and clenching every muscle in her body. She took a deep breath and screeched at the top of her lungs, "No!"

She rolled onto her side again, curling back up into a ball, and continued sobbing while muttering quietly, "No. Please don't take him. I love him."

* * *

Yolken clenched his teeth and launched himself toward the cliff. He took four Energy-fueled steps, each one propelling him faster toward the edge. He wanted to jump as far away from the cliff-side as he could in case it took him some time to get the air to do what he wanted. His foot hit the ground on the edge, and in a fluid motion his knee bent as his muscles tensed like a coil then exploded back up. He soared into the air and looked out at the northern plains far below.

Something snaked around his torso and yanked him back, doubling him in half. Instead of soaring further out into the air, he flew back and hit the ground. The air he had gathered around him cushioned his fall, saving him from what he knew would have seriously hurt.

He looked up and saw the man in gray—his pants were a few shades darker than the shirt, which was embroidered to resemble dragon scales—walking toward him. He tried scrambling away, but the invisible force pulled him from the edge. Yolken used Energy to strengthen his arms and clawed against the force. Not making any progress, and seeing the man walking toward him, he grabbed a loose piece of shale and threw it at the man with an Energy-strengthened arm. The man easily dodged the threat and kept pulling Yolken further back from the edge.

Fire erupted in front of the man and started to grow. Remembering what Jax taught him about protecting himself from such a threat, Yolken realized he still controlled most of the air he'd gathered in preparation for his big jump. But instead of waiting until the man threw the fire at him and using the air to divert the fire away, he threw all of it straight at the man. The man stumbled back and fell to the ground, breaking his invisible hold on Yolken.

Yolken scrambled to his feet and started gathering in more air.

"It's impossible to hide from the Regency," the man said, pushing himself up onto a knee. "If not now, we will catch you eventually."

"I won't kill you if you turn around and go back to wherever you came from," Yolken said, even though he really had no idea how he might accomplish that. But he had seen the look in the man's eyes when they'd locked earlier: He was afraid of Yolken.

Despite Yolken's threat, the man pushed himself to his feet and started walking toward him.

Yolken stepped backward and gathered air as quickly as he could, pushing it at the man as it swirled toward him. The force was nowhere near as powerful as it had been before. He wasn't controlling nearly as much air, and he didn't have the time to gather it again for a stronger attack.

"I'm dead either way," the man said. "So I might as well take you with me to meet Draego."

The man ran toward Yolken and, for the first time, Yolken saw the blade he carried in his hand. When he was only a few paces away, the man lifted the blade and swung it down toward Yolken. Yolken instinctively filled the bones in his arm with Energy and held it up in defense. A sickening crunch reverberated in the air surrounding him when their arms collided. Pain shot up his arm at the same instant the man crashed into him, throwing them both over the cliff.

With their bodies entangled, they reflexively grasped for handholds that weren't there. They spun end over end, and Yolken lost his connection with the sun when it disappeared behind the cliff. Energy still burned in his Core, but the little pressure he had managed to gather around himself was gone.

His mind raced, frantically trying to remember the techniques Jax had been teaching him about controlling the air. When he finally managed to regain some focus, a fist buried itself into his side. He groaned in pain.

The world spun. Yolken fought to ignore the dizzying motion and pain in his side and brought his attention closer in, to his assailant. The man's head was buried into his side, just below the crook of his left arm and chest. The man's right arm hung lifeless as they fell. However, he repeatedly buried his left fist into Yolken's side. The pain and disorientation kept him from concentrating.

They were falling to their death. He *would* die if he didn't do something. Then he realized his assailant wasn't trying to stop their fall either.

He can't.

But I can. And I'm not dying.

Not today.

The blue sky faded to gray. They were in the mist, he knew. *How much farther?* He didn't want to find out.

Yolken grabbed his assailant by the hair on the back of his head and pulled back sharply.

The pounding on his side stopped.

With every ounce of Energy burning within him, Yolken pushed out against his attacker. The man flew away from him explosively, and the recoil changed his own direction of movement.

The sky turned blue again.

It took Yolken a second to orient himself, and when he did, he saw he was now traveling mostly horizontally, away from the falls. He looked between his feet and laughed when he realized he was looking at the scene hanging behind the bar in his tavern.

When he felt himself fall downward again, he pushed the thought from his mind. He was free from his assailant, but he was still falling.

Yolken twisted himself in the air until he was looking down. He was far enough away from the cliff horizontally now he once again felt the warmth of the sun on his skin. He drew Energy in as the river below rapidly approached. Just before hitting the water, he pushed downward with the same force he had used to free himself from his attacker. The water exploded beneath him, parting in two large waves, each moving toward their respective shores. The reaction jerked him sharply and sent him flying higher into the air.

He gathered his wits about himself and remembered the techniques Jax had spent the last few days teaching him. As his upward movement slowed and he once again fell toward the river, he gathered air around himself. As he fell, he pushed down with the air and slowed his descent.

He hit the water harder than he had intended.

He desperately clawed toward the surface, his lungs immediately starting to burn, but became entangled in his cloak. His boots felt like someone had tied rocks to his feet. As his lungs burned, his efforts became more frantic.

Something grabbed Yolken by the ankle and pulled against the current of the river. He increased his struggle to free himself from the man's invisible hold but couldn't shake it. In desperation, Yolken wondered how the man had not only survived a blow so strong that it sent Yolken hurling through the air in the opposite direction but managed to find him again so quickly.

He emerged from the river and sucked air into his lungs. His cloak hung down over his head, and streams of water ran off it to the river. The Harachin sword hung awkwardly from his belt. The invisible force was holding him by the heel upside-down over the water. He grabbed hold of the hilt as he twisted and turned to try and find his assailant. He began to move over the river toward the bank then found himself face to upside-down face with Jax.

"What in Draego's Fire was that?" Jax said.

CHAPTER 45

Yolken stared into the flames, thankful for the heat of the fire.

The encounter with the man kept replaying in his mind, beginning when he had turned around and locked eyes with him. The moment his head went into the water, he was once again staring eye to eye with his assailant. The scene repeated over and over. It wasn't the fall itself that bothered him, or that he had nearly died—though the experience left his body shaking uncontrollably. It was the fate of the man Jax was out looking for, though he already knew the answer.

As he sat warming himself, Yolken held his right arm close to his body and tried not to move it too much. Jax had inspected it and ensured him it wasn't broken, but it still ached. The crunch he still clearly heard each time the scene reset itself and started over must have been his attacker's arm breaking. The man's resolve amazed him; whereas it had been all he could do to regain his own focus, that man had somehow managed to still beat him as they fell toward certain death—even with a broken arm. Yolken felt where the man had hit him and winced. He hoped he didn't have any broken ribs.

Before going out to search for the body, Jax had questioned him in depth about what happened. He'd told Jax everything he could. Specifically, Jax wanted to know if there were others. Despite his insistence that he didn't know, Jax kept asking, prodding from different angles. It had all happened so fast he hadn't really had the chance to see if there were others before his assailant threw him over the cliff. Finally, Jax resigned himself to the fact that it no longer mattered if they remained hidden and quit asking—if there were others, they would now know where Yolken was since they were missing one of their own.

"Don't let that man's death bother you," Jax said, emerging from the darkness waiting at the edge of the fire's light.

"You found him, then?" Yolken said, looking up at Jax.

"I did."

Yolken frowned and returned his gaze to the fire. "I've never killed anyone before."

"He was the enemy, Yolken. His mission was to kill you, and he almost succeeded."

Yolken knew the truth of what Jax said. The thought helped a little. He had grown up with an innate joy of hunting, but Selena instilled in him a strong respect for life. He did not take life frivolously. Hunting was a means by which he and Javen provided for their family, and they hunted only when necessary. As he stared into the fire, he decided this situation was no different. He had taken the life of that man because it was necessary. If he hadn't defended himself, he would also be dead. He shared this conclusion with Jax.

"It *is* true that sometimes it becomes necessary to kill—such as today, when there is an immediate threat to your life," Jax said. "However, if you wish to become a part of the Order, one day you might be called upon to kill someone who, though they might not be immediately threatening you, is a threat to our ultimate purpose."

Yolken considered what Jax said. The truth was, he hadn't put much thought into whether he wanted to join the Order.

"Right now, I just want to focus on finding Javen."

"You realize any attempt to rescue him will likely result in some sort of a confrontation with the Regency."

"I know," Yolken said. "I'll do what needs to be done to get my brother back, but that won't make killing people any easier."

"Nor should it," Jax said. "The ruthlessness of the Regency is well established. They kill without thinking twice, and their subjects accept it because they believe they rule with the Great Dragon's blessing. And because they know the secret of Regeneration, they have long forgotten the value of life. So long as you continue to feel the way you do now, then you will know respect for life remains within you. The unfortunate reality is that those of us who push back against the Regency are often put into the position of having to choose between our own life or that of another."

"How many people have you killed?" Yolken said.

"Too many."

"Do you still value life after having lived so long?"

"Very much so," Jax said. "Even though I'm one hundred seventeen years old and have been a part of the Order for much of that, it still weighs heavily on me when I take a life." Jax sat across from Yolken and stared into the fire. "I remember thinking just before I descended into sleep after taking the Harachin sword from Drenan that I was willing to take the life of every member of the Regency if I thought it would somehow redeem the deaths of your father and mother. However, even though I was, and still am, willing to shed blood, it didn't mean it wouldn't have at the same time weighed heavily on my conscience."

"Is revenge the answer, then?" Yolken asked. "I mean, if it would weigh so heavily on your conscience, then perhaps it isn't what my father and mother would have wanted."

"Perhaps not," Jax said.

Yolken looked up at the cliffs concealed by darkness and looked for any sign there might be pursuers attempting to descend. The light of their fire would be a beacon identifying their location if anyone still looked for them; however, so would the light needed to descend the cliffs safely. Jax assured him that even in daylight the path down wasn't easy, and without proper illumination at night, it would be impossible. All he saw was darkness.

Yolken looked back into the flames. All the talk of death made him think of something Relan had said to him the morning Dorlan arrived in Lonely Oak. He used to think that Relan was just a drunkard who talked nonsense, but now he wasn't so sure. He was always talking about how evil the Regency was, and it turned out that most of what he said was true. "Jax?"

"Yes?"

"Is the sun dying?"

"What?" Jax looked up at Yolken, betraying what Yolken thought was surprise. "What would give you an idea like that?"

"It's just something I heard."

"From who? Selena?"

"No."

"Well, I would hope she didn't fill your head with such foolishness."

"So it's not dying?"

"Of course not. Even I couldn't come up with something so outlandish," Jax said. "Now, how do you feel?"

"Pretty good," Yolken said. *Did he just change the subject?*

"Good," Jax said. "Let's put some distance between us and the cliffs just in case there are more of them up there. Before dawn, I want to be as far from them as we can be."

Jax stood and began kicking dirt over the fire.

Yolken frowned at the idea of leaving. A part of him wanted to wait so he could finally see the waterfall as it was depicted in his painting. However, he smirked at the memory of seeing the falls as he flew through the air and concluded it could never be better than that.

He stood up and gripped the hilt of the Harachin sword. He used Synthesis to draw water from the Mindon to douse the fire. It went out with a loud hiss. Just before the light of the fire went out, he saw Jax look at him crossly. "What? You said you weren't worried about them knowing we were here anymore."

"I guess you're right," Jax said in the darkness. A small flame appeared before Jax, and he started walking with his back to the north-flowing river.

Yolken followed closely enough behind him that he didn't have to light his own fire. He thought it would be prudent to conserve the Energy remaining in the sword from his day of practicing. He could still feel it push toward him when he gripped the hilt, but it wasn't nearly as forceful as when it was full. They walked in the darkness for a while then he asked, "What exactly were you looking for back there?"

"To verify if he was dead or not. And to see if he had anything that might have been of value."

"Did you find anything?"

"No."

"Where did you find him?"

"I wasn't sure I was going to find anything at all, as large and swift as the river is. However, his body had become lodged between some rocks jutting out of the water not far from the base of the falls."

"Was his arm broken?"

"Yes, and his chest cavity was caved in. The back of his skull was also crushed. If I had to guess," Jax said, "based on what you described, the force you used to push him is what caved in his chest. His skull was probably crushed when he flew into the rocks behind him."

Yolken grimaced at the thought. "Did you recognize him?"

"I did."

"Was he a regent?"

"Drenan's bastard, actually. I've seen him around before. He was a Watcher in Dorlan's guard."

"Hmm," Yolken said. "I still can't believe you just jumped and left me up there."

"I told you I thought you were right behind me."

"How could you be so certain I was just going to jump off a cliff?"

"I knew you'd jump," Jax said.

"How?"

"Because you have in you Draego's Gift, Yolken."

"I almost died."

"But you didn't. And you said yourself that you were about to jump, so I was right."

"Then you should have waited and let me go first," Yolken said.

"Would you have?"

"I… probably."

They continued to walk through the night. As the pre-dawn light began illuminating their surroundings, Jax let the small flame he had used to guide them in the dark go out. They walked through grassy fields that reminded Yolken of the terrain surrounding Lonely Oak; the main difference being that the ground here was much flatter, lacking the rolling hills that surrounded the town that used to be his home. Yolken could see almost indefinitely in all directions except to his left, where the Mindon Mountains rose high into the sky.

When the sun crested the horizon behind them, Jax took off in a sprint while shouting over his shoulder, "Race ya!"

At the rate Jax moved away from him, Yolken knew Jax was Synthesizing. His side ached, but he opened himself to the warmth of the sun and directed Energy to his sore ribs. The pain abated. He sent more Energy to his legs and chased after Jax. He flew through the grass. He ran until the sun stood high in the sky and never caught up to Jax. He leaped over a creek and stopped abruptly on the opposite side when he saw a figure sitting by the water.

"Are you going to let an old man outrun you all day?" Jax said.

Yolken breathed heavily, unable to speak. He raised his arms up and interlocked his hands on top of his head to help him take deeper breaths. His side ached with each breath. While he waited for his breathing to slow and the pain to subside, he looked around. The scenery was virtually unchanged, except that the Mindons had faded into the distance. "How… far… have we… run?" he said between breaths.

"I'd guess about twenty leagues."

Yolken's eyes widened in surprise—they had already covered twice what was normally possible for someone to travel in a day by foot.

"This far south of the road to Tieger is mostly uninhabited, so if you can keep up, you should be able to kiss your fair lass by tomorrow evening."

"Won't Synthesizing that long wear us out?"

"You'll have plenty of time to rest once you're under the Order's protection."

They rested by the creek and ate a meal. Then they resumed their unnatural sprint toward Croff, Jax's coat and his cloak flying out behind them, which brought a smile to Yolken's face.

He had some misgivings as he ran toward the mysterious group which had cost his parents their lives—the Order of the Dragon. But then he thought of Kaylan, and his trepidation melted away.

INTERIM

Drenan followed the guard carrying Danavin's unconscious son down the cobbled road. The guard arrived at a set of weathered stairs made from cut stone and proceeded down them, while Drenan stopped and stood next to Devin. He watched the guard step onto the stone dock at the bottom and walk toward a regal ship. It had a tall mast flying green flags with a large clump of purple grapes in the middle—the official emblem of Onta Province.

"He's in good hands, brother," Devin said.

"I don't want him to be in good hands," Drenan said. "I want him to be hanging from a tree by his neck. Or better yet, burning on a pyre, suffering the same fate as his father."

"For some reason, the emperor has chosen a different fate for the boy."

"What could he possibly be thinking making Danavin's get a regent?"

"It makes sense."

Drenan gave Devin a side look.

"Consider how demoralizing it will be for the rebels when they find out," Devin said.

"He should be suffering a rebel's death, not living as one of the Blessed in Onta."

"I'm certainly not going to disobey the emperor."

"And what does Karina think of taking a rebel into her home?"

"She seemed quite pleased when I told her he would be going with us."

"The woman Father's bedding must be clouding his head," Drenan said, still trying to figure out what the emperor could possibly be thinking.

"Careful," Devin said. "She may soon be his wife."

"He won't marry her."

"That's not what I've been hearing."

"Rumors…" Drenan said, shaking his head in disgust. That was exactly why he had never taken another wife; it was easier to satisfy his needs with whores than to fall in love with a woman a fraction of his age and let her influence cloud his judgment. He watched the guard climb the gangplank and step onto Devin's ship. Thinking of wives and whores, he said, "Where is Karina? After all this, I need a good bedding."

Devin snorted. "She's preoccupied."

"With what?"

"Someone has to look after the boy."

This time Drenan snorted. "You have your wife tending to the son of the most troublesome rebel in the history of the empire?"

"We can't have the sailors looking after him, now can we?" Devin said. "That wouldn't be treating him as one of us. And besides, you know how she feels about you."

"I don't know what she has against me; she seems to bed just about everybody else."

When Drenan's guard reappeared on the gangplank and started his way back up the dock, Devin said, "And what of the girl he was with?"

"I sent her away."

"She won't trouble us?"

"She knows better. She also knows things go unpleasantly

for those who interfere with the Regency."

"Good. We had best be going," Devin said when the guard rejoined them. "They'll be waiting for us at Dunlor's mansion. Apparently, several regents from around the realm have come to herald Dorlan's return."

"He better have a proper selection of whores," Drenan said, turning from the stairs.

The two regents joined back up with the rest of their guards waiting for them by their carriages. Flanked on all sides, they made their way through the dingy streets of the small fishing town.

As they walked, Drenan couldn't help but feel he was being punished by the chancellor. In the end, it didn't matter; he had accomplished what he'd been instructed to do. It wasn't his fault Dorlan disapproved of his method.

The group tromped down a muddy alley smelling of sewage. Drenan drew Energy from the dagger on his belt and used Synthesis to plug his nose—breathing through his mouth made the smell less putrid.

Walking down the alley made him think about the night he had last worn black. The information he'd had from the Synod was spot on, so he wondered how they could have missed knowing Danavin had had children; Nera would have to answer. He didn't appreciate being caught up in someone else's loose ends. This whole debacle made him want to return to Lonely Oak and burn the entire town to the ground.

They emerged from the alley and joined with another cobbled road. They followed it up a hill, into the trees, and away from the grimy town. As they climbed above the town, the smell lessened, so Drenan opened his nasal passages to breathe normally again. He took a deep breath and, although he could still smell sewage intermingled with the smell of fish, he could smell the salt in the air as well.

When Dunlor's mansion came into view at the top of the

hill, Drenan found himself thinking about his bastard. It had been nearly a month, so he expected to hear from him any day. He hoped Crin had good news; his already sour mood would only worsen if he lost both of Danavin's children.

The front door of the mansion opened, and Dunlor—the regent of the Portstown province—greeted them, wearing a light blue robe tied closed with a matching silk belt.

While Dunlor greeted Devin, Drenan flexed his hands inside his blue dragon-scaled gloves and felt the scars on the backs of his hands stretch. Dorlan might have sent Danavin's get away, but he had only succeeded in delaying Drenan's gratification. *I will see to it that both of your boys suffer, Danavin.*

Dunlor turned to him, and Drenan shook Dunlor's hand and feigned excitement at seeing his half-brother. Dunlor ushered them into his mansion, and Drenan followed him inside. The sight of naked women strolling around made him smile. His frustrations were about to be alleviated—at least temporarily.

I promise you, Danavin—for Therese, for Cara—they will suffer.

THE END
of Book One of
THE BLESSED OF THE DRAGON

DRAKE FAMILY TREE

Previous Era (PE): the era prior to the establishment of the Dragon Throne became known as the Previous Era

Dragon King Era (DKE): the Dragon King Era commenced when Draeko established the Dragon Throne.

United Era (UE): the United Era commenced when Drakonias sat upon the Dragon Throne and proclaimed himself emperor of Dradonia.

Note: Provided below is the first and second generations of the Blessed of the Dragon. A complete genealogy of those loyal to the emperor is maintained at the palace in Kyinth.

(L) indicates those that pledged their loyalty to Drakonias during Drakonias' war.

GENERATION 1

Draeko Dairion Drake (m) (b. unknown d. 1150 DKE)
   Married to:
      Aliza Varias (f) (b 61 PE d. 1148 DKE)
   Children:
      Drakonias Draeko Arvarin Drake (m) (b. 42 PE d.)
      Deanna Aliza Drake (f) (b. 41 PE d. 1150 DKE)
      Eagan Draeko Calavin Drake (m) (b. 39 PE d. 1150 DKE)
      Reago Draeko Yarin Drake (m) (b. 37 PE d.) (L)
      Anshar Draeko Olivar Drake (m) (b. 35 PE d. 1150 DKE)
      Drae Draeko Harachin Drake (m) (b. 34 PE d. 44 UE)
      Reega Aliza Drake (f) (b. 31 PE d. 1150 DKE)
      Orlan Draeko Dairion Drake (m) (b. 29 PE d. 289 UE) (L)
      Thena Aliza Drake (f) (b. 835 DKE d.) (L)
      Nera Aliza Drake (f) (b. 837 DKE d.) (L)
      Lio Draeko Mattath Drake (m) (b. 980 DKE d. 30 UE)
      Atter Draeko Eber Drake (m) (b. 983 DKE d. 1138 DKE) (L)
      Mattha Aliza Drake (f) (b. 984 DKE d. 1150 DKE)
      Sheal Draeko Kena Drake (m) (b. 986 DKE d.) (L)
      Akim Draeko Nash Drake (m) (b. 992 DKE d. 33 UE) (L)
      Bathsheth Aliza Drake (f) (b. 995 DKE d. 80 UE)
      Esli Draeko Elish Drake (m) (b. 1001 DKE d. 19 UE)

GENERATION 2

Drakonias Draeko Arvarin Drake (m) (b. 42 PE d.)
    Married to:
        Mariana Hargen (b. 20 PE d. 1120 DKE)
    Children:
        Drashon Drakonias Irigwin Drake (m) (b 14 DKE d. 295 UE)
        Dorlan Drakonias Irigwin Drake (m) (b 150 DKE d.)
        Devin Drakonias Metra Drake (m) (b. 820 DKE d.)
        Drenan Drakonias Loid Drake (m) (b. 954 DKE d.)
        Darsi Mariana Drake (f) (b. 960 DKE d. 1142 DKE)
        Donlin Drakonias Ronn Drake (m) (b. 980 DKE d. 1128 DKE)
        Dalia Mariana Drake (f) (b. 982 DKE d.)
    Married to:
        Ceena Realag (b. 1101 DKE d. 40 UE)
    Children:
        Darek Drakonias Proogan Drake (m)(b. 1 UE d.)
        Dreanna Ceena Drake (f)(b. 3 UE d.)
        Dunlor Drakonias Metra Drake (m) (b. 3 UE d.)

Please enjoy an excerpt from:
THE ISLAND OF KVORGA
Book Two of
THE BLESSED OF THE DRAGON

BEFORE

245 United Era

Drakonias stood on the palace balcony, high above the sprawling city below, his hands clasped behind his back. Stoic. Regal.

In the pre-dawn light, he gazed down upon the slumbering city. He'd long been fond of the quietness of this early hour. The night's peacefulness lingered, not yet vanquished by the bustle of governing such a vast realm. But as much as he enjoyed this early hour, that wasn't the reason he ritually rose so early every day.

The emperor shifted his gaze from the sleeping city below to the horizon above. The transition from night to day was underway. The predawn light that signaled the coming of the sun pushed the darkness farther and farther from the horizon. Blackness gradually gave way to varying shades of purples and dark blues, and they, in turn, became the oranges and reds of dawn. The dimmest of the stars that peppered the night sky were fading in the growing light. Only the body and tail of the Great Dragon constellation, diving into the western horizon, still shone brightly.

This ritual of rising early to await the coming of the sun had begun many years ago as a sort of homage to the source of his power. Homage was not something he had felt the need to pay in a very long time—after all, one paid homage to show respect for someone of higher authority, and he was the emperor, so there *was* no higher authority. However, he knew that he would not be standing here, high above his realm, were it not for the sun.

His father would have told him that he was misguided—that it was not the sun to whom he should pay his homage. Rather, he should be honoring Draego, the Great Dragon. Whether or not Draego had given them their gift was anyone's guess. What he did know, however, was that the sun was what kept him in power. Where his gift came from didn't matter.

His daily ritual began when the sky was still black—when the Great Dragon constellation still shared the night sky with the other stars—and ended when the sun had fully risen. He'd been doing it so long he'd memorized the sun's pattern as it changed with the seasons. He knew the exact moment to expect it each and every day.

Lately, though, the serenity he had originally found in performing the ritual was eluding him. Instead, the process had become an exercise of patience. Something about it had recently begun to itch at him. Something about it was not quite right. It was… off.

When he had first noticed the feeling, he'd shrugged it off as an anomaly. However, the itch wouldn't go away. With each passing day, it became stronger.

With hands clasped behind his back—in part to prevent himself from fidgeting—he impatiently waited for the ritual to conclude. He wanted it to be over so he could return to the woman in his bed and put it out of his mind until the morrow.

At last, the sun began to crest the horizon. Drakonias watched intently as it slowly inched its way higher and higher into the sky. As expected, the itch in the back of his mind returned. *What is it? What are you trying to tell me?* He directed his thoughts at the sun as if the sun could converse with him, but it never did. Since the day it had begun, the meaning of the itch eluded him. Daily, it frustrated him.

The sunrise was just like every other sunrise he had watched—the thousands and thousands of them. Were it not for the presence of the itch, this particular sunrise would have seemed no different from any of those that had preceded it. But for months, the irregularity had been playing at the fringes of his consciousness.

Drakonias shifted his stance. Something felt different. Unlike the previous days, when he'd left the balcony frustrated at not being able to solve the puzzle, now the itch began to grow. His eyes narrowed in concentration as it began to claw and gnaw with ever-increasing intensity, slowly boring its way into his consciousness. As the sun continued to creep higher, the itch that had been plaguing him began coalescing into realization.

Drakonias' eyes went wide as a flood of images rushed into his mind—images of every sunrise he had witnessed for the last two hundred years.

Drakonias fell to his knees under the crushing burden. He felt as though the full weight of the palace atop which he perched had suddenly crashed down upon him.

He realized, after all this time, what he had done.

ABOUT THE AUTHOR

Patrik grew up in the southwest and presently lives in Idaho. Earlier in life he almost exclusively read fantasy novels but has since broadened his horizon and enjoys many genres, both fiction and nonfiction. He has wanted to write a book for a long time but never really had any ideas. Then, one random day, when he least expected it, he had an inkling and started writing. In his spare time, he enjoys hanging out with his family and entertaining his exuberant dog Pearl (or the Black Pearl when she is naughty, and yes, she is black). He also enjoys a good beer. He occasionally brews it as well, but he's not nearly as good as Yolken.